the best of

C.M.
KORNBLUTH

CLASSIC SCIENCE FICTION

edited by **Frederik Pohl**

the best of
C.M.
KORNBLUTH

Taplinger Publishing Company | New York

This edition first published in the United States in 1977 by
TAPLINGER PUBLISHING CO., INC.
New York, New York

Copyright © 1976 by Mary Kornbluth, John Kornbluth,
and David Kornbluth
Introduction: *An Appreciation* Copyright © 1976 by Frederik Pohl
All rights reserved. Printed in the U.S.A.

Published simultaneously in Canada by
Burns & MacEachern, Limited, Ontario

Published by arrangement with Ballantine Books
A Division of Random House, Inc.
201 East 50th Street
New York, New York 10022

Library of Congress Cataloging in Publication Data
Kornbluth, Cyril M.
    The best of C. M. Kornbluth.

    CONTENTS: The rocket of 1955.—The words of guru.—The only
thing we learn.—The adventurer. [etc.]
    1. Science fiction, American. I. Title.
PZ4.K85Bd3   [PS3561.067]   813'.5'4   77-5294
ISBN 0-8008-0723-5

Contents

the best of
C. M.
KORNBLUTH

AN APPRECIATION
by Frederik Pohl

CYRIL KORNBLUTH was my friend from the time we were both in our middle teens until the day of his death, and for most of that time we were collaborators as well.

It isn't easy for me to speak of him objectively. A collaboration is too close a relationship for impersonal appraisal. And yet I have no doubt that Kornbluth's work deserves critical study. From first to last, it was lucid, inventive, economical, and informed. Cyril was a wise as well as a talented man.

He was also a sardonic soul. The comedy present in almost everything he wrote relates to the essential hypocrisies and foolishnesses of mankind. His target was not always Man in the abstract and general. Sometimes it was one particular man, or woman, thinly disguised as a character in a story—and thinly sliced, into quivering bits. Once or twice it was me. Cyril and I were good friends, but there was too much ego in both of our cosmoses for the relationship to be always tranquil. We had our differences, and one of the periods when we were having them coincided with his writing the novel *Gunner Cade,* in collaboration with Judith Merril. There is a character in the book who is pitifully corrupt and whiningly ineffectual. It is not an accident that the character's name is what Judy's first daughter called me when she was first learning to talk: Threadwick.

Cyril's total catalogue comprises about a dozen novels and about fifty shorter stories, alone or in collaboration. Nearly all were science fiction. Of the novels, seven were done with me and two with Judith Merril (in one of which I had some slight part).

Of his own science-fiction novels, there were three. The first was *Takeoff.* Events have outrun *Takeoff*—it is about the machinations by which the first manned launch into space occurs—and so it is not widely read these days; but it is a good story, and parts of it are brilliant. I remember Cyril writing it. Walter Bradbury, then the science-fiction editor at Doubleday, read the first couple of chapters and liked them; he offered Cyril a contract on condition that he write an outline of the balance of the book, preferably over the weekend, so that Brad could present it at the Doubleday editorial conference on Monday morning. Cyril wanted the contract but he didn't want to write outlines, then or ever; so he took his typewriter to the Hotel Latham on East Twenty-eighth Street in New York, holed up in a tiny attic room next to the elevators (I know the room well; I've used it myself from time to time) and wrote the balance of the novel in seventy-two sleepless hours.

Takeoff did well, so Cyril wrote another one, *The Syndic.* That also did well. Then he wrote a third, *Not This August,* and for a while it looked as though that novel might do at least an order of magnitude better than anything of his before. To begin with, this one was not serialized in a science-fiction magazine, but in a large-circulation slick. Then the New York Sunday *News* took it up. *Not This August* is a cold-war story of the purest ray serene. The Commies have conquered America, and in the novel the Americans, with wit and spunk and good old U.S. knowhow, regather their strength and destroy the invaders. The *News's* editorial writer was turned on by all this, and he devoted his whole Sunday column to a glowing plug for this real Amurrican type of book. However, the people who read *News* editorials apparently don't read books, for in the long run, the bottom line for *Not This August* was just as good as, but not visibly better than, that for *Takeoff.*

These are good novels; but, for my taste, they are not the best there is of Cyril Kornbluth. His unique contribution to science fiction is in the shorter stories. One of the words I used to describe Kornbluth's work was "economical." He did not ramble, and he did not digress. If he used ten words to describe a character or set a scene, every word of the ten worked.

Perhaps if Kornbluth's major work had been written in the 1960s and 70s instead of in the 40s and 50s he might have been corrupted, as many writers have been, by the hard market fact that it is as easy to get a novel published as a short story . . . and a novel brings in a lot more money—wherefore so many bad sf novels get published. He might have been tempted, but I don't think so. I think Cyril was too much a craftsman to do that.

In any case, when Cyril was writing, that particular temptation did not exist. There were many, many markets for science-fiction short stories and novelettes—something like thirty-five magazines just before his death—so he was free to write his stories to the length they themselves dictated.

He began by filling up the Futurian magazines (the ones edited by Donald A. Wollheim, Robert A. W. Lowndes, and myself) with stories that were often somewhat slim, tricksy, and special ("The Rocket of 1955," "The City in the Sofa," "Thirteen O'Clock") but always bright and brightly written. He was in his teens when he wrote them. The best and worst that can be said of them is that they were damn good teenage stories. Cyril didn't write for several years during World War II. When he began again, in the early 40s, he had matured. He wrote "The Luckiest Man in Denv," "The Adventurer," and "That Share of Glory," and then began to hit his stride, in the novelettes and novellas of the 50s.

I had a little to do with a couple of his best stories. I say it with some pride, maybe more pride than is justified, but it is something I feel good about.

Once, I think while he was still in Chicago, possibly even earlier, Cyril mentioned to me that he had thought of writing a story about medical instruments of the future coming back to the present. Years later, when Horace Gold was badgering Cyril for stories for *Galaxy* and Cyril complained that he couldn't think of anything he felt like writing at that moment, I reminded him of the notion. A week later he had written "The Little Black Bag" (which, as it happened, appeared in John Campbell's *Astounding* instead of Horace Gold's *Galaxy* anyway). I think "The Little Black Bag" is my very favorite of Cyril's stories. It has been reprinted endlessly and adapted for TV by Rod Serling, and I think it will go on for a long time.

In it there is a throwaway scene about the human population of the future, ludicrous dummies all, and I thought they were interesting enough to deserve a story of their own. I told that to Cyril. He poured himself another shot of Hiram Walker's Imperial—or vanilla extract, or elixir of terpin hydrate or whatever we were drinking that night—and pursed his lips. He could see doing that, he said. Maybe bring a man from the present into the future for contrast; but how could he get the man from the present there? "Steal," I advised him. In the old, bad sf film *Just Imagine* the comedian, El Brendel, had gone from 1930 to 1980 simply by being hit by lightning and paralyzed for fifty years. If you're writing farce, I said, why worry about inviting time machines? So Cyril went away, and came back with a man who had been paralyzed by a malfunction of the anesthesia systems in his dentist's office and woke up in the future; he called the story "The Marching Morons."

I have seen the criticism directed against "The Marching Morons," including a quite recent article that points out it is bad genetics (the plot implies that the tendency of lower-class families to be larger than upper-class ones is selective breeding for dumbness). True. But I have also had grown men say to me, with tears in their eyes, that "The Marching Morons" was the best story of any kind they had ever read, and that it had changed their lives. What the story warns against is not the degradation of the human germ plasm, but the degradation of human life, by cheapening values and substituting what is meretricious for what is true.

There were more stories—many, many more, and all good. Cyril had never written better than he was writing in the 50s, right up to the day his wife called to say that he had shoveled snow out of his driveway and then run to catch a train; he had a heart attack on the station platform and died on the spot.

Cyril died too young. There isn't any doubt about that. He was growing and developing every year. It's interesting, as an intellectual exercise, to wonder what he might have written for us if he had lived a normal span.

I do know some of what his intention was, and that was that a good deal of what he was intending to write would not have been science fiction. He had already published four novels of his own outside the sf field (and three in collaboration with me: *Presidential Year, A Town Is Drowning,* and *Sorority House*—the last under Cyril's potboiler pseudonym, Jordan Park). One of his own novels was called *The Naked Storm,* in which a trainful of people is marooned by a blizzard in the Donner Pass. One was *Valerie,* about a Scottish girl accused of witchcraft in the days of the burnings. *Man of Cold Rages* was about an ex-dictator; *Half* was about a sexually incomplete man. Except for *Presidential Year* and *A Town Is Drowning,* all had appeared under somewhat tongue-in-cheek pseudonyms like "Simon Eisner" and "Jordan Park," and none had broken through the paperback-original barrier, and gained a mass readership. But Cyril had established to his own satisfaction what none of the rest of us had ever doubted, that he could write successfully in modes other than science fiction if he chose. And he chose.

When he died he left two incomplete major projects that were not science fiction. One was a novel, some two hundred pages of it written, called *The Crater*. "The crater" was a real event of the Civil War. It took place in the fortifications outside Petersburg just before the defeat of the Confederate States, when some Pennsylvania miners used gunpowder to blow a solid hole in the Southron defenses, only to see their efforts go for nothing because of cowardice and incompetence on the part of two Union generals. And he had signed a contract for another historical novel, a good deal farther back in time; as far as I know nothing was ever put on paper.

The Crater was a disappointment to me when I read the manuscript. It has not been published, and I suspect it never will be. Where Cyril was quicksilver bright in everything he wrote, *The Crater* plods. I don't know why. I do know that he went to immense pains to research every aspect of the battle and the times; perhaps he was smothered in his research.

I think he would have written science fiction again, because it was the thing he did so very well. I am tempted to wonder what kind.

Cyril died before the Wars of the New Wave began. I am not sure which side he would have taken. Everything he wrote is a perfectly polished example of the structured *Galaxy* or *Astounding* story of the 50s—which is, after all, what the New Wave was fighting against. But Cyril might have elected to fight on the same side. He was a poet before he was a science-fiction writer, and the fact that he mastered form does not mean he worshipped it.

In a sense, I don't think his choice of sides would have made much difference. I don't think it really did for any of us.

A fundamental characteristic of most wars is that nobody wins them. It seems to me that the War of the New Wave was unique—everybody won. The old stalwarts learned how to break free of the formal pulp structure. The New Wavers learned—or at least the educable ones learned—how to include some of the special content of sf, which is irreplaceably valuable, in their experiments with form and style.

All of us learned something from the New Wave. I know I did. I think that in that struggle Cyril would have produced some richly rewarding works, even finer than the stories that survive. If he were writing now he might not choose between being poet and sciencefiction writer. He might at the same time be both.

It's hard for me to realize that if Cyril Kornbluth were alive today he would be in his fifties.

My memories of him are very clear, and we were both so young. I have a vagrant recollection of a particular Sunday morning—it must have been around 1939—in the summer. We had stayed up all night— to talk, or for no reason at all. (We did that a lot.) I lived in Brooklyn at the time, at one corner of Prospect Park, and Isaac Asimov's family owned a candy store at the opposite corner, and Cyril and I decided to walk across the park to call on the Asimovs. We had powerful motives for this. Isaac's mother could always be counted on to supply us with free chocolate malteds. And I can remember our wandering across the park in the bright summer dawn, pausing now and then to climb trees and practice the call of the plover-tailed teal. We must not have been very good at it. No teal ever came down to investigate.

Dawns were bright and warm, in the summer of 1939.

So it is not only as a writer that I remember Cyril Kornbluth. He was part of my growing up. As a person he was what he was as a writer: bright, sardonic, and immensely rewarding. Cyril had a great deal to say, and he said it all tersely, wittily, and with grace. I do not think we shall soon see his like again.

The Rocket of 1955

IT IS always a mistake to put a date on a science-fiction story, and now that 1955 is embalmed in history we know that the first attempt at space travel didn't go this way at all. But when it was written—when Cyril was in his teens, World War II was just settling into the routine of grinding human beings into garbage, and space travel was still only a crazy science-fiction idea—it might have.

THE SCHEME was all Fein's, but the trimmings that made it more than a pipe dream and its actual operation depended on me. How long the plan had been in incubation I do not know, but Fein, one spring day, broke it to me in crude form. I pointed out some errors, corrected and amplified on the thing in general, and told him that I'd have no part of it—and changed my mind when he threatened to reveal certain indiscretions committed by me some years ago.

It was necessary that I spend some months in Europe, conducting research work incidental to the scheme. I returned with recorded statements, old newspapers, and photostatic copies of certain documents. There was a brief, quiet interview with that old, bushy-haired Viennese worshipped incontinently by the mob; he was convinced by the evidence I had compiled that it would be wise to assist us.

You all know what happened next—it was the professor's historic radio broadcast. Fein had drafted the thing, I had rewritten it, and told the astronomer to assume a German accent while reading. Some of the phrases were beautiful: "American dominion over the very planets! . . . veil at last ripped aside . . . man defies gravity . . . travel through limitless space . . . plant the red-white-and-blue banner in the soil of Mars!"

The requested contributions poured in. Newspapers and magazines ostentatiously donated yard-long checks of a few thousand dollars;

the government gave a welcome half-million; heavy sugar came from the "Rocket Contribution Week" held in the nation's public schools; but independent contributions were the largest. We cleared seven million dollars, and then started to build the spaceship.

The virginium that took up most of the money was tin plate; the monoatomic fluorine that gave us our terrific speed was hydrogen. The take-off was a party for the newsreels: the big, gleaming bullet extravagant with vanes and projections; speeches by the professor; Farley, who was to fly it to Mars, grinning into the cameras. He climbed an outside ladder to the nose of the thing, then dropped into the steering compartment. I screwed down the sound-proof door, smiling as he hammered to be let out. To his surprise, there was no duplicate of the elaborate dummy controls he had been practicing on for the past few weeks.

I cautioned the pressmen to stand back under the shelter, and gave the professor the knife switch that would send the rocket on its way. He hesitated too long—Fein hissed into his ear: "Anna Pareloff of Cracow, Herr Professor . . ."

The triple blade clicked into the sockets. The vaned projectile roared a hundred yards into the air with a wobbling curve—then exploded.

A photographer, eager for an angle shot, was killed; so were some kids. The steel roof protected the rest of us. Fein and I shook hands, while the pressmen screamed into the telephones which we had provided.

But the professor got drunk, and, disgusted with the part he had played in the affair, told all and poisoned himself. Fein and I left the cash behind and hopped a freight. We were picked off it by a vigilance committee (headed by a man who had lost fifty cents in our rocket). Fein was too frightened to talk or write so they hanged him first, and gave me a paper and pencil to tell the story as best I could.

Here they come, with an insulting thick rope.

The Words of Guru

THE SECOND Futurian to get his own professional
science-fiction magazines to edit was Donald A.
Wollheim (now editor and publisher of his own
line of paperbacks, DAW Books). Over the life-
times of his two magazines, *Stirring* and *Cosmic,*
Cyril wrote (under one penname or another, with
or without collaborators) probably half the total
contents. This is the one I like best.

YESTERDAY, when I was going to meet Guru in the woods a man
stopped me and said: "Child, what are you doing out at one in the
morning? Does your mother know where you are? How old are you,
walking around this late?"

I looked at him, and saw that he was white-haired, so I laughed.
Old men never see; in fact men hardly see at all. Sometimes young
women see part, but men rarely ever see at all. "I'm twelve on my
next birthday," I said. And then, because I would not let him live to
tell people, I said, "and I'm out this late to see Guru."

"Guru?" he asked. "Who is Guru? Some foreigner, I suppose? Bad
business mixing with foreigners, young fellow. Who is Guru?"

So I told him who Guru was, and just as he began talking about
cheap magazines and fairy tales I said one of the words that Guru
taught me and he stopped talking. Because he was an old man and
his joints were stiff he didn't crumple up but fell in one piece, hitting
his head on the stone. Then I went on.

Even though I'm going to be only twelve on my next birthday I
know many things that old people don't. And I remember things that
other boys can't. I remember being born out of darkness, and I
remember the noises that people made about me. Then when I was
two months old I began to understand that the noises meant things
like the things that were going on inside my head. I found out that I

could make the noises too, and everybody was very much surprised. "Talking!" they said, again and again. "And so very young! Clara, what do you make of it?" Clara was my mother.

And Clara would say: "I'm sure I don't know. There never was any genius in my family, and I'm sure there was none in Joe's." Joe was my father.

Once Clara showed me a man I had never seen before, and told me that he was a reporter—that he wrote things in newspapers. The reporter tried to talk to me as if I were an ordinary baby; I didn't even answer him, but just kept looking at him until his eyes fell and he went away. Later Clara scolded me and read me a little piece in the reporter's newspaper that was supposed to be funny—about the reporter asking me very complicated questions and me answering with baby noises. It was not true, of course. I didn't say a word to the reporter, and he didn't ask me even one of the questions.

I heard her read the little piece, but while I listened I was watching the slug crawling on the wall. When Clara was finished I asked her: "What is that grey thing?"

She looked where I pointed, but couldn't see it. "What grey thing, Peter?" she asked. I had her call me by my whole name, Peter, instead of anything silly like Petey. "What grey thing?"

"It's as big as your hand, Clara, but soft. I don't think it has any bones at all. It's crawling up, but I don't see any face on the topwards side. And there aren't any legs."

I think she was worried, but she tried to baby me by putting her hand on the wall and trying to find out where it was. I called out whether she was right or left of the thing. Finally she put her hand right through the slug. And then I realized that she really couldn't see it, and didn't believe it was there. I stopped talking about it then and only asked her a few days later: "Clara, what do you call a thing which one person can see and another person can't?"

"An illusion, Peter," she said. "If that's what you mean." I said nothing, but let her put me to bed as usual, but when she turned out the light and went away I waited a little while and then called out softly. "Illusion! Illusion!"

At once Guru came for the first time. He bowed, the way he always has since, and said: "I have been waiting."

"I didn't know that was the way to call you," I said.

"Whenever you want me I will be ready. I will teach you, Peter—if you want to learn. Do you know what I will teach you?"

"If you will teach me about the grey thing on the wall," I said, "I will listen. And if you will teach me about real things and unreal things I will listen."

"These things," he said thoughtfully, "very few wish to learn. And there are some things that nobody ever wished to learn. And there are some things that I will not teach."

Then I said: "The things nobody has ever wished to learn I will learn. And I will even learn the things you do not wish to teach."

He smiled mockingly. "A master has come," he said, half-laughing. "A master of Guru."

That was how I learned his name. And that night he taught me a word which would do little things, like spoiling food.

From that day to the time I saw him last night he has not changed at all, though now I am as tall as he is. His skin is still as dry and shiny as ever it was, and his face is still bony, crowned by a head of very coarse, black hair.

When I was ten years old I went to bed one night only long enough to make Joe and Clara suppose I was fast asleep. I left in my place something which appears when you say one of the words of Guru and went down the drainpipe outside my window. It always was easy to climb down and up, ever since I was eight years old.

I met Guru in Inwood Hill Park. "You're late," he said.

"Not too late," I answered. "I know it's never too late for one of these things."

"How do you know?" he asked sharply. "This is your first."

"And maybe my last," I replied. "I don't like the idea of it. If I have nothing more to learn from my second than my first I shan't go to another."

"You don't know," he said. "You don't know what it's like—the voices, and the bodies slick with unguent, leaping flames; mind-filling ritual! You can have no idea at all until you've taken part."

"We'll see," I said. "Can we leave from here?"

"Yes," he said. Then he taught me the word I would need to know, and we both said it together.

The place we were in next was lit with red lights, and I think that the walls were of rock. Though of course there was no real seeing there, and so the lights only seemed to be red, and it was not real rock.

As we were going to the fire one of them stopped us. "Who's with you?" she asked, calling Guru by another name. I did not know that he was also the person bearing that name, for it was a very powerful one.

He cast a hasty, sidewise glance at me and then said: "This is Peter of whom I have often told you."

She looked at me then and smiled, stretching out her oily arms. "Ah," she said, softly, like the cats when they talk at night to me. "Ah, this is Peter. Will you come to me when I call you, Peter? And sometimes call for me—in the dark—when you are alone?"

"Don't do that!" said Guru, angrily pushing past her. "He's very young—you might spoil him for his work."

She screeched at our backs: "Guru and his pupil—fine pair! Boy, he's no more real than I am—you're the only real thing here!"

"Don't listen to her," said Guru. "She's wild and raving. They're always tight-strung when this time comes around."

We came near the fires then, and sat down on rocks. They were killing animals and birds and doing things with their bodies. The blood was being collected in a basin of stone, which passed through the crowd. The one to my left handed it to me. "Drink," she said, grinning to show me her fine, white teeth. I swallowed twice from it and passed it to Guru.

When the bowl had passed all around we took off our clothes. Some, like Guru, did not wear them, but many did. The one to my left sat closer to me, breathing heavily at my face. I moved away. "Tell her to stop, Guru," I said. "This isn't part of it, I know."

Guru spoke to her sharply in their own language, and she changed her seat, snarling.

Then we all began to chant, clapping our hands and beating our thighs. One of them rose slowly and circled about the fires in a slow pace, her eyes rolling wildly. She worked her jaws and flung her arms about so sharply that I could hear the elbows crack. Still shuffling her feet against the rock floor she bent her body backwards down to her feet. Her belly muscles were bands nearly standing out from her skin, and the oil rolled down her body and legs. As the palms of her hands touched the ground, she collapsed in a twitching heap and began to set up a thin wailing noise against the steady chant and hand beat that the rest of us were keeping up. Another of them did the same as the first, and we chanted louder for her and still louder for the third. Then, while we still beat our hands and thighs, one of them took up the third, laid her across the altar, and made her ready with a stone knife. The fire's light gleamed off the chipped edge of obsidian. As her blood drained down the groove, cut as a gutter into the rock of the altar, we stopped our chant and the fires were snuffed out.

But still we could see what was going on, for these things were, of course, not happening at all—only seeming to happen, really, just as all the people and things there only seemed to be what they were. Only I was real. That must be why they desired me so.

As the last of the fires died Guru excitedly whispered: "The Presence!" He was very deeply moved.

From the pool of blood from the third dancer's body there issued the Presence. It was the tallest one there, and when it spoke its voice was deeper, and when it commanded its commands were obeyed.

"Let blood!" it commanded, and we gashed ourselves with flints. It smiled and showed teeth bigger and sharper and whiter than any of the others.

"Make water!" it commanded, and we all spat on each other. It flapped its wings and rolled its eyes, which were bigger and redder than any of the others.

"Pass flame!" it commanded, and we breathed smoke and fire on our limbs. It stamped its feet, let blue flames roar from its mouth, and they were bigger and wilder than any of the others.

Then it returned to the pool of blood and we lit the fires again. Guru was staring straight before him; I tugged his arm. He bowed as though we were meeting for the first time that night.

"What are you thinking of?" I asked. "We shall go now."

"Yes," he said heavily. "Now we shall go." Then we said the word that had brought us there.

The first man I killed was Brother Paul, at the school where I went to learn the things that Guru did not teach me.

It was less than a year ago, but it seems like a very long time. I have killed so many times since then.

"You're a very bright boy, Peter," said the brother.

"Thank you, brother."

"But there are things about you that I don't understand. Normally

I'd ask your parents but—I feel that they don't understand either. You were an infant prodigy, weren't you?"

"Yes, brother."

"There's nothing very unusual about that—glands, I'm told. You know what glands are?"

Then I was alarmed. I had heard of them, but I was not certain whether they were the short, thick green men who wear only metal or the things with many legs with whom I talked in the woods.

"How did you find out?" I asked him.

"But Peter! You look positively frightened, lad! I don't know a thing about them myself, but Father Frederick does. He has whole books about them, though I sometimes doubt whether he believes them himself."

"They aren't good books, brother," I said. "They ought to be burned."

"That's a savage thought, my son. But to return to your own problem—"

I could not let him go any further knowing what he did about me. I said one of the words Guru taught me and he looked at first very surprised and then seemed to be in great pain. He dropped across his desk and I felt his wrist to make sure, for I had not used that word before. But he was dead.

There was a heavy step outside and I made myself invisible. Stout Father Frederick entered, and I nearly killed him too with the word, but I knew that that would be very curious. I decided to wait, and went through the door as Father Frederick bent over the dead monk. He thought he was asleep.

I went down the corridor to the book-lined office of the stout priest and, working quickly, piled all his books in the center of the room and lit them with my breath. Then I went down to the schoolyard and made myself visible again when there was nobody looking. It was very easy. I killed a man I passed on the street the next day.

There was a girl named Mary who lived near us. She was fourteen then, and I desired her as those in the Cavern out of Time and Space had desired me.

So when I saw Guru and he had bowed, I told him of it, and he looked at me in great surprise. "You are growing older, Peter," he said.

"I am, Guru. And there will come a time when your words will not be strong enough for me."

He laughed. "Come, Peter," he said. "Follow me if you wish. There is something that is going to be done—" He licked his thin, purple lips and said: "I have told you what it will be like."

"I shall come," I said. "Teach me the word." So he taught me the word and we said it together.

The place we were in next was not like any of the other places I had been to before with Guru. It was No-place. Always before there had been the seeming passage of time and matter, but here there was not even that. Here Guru and the others cast off their forms and were what they were, and No-place was the only place where they could do this.

It was not like the Cavern, for the Cavern had been out of Time and Space, and this place was not enough of a place even for that. It was No-place.

What happened there does not bear telling, but I was made known to certain ones who never departed from there. All came to them as they existed. They had not color or the seeming of color, or any seeming of shape.

There I learned that eventually I would join with them; that I had been selected as the one of my planet who was to dwell without being forever in that No-place.

Guru and I left, having said the word.

"Well?" demanded Guru, staring me in the eye.

"I am willing," I said. "But teach me one word now—"

"Ah," he said grinning. "The girl?"

"Yes," I said. "The word that will mean much to her."

Still grinning, he taught me the word.

Mary, who had been fourteen, is now fifteen and what they call incurably mad.

Last night I saw Guru again and for the last time. He bowed as I approached him. "Peter," he said warmly.

"Teach me the word," said I.

"It is not too late."

"Teach me the word."

"You can withdraw—with what you master you can master also

this world. Gold without reckoning; sardonyx and gems, Peter! Rich crushed velvet—stiff, scraping, embroidered tapestries!"

"Teach me the word."

"Think, Peter, of the house you could build. It could be of white marble, and every slab centered by a winking ruby. Its gate could be of beaten gold within and without and it could be built about one slender tower of carven ivory, rising mile after mile into the turquoise sky. You could see the clouds float underneath your eyes."

"Teach me the word."

"Your tongue could crush the grapes that taste like melted silver. You could hear always the song of the bulbul and the lark that sounds like the dawnstar made musical. Spikenard that will bloom a thousand thousand years could be ever in your nostrils. Your hands could feel the down of purple Himalayan swans that is softer than a sunset cloud."

"Teach me the word."

"You could have women whose skin would be from the black of ebony to the white of snow. You could have women who would be as hard as flints or as soft as a sunset cloud."

"Teach me the word."

Guru grinned and said the word.

Now, I do not know whether I will say that word, which was the last that Guru taught me, today or tomorrow or until a year has passed.

It is a word that will explode this planet like a stick of dynamite in a rotten apple.

The Only Thing We Learn

ANOTHER MEMBER of the Futurians was a tall,
good-looking young man named Dirk Wylie. Like
Cyril Kornbluth, Dirk was in the Battle of the
Bulge; like him, he received there the injuries that
ultimately killed him. (And like Cyril, it was not a
wound. What Cyril got was a strained heart. What
Dirk got was a back disability that developed by
slow and painful stages into tuberculosis of the
spine—apparently from getting hurt jumping off a
truck.) Dirk, with some help from me, started a
literary agency in the last two years of his life, and
one of his first clients was Cyril Kornbluth, off in
Chicago writing stories when his news-wire job
permitted. The first sale for Cyril the agency made
was a long mystery novelette called *The Yogi Says
Yes* to the Trojan magazine group in July 1948;
three months later it sold his first post-war sf story,
"The Only Thing We Learn."

THE PROFESSOR, though he did not know the actor's phrase for it,
was counting the house—peering through a spyhole in the door
through which he would in a moment appear before the class. He was
pleased with what he saw. Tier after tier of young people, ready with
notebooks and styli, chattering tentatively, glancing at the door
against which his nose was flattened, waiting for the pleasant inter-
lude known as "Archaeo-Literature 203" to begin.

The professor stepped back, smoothed his tunic, crooked four
books on his left elbow, and made his entrance. Four swift strides
brought him to the lectern and, for the thousandth-odd time, he
impassively swept the lecture hall with his gaze. Then he gave a wry
little smile. Inside, for the thousandth-odd time, he was nagged by the

irritable little thought that the lectern really ought to be a foot or so higher.

The irritation did not show. He was out to win the audience, and he did. A dead silence, the supreme tribute, gratified him. Imperceptibly, the lights of the lecture hall began to dim and the light on the lectern to brighten.

He spoke.

"Young gentlemen of the Empire, I ought to warn you that this and the succeeding lectures will be most subversive."

There was a little rustle of incomprehension from the audience— but by then the lectern light was strong enough to show the twinkling smile about his eyes that belied his stern mouth, and agreeable chuckles sounded in the gathering darkness of the tiered seats. Glow lights grew bright gradually at the students' tables, and they adjusted their notebooks in the narrow ribbons of illumination. He waited for the small commotion to subside.

"Subversive—" He gave them a link to cling to. "Subversive because I shall make every effort to tell both sides of our ancient beginnings with every resource of archaeology and with every clue my diligence has discovered in our epic literature.

"There *were* two sides, you know—difficult though it may be to believe that if we judge by the Old Epic alone—such epics as the noble and tempestuous *Chant of Remd,* the remaining fragments of *Krall's Voyage,* or the gory and rather out-of-date *Battle For the Ten Suns.*" He paused while styli scribbled across the notebook pages.

"The Middle Epic is marked, however, by what I might call the rediscovered ethos." From his voice, every student knew that that phrase, surer than death and taxes, would appear on an examination paper. The styli scribbled. "By this I mean an awakening of fellow-feeling with the Home Suns People, which had once been filial loyalty to them when our ancestors were few and pioneers, but which turned into contempt when their numbers grew.

"The Middle Epic writers did not despise the Home Suns People, as did the bards of the Old Epic. Perhaps this was because they did not have to—since their long war against the Home Suns was drawing to a victorious close.

"Of the New Epic I shall have little to say. It was a literary fad, a pose, and a silly one. Written within historic times, the some two score pseudo-epics now moulder in their cylinders, where they belong. Our ripening civilization could not with integrity work in the epic form, and the artistic failures produced so indicate. Our genius turned to the lyric and to the unabashedly romantic novel.

"So much, for the moment, of literature. What contribution, you must wonder, have archaeological studies to make in an investigation of the wars from which our ancestry emerged?

"Archaeology offers—one—a check in historical matters in the epics—confirming or denying. Two—it provides evidence glossed over in the epics—for artistic or patriotic reasons. Three—it provides evidence which has been lost, owing to the fragmentary nature of some of the early epics."

All this he fired at them crisply, enjoying himself. Let them not think him a dreamy litterateur, or, worse, a flat precisionist, but let them be always a little off-balance before him, never knowing what came next, and often wondering, in class and out. The styli paused after heading Three.

"We shall examine first, by our archaeo-literary technique, the second book of the *Chant of Remd.* As the selected youth of the Empire, you know much about it, of course—much that is false, some that is true, and a great deal that is irrelevant. You know that Book One hurls us into the middle of things, aboard ship with Algan and his great captain, Remd, on their way from the triumph over a Home Suns stronghold, the planet Telse. We watch Remd on his diversionary action that splits the Ten Suns Fleet into two halves. But before we see the destruction of those halves by the Horde of Algan, we are told in Book Two of the battle for Telse."

He opened one of his books on the lectern, swept the amphitheater again, and read sonorously.

"Then battle broke
And high the blinding blast
Sight-searing leaped
While folk in fear below
Cowered in caverns
From the wrath of Remd—

"Or, in less sumptuous language, one fission bomb—or a stick of time-on-target bombs—was dropped. An unprepared and disorganized populace did not take the standard measure of dispersing, but huddled foolishly to await Algan's gunfighters and the death they brought.

"One of the things you believe because you have seen them in notes to elementary-school editions of *Remd* is that Telse was the fourth planet of the star, Sol. Archaeology denies it by establishing that the fourth planet—actually called Marse, by the way—was in those days weather-roofed at least, and possibly atmosphere-roofed as well. As potential warriors, you know that one does not waste fissionable material on a roof, and there is no mention of chemical explosives being used to crack the roof. Marse, therefore, was not the locale of *Remd,* Book Two.

"Which planet was? The answer to that has been established by X-radar, differential decay analyses, video-coring, and every other resource of those scientists still quaintly called 'diggers.' We know and can prove that Telse was the *third* planet of Sol. So much for the opening of the attack. Let us jump to Canto Three, the Storming of the Dynastic Palace.

> "Imperial purple wore they
> Fresh from the feast
> Grossly gorged
> They sought to slay—

"And so on. Now, as I warned you, Remd is of the Old Epic, and makes no pretense at fairness. The unorganized huddling of Telse's population was read as cowardice instead of poor A.R.P. The same is true of the Third Canto. Video-cores show on the site of the palace a hecatomb of dead in once-purple livery, but also shows impartially that they were not particularly gorged and that digestion of their last meals had been well advanced. They didn't give such a bad accounting of themselves, either. I hesitate to guess, but perhaps they accounted for one of our ancestors apiece and were simply outnumbered. The study is not complete.

"That much we know." The professor saw they were tiring of the terse scientist and shifted gears. "If but the veil of time were rent that shrouds the years between us and the Home Suns People, how much more would we learn? Would we despise the Home Suns People as our frontiersman ancestors did, or would we cry: '*This* is our spiritual home—this world of rank and order, this world of formal verse and exquisitely patterned arts'?"

If the veil of time were rent—?

We can try to rend it . . .

Wing Commander Arris heard the clear jangle of the radar net alarm as he was dreaming about a fish. Struggling out of his too-deep, too-soft bed, he stepped into a purple singlet, buckled on his Sam Browne belt with its holstered .45 automatic, and tried to read the radar screen. Whatever had set it off was either too small or too distant to register on the five-inch C.R.T.

He rang for his aide, and checked his appearance in a wall mirror while waiting. His space tan was beginning to fade, he saw, and made a mental note to get it renewed at the parlor. He stepped into the corridor as Evan, his aide, trotted up—younger, browner, thinner, but the same officer type that made the Service what it was, Arris thought with satisfaction.

Evan gave him a bone-cracking salute, which he returned. They set off for the elevator that whisked them down to a large, chilly, dark underground room where faces were greenly lit by radar screens and the lights of plotting tables. Somebody yelled "Attention!" and the tecks snapped. He gave them "At ease" and took the brisk salute of the senior teck, who reported to him in flat, machine-gun delivery:

"Object-becoming-visible-on-primary-screen-sir."

He studied the sixty-inch disk for several seconds before he spotted the intercepted particle. It was coming in fast from zenith, growing while he watched.

"Assuming it's now traveling at maximum, how long will it be before it's within striking range?" he asked the teck.

"Seven hours, sir."

"The interceptors at Idlewild alerted?"

"Yessir."

Arris turned on a phone that connected with Interception. The boy at Interception knew the face that appeared on its screen, and was already capped with a crash helmet.

"Go ahead and take him, Efrid," said the wing commander.

"Yessir!" and a punctilious salute, the boy's pleasure plain at being known by name and a great deal more at being on the way to a fight that might be first-class.

Arris cut him off before the boy could detect a smile that was forming on his face. He turned from the pale lunar glow of the sixty-incher to enjoy it. Those kids—when every meteor was an invading dreadnaught, when every ragged scouting ship from the rebels was an armada!

He watched Efrid's squadron soar off on the screen and then he retreated to a darker corner. This was his post until the meteor or scout or whatever it was got taken care of. Evan joined him, and they silently studied the smooth, disciplined functioning of the plot room, Arris with satisfaction and Evan doubtless with the same. The aide broke silence, asking:

"Do you suppose it's a Frontier ship, sir?" He caught the wing commander's look and hastily corrected himself: "I mean rebel ship, sir, of course."

"Then you should have said so. Is that what the junior officers generally call those scoundrels?"

Evan conscientiously cast his mind back over the last few junior messes and reported unhappily: "I'm afraid we do, sir. We seem to have got into the habit."

"I shall write a memorandum about it. How do you account for that very peculiar habit?"

"Well, sir, they do have something like a fleet, and they did take over the Regulus Cluster, didn't they?"

What had got into this incredible fellow, Arris wondered in amazement. Why, the thing was self-evident! They had a few ships—accounts differed as to how many—and they had, doubtless by raw sedition, taken over some systems temporarily.

He turned from his aide, who sensibly became interested in a screen and left with a murmured excuse to study it very closely.

The brigands had certainly knocked together some ramshackle league or other, but—The wing commander wondered briefly if it could last, shut the horrid thought from his head, and set himself to composing mentally a stiff memorandum that would be posted in the junior officer's mess and put an end to this absurd talk.

His eyes wandered to the sixty-incher, where he saw the interceptor squadron climbing nicely toward the particle—which, he noticed, had become three particles. A low crooning distracted him. Was one of the tecks singing at work? It couldn't be!

It wasn't. An unsteady shape wandered up in the darkness, murmuring a song and exhaling alcohol. He recognized the Chief Archivist, Glen.

"This is Service country, mister," he told Glen.

"Hullo, Arris," the round little civilian said, peering at him. "I come down here regularly—regularly against regulations—to wear off my regular irregularities with the wine bottle. That's all right, isn't it?"

He was drunk and argumentative. Arris felt hemmed in. Glen couldn't be talked into leaving without loss of dignity to the wing commander, and he couldn't be chucked out because he was writing a biography of the chamberlain and could, for the time being, have any head in the palace for the asking. Arris sat down unhappily, and Glen plumped down beside him.

The little man asked him.

"Is that a fleet from the Frontier League?" He pointed to the big screen. Arris didn't look at his face, but felt that Glen was grinning maliciously.

"I know of no organization called the Frontier League," Arris said. "If you are referring to the brigands who have recently been operating in Galactic East, you could at least call them by their proper names." Really, he thought—civilians!

"So sorry. But the brigands should have the Regulus Cluster by now, shouldn't they?" he asked, insinuatingly.

This was serious—a grave breach of security. Arris turned to the little man.

"Mister, I have no authority to command you," he said measuredly. "Furthermore, I understand you are enjoying a temporary eminence in the non-Service world which would make it very difficult for me to—ah—tangle with you. I shall therefore refer only to your altruism. How did you find out about the Regulus Cluster?"

"Eloquent!" murmured the little man, smiling happily. "I got it from Rome."

Arris searched his memory. "You mean Squadron Commander Romo broke security? I can't believe it!"

"No, commander. I mean Rome—a place—a time—a civilization. I got it also from Babylon, Assyria, the Mogul Raj—every one of them. You don't understand me, of course."

"I understand that you're trifling with Service security and that you're a fat little, malevolent, worthless drone and scribbler!"

"Oh, commander!" protested the archivist. "I'm not so little!" He wandered away, chuckling.

Arris wished he had the shooting of him, and tried to explore the chain of secrecy for a weak link. He was tired and bored by this harping on the Fron—on the brigands.

His aide tentatively approached him. "Interceptors in striking range, sir," he murmured.

"Thank you," said the wing commander, genuinely grateful to be back in the clean, etched-line world of the Service and out of that blurred, water-color, civilian land where long-dead Syrians apparently retailed classified matter to nasty little drunken warts who had no business with it. Arris confronted the sixty-incher. The particle that had become three particles was now—he counted—eighteen particles. Big ones. Getting bigger.

He did not allow himself emotion, but turned to the plot on the interceptor squadron.

"Set up Lunar relay," he ordered.

"Yessir."

Half the plot room crew bustled silently and efficiently about the delicate job of applied relativistic physics that was 'lunar relay.' He knew that the palace power plant could take it for a few minutes, and he wanted to *see*. If he could not believe radar pips, he might believe a video screen.

On the great, green circle, the eighteen—now twenty-four—particles neared the thirty-six smaller particles that were interceptors, led by the eager young Efrid.

"Testing Lunar relay, sir," said the chief teck.

The wing commander turned to a twelve-inch screen. Unobtrusively, behind him, tecks jockeyed for position. The picture on the screen was something to see. The chief let mercury fill a thick-walled, ceramic tank. There was a sputtering and contact was made.

"Well done," said Arris. "Perfect seeing."

He saw, upper left, a globe of ships—what ships! Some were Service jobs, with extra turrets plastered on them wherever there was room. Some were orthodox freighters, with the same porcupine-bristle of weapons. Some were obviously home-made crates, hideously ugly—and as heavily armed as the others.

Next to him, Arris heard his aide murmur, "It's all wrong, sir.

They haven't got any pick-up boats. They haven't got any hospital ships. What happens when one of them gets shot up?"

"Just what ought to happen, Evan," snapped the wing commander. "They float in space until they desiccate in their suits. Or if they get grappled inboard with a boat hook, they don't get any medical care. As I told you, they're brigands, without decency even to care of their own." He enlarged on the theme. "Their morale must be insignificant compared with our men's. When the Service goes into action, every rating and teck knows he'll be cared for if he's hurt. Why, if we didn't have pick-up boats and hospital ships the men wouldn't—" He almost finished it with "fight," but thought, and lamely ended,—"wouldn't like it."

Evan nodded, wonderingly, and crowded his chief a little as he craned his neck for a look at the screen.

"Get the hell away from here!" said the wing commander in a restrained yell, and Evan got.

The interceptor squadron swam into the field—a sleek, deadly needle of vessels in perfect alignment, with its little cloud of pick-ups trailing, and farther astern a white hospital ship with the ancient red cross.

The contact was immediate and shocking. One of the rebel ships lumbered into the path of the interceptors, spraying fire from what seemed to be as many points as a man has pores. The Service ships promptly riddled it and it should have drifted away—but it didn't. It kept on fighting. It rammed an interceptor with a crunch that must have killed every man before the first bulwark, but aft of the bulwark the ship kept fighting.

It took a torpedo portside and its plumbing drifted through space in a tangle. Still the starboard side kept squirting fire. Isolated weapon blisters fought on while they were obviously cut off from the rest of the ship. It was a pounded tangle of wreckage, and it had destroyed two interceptors, crippled two more, and kept fighting.

Finally, it drifted away, under feeble jets of power. Two more of the fantastic rebel fleet wandered into action, but the wing commander's horrified eyes were on the first pile of scrap. It was going *somewhere—*

The ship neared the thin-skinned, unarmored, gleaming hospital vessel, rammed it amidships, square in one of the red crosses, and then blew itself up, apparently with everything left in its powder magazine, taking the hospital ship with it.

The sickened wing commander would never have recognized what he had seen as it was told in a later version, thus:

> "The crushing course they took
> And nobly knew
> Their death undaunted
> By heroic blast
> The hospital's host
> They dragged to doom
> Hail! Men without mercy
> From the far frontier!"

Lunar relay flickered out as overloaded fuses flashed into vapor. Arris distractedly paced back to the dark corner and sank into a chair.

"I'm sorry," said the voice of Glen next to him, sounding quite sincere. "No doubt it was quite a shock to you."

"Not to you?" asked Arris bitterly.

"Not to me."

"Then how did they do it?" the wing commander asked the civilian in a low, desperate whisper. "They don't even wear .45's. Intelligence says their enlisted men have hit their officers and got away with it. They *elect* ship captains! Glen, what does it all mean?"

"It means," said the fat little man with a timbre of doom in his voice, "that they've returned. They always have. They always will. You see, commander, there is always somewhere a wealthy, powerful city, or nation, or world. In it are those whose blood is not right for a wealthy, powerful place. They must seek danger and overcome it. So they go out—on the marshes, in the desert, on the tundra, the planets, or the stars. Being strong, they grow stronger by fighting the tundra, the planets, or the stars. They—they change. They sing new songs. They know new heroes. And then, one day, they return to their old home.

"They return to the wealthy, powerful city, or nation or world. They fight its guardians as they fought the tundra, the planets, or the stars—a way that strikes terror to the heart. Then they sack the city, nation, or world and sing great, ringing sagas of their deeds. They always have. Doubtless they always will."

"But what shall we do?"

"We shall cower, I suppose, beneath the bombs they drop on us, and we shall die, some bravely, some not, defending the palace within a very few hours. But you will have your revenge."

"How?" asked the wing commander, with haunted eyes.

The fat little man giggled and whispered in the officer's ear. Arris irritably shrugged it off as a bad joke. He didn't believe it. As he died, drilled through the chest a few hours later by one of Algan's gunfighters, he believed it even less.

The professor's lecture was drawing to a close. There was time for only one more joke to send his students away happy. He was about to spring it when a messenger handed him two slips of paper. He raged inwardly at his ruined exit and poisonously read from them:

"I have been asked to make two announcements. One, a bulletin from General Sleg's force. He reports that the so-called Outland Insurrection is being brought under control and that there is no cause for alarm. Two, the gentlemen who are members of the S.O.T.C. will please report to the armory at 1375 hours—whatever that may mean—for blaster inspection. The class is dismissed."

Petulantly, he swept from the lectern and through the door.

The Adventurer

AT THE TIME "The Adventurer" was written, R*ch*rd M. N*x*n was not quite yet even Vice-President. So it isn't about him. Is it?

PRESIDENT FOLSOM XXIV said petulantly to his Secretary of the Treasury: "Blow me to hell, Bannister, if I understood a single word of that. *Why* can't I buy the Nicolaides Collection? And don't start with the rediscount and the Series W business again. Just tell me *why*."

The Secretary of the Treasury said with an air of apprehension and a thread-like feeling across his throat: "It boils down to—no money, Mr. President."

The President was too engrossed in thoughts of the marvelous collection to fly into a rage. "It's *such* a bargain," he said mournfully. "An archaic Henry Moore figure—really too big to finger, but I'm no culture-snob, thank God—and fifteen early Morrisons and I can't begin to tell you what else." He looked hopefully at the Secretary of Public Opinion. "Mightn't I seize it for the public good or something?"

The Secretary of Public Opinion shook his head. His pose was gruffly professional. "Not a chance, Mr. President. We'd never get away with it. The art lovers would scream to high Heaven."

"I suppose so . . . *Why* isn't there any money?" He had swiveled dangerously on the Secretary of the Treasury again.

"Sir, purchases of the new Series W bond issue have lagged badly because potential buyers have been attracted to—"

"Stop it, stop it, *stop* it! You know I can't make head or tail of that stuff. Where's the money *going?*"

The Director of the Budget said cautiously: "Mr. President, during the biennium just ending, the Department of Defense accounted for seventy-eight per cent of expenditures—"

The Secretary of Defense growled: "Now wait a minute, Felder! We were voted—"

The President interrupted, raging weakly: "Oh, you rascals! My father would have known what to do with you! But don't think I can't handle it. *Don't* think you can hoodwink me." He punched a button ferociously; his silly face was contorted with rage and there was a certain tension on all the faces around the Cabinet table.

Panels slid down abruptly in the walls, revealing grim-faced Secret Servicemen. Each Cabinet officer was covered by at least two automatic rifles.

"Take that—that traitor away!" the President yelled. His finger pointed at the Secretary of Defense, who slumped over the table, sobbing. Two Secret Servicemen half-carried him from the room.

President Folsom XXIV leaned back, thrusting out his lower lip. He told the Secretary of the Treasury: "*Get* me the money for the Nicolaides Collection. Do you understand? I don't care how you do it. *Get* it." He glared at the Secretary of Public Opinion. "Have you any comments?"

"No, Mr. President."

"All right, then." The President unbent and said plaintively: "I don't see why you can't all be more reasonable. I'm a very reasonable man. I don't see why I can't have a few pleasures along with my responsibilities. Really I don't. And I'm sensitive. I don't *like* these scenes. Very well. That's all. The Cabinet meeting is adjourned."

They rose and left silently in the order of their seniority. The President noticed that the panels were still down and pushed the button that raised them again and hid the granite-faced Secret Servicemen. He took out of his pocket a late Morrison fingering-piece and turned it over in his hand, a smile of relaxation and bliss spreading over his face. *Such* amusing textural contrast! *Such* unexpected variations on the classic sequences!

The Cabinet, less the Secretary of Defense, was holding a rump meeting in an untapped corner of the White House gymnasium.

"God," the Secretary of State said, white-faced. "Poor old Willy!"

The professionally gruff Secretary of Public Opinion said: "We should murder the bastard. I don't care what happens—"

The Director of the Budget said dryly: "We all know what would happen. President Folsom XXV would take office. No; we've got to keep plugging as before. Nothing short of the invincible can topple the Republic . . ."

"What about a war?" the Secretary of Commerce demanded fiercely. "We've no proof that our program will work. What about a war?"

State said wearily: "Not while there's a balance of power, my dear man. The Io–Callisto Question proved that. The Republic and the Soviet fell all over themselves trying to patch things up as soon as it seemed that there would be real shooting. Folsom XXIV and his excellency Premier Yersinsky know at least that much."

The Secretary of the Treasury said: "What would you all think of Steiner for Defense?"

The Director of the Budget was astonished. "Would he take it?"

Treasury cleared his throat. "As a matter of fact, I've asked him to stop by right about now." He hurled a medicine ball into the budgetary gut.

"Oof!" said the Director. "You bastard. Steiner would be perfect. He runs Standards like a watch." He treacherously fired the medicine ball at the Secretary of Raw Materials, who blandly caught it and slammed it back.

"Here he comes," said the Secretary of Raw Materials. "Steiner! Come and sweat some oleo off!"

Steiner ambled over, a squat man in his fifties, and said: "I don't mind if I do. Where's Willy?"

State said: "The President unmasked him as a traitor. He's probably been executed by now."

Steiner looked grim, and grimmer yet when the Secretary of the Treasury said, deadpan: "We want to propose you for Defense."

"I'm happy in Standards," Steiner said. "Safer, too. The Man's father took an interest in science, but The Man never comes around. Things are very quiet. Why don't you invite Winch, from the National Art Commission? It wouldn't be much of a change for the worse for him."

"No brains," the Secretary for Raw Materials said briefly. "Heads up!"

Steiner caught the ball and slugged it back at him. "What good are brains?" he asked quietly.

"Close the ranks, gentlemen," State said. "These long shots are too hard on my arms."

The ranks closed and the Cabinet told Steiner what good were brains. He ended by accepting.

The Moon is all Republic. Mars is all Soviet. Titan is all Republic. Ganymede is all Soviet. But Io and Callisto, by the Treaty of Greenwich, are half-and-half Republic and Soviet.

Down the main street of the principal settlement on Io runs an invisible line. On one side of the line, the principal settlement is known as New Pittsburgh. On the other side it is known as Nizhni-Magnitogorsk.

Into a miner's home in New Pittsburgh one day an eight-year-old boy named Grayson staggered, bleeding from the head. His eyes were swollen almost shut.

His father lurched to his feet, knocking over a bottle. He looked stupidly at the bottle, set it upright too late to save much of the alcohol, and then stared fixedly at the boy. "See what you made me do, you little bastard?" he growled, and fetched the boy a clout on his bleeding head that sent him spinning against the wall of the hut. The boy got up slowly and silently—there seemed to be something wrong with his left arm—and glowered at his father.

He said nothing.

"Fighting again," the father said, in a would-be fierce voice. His eyes fell under the peculiar fire in the boy's stare. "Damn fool—"

A woman came in from the kitchen. She was tall and thin. In a flat voice she said to the man: "Get out of here." The man hiccupped and said: "Your brat spilled my bottle. Gimme a dollar."

In the same flat voice: "I have to buy food."

"*I said gimme a dollar!*" The man slapped her face—it did not change—and wrenched a small purse from the string that suspended it around her neck. The boy suddenly was a demon, flying at his father with fists and teeth. It lasted only a second or two. The father kicked him into a corner where he lay, still glaring, wordless and dry-eyed. The mother had not moved; her husband's handmark was still red on her face when he hulked out, clutching the money bag.

Mrs. Grayson at last crouched in the corner with the eight-year-old boy. "Little Tommy," she said softly. "My little Tommy! Did you cross the line again?"

He was blubbering in her arms, hysterically, as she caressed him. At last he was able to say: "I didn't cross the line, Mom. Not this time. It was in school. They said our name was really Krasinsky. God damn him!" the boy shrieked. "They said his grandfather was named Krasinsky and he moved over the line and changed his name to Grayson! God damn him! Doing that to us!"

"Now darling," his mother said, caressing him. "Now, darling." His trembling began to ebb. She said: "Let's get out the spools, Tommy. You mustn't fall behind in school. You owe that to me, don't you, darling?"

"Yes, Mom," he said. He threw his spindly arms around her and kissed her. "Get out the spools. We'll show him. I mean them."

President Folsom XXIV lay on his deathbed, feeling no pain, mostly because his personal physician had pumped him full of morphine. Dr. Barnes sat by the bed holding the presidential wrist and waiting, occasionally nodding off and recovering with a belligerent stare around the room. The four wire service men didn't care whether he fell asleep or not; they were worriedly discussing the nature and habits of the President's first born, who would shortly succeed to the highest office in the Republic.

"A firebrand, they tell me," the A.P. man said unhappily.

"Firebrands I don't mind," the U.P. man said. "He can send out all the inflammatory notes he wants just as long as he isn't a fiend for exercise. I'm not as young as I once was. You boys wouldn't remember the *old* President, Folsom XXII. He used to do point-to-point hiking. He worshipped old F.D.R."

The I.N.S. man said, lowering his voice: "Then he was worshipping the wrong Roosevelt. Teddy was the athlete."

Dr. Barnes started, dropped the presidential wrist, and held a mirror to the mouth for a moment. "Gentlemen," he said, "the President is dead."

"O.K.," the A.P. man said. "Let's go, boys. I'll send in the flash. U.P., you go cover the College of Electors. I.N.S., get onto the President Elect. Trib, collect some interviews and background—"

The door opened abruptly; a colonel of infantry was standing there, breathing hard, with an automatic rifle at port. "Is he dead?" he asked.

"Yes," the A.P. man said. "If you'll let me past—"

"Nobody leaves the room," the colonel said grimly. "I represent General Slocum, Acting President of the Republic. The College of Electors is acting now to ratify—"

A burst of gunfire caught the colonel in the back; he spun and fell, with a single hoarse cry. More gunfire sounded through the White House. A Secret Serviceman ducked his head through the door: "President's dead? You boys stay put. We'll have this thing cleaned up in an hour—" He vanished.

The doctor sputtered his alarm and the newsmen ignored him with professional poise. The A.P. man asked: "Now who's Slocum? Defense Command?"

I.N.S. said: "I remember him. Three stars. He headed up the Tactical Airborne Force out in Kansas four–five years ago. I think he was retired since then."

A phosphorus grenade crashed through the window and exploded with a globe of yellow flame the size of a basketball; dense clouds of phosphorus pentoxide gushed from it and the sprinkler system switched on, drenching the room.

"Come on!" hacked the A.P. man, and they scrambled from the room and slammed the door. The doctor's coat was burning in two or three places, and he was retching feebly on the corridor floor. They tore his coat off and flung it back into the room.

The U.P. man, swearing horribly, dug a sizzling bit of phosphorus from the back of his hand with a penknife and collapsed, sweating, when it was out. The I.N.S. man passed him a flask and he gurgled down half a pint of liquor. "Who flang that brick?" he asked faintly.

"Nobody," the A.P. man said gloomily. "That's the hell of it. None of this is happening. Just the way Taft the Pretender never happened in nineteen oh three. Just the way the Pentagon Mutiny never happened in sixty-seven."

"Sixty-eight," the U.P. man said faintly. "It didn't happen in sixty-eight, not sixty-seven."

The A.P. man smashed a fist into the palm of his hand and swore. "*God* damn," he said. "Some day I'd like to—" He broke off and was bitterly silent.

The U.P. man must have been a little dislocated with shock and quite drunk to talk the way he did. "Me too," he said. "Like to tell the story. Maybe it was sixty-seven not sixty-eight. I'm not sure now. Can't write it down so the details get lost and then after a while it didn't happen at all. Revolution'd be good deal. But it takes people t' make revolution. *People.* With eyes 'n ears. 'N memories. We make things not-happen an' we make people not-see an' not-hear . . ."

He slumped back against the corridor wall, nursing his burned hand. The others were watching him, very scared.

Then the A.P. man caught sight of the Secretary of Defense striding down the corridor, flanked by Secret Servicemen. "Mr. Steiner!" he called. "What's the picture?"

Steiner stopped, breathing heavily, and said: "Slocum's barricaded in the Oval Study. They don't want to smash in. He's about the only one left. There were only fifty or so. The Acting President's taken charge at the Study. You want to come along?"

They did, and even hauled the U.P. man after them.

The Acting President, who would be President Folsom XXV as soon as the Electoral College got around to it, had his father's face— the petulant lip, the soft jowl—on a hard young body. He also had an auto-rifle ready to fire from the hip. Most of the Cabinet was present. When the Secretary of Defense arrived, he turned on him. "Steiner," he said nastily, "can you explain why there should be a rebellion against the Republic in your department?"

"Mr. President," Steiner said, "Slocum was retired on my recommendation two years ago. It seems to me that my responsibility ended there and Security should have taken over."

The President Elect's finger left the trigger of the auto-rifle and his lip drew in a little. "Quite so," he said curtly, and turned to the door. "Slocum!" he shouted. "Come out of there. We can use gas if we want."

The door opened unexpectedly and a tired-looking man with three stars on each shoulder stood there, bare-handed. "All right," he said drearily. "I was fool enough to think something could be done about the regime. But you fat-faced imbeciles are going to go on and on and and—"

The stutter of the auto-rifle cut him off. The President Elect's knuckles were white as he clutched the piece's forearm and grip; the torrent of slugs continued to hack and plow the general's body until the magazine was empty. "Burn that," he said curtly, turning his back on it. "Dr. Barnes, come here. I want to know about my father's passing."

The doctor, hoarse and red-eyed from the whiff of phosphorus smoke, spoke with him. The U.P. man had sagged drunkenly into a chair, but the other newsmen noted that Dr. Barnes glanced at them as he spoke, in a confidential murmur.

"Thank you, doctor," the President Elect said at last, decisively. He gestured to a Secret Serviceman. "Take those traitors away." They went, numbly.

The Secretary of State cleared his throat. "Mr. President," he said, "I take this opportunity to submit the resignations of myself and fellow Cabinet members according to custom."

"That's all right," the President Elect said. "You may as well stay on. I intend to run things myself anyway." He hefted the auto-rifle. "You," he said to the Secretary of Public Opinion. "You have some work to do. Have the memory of my father's—artistic—preoccupations obliterated as soon as possible. I wish the Republic to assume a warlike posture—yes; what is it?"

A trembling messenger said: "Mr. President, I have the honor to inform you that the College of Electors has elected you President of the Republic—unanimously."

Cadet Fourth Classman Thomas Grayson lay on his bunk and sobbed in an agony of loneliness. The letter from his mother was crumpled in his hand: "—prouder than words can tell of your appointment to the Academy. Darling, I hardly knew my grandfather but I know that you will serve as brilliantly as he did, to the eternal credit of the Republic. You must be brave and strong for my sake—"

He would have given everything he had or ever could hope to have to be back with her, and away from the bullying, sneering fellow-cadets of the Corps. He kissed the letter—and then hastily shoved it under his mattress as he heard footsteps.

He popped to a brace, but it was only his roommate Ferguson. Ferguson was from Earth, and rejoiced in the lighter Lunar gravity which was punishment to Grayson's Io-bred muscles.

"Rest, mister," Ferguson grinned.

"Thought it was night inspection."

"Any minute now. They're down the hall. Lemme tighten your bunk or you'll be in trouble—" Tightening the bunk he pulled out the letter and said, calfishly: "Ah-*hah!* Who is she?—" and opened it.

When the cadet officers reached the room they found Ferguson on the floor being strangled black in the face by spidery little Grayson. It took all three of them to pull him off. Ferguson went to the infirmary and Grayson went to the Commandant's office.

The Commandant glared at the cadet from under the most spectacular pair of eyebrows in the Service. "Cadet Grayson," he said, "explain what occurred."

"Sir, Cadet Ferguson began to read a letter from my mother without my permission."

"That is not accepted by the Corps as grounds for mayhem. Do you have anything further to say?"

"Sir, I lost my temper. All I thought of was that it was an act of disrespect to my mother and somehow to the Corps and the Republic too—that Cadet Ferguson was dishonoring the Corps."

Bushwah, the Commandant thought. *A snow job and a crude one.* He studied the youngster. He had never seen such a brace from an Io-bred fourth-classman. It must be torture to muscles not yet toughened up to even Lunar gravity. Five minutes more and the boy would have to give way, and serve him right for showing off.

He studied Grayson's folder. It was too early to tell about academic work, but the fourth-classman was a bear—or a fool—for extra duty. He had gone out for half a dozen teams and applied for membership in the exacting Math Club *and* Writing Club. The Commandant glanced up; Grayson was still in his extreme brace. The Commandant suddenly had the queer idea that Grayson could hold it until it killed him.

"One hundred hours of pack drill," he barked, "to be completed before quarter-term. Cadet Grayson, if you succeed in walking off your tours, remember that there is a tradition of fellowship in the Corps which its members are expected to observe. Dismiss."

After Grayson's steel-sharp salute and exit the Commandant dug deeper into the folder. Apparently there was something wrong with the boy's left arm, but it had been passed by the examining team that visited Io. Most unusual. Most irregular. But nothing could be done about it now.

The President, softer now in body than on his election day, and infinitely more cautious, snapped: "It's all very well to create an incident. But where's the money to come from? Who wants the rest of Io anyway? And what will happen if there's war?"

Treasury said: "The hoarders will supply the money, Mr. President. A system of percentage bounties for persons who report currency hoarders, and then enforced purchase of a bond issue."

Raw Materials said: "We need that iron, Mr. President. We need it desperately."

State said: "All our evaluations indicate that the Soviet Premier would consider nothing less than armed invasion of his continental borders as occasion for all-out war. The consumer-goods party in the Soviet has gained immensely during the past five years and of course their armaments have suffered. Your shrewd directive to put the Republic in a warlike posture has borne fruit, Mr. President . . ."

President Folsom XXV studied them narrowly. To him the need for a border incident culminating in a forced purchase of Soviet Io did not seem as pressing as they thought, but they were, after all, specialists. And there was no conceivable way they could benefit from it personally. The only alternative was that they were offering their professional advice and that it would be best to heed it. Still, there was a vague, nagging something . . .

Nonsense, he decided. The spy dossiers on his Cabinet showed nothing but the usual. One had been blackmailed by an actress after an affair and railroaded her off the Earth. Another had a habit of taking bribes to advance favorite sons in civil and military service. And so on. The Republic could not suffer at their hands; the Republic and the dynasty were impregnable. You simply spied on everybody— including the spies—and ordered summary executions often enough to show that you meant it, and kept the public ignorant: deaf-dumb-blind ignorant. The spy system was simplicity itself; you had only to let things get as tangled and confused as possible until *nobody* knew who was who. The executions were literally no problem, for guilt or innocence made no matter. And mind control, when there were four newspapers, six magazines, and three radio and television stations, was a job for a handful of clerks.

No; the Cabinet couldn't be getting away with anything. The system was unbeatable.

President Folsom XXV said: "Very well. Have it done."

Mrs. Grayson, widow, of New Pittsburgh, Io, disappeared one night. It was in all the papers and on all the broadcasts. Some time later she was found dragging herself back across the line between Nizhni-Magnitogorsk and New Pittsburgh in sorry shape. She had a terrible tale to tell about what she had suffered at the hands and so forth of the Nizhni-Magnitogorskniks. A diplomatic note from the Republic to the Soviet was answered by another note which was answered by the dispatch of the Republic's First Fleet to Io which was answered by the dispatch of the Soviet's First and Fifth Fleets to Io.

The Republic's First Fleet blew up the customary deserted target hulk, fulminated over a sneak sabotage attack, and moved in its destroyers. Battle was joined.

Ensign Thomas Grayson took over the command of his destroyer when its captain was killed on his bridge. An electrified crew saw the strange, brooding youngster perform prodigies of skill and courage, and responded to them. In one week of desultory action the battered destroyer had accounted for seven Soviet destroyers and a cruiser.

As soon as this penetrated to the flagship Grayson was decorated and given a flotilla. His weird magnetism extended to every officer and man aboard the seven craft. They struck like phantoms, cutting out cruisers and battlewagons in wild unorthodox actions that couldn't have succeeded but did—every time. Grayson was badly wounded twice, but his driving nervous energy carried him through.

He was decorated again and given the battlewagon of an ailing four-striper.

Without orders he touched down on the Soviet side of Io, led out a landing party of marines and bluejackets, cut through two regiments of Soviet infantry, and returned to his battlewagon with prisoners: the top civil and military administrators of Soviet Io.

They discussed him nervously aboard the flagship.

"He had a mystical quality, Admiral. His men would follow him into an atomic furnace. And—and I almost believe he could bring them through safely if he wanted to." The laugh was nervous.

"He doesn't look like much. But when he turns on the charm—watch out!"

"He's—he's a *winner*. Now I wonder what I mean by that?"

"I know what you mean. They turn up every so often. People who can't be stopped. People who have everything. Napoleons. Alexanders. Stalins. Up from nowhere."

"Suleiman. Hitler. Folsom I. Jenghiz Khan."

"Well, let's get it over with."

They tugged at their gold-braided jackets and signalled the honor guard.

Grayson was piped aboard, received another decoration and another speech. This time he made a speech in return.

President Folsom XXV, not knowing what else to do, had summoned his Cabinet. "Well?" he rasped at the Secretary of Defense. Steiner said with a faint shrug: "Mr. President, there is nothing to be done. He has the fleet, he has the broadcasting facilities, he has the people."

"People!" snarled the President. His finger stabbed at a button and the wall panels snapped down to show the Secret Servicemen standing in their niches. The finger shot tremulously out at Steiner. "Kill that traitor!" he raved.

The chief of the detail said uneasily: "Mr. President, we were listening to Grayson before we came on duty. He says he's de facto President now—"

"Kill him! Kill him!"

The chief went doggedly on: "—and we liked what he had to say about the Republic and he said citizens of the Republic shouldn't take orders from you and he'd relieve you—"

The President fell back.

Grayson walked in, wearing his plain ensign's uniform and smiling faintly. Admirals and four-stripers flanked him.

The chief of the detail said: "Mr. Grayson! Are you taking over?"

The man in the ensign's uniform said gravely: "Yes. And just call me 'Grayson,' please. The titles come later. You can go now."

The chief gave a pleased grin and collected his detail. The rather slight, youngish man who had something wrong with one arm was in charge—*complete* charge.

Grayson said: "Mr. Folsom, you are relieved of the presidency. Captain, take him out and—" He finished with a whimsical shrug. A portly four-striper took Folsom by one arm. Like a drugged man the deposed president let himself be led out.

Grayson looked around the table. "Who are you gentlemen?"

They felt his magnetism, like the hum when you pass a power station.

Steiner was the spokesman. "Grayson," he said soberly, "we were Folsom's Cabinet. However, there is more that we have to tell you. Alone, if you will allow it."

"Very well, gentlemen." Admirals and captains backed out, looking concerned.

Steiner said: "Grayson, the story goes back many years. My predecessor, William Malvern, determined to overthrow the regime, holding that it was an affront to the human spirit. There have been many such attempts. All have broken up on the rocks of espionage, terrorism, and opinion control—the three weapons which the regime holds firmly in its hands.

"Malvern tried another approach than espionage versus espionage, terrorism versus terrorism, and opinion control versus opinion control. He determined to use the basic fact that certain men make history: that there are men born to be mould breakers. They are the Philips of Macedon, the Napoleons, Stalins and Hitlers, the Suleimans—the adventurers. Again and again they flash across history, bringing down an ancient empire, turning ordinary soldiers of the line into unkillable demons of battle, uprooting cultures, breathing new life into moribund peoples.

"There are common denominators among all the adventurers. Intelligence, of course. Other things are more mysterious but are always present. They are foreigners. Napoleon the Corsican. Hitler the Austrian. Stalin the Georgian. Philip the Macedonian. Always there is an Oedipus complex. Always there is physical deficiency. Napoleon's stature. Stalin's withered arm—and yours. Always there is a minority disability, real or fancied.

"This is a shock to you, Grayson, but you must face it. *You were manufactured.*

"Malvern packed the Cabinet with the slyest double-dealers he could find and they went to work. Eighty-six infants were planted on the outposts of the Republic in simulated family environments. Your mother was not your mother but one of the most brilliant actresses ever to drop out of sight on Earth. Your intelligence heredity was so good that we couldn't turn you down for lack of a physical deficiency. We withered your arm with gamma radiation. I hope you will forgive us. There was no other way.

"Of the eighty-six you are the one that worked. Somehow the combination for you was minutely different from all the other combinations, genetically or environmentally, and it worked. That is all we were after. The mould has been broken, you know now what you are.

Let come whatever chaos is to come; the dead hand of the past no longer lies on—"

Grayson went to the door and beckoned; two captains came in. Steiner broke off his speech as Grayson said to them: "These men deny my godhood. Take them out and—" he finished with a whimsical shrug.

"Yes, your divinity," said the captains, without a trace of humor in their voices.

The Little Black Bag

In 1971 I was speaking at the First General Assembly of the World Future Society at the Washington Hilton. One evening I went up to my room to make a phone call and, waiting for the person at the other end to get off the phone, flipped on the television. What turned up on the screen was "The Little Black Bag." I hadn't expected it. It was Rod Serling's adaptation, faithful to the text and very good. So I forgot to make my phone call, and was late joining friends downstairs . . . but it was worth it.

OLD DR. FULL felt the winter in his bones as he limped down the alley. It was the alley and the back door he had chosen rather than the sidewalk and the front door because of the brown paper bag under his arm. He knew perfectly well that the flat-faced, stringy-haired women of his street and their gap-toothed, sour-smelling husbands did not notice if he brought a bottle of cheap wine to his room. They all but lived on the stuff themselves, varied with whiskey when pay checks were boosted by overtime. But Dr. Full, unlike them, was ashamed. A complicated disaster occurred as he limped down the littered alley. One of the neighborhood dogs—a mean little black one he knew and hated, with its teeth always bared and always snarling with menace—hurled at his legs through a hole in the board fence that lined his path. Dr. Full flinched, then swung his leg in what was to have been a satisfying kick to the animal's gaunt ribs. But the winter in his bones weighed down the leg. His foot failed to clear a half-buried brick, and he sat down abruptly, cursing. When he smelled unbottled wine and realized his brown paper package had slipped from under his arm and smashed, his curses died on his lips. The snarling black dog was circling him at a yard's distance, tensely stalking, but he ignored it in the greater disaster.

With stiff fingers as he sat on the filth of the alley, Dr. Full unfolded the brown paper bag's top, which had been crimped over, grocer-wise. The early autumnal dusk had come; he could not see plainly what was left. He lifted out the jug-handled top of his half gallon, and some fragments, and then the bottom of the bottle. Dr. Full was far too occupied to exult as he noted that there was a good pint left. He had a problem, and emotions could be deferred until the fitting time.

The dog closed in, its snarl rising in pitch. He set down the bottom of the bottle and pelted the dog with the curved triangular glass fragments of its top. One of them connected, and the dog ducked back through the fence, howling. Dr. Full then placed a razor-like edge of the half-gallon bottle's foundation to his lips and drank from it as though it were a giant's cup. Twice he had to put it down to rest his arms, but in one minute he had swallowed the pint of wine.

He thought of rising to his feet and walking through the alley to his room, but a flood of well-being drowned the notion. It was, after all, inexpressibly pleasant to sit there and feel the frost-hardened mud of the alley turn soft, or seem to, and to feel the winter evaporating from his bones under a warmth which spread from his stomach through his limbs.

A three-year-old girl in a cut-down winter coat squeezed through the same hole in the board fence from which the black dog had sprung its ambush. Gravely she toddled up to Dr. Full and inspected him with her dirty forefinger in her mouth. Dr. Full's happiness had been providentially made complete; he had been supplied with an audience.

"Ah, my dear," he said hoarsely. And then: "Preposserous accusation. 'If that's what you call evidence,' I should have told them, 'you better stick to your doctoring.' I should have told them: 'I was here before your County Medical Society. And the License Commissioner never proved a thing on me. So, gennulmen, doesn't it stand to reason? I appeal to you as fellow memmers of a great profession—'"

The little girl, bored, moved away, picking up one of the triangular pieces of glass to play with as she left. Dr. Full forgot her immediately, and continued to himself earnestly: "But so help me, they *couldn't* prove a thing. Hasn't a man got any *rights?*" He brooded over the question, of whose answer he was so sure, but on which the Committee on Ethics of the County Medical Society had been equally certain. The winter was creeping into his bones again, and he had no money and no more wine.

Dr. Full pretended to himself that there was a bottle of whiskey somewhere in the fearful litter of his room. It was an old and cruel trick he played on himself when he simply had to be galvanized into getting up and going home. He might freeze there in the alley. In his room he would be bitten by bugs and would cough at the moldy reek from his sink, but he would not freeze and be cheated of the hundreds of bottles of wine that he still might drink, the thousands of hours of glowing content he still might feel. He thought about that bottle of whiskey—was it back of a mounded heap of medical journals? No; he had looked there last time. Was it under the sink, shoved well to the rear, behind the rusty drain? The cruel trick began to play itself out again. Yes, he told himself with mounting excitement, yes, it might be! Your memory isn't so good nowadays, he told himself with rueful good fellowship. You know perfectly well you might have bought a bottle of whiskey and shoved it behind the sink drain for a moment just like this.

The amber bottle, the crisp snap of the sealing as he cut it, the pleasurable exertion of starting the screw cap on its threads, and then the refreshing tangs in his throat, the warmth in his stomach, the dark, dull happy oblivion of drunkenness—they became real to him. You *could* have, you know! You *could* have! he told himself. With the blessed conviction growing in his mind—It *could* have happened, you know! It *could* have!—he struggled to his right knee. As he did, he heard a yelp behind him, and curiously craned his neck around while resting. It was the little girl, who had cut her hand quite badly on her toy, the piece of glass. Dr. Full could see the rilling bright blood down her coat, pooling at her feet.

He almost felt inclined to defer the image of the amber bottle for her, but not seriously. He knew that it was there, shoved well to the rear under the sink, behind the rusty drain where he had hidden it. He would have a drink and then magnanimously return to help the child. Dr. Full got to his other knee and then his feet, and proceeded at a rapid totter down the littered alley toward his room, where he would hunt with calm optimism at first for the bottle that was not there, then with anxiety, and then with frantic violence. He would hurl books and dishes about before he was done looking for the amber bottle of whiskey, and finally would beat his swollen knuckles against the brick wall until old scars on them opened and his thick old blood oozed over his hands. Last of all, he would sit down somewhere on the floor, whimpering, and would plunge into the abyss of purgative nightmare that was his sleep.

After twenty generations of shilly-shallying and "we'll cross that bridge when we come to it," genus homo had bred himself into an impasse. Dogged biometricians had pointed out with irrefutable logic that mental subnormals were outbreeding mental normals and supernormals, and that the process was occurring on an exponential curve. Every fact that could be mustered in the argument proved the biometricians' case, and led inevitably to the conclusion that genus homo was going to wind up in a preposterous jam quite soon. If you think that had any effect on breeding practices, you do not know genus homo.

There was, of course, a sort of masking effect produced by that other exponential function, the accumulation of technological devices. A moron trained to punch an adding machine seems to be a more skillful computer than a medieval mathematician trained to count on his fingers. A moron trained to operate the twenty-first century equivalent of a linotype seems to be a better typographer than a Renaissance printer limited to a few fonts of movable type. This is also true of medical practice.

It was a complicated affair of many factors. The supernormals "improved the product" at greater speed than the subnormals degraded it, but in smaller quantity because elaborate training of their children was practiced on a custom-made basis. The fetish of higher education had some weird avatars by the twentieth generation: "colleges" where not a member of the student body could read words of three syllables; "universities" where such degrees as "Bachelor of Typewriting," "Master of Shorthand" and "Doctor of Philosophy (Card Filing)" were conferred with the traditional pomp. The handful of supernormals used such devices in order that the vast majority might keep some semblance of a social order going.

Some day the supernormals would mercilessly cross the bridge; at the twentieth generation they were standing irresolutely at its approaches wondering what had hit them. And the ghosts of twenty generations of biometricians chuckled malignantly.

It is a certain Doctor of Medicine of this twentieth generation that we are concerned with. His name was Hemingway—John Hemingway, B.Sc., M.D. He was a general practitioner, and did not hold with running to specialists with every trifling ailment. He often said as much, in approximately these words: "Now, uh, what I mean is you got a good old G.P. See what I mean? Well, uh, now a good old G.P. don't claim he knows all about lungs and glands and them things, get me? But you got a G.P., you got, uh, you got a, well, you got a . . . *all-around man!* That's what you got when you got a G.P. —you got a all-around man."

But from this, do not imagine that Dr. Hemingway was a poor doctor. He could remove tonsils or appendixes, assist at practically any confinement and deliver a living, uninjured infant, correctly diagnose hundreds of ailments, and prescribe and administer the correct medication or treatment for each. There was, in fact, only one thing he could not do in the medical line, and that was violate the ancient canons of medical ethics. And Dr. Hemingway knew better than to try.

Dr. Hemingway and a few friends were chatting one evening when the event occurred that precipitates him into our story. He had been through a hard day at the clinic, and he wished his physicist friend Walter Gillis, B.Sc., M.Sc., Ph.D., would shut up so he could tell everybody about it. But Gillis kept rambling on, in his stilted fashion: "You got to hand it to old Mike; he don't have what we call the scientific method, but you got to hand it to him. There this poor little dope is, puttering around with some glassware and I come up and I ask him, kidding of course, 'How's about a time-travel machine, Mike?'"

Dr. Gillis was not aware of it, but "Mike" had an I.Q. six times his own, and was—to be blunt—his keeper. "Mike" rode herd on the pseudo-physicists in the pseudo-laboratory, in the guise of a bottle washer. It was a social waste—but as has been mentioned before, the supernormals were still standing at the approaches to a bridge. Their irresolution led to many such preposterous situations. And it happens that "Mike," having grown frantically bored with his task, was malevolent enough to—but let Dr. Gillis tell it:

"So he gives me these here tube numbers and says, 'Series circuit. Now stop bothering me. Build your time machine, sit down at it and turn on the switch. That's all I ask, Dr. Gillis—that's all I ask.'"

"Say," marveled a brittle and lovely blond guest, "you remember real good, don't you, doc?" She gave him a melting smile.

"Heck," said Gillis modestly, "I always remember good. It's what you call an inherent facility. And besides I told it quick to my secretary, so she wrote it down. I don't read so good, but I sure remember good, all right. Now, where was I?"

Everybody thought hard, and there were various suggestions:

"Something about bottles, doc?"

"You was starting a fight. You said 'time somebody was traveling.' "

"Yeah—you called somebody a swish. Who did you call a swish?"

"Not swish—*switch.*"

Dr. Gillis's noble brow grooved with thought, and he declared: "Switch is right. It was about time travel. What we call travel through time. So I took the tube numbers he gave me and I put them into the circuit builder; I set it for 'series' and there it is—my time-traveling machine. It travels things through time real good." He displayed a box.

"What's in the box?" asked the lovely blonde.

Dr. Hemingway told her: "Time travel. It travels things through time."

"Look," said Gillis, the physicist. He took Dr. Hemingway's little black bag and put it on the box. He turned on the switch and the little black bag vanished.

"Say," said Dr. Hemingway, "that was, uh, swell. Now bring it back."

"Huh?"

"Bring back my little black bag."

"Well," said Dr. Gillis, "they don't come back. I tried it backwards and they don't come back. I guess maybe that dummy Mike give me a bum steer."

There was wholesale condemnation of "Mike" but Dr. Hemingway took no part in it. He was nagged by a vague feeling that there was something he would have to do. He reasoned: "I am a doctor, and a doctor has got to have a little black bag. I ain't got a little black bag—so ain't I a doctor no more?" He decided that this was absurd. He *knew* he was a doctor. So it must be the bag's fault for not being there. It was no good, and he would get another one tomorrow from that dummy Al, at the clinic. Al could find things good, but he was a dummy—never liked to talk sociable to you.

So the next day Dr. Hemingway remembered to get another little black bag from his keeper—another little black bag with which he could perform tonsillectomies, appendectomies, and the most difficult confinements, and with which he could diagnose and cure his kind until the day when the supernormals could bring themselves to cross that bridge. Al was kinda nasty about the missing little black bag, but Dr. Hemingway didn't exactly remember what had happened, so no tracer was sent out, so—

Old Dr. Full awoke from the horrors of the night to the horrors of the day. His gummy eyelashes pulled apart convulsively. He was propped against a corner of his room, and something was making a little drumming noise. He felt very cold and cramped. As his eyes focused on his lower body, he croaked out a laugh. The drumming noise was being made by his left heel, agitated by fine tremors against the bare floor. It was going to be the D.T.'s again, he decided dispassionately. He wiped his mouth with his bloody knuckles, and the fine tremor coarsened; the snare-drum beat became louder and slower. He was getting a break this fine morning, he decided sardonically. You didn't get the horrors until you had been tightened like a violin string, just to the breaking point. He had a reprieve, if a reprieve into his old body with the blazing, endless headache just back of the eyes and the screaming stiffness in the joints were anything to be thankful for.

There was something or other about a kid, he thought vaguely. He was going to doctor some kid. His eyes rested on a little black bag in the center of the room, and he forgot about the kid. "I could have sworn," said Dr. Full, "I hocked that two years ago!" He hitched over and reached the bag, and then realized it was some stranger's kit, arriving here he did not know how. He tentatively touched the lock and it snapped open and lay flat, rows and rows of instruments and medications tucked into loops in its four walls. It seemed vastly larger open than closed. He didn't see how it could possibly fold up into that compact size again, but decided it was some stunt of the instrument makers. Since his time—that made it worth more at the hock shop, he thought with satisfaction.

Just for old times' sake, he let his eyes and fingers rove over the instruments before he snapped the bag shut and headed for Uncle's. More than a few were a little hard to recognize—exactly that is. You could see the things with blades for cutting, the forceps for holding and pulling, the retractors for holding fast, the needles and gut for suturing, the hypos—a fleeting thought crossed his mind that he could peddle the hypos separately to drug addicts.

Let's go, he decided, and tried to fold up the case. It didn't fold until he happened to touch the lock, and then it folded all at once into a little black bag. Sure have forged ahead, he thought, almost able to forget that what he was primarily interested in was its pawn value.

With a definite objective, it was not too hard for him to get to his feet. He decided to go down the front steps, out the front door, and down the sidewalk. But first—

He snapped the bag open again on his kitchen table, and pored through the medication tubes. "Anything to sock the autonomic nervous system good and hard," he mumbled. The tubes were numbered, and there was a plastic card which seemed to list them. The left margin of the card was a run-down of the systems—vascular, muscular, nervous. He followed the last entry across to the right. There were columns for "stimulant," "depressant," and so on. Under "nervous system" and "depressant" he found the number 17, and shakily located the little glass tube which bore it. It was full of pretty blue pills and he took one.

It was like being struck by a thunderbolt.

Dr. Full had so long lacked any sense of well-being except the brief glow of alcohol that he had forgotten its very nature. He was panic-stricken for a long moment at the sensation that spread through him slowly, finally tingling in his fingertips. He straightened up, his pains gone and his leg tremor stilled.

That was great, he thought. He'd be able to *run* to the hock shop, pawn the little black bag, and get some booze. He started down the stairs. Not even the street, bright with mid-morning sun, into which he emerged made him quail. The little black bag in his left hand had a satisfying, authoritative weight. He was walking erect, he noted, and not in the somewhat furtive crouch that had grown on him in recent years. A little self-respect, he told himself, that's what I need. Just because a man's down doesn't mean—

"Docta, please-a come wit'!" somebody yelled at him, tugging his arm. "Da litt-la girl, she's-a burn' up!" It was one of the slum's innumerable flat-faced, stringy-haired women, in a slovenly wrapper.

"Ah, I happen to be retired from practice—" he began hoarsely, but she would not be put off.

"In by here, Docta!" she urged, tugging him to a doorway. "You come look-a da litt-la girl. I got two dolla, you come look!" That put a different complexion on the matter. He allowed himself to be towed through the doorway into a mussy, cabbage-smelling flat. He knew the woman now, or rather knew who she must be—a new arrival who had moved in the other night. These people moved at night, in motorcades of battered cars supplied by friends and relations, with furniture lashed to the tops, swearing and drinking until the small hours. It explained why she had stopped him: she did not yet know he was old Dr. Full, a drunken reprobate whom nobody would trust. The little black bag had been his guarantee, outweighing his whiskery face and stained black suit.

He was looking down on a three-year-old girl who had, he rather suspected, just been placed in the mathematical center of a freshly changed double bed. God knew what sour and dirty mattress she usually slept on. He seemed to recognize her as he noted a crusted bandage on her right hand. Two dollars, he thought— An ugly flush had spread up her pipe-stem arm. He poked a finger into the socket of her elbow, and felt little spheres like marbles under the skin and ligaments roll apart. The child began to squall thinly; beside him, the woman gasped and began to weep herself.

"Out," he gestured briskly at her, and she thudded away, still sobbing.

Two dollars, he thought— Give her some mumbo jumbo, take the money and tell her to go to a clinic. Strep, I guess, from that stinking alley. It's a wonder any of them grow up. He put down the little black bag and forgetfully fumbled for his key, then remembered and touched the lock. It flew open, and he selected a bandage shears, with a blunt wafer for the lower jaw. He fitted the lower jaw under the bandage, trying not to hurt the kid by its pressure on the infection, and began to cut. It was amazing how easily and swiftly the shining shears snipped through the crusty rag around the wound. He hardly seemed to be driving the shears with fingers at all. It almost seemed as though the shears were driving his fingers instead as they scissored a clean, light line through the bandage.

Certainly have forged ahead since my time, he thought—sharper than a microtome knife. He replaced the shears in their loop on the extraordinarily big board that the little black bag turned into when it unfolded, and leaned over the wound. He whistled at the ugly gash, and the violent infection which had taken immediate root in the sickly child's thin body. Now what can you do with a thing like that? He pawed over the contents of the little black bag, nervously. If he lanced it and let some of the pus out, the old woman would think he'd done something for her and he'd get the two dollars. But at the clinic they'd want to know who did it and if they got sore enough they might send a cop around. Maybe there was something in the kit—

He ran down the left edge of the card to "lymphatic" and read across to the column under "infection." It didn't sound right at all to him; he checked again, but it still said that. In the square to which the line and column led were the symbols: "IV-g-3cc." He couldn't find any bottles marked with Roman numerals, and then noticed that that was how the hypodermic needles were designated. He lifted number IV from its loop, noting that it was fitted with a needle already and even seemed to be charged. What a way to carry those things around! So—three cc. of whatever was in hypo number IV ought to do something or other about infections settled in the lymphatic system— which, God knows, this one was. What did the lower-case "g" mean, though? He studied the glass hypo and saw letters engraved on what looked like a rotating disk at the top of the barrel. They ran from "a" to "i," and there was an index line engraved on the barrel on the op- posite side from the calibrations.

Shrugging, old Dr. Full turned the disk until "g" coincided with the index line, and lifted the hypo to eye level. As he pressed in the plunger he did not see the tiny thread of fluid squirt from the tip of the needle. There was a sort of dark mist for a moment about the tip. A closer inspection showed that the needle was not even pierced at the tip. It had the usual slanting cut across the bias of the shaft, but the cut did not expose an oval hole. Baffled, he tried pressing the plunger again. Again *something* appeared around the tip and vanished. "We'll settle this," said the doctor. He slipped the needle into the skin of his forearm. He thought at first that he had missed— that the point had glided over the top of his skin instead of catching and slipping under it. But he saw a tiny blood-spot and realized that somehow he just hadn't felt the puncture. Whatever was in the barrel, he decided, couldn't do him any harm if it lived up to its billing—and if it could come out through a needle that had no hole. He gave him- self three cc. and twitched the needle out. There was the swelling— painless, but otherwise typical.

Dr. Full decided it was his eyes or something, and gave three cc. of "g" from hypodermic IV to the feverish child. There was no interruption to her wailing as the needle went in and the swelling rose. But a long instant later, she gave a final gasp and was silent.

Well, he told himself, cold with horror, you did it that time. You killed her with that stuff.

Then the child sat up and said: "Where's my mommy?"

Incredulously, the doctor seized her arm and palpated the elbow. The gland infection was zero, and the temperature seemed normal. The blood-congested tissues surrounding the wound were subsiding as he watched. The child's pulse was stronger and no faster than a child's should be. In the sudden silence of the room he could hear the little girl's mother sobbing in her kitchen, outside. And he also heard a girl's insinuating voice:

"She gonna be O.K., doc?"

He turned and saw a gaunt-faced, dirty-blond sloven of perhaps eighteen leaning in the doorway and eying him with amused contempt. She continued: "I heard about you, *Doc-tor* Full. So don't go try and put the bite on the old lady. You couldn't doctor up a sick cat."

"Indeed?" he rumbled. This young person was going to get a lesson she richly deserved. "Perhaps you would care to look at my patient?"

"Where's my mommy?" insisted the little girl, and the blonde's jaw fell. She went to the bed and cautiously asked: "You O.K. now, Teresa? You all fixed up?"

"Where's my mommy?" demanded Teresa. Then, accusingly, she gestured with her wounded hand at the doctor. "You *poke* me!" she complained, and giggled pointlessly.

"Well—" said the blond girl, "I guess I got to hand it to you, doc. These loud-mouth women around here said you didn't know your . . . I mean, didn't know how to cure people. They said you ain't a real doctor."

"I *have* retired from practice," he said. "But I happened to be taking this case to a colleague as a favor, your good mother noticed me, and—" a deprecating smile. He touched the lock of the case and it folded up into the little black bag again.

"You stole it," the girl said flatly.

He sputtered.

"Nobody'd trust you with a thing like that. It must be worth plenty. You stole that case. I was going to stop you when I come in and saw you working over Teresa, but it looked like you wasn't doing her any harm. But when you give me that line about taking that case to a colleague I know you stole it. You gimme a cut or I go to the cops. A thing like that must be worth twenty–thirty dollars."

The mother came timidly in, her eyes red. But she let out a whoop of joy when she saw the little girl sitting up and babbling to herself, embraced her madly, fell on her knees for a quick prayer, hopped up to kiss the doctor's hand, and then dragged him into the kitchen, all the while rattling in her native language while the blond girl let her eyes go cold with disgust. Dr. Full allowed himself to be towed into the kitchen, but flatly declined a cup of coffee and a plate of anise cakes and St. John's Bread.

"Try him on some wine, ma," said the girl sardonically.

"Hyass! Hyass!" breathed the woman delightedly. "You like-a wine, docta?" She had a carafe of purplish liquid before him in an instant, and the blond girl snickered as the doctor's hand twitched out at it. He drew his hand back, while there grew in his head the old image of how it would smell and then taste and then warm his stomach and limbs. He made the kind of calculation at which he was practiced; the delighted woman would not notice as he downed two tumblers, and he could overawe her through two tumblers more with his tale of Teresa's narrow brush with the Destroying Angel, and then —why, then it would not matter. He would be drunk.

But for the first time in years, there was a sort of counter-image: a blend of the rage he felt at the blond girl to whom he was so transparent, and of pride at the cure he had just effected. Much to his own surprise, he drew back his hand from the carafe and said, luxuriating in the words: "No, thank you. I don't believe I'd care for any so early in the day." He covertly watched the blond girl's face, and was gratified at her surprise. Then the mother was shyly handing him two bills and saying: "Is no much-a money, docta—but you come again, see Teresa?"

"I shall be glad to follow the case through," he said. "But now excuse me—I really must be running along." He grasped the little black bag firmly and got up; he wanted very much to get away from the wine and the older girl.

"Wait up, doc," said she, "I'm going your way." She followed him out and down the street. He ignored her until he felt her hand on the black bag. Then old Dr. Full stopped and tried to reason with her: "Look, my dear. Perhaps you're right. I might have stolen it. To be perfectly frank, I don't remember how I got it. But you're young and you can earn your own money—"

"Fifty–fifty," she said, "or I go to the cops. And if I get another word outta you, it's sixty–forty. And you know who gets the short end, don't you, doc?"

Defeated, he marched to the pawnshop, her impudent hand still on the handle with his, and her heels beating out a tattoo against his stately tread.

In the pawnshop, they both got a shock.

"It ain't stendard," said Uncle, unimpressed by the ingenious lock. "I ain't nevva seen one like it. Some cheap Jap stuff, maybe? Try down the street. This I nevva could sell."

Down the street they got an offer of one dollar. The same complaint was made: "I ain't a collecta, mista—I buy stuff that got resale value. Who could I sell this to, a Chinaman who don't know medical instruments? Every one of them looks funny. You sure you didn't make these yourself?" They didn't take the one-dollar offer.

The girl was baffled and angry; the doctor was baffled too, but triumphant. He had two dollars, and the girl had a half-interest in something nobody wanted. But, he suddenly marveled, the thing had been all right to cure the kid, hadn't it?

"Well," he asked her, "do you give up? As you see, the kit is practically valueless."

She was thinking hard. "Don't fly off the handle, doc. I don't get this but something's going on all right . . . would those guys know good stuff if they saw it?"

"They would. They make a living from it. Wherever this kit came from—"

She seized on that, with a devilish faculty she seemed to have of eliciting answers without asking questions. "I thought so. You don't know either, huh? Well, maybe I can find out for you. C'mon in here. I ain't letting go of that thing. There's money in it—some way, I don't know how, there's money in it." He followed her into a cafeteria and to an almost-empty corner. She was oblivious to stares and snickers from the other customers as she opened the little black bag—it almost covered a cafeteria table—and ferreted through it. She picked out a retractor from a loop, scrutinized it, contemptuously threw it down, picked out a speculum, threw it down, picked out the lower half of an O.B. forceps, turned it over, close to her sharp young eyes—and saw what the doctor's dim old ones could not have seen.

All old Dr. Full knew was that she was peering at the neck of the forceps and then turned white. Very carefully, she placed the half of the forceps back in its loop of cloth and then replaced the retractor and the speculum. "Well?" he asked. "What did you see?"

" 'Made in U.S.A.,' " she quoted hoarsely. " 'Patent Applied for July 2450.' "

He wanted to tell her she must have misread the inscription, that it must be a practical joke, that—

But he knew she had read correctly. Those bandage shears: they *had* driven his fingers, rather than his fingers driving them. The hypo needle that had no hole. The pretty blue pill that had struck him like a thunderbolt.

"You know what I'm going to do?" asked the girl, with sudden animation. "I'm going to go to charm school. You'll like that, won't ya, doc? Because we're sure going to be seeing a lot of each other."

Old Dr. Full didn't answer. His hands had been playing idly with that plastic card from the kit on which had been printed the rows and columns that had guided him twice before. The card had a slight convexity; you could snap the convexity back and forth from one side to the other. He noted, in a daze, that with each snap a different text appeared on the cards. *Snap.* "The knife with the blue dot in the handle is for tumors only. Diagnose tumors with your Instrument Seven, the Swelling Tester. Place the Swelling Tester—" *Snap.* "An overdose of the pink pills in Bottle 3 can be fixed with one white pill from Bottle—" *Snap.* "Hold the suture needle by the end without the hole in it. Touch it to one end of the wound you want to close and let go. After it has made the knot, touch it—" *Snap.* "Place the top half of the O.B. Forceps near the opening. Let go. After it has entered and conformed to the shape of—" *Snap.*

The slot man saw "FLANNERY 1—MEDICAL" in the upper left corner of the hunk of copy. He automatically scribbled "trim to .75" on it and skimmed it across the horseshoe-shaped copy desk to Piper, who had been handling Edna Flannery's quack-exposé series. She was a nice youngster, he thought, but like all youngsters she overwrote. Hence, the "trim."

Piper dealt back a city hall story to the slot, pinned down Flannery's feature with one hand and began to tap his pencil across it, one tap to a word, at the same steady beat as a teletype carriage traveling across the roller. He wasn't exactly reading it this first time. He was just looking at the letters and words to find out whether, as letters and words, they conformed to *Herald* style. The steady tap of his pencil ceased at intervals as it drew a black line ending with a stylized letter "d" through the word "breast" and scribbled in "chest" instead, or knocked down the capital "E" in "East" to lower case with a diagonal, or closed up a split word—in whose middle Flannery had bumped the space bar of her typewriter—with two curved lines like parentheses rotated through ninety degrees. The thick black pencil zipped a ring around the "30," which, like all youngsters, she put at the end of her stories. He turned back to the first page for the second reading. This time the pencil drew lines with the stylized "d's" at the end of them through adjectives and whole phrases, printed big "L's" to mark paragraphs, hooked some of Flannery's own paragraphs together with swooping recurved lines.

At the bottom of "FLANNERY ADD 2—MEDICAL" the pencil slowed down and stopped. The slot man, sensitive to the rhythm of his beloved copy desk, looked up almost at once. He saw Piper squinting at the story, at a loss. Without wasting words, the copy reader skimmed it back across the Masonite horseshoe to the chief, caught a police story in return and buckled down, his pencil tapping. The slot man read as far as the fourth add, barked at Howard, on the rim: "Sit in for me," and stumped through the clattering city room toward the alcove where the managing editor presided over his own bedlam.

The copy chief waited his turn while the make-up editor, the pressroom foreman, and the chief photographer had words with the M.E. When his turn came, he dropped Flannery's copy on his desk and said: "She says this one isn't a quack."

The M.E. read:

"FLANNERY 1—MEDICAL, by Edna Flannery, *Herald* Staff Writer.

"The sordid tale of medical quackery which the *Herald* has exposed in this series of articles undergoes a change of pace today which the reporter found a welcome surprise. Her quest for the facts in the case of today's subject started just the same way that her exposure of one dozen shyster M.D.'s and faith-healing phonies did. But she can report for a change that Dr. Bayard Full is, despite unorthodox practices which have drawn the suspicion of the rightly hypersensitive medical associations, a true healer living up to the highest ideals of his profession.

"Dr. Full's name was given to the *Herald's* reporter by the ethical committee of a county medical association, which reported that he had been expelled from the association on July 18, 1941, for allegedly 'milking' several patients suffering from trivial complaints. According to sworn statements in the committee's files, Dr. Full had told them they suffered from cancer, and that he had a treatment which would prolong their lives. After his expulsion from the association, Dr. Full dropped out of their sight—until he opened a midtown 'sanitarium' in a brownstone front which had for years served as a rooming house.

"The *Herald's* reporter went to that sanitarium, on East 89th Street, with the full expectation of having numerous imaginary ailments diagnosed and of being promised a sure cure for a flat sum of money. She expected to find unkempt quarters, dirty instruments, and the mumbo-jumbo paraphernalia of the shyster M.D. which had seen a dozen times before.

"She was wrong.

"Dr. Full's sanitarium is spotlessly clean, from its tastefully furnished entrance hall to its shining, white treatment rooms. The attractive, blond receptionist who greeted the reporter was soft-spoken and correct, asking only the reporter's name, address, and the general nature of her complaint. This was given, as usual, as 'nagging backache.' The receptionist asked the *Herald's* reporter to be seated, and a short while later conducted her to a second-floor treatment room and introduced her to Dr. Full.

"Dr. Full's alleged past, as described by the medical society spokesman, is hard to reconcile with his present appearance. He is a clear-eyed, white-haired man in his sixties, to judge by his appearance—a little above middle height and apparently in good physical condition. His voice was firm and friendly, untainted by the ingratiating whine of the shyster M.D. which the reporter has come to know too well.

"The receptionist did not leave the room as he began his examination after a few questions as to the nature and location of the pain. As the reporter lay face down on a treatment table the doctor pressed some instrument to the small of her back. In about one minute he made this astounding statement: 'Young woman, there is no reason for you to have any pain where you say you do. I understand they're saying nowadays that emotional upsets cause pains like that. You'd better go to a psychologist or psychiatrist if the pain keeps up. There is no physical cause for it, so I can do nothing for you.'

"His frankness took the reporter's breath away. Had he guessed she was, so to speak, a spy in his camp? She tried again: 'Well, doctor, perhaps you'd give me a physical checkup, I feel run down all the time, besides the pains. Maybe I need a tonic.' This is never-failing bait to shyster M.D.'s—an invitation for them to find all sorts of mysterious conditions wrong with a patient, each of which 'requires' an expensive treatment. As explained in the first article of this series, of course, the reporter underwent a thorough physical checkup before she embarked on her quack hunt, and was found to be in one hundred percent perfect condition, with the exception of a 'scarred' area at the bottom tip of her left lung resulting from a childhood attack of tuberculosis and a tendency toward 'hyperthyroidism'—overactivity of the thyroid gland which makes it difficult to put on weight and sometimes causes a slight shortness of breath.

"Dr. Full consented to perform the examination, and took a number of shining, spotlessly clean instruments from loops in a large board literally covered with instruments—most of them unfamiliar to the reporter. The instrument with which he approached first was a tube with a curved dial in its surface and two wires that ended on flat disks growing from its ends. He placed one of the disks on the back of the reporter's right hand and the other on the back of her left. 'Reading the meter,' he called out some number which the attentive receptionist took down on a ruled form. The same procedure was repeated several times, thoroughly covering the reporter's anatomy and thoroughly convincing her that the doctor was a complete quack. The reporter had never seen any such diagnostic procedure practiced during the weeks she put in preparing for this series.

"The doctor then took the ruled sheet from the receptionist, conferred with her in low tones, and said: 'You have a slightly overactive thyroid, young woman. And there's something wrong with your left lung—not seriously, but I'd like to take a closer look.'

"He selected an instrument from the board which, the reporter knew, is called a 'speculum'—a scissorlike device which spreads apart body openings such as the orifice of the ear, the nostril, and so on, so that a doctor can look in during an examination. The instrument was, however, too large to be an aural or nasal speculum but too small to be anything else. As the *Herald's* reporter was about to ask further questions, the attending receptionist told her: 'It's customary for us to blindfold our patients during lung examinations—do you mind?' The reporter, bewildered, allowed her to tie a spotlessly clean bandage over her eyes, and waited nervously for what would come next.

"She still cannot say exactly what happened while she was blindfolded—but X rays confirm her suspicions. She felt a cold sensation at her ribs on the left side—a cold that seemed to enter inside her body. Then there was a snapping feeling, and the cold sensation was gone. She heard Dr. Full say in a matter-of-fact voice: 'You have an old tubercular scar down there. It isn't doing any particular harm, but an active person like you needs all the oxygen she can get. Lie still and I'll fix it for you.'

"Then there was a repetition of the cold sensation, lasting for a longer time. 'Another batch of alveoli and some more vascular glue,' the *Herald's* reporter heard Dr. Full say, and the receptionist's crisp response to the order. Then the strange sensation departed and the eye bandage was removed. The reporter saw no scar on her ribs, and yet the doctor assured her: 'That did it. We took out the fibrosis— and a good fibrosis it was, too; it walled off the infection so you're still alive to tell the tale. Then we planted a few clumps of alveoli— they're the little gadgets that get the oxygen from the air you breathe into your blood. I won't monkey with your thyroxin supply. You've got used to being the kind of person you are, and if you suddenly found yourself easygoing and all the rest of it, chances are you'd only be upset. About the backache: just check with the county medical society for the name of a good psychologist or psychiatrist. And look out for quacks; the woods are full of them.'

"The doctor's self-assurance took the reporter's breath away. She asked what the charge would be, and was told to pay the receptionist fifty dollars. As usual, the reporter delayed paying until she got a receipt signed by the doctor himself, detailing the services for which it paid. Unlike most, the doctor cheerfully wrote: 'For removal of fibrosis from left lung and restoration of alveoli,' and signed it.

"The reporter's first move when she left the sanitarium was to head for the chest specialist who had examined her in preparation for this series. A comparison of X rays taken on the day of the 'operation' and those taken previously would, the *Herald's* reporter then thought, expose Dr. Full as a prince of shyster M.D.'s and quacks.

"The chest specialist made time on his crowded schedule for the reporter, in whose series he has shown a lively interest from the planning stage on. He laughed uproariously in his staid Park Avenue examining room as she described the weird procedure to which she had been subjected. But he did not laugh when he took a chest X ray of the reporter, developed it, dried it, and compared it with the ones he had taken earlier. The chest specialist took six more X rays that afternoon, but finally admitted that they all told the same story. The *Herald's* reporter has it on his authority that the scar she had eighteen days ago from her tuberculosis is now gone and has been replaced by healthy lung tissue. He declares that this is a happening unparalleled in medical history. He does not go along with the reporter in her firm conviction that Dr. Full is responsible for the change.

"The *Herald's* reporter, however, sees no two ways about it. She concludes that Dr. Bayard Full—whatever his alleged past may have been—is now an unorthodox but highly successful practitioner of medicine, to whose hands the reporter would trust herself in any emergency.

"Not so is the case of 'Rev.' Annie Dimsworth—a female harpy who, under the guise of 'faith' preys on the ignorant and suffering who come to her sordid 'healing parlor' for help and remain to feed 'Rev.' Annie's bank account, which now totals up to $53,238.64. Tomorrow's article will show, with photostats of bank statements and sworn testimony that—"

The managing editor turned down "FLANNERY LAST ADD—MEDICAL" and tapped his front teeth with a pencil, trying to think straight. He finally told the copy chief: "Kill the story. Run the teaser as a box." He tore off the last paragraph—the "teaser" about "Rev." Annie—and handed it to the desk man, who stumped back to his Masonite horseshoe.

The make-up editor was back, dancing with impatience as he tried to catch the M.E.'s eye. The interphone buzzed with the red light which indicated that the editor and publisher wanted to talk to him. The M.E. thought briefly of a special series on this Dr. Full, decided nobody would believe it and that he probably was a phony anyway. He spiked the story on the "dead" hook and answered his interphone.

Dr. Full had become almost fond of Angie. As his practice had grown to engross the neighborhood illnesses, and then to a corner suite in an uptown taxpayer building, and finally to the sanitarium, she seemed to have grown with it. Oh, he thought, we have our little disputes—

The girl, for instance, was too much interested in money. She had wanted to specialize in cosmetic surgery—removing wrinkles from wealthy old women and whatnot. She didn't realize, at first, that a thing like this was in their trust, that they were the stewards and not the owners of the little black bag and its fabulous contents.

He had tried, ever so cautiously, to analyze them, but without success. All the instruments were slightly radioactive, for instance, but not quite so. They would make a Geiger-Mueller counter indicate, but they would not collapse the leaves of an electroscope. He didn't pretend to be up on the latest developments, but as he understood it, that was just plain *wrong*. Under the highest magnification there were lines on the instruments' superfinished surfaces: incredibly fine lines, engraved in random hatchments which made no particular sense. Their magnetic properties were preposterous. Sometimes the instruments were strongly attracted to magnets, sometimes less so, and sometimes not at all.

Dr. Full had taken X rays in fear and trembling lest he disrupt whatever delicate machinery worked in them. He was *sure* they were not solid, that the handles and perhaps the blades must be mere shells filled with busy little watchworks—but the X rays showed nothing of the sort. Oh, yes—and they were always sterile, and they wouldn't rust. Dust *fell* off them if you shook them: now, that was something he understood. They ionized the dust, or were ionized themselves, or something of the sort. At any rate, he had read of something similar that had to do with phonograph records.

She wouldn't know about that, he proudly thought. She kept the books well enough, and perhaps she gave him a useful prod now and then when he was inclined to settle down. The move from the neighborhood slum to the uptown quarters had been her idea, and so had the sanitarium. Good, good, it enlarged his sphere of usefulness. Let the child have her mink coats and her convertible, as they seemed to be calling roadsters nowadays. He himself was too busy and too old. He had so much to make up for.

Dr. Full thought happily of his Master Plan. She would not like it much, but she would have to see the logic of it. This marvelous thing that had happened to them must be handed on. She was herself no doctor; even though the instruments practically ran themselves, there was more to doctoring than skill. There were the ancient canons of the healing art. And so, having seen the logic of it, Angie would yield; she would assent to his turning over the little black bag to all humanity.

He would probably present it to the College of Surgeons, with as little fuss as possible—well, perhaps a *small* ceremony, and he would like a souvenir of the occasion, a cup or a framed testimonial. It would be a relief to have the thing out of his hands, in a way; let the giants of the healing art decide who was to have its benefits. No, Angie would understand. She was a goodhearted girl.

It was nice that she had been showing so much interest in the surgical side lately—asking about the instruments, reading the instruction card for hours, even practicing on guinea pigs. If something of his love for humanity had been communicated to her, old Dr. Full sentimentally thought, his life would not have been in vain. Surely she would realize that a greater good would be served by surrendering the instruments to wiser hands than theirs, and by throwing aside the cloak of secrecy necessary to work on their small scale.

Dr. Full was in the treatment room that had been the brownstone's front parlor; through the window he saw Angie's yellow convertible roll to a stop before the stoop. He liked the way she looked as she climbed the stairs; neat, not flashy, he thought. A sensible girl like her, she'd understand. There was somebody with her—a fat woman, puffing up the steps, overdressed and petulant. Now, what could she want?

Angie let herself in and went into the treatment room, followed by the fat woman. "Doctor," said the blond girl gravely, "may I present Mrs. Coleman?" Charm school had not taught her everything, but Mrs. Coleman, evidently *nouveau riche,* thought the doctor, did not notice the blunder.

"Miss Aquella told me *so* much about you, doctor, and your remarkable system!" she gushed.

Before he could answer, Angie smoothly interposed: "Would you excuse us for just a moment, Mrs. Coleman?"

She took the doctor's arm and led him into the reception hall. "Listen," she said swiftly, "I know this goes against your grain, but I couldn't pass it up. I met this old thing in the exercise class at Elizabeth Barton's. Nobody else'll talk to her there. She's a widow. I guess her husband was a black marketeer or something, and she has a pile of dough. I gave her a line about how you had a system of massaging wrinkles out. My idea is, you blindfold her, cut her neck open with the Cutaneous Series knife, shoot some Firmol into the muscles, spoon out some of that blubber with an Adipose Series curette and spray it all with Skintite. When you take the blindfold off she's got rid of a wrinkle and doesn't know what happened. She'll pay five hundred dollars. Now, don't say 'no,' doc. Just this once, let's do it my way, can't you? I've been working on this deal all along too, haven't I?"

"Oh," said the doctor, "very well." He was going to have to tell her about the Master Plan before long anyway. He would let her have it her way this time.

Back in the treatment room, Mrs. Coleman had been thinking things over. She told the doctor sternly as he entered: "Of course, your system is permanent, isn't it?"

"It is, madam," he said shortly. "Would you please lie down there? Miss Aquella, get a sterile three-inch bandage for Mrs. Coleman's eyes." He turned his back on the fat woman to avoid conversation, and pretended to be adjusting the lights. Angie blindfolded the woman, and the doctor selected the instruments he would need. He handed the blond girl a pair of retractors, and told her: "Just slip the corners of the blades in as I cut—" She gave him an alarmed look, and gestured at the reclining woman. He lowered his voice: "Very well. Slip in the corners and rock them along the incision. I'll tell you when to pull them out."

Dr. Full held the Cutaneous Series knife to his eyes as he adjusted the little slide for three centimeters depth. He sighed a little as he recalled that its last use had been in the extirpation of an "inoperable" tumor of the throat.

"Very well," he said, bending over the woman. He tried a tentative pass through her tissues. The blade dipped in and flowed through them, like a finger through quicksilver, with no wound left in the wake. Only the retractors could hold the edges of the incision apart.

Mrs. Coleman stirred and jabbered: "Doctor, that felt so peculiar! Are you sure you're rubbing the right way?"

"Quite sure, madam," said the doctor wearily. "Would you please try not to talk during the massage?"

He nodded at Angie, who stood ready with the retractors. The blade sank in to its three centimeters, miraculously cutting only the dead horny tissues of the epidermis and the live tissue of the dermis, pushing aside mysteriously all major and minor blood vessels and muscular tissue, declining to affect any system or organ except the one it was—tuned to, could you say? The doctor didn't know the answer, but he felt tired and bitter at this prostitution. Angie slipped in the retractor blades and rocked them as he withdrew the knife, then pulled to separate the lips of the incision. It bloodlessly exposed an unhealthy string of muscle, sagging in a dead-looking loop from blue-gray ligaments. The doctor took a hypo. Number IX, pre-set to "g," and raised it to his eye level. The mist came and went; there probably was no possibility of an embolus with one of these gadgets, but why take chances? He shot one cc. of "g"—identified as "Firmol" by the card—into the muscle. He and Angie watched as it tightened up against the pharynx.

He took the Adipose Series curette, a small one, and spooned out yellowish tissue, dropping it into the incinerator box, and then nodded to Angie. She eased out the retractors and the gaping incision slipped together into unbroken skin, sagging now. The doctor had the atomizer—dialed to "Skintite"—ready. He sprayed, and the skin shrank up into the new firm throat line.

As he replaced the instruments, Angie removed Mrs. Coleman's bandage and gaily announced: "We're finished! And there's a mirror in the reception hall—"

Mrs. Coleman didn't need to be invited twice. With incredulous fingers she felt her chin, and then dashed for the hall. The doctor grimaced as he heard her yelp of delight, and Angie turned to him with a tight smile. "I'll get the money and get her out," she said. "You won't have to be bothered with her any more."

He was grateful for that much.

She followed Mrs. Coleman into the reception hall, and the doctor dreamed over the case of instruments. A ceremony, certainly—he was *entitled* to one. Not everybody, he thought, would turn such a sure source of money over to the good of humanity. But you reached an age when money mattered less, and when you thought of these things you had done that *might* be open to misunderstanding if, just if, there chanced to be any of that, well, that judgment business. The doctor wasn't a religious man, but you certainly found yourself thinking hard about some things when your time drew near—

Angie was back, with a bit of paper in her hands. "Five hundred dollars," she said matter-of-factly. "And you realize, don't you, that we could go over her an inch at a time—at five hundred dollars an inch?"

"I've been meaning to talk to you about that," he said.

There was bright fear in her eyes, he thought—but why?

"Angie, you've been a good girl and an understanding girl, but we can't keep this up forever, you know."

"Let's talk about it some other time," she said flatly. "I'm tired now."

"No—I really feel we've gone far enough on our own. The instruments—"

"Don't say it, doc!" she hissed. "Don't say it, or you'll be sorry!" In her face there was a look that reminded him of the hollow-eyed, gaunt-faced, dirty-blond creature she had been. From under the charm-school finish there burned the guttersnipe whose infancy had been spent on a sour and filthy mattress, whose childhood had been play in the littered alley, and whose adolescence had been the sweat-shops and the aimless gatherings at night under the glaring street lamps.

He shook his head to dispel the puzzling notion. "It's this way," he patiently began. "I told you about the family that invented the O.B. forceps and kept them a secret for so many generations, how they could have given them to the world but didn't?"

"They knew what they were doing," said the guttersnipe flatly.

"Well, that's neither here nor there," said the doctor, irritated. "My mind is made up about it. I'm going to turn the instruments over to the College of Surgeons. We have enough money to be comfortable. You can even have the house. I've been thinking of going to a warmer climate, myself." He felt peeved with her for making the unpleasant scene. He was unprepared for what happened next.

Angie snatched the little black bag and dashed for the door, with panic in her eyes. He scrambled after her, catching her arm, twisting it in a sudden rage. She clawed at his face with her free hand, babbling curses. Somehow, somebody's finger touched the little black bag, and it opened grotesquely into the enormous board, covered with shining instruments, large and small. Half a dozen of them joggled loose and fell to the floor.

"*Now* see what you've done!" roared the doctor, unreasonably. Her hand was still viselike on the handle, but she was standing still, trembling with choked-up rage. The doctor bent stiffly to pick up the fallen instruments. Unreasonable girl! he thought bitterly. Making a scene—

Pain drove in between his shoulderblades and he fell face down. The light ebbed. "Unreasonable girl!" he tried to croak. And then: "They'll know I tried, anyway—"

Angie looked down on his prone body, with the handle of the Number Six Cautery Series knife protruding from it. "—will cut through all tissues. Use for amputations before you spread on the Re-Gro. Extreme caution should be used in the vicinity of vital organs and major blood vessels or nerve trunks—"

"I didn't mean to do that," said Angie, dully, cold with horror. Now the detective would come, the implacable detective who would reconstruct the crime from the dust in the room. She would run and turn and twist, but the detective would find her out and she would be tried in a courtroom before a judge and jury; the lawyer would make speeches, but the jury would convict her anyway, and the headlines would scream: "BLOND KILLER GUILTY!" and she'd maybe get the chair, walking down a plain corridor where a beam of sunlight struck through the dusty air, with an iron door at the end of it. Her mink, her convertible, her dresses, the handsome man she was going to meet and marry—

The mist of cinematic clichés cleared, and she knew what she would do next. Quite steadily, she picked the incinerator box from its loop in the board—a metal cube with a different-textured spot on one side. "—to dispose of fibroses or other unwanted matter, simply touch the disk—" You dropped something in and touched the disk. There was a sort of soundless whistle, very powerful and unpleasant if you were too close, and a sort of lightless flash. When you opened the box again, the contents were gone. Angie took another of the Cautery

Series knives and went grimly to work. Good thing there wasn't any blood to speak of— She finished the awful task in three hours.

She slept heavily that night, totally exhausted by the wringing emotional demands of the slaying and the subsequent horror. But in the morning, it was as though the doctor had never been there. She ate breakfast, dressed with unusual care—and then undid the unusual care. Nothing out of the ordinary, she told herself. Don't do one thing different from the way you would have done it before. After a day or two, you can phone the cops. Say he walked out spoiling for a drunk, and you're worried. But don't rush it, baby—*don't rush it.*

Mrs. Coleman was due at 10:00 a.m. Angie had counted on being able to talk the doctor into at least one more five-hundred-dollar session. She'd have to do it herself now—but she'd have to start sooner or later.

The woman arrived early. Angie explained smoothly: "The doctor asked me to take care of the massage today. Now that he has the tissue-firming process beginning, it only requires somebody trained in his methods—" As she spoke, her eyes swiveled to the instrument case—open! She cursed herself for the single flaw as the woman followed her gaze and recoiled.

"What are those things!" she demanded. "Are you going to cut me with them? I *thought* there was something fishy—"

"Please, Mrs. Coleman," said Angie, "please, *dear* Mrs. Coleman —you don't understand about the . . . the massage instruments!"

"Massage instruments, my foot!" squabbled the woman shrilly. "That doctor *operated* on me. Why, he might have killed me!"

Angie wordlessly took one of the smaller Cutaneous Series knives and passed it through her forearm. The blade flowed like a finger through quicksilver, leaving no wound in its wake. *That* should convince the old cow!

It didn't convince her, but it did startle her. "What did you do with it? The blade folds up into the handle—that's it!"

"Now look closely, Mrs. Coleman," said Angie, thinking desperately of the five hundred dollars. "Look very closely and you'll see that the, uh, the sub-skin massager simply slips beneath the tissues without doing any harm, tightening and firming the muscles themselves instead of having to work through layers of skin and adipose tissue. It's the secret of the doctor's method. Now, how can outside massage have the effect that we got last night?"

Mrs. Coleman was beginning to calm down. "It *did* work, all right," she admitted, stroking the new line of her neck. But your arm's one thing and my neck's another! Let me see you do that with your neck!"

Angie smiled—

Al returned to the clinic after an excellent lunch that had almost reconciled him to three more months he would have to spend on duty. And then, he thought, and then a blessed year at the blessedly super-normal South Pole working on his specialty—which happened to be telekinesis exercises for ages three to six. Meanwhile, of course, the world had to go on and of course he had to shoulder his share in the running of it.

Before settling down to desk work he gave a routine glance at the bag board. What he saw made him stiffen with shocked surprise. A red light was on next to one of the numbers—the first since he couldn't think when. He read off the number and murmured "O.K., 674,101. That fixes *you*." He put the number on a card sorter and in a moment the record was in his hand. Oh, yes—Hemingway's bag. The big dummy didn't remember how or where he had lost it; none of them ever did. There were hundreds of them floating around.

Al's policy in such cases was to leave the bag turned on. The things practically ran themselves, it was practically impossible to do harm with them, so whoever found a lost one might as well be allowed to use it. You turn it off, you have a social loss—you leave it on, it may do some good. As he understood it, and not very well at that, the stuff wasn't "used up." A temporalist had tried to explain it to him with little success that the prototypes in the transmitter *had been transducted* through a series of point-events of transfinite cardinality. Al had innocently asked whether that meant prototypes had been stretched, so to speak, through all time, and the temporalist had thought he was joking and left in a huff.

"Like to see him do this," thought Al darkly, as he telekinized himself to the combox, after a cautious look to see that there were no medics around. To the box he said: "Police chief," and then to the police chief: "There's been a homicide committed with Medical Instrument Kit 674,101. It was lost some months ago by one of my people, Dr. John Hemingway. He didn't have a clear account of the circumstances."

The police chief groaned and said: "I'll call him in and question him." He was to be astonished by the answers, and was to learn that the homicide was well out of his jurisdiction.

Al stood for a moment at the bag board by the glowing red light that had been sparked into life by a departing vital force giving, as its last act, the warning that Kit 674,101 was in homicidal hands. With a sigh, Al pulled the plug and the light went out.

"Yah," jeered the woman. "You'd fool around with my neck, but you wouldn't risk your own with that thing!"

Angie smiled with serene confidence a smile that was to shock hardened morgue attendants. She set the Cutaneous Series knife to three centimeters before drawing it across her neck. Smiling, knowing the blade would cut only the dead horny tissue of the epidermis and the live tissue of the dermis, mysteriously push aside all major and minor blood vessels and muscular tissue—

Smiling, the knife plunging in and its microtomesharp metal shearing through major and minor blood vessels and muscular tissue and pharynx, Angie cut her throat.

In the few minutes it took the police, summoned by the shrieking Mrs. Coleman, to arrive, the instruments had become crusted with rust, and the flasks which had held vascular glue and clumps of pink, rubbery alveoli and spare gray cells and coils of receptor nerves held only black slime, and from them when opened gushed the foul gases of decomposition.

The Luckiest Man in Denv

ONE OF the words that seems most applicable to
Kornbluth's work is "economical." For some audiences this is not a virtue; Kornbluth grew up in
science fiction and made full use of its short-hand
vocabulary: he expected his audience to understand it without explanation, and so is sometimes
too telegraphic and too compact for readers who
expect to be told everything in full detail, and
twice. *The Luckiest Man in Denv* contains six
major characters, almost as many plot turns, a
working model of a whole new social structure,
and the germ of a textbook's worth of warning
about the waste of scarce resources . . . all in five
thousand words!

MAY'S MAN Reuben, of the eighty-third level, Atomist, knew there
was something wrong when the binoculars flashed and then went
opaque. Inwardly he cursed, hoping that he had not committed himself to anything. Outwardly he was unperturbed. He handed the binoculars back to Rudolph's man Almon, of the eighty-ninth level,
Maintainer, with a smile.

"They aren't very good," he said.

Almon put them to his own eyes, glanced over the parapet, and
swore mildly. "Blacker than the heart of a crazy Angelo, eh? Never
mind; here's another pair."

This pair was unremarkable. Through it, Reuben studied the thousand setbacks and penthouses of Denv that ranged themselves below.
He was too worried to enjoy his first sight of the vista from the
eighty-ninth level, but he let out a murmur of appreciation. Now to
get away from this suddenly sinister fellow and try to puzzle it out.

"Could we—?" he asked cryptically, with a little upward jerk of his
chin.

"It's better not to," Almon said hastily, taking the glasses from his hands. "What if somebody with stars happened to see, you know? How'd *you* like it if you saw some impudent fellow peering up at you?"

"He wouldn't dare!" said Reuben, pretending to be stupid and indignant, and joined a moment later in Almon's sympathetic laughter.

"Never mind," said Almon. "We are young. Some day, who knows? Perhaps we shall look from the ninety-fifth level, or the hundredth."

Though Reuben knew that the Maintainer was no friend of his, the generous words sent blood hammering through his veins; ambition for a moment.

He pulled a long face and told Almon: "Let us hope so. Thank you for being my host. Now I must return to my quarters."

He left the windy parapet for the serene luxury of an eighty-ninth-level corridor and descended slow-moving stairs through gradually less luxurious levels to his own Spartan floor. Selene was waiting, smiling, as he stepped off the stairs.

She was decked out nicely—too nicely. She wore a steely hued corselet and a touch of scent; her hair was dressed long. The combination appealed to him, and instantly he was on his guard. Why had she gone to the trouble of learning his tastes? What was she up to? After all, she was Griffin's woman.

"Coming *down?*" she asked, awed. "Where have you been?"

"The eighty-ninth, as a guest of that fellow Almon. The vista is immense."

"I've never been . . ." she murmured, and then said decisively: "You belong up there. And higher. Griffin laughs at me, but he's a fool. Last night in chamber we got to talking about you, I don't know how, and he finally became quite angry and said he didn't want to hear another word." She smiled wickedly. "I was revenged, though."

Blank-faced, he said: "You must be a good hand at revenge, Selene, and at stirring up the need for it."

The slight hardening of her smile meant that he had scored and he hurried by with a rather formal salutation.

Burn him for an Angelo, but she was easy enough to take! The contrast of the metallic garment with her soft, white skin was disturbing, and her long hair suggested things. It was hard to think of her as scheming something or other; scheming Selene was displaced in his mind by Selene in chamber.

But what was she up to? Had she perhaps heard that he was to be elevated? Was Griffin going to be swooped on by the Maintainers? Was he to kill off Griffin so she could leech onto some rising third party? Was she perhaps merely giving her man a touch of the lash?

He wished gloomily that the binoculars problem and the Selene problem had not come together. That trickster Almon had spoken of youth as though it were something for congratulation; he hated being young and stupid and unable to puzzle out the faulty binoculars and the warmth of Griffin's woman.

The attack alarm roared through the Spartan corridor. He ducked through the nearest door into a vacant bedroom and under the heavy steel table. Somebody else floundered under the table a moment later, and a third person tried to join them.

The firstcomer roared: "Get out and find your own shelter! I don't propose to be crowded out by you or to crowd you out either and see your ugly blood and brains if there's a hit. Go, now!"

"Forgive me, sir! At once, sir!" the latecomer wailed; and scrambled away as the alarm continued to roar.

Reuben gasped at the "sirs" and looked at his neighbor. It was May! Trapped, no doubt, on an inspection tour of the level.

"Sir," he said respectfully, "if you wish to be alone, I can find another room."

"You may stay with me for company. Are you one of mine?" There was power in the general's voice and on his craggy face.

"Yes, sir. May's man Reuben, of the eighty-third level, Atomist."

May surveyed him, and Reuben noted that there were pouches of skin depending from cheekbones and the jaw line—dead-looking, coarse-pored skin.

"You're a well-made boy, Reuben. Do you have women?"

"Yes, sir," said Reuben hastily. "One after another—I *always* have women. I'm making up at this time to a charming thing called Selene. Well-rounded, yet firm, soft but supple, with long red hair and long white legs—"

"Spare me the details," muttered the general. "It takes all kinds. An Atomist, you said. That has a future, to be sure. I myself was a Controller long ago. The calling seems to have gone out of fashion—"

Abruptly the alarm stopped. The silence was hard to bear.

May swallowed and went on: "—for some reason or other. Why don't youngsters elect for Controller any more? Why didn't you, for instance?"

Reuben wished he could be saved by a direct hit. The binoculars, Selene, the raid, and now he was supposed to make intelligent conversation with a general.

"I really don't know, sir," he said miserably. "At the time there seemed to be very little difference—Controller, Atomist, Missiler, Maintainer. We have a saying, 'The buttons are different,' which usually ends any conversation on the subject."

"Indeed?" asked May distractedly. His face was thinly filmed with sweat. "Do you suppose Ellay intends to clobber us this time?" he asked almost hoarsely. "It's been some weeks since they made a maximum effort, hasn't it?"

"Four," said Reuben. "I remember because one of my best Servers was killed by a falling corridor roof—the only fatality and it had to happen to my team!"

He laughed nervously and realized that he was talking like a fool, but May seemed not to notice.

Far below them, there was a series of screaming whistles as the interceptors were loosed to begin their intricate, double basketwork wall of defense in a towering cylinder about Denv.

"Go on, Reuben," said May. "That was most interesting." His eyes were searching the underside of the steel table.

Reuben averted his own eyes from the frightened face, feeling some awe drain out of him. Under a table with a general! It didn't seem so strange now.

"Perhaps, sir, you can tell me what a puzzling thing, that happened this afternoon, means. A fellow—Rudolph's man Almon, of the eighty-ninth level—gave me a pair of binoculars that flashed in my eyes and then went opaque. Has your wide experience—"

May laughed hoarsely and said in a shaky voice: "That old trick! He was photographing your retinas for the blood-vessel pattern. One of Rudolph's men, eh? I'm glad you spoke to me; I'm old enough to spot a revival like that. Perhaps my good friend Rudolph plans—"

There was a thudding volley in the air and then a faint jar. One had got through, exploding, from the feel of it, far down at the foot of Denv.

The alarm roared again, in bursts that meant all clear; only one flight of missiles and that disposed of.

The Atomist and the general climbed out from under the table; May's secretary popped through the door. The general waved him out again and leaned heavily on the table, his arms quivering. Reuben hastily brought a chair.

"A glass of water," said May.

The Atomist brought it. He saw the general wash down what looked like a triple dose of xxx—green capsules which it was better to leave alone.

May said after a moment: "That's better. And don't look so shocked, youngster; you don't know the strain we're under. It's only a temporary measure which I shall discontinue as soon as things ease up a bit. I was saying that perhaps my good friend Rudolph plans to substitute one of his men for one of mine. Tell me, how long has this fellow Almon been a friend of yours?"

"He struck up an acquaintance with me only last week. I should have realized—"

"You certainly should have. One week. Time enough and more. By now you've been photographed, your fingerprints taken, your voice recorded, and your gait studied without your knowledge. Only the retinascope is difficult, but one must risk it for a real double. Have you killed your man, Reuben?"

He nodded. It had been a silly brawl two years ago over precedence at the refectory; he disliked being reminded of it.

"Good," said May grimly. "The way these things are done, your double kills you in a secluded spot, disposes of your body, and takes over your role. We shall reverse it. You will kill the double and take over *his* role."

The powerful, methodical voice ticked off possibilities and contingencies, measures and countermeasures. Reuben absorbed them and felt his awe return. Perhaps May had not really been frightened under the table; perhaps it had been he reading his own terror in the general's face. May was actually talking to him of backgrounds and policies. "Up from the eighty-third level!" he swore to himself as the great names were uttered.

"My good friend Rudolph, of course, wants the five stars. You would not know this, but the man who wears the stars is now eighty years old and failing fast. I consider myself a likely candidate to replace him. So, evidently, must Rudolph. No doubt he plans to have your double perpetrate some horrible blunder on the eve of the election, and the discredit would reflect on me. Now what you and I must do—"

You and I—May's man Reuben and May—up from the eighty-third! Up from the bare corridors and cheerless bedrooms to marble halls and vaulted chambers! From the clatter of the crowded refectory to small and glowing restaurants where you had your own table and servant and where music came softly from the walls! Up from the scramble to win this woman or that, by wit or charm or the poor bribes you could afford, to the eminence from which you could calmly command your pick of the beauty of Denv! From the moiling intrigue of tripping your fellow Atomist and guarding against him tripping you to the heroic thrust and parry of generals!

Up from the eighty-third!

Then May dismissed him with a speech whose implications were deliriously exciting. "I need an able man and a young one, Reuben. Perhaps I've waited too long looking for him. If you do well in this touchy business, I'll consider you very seriously for an important task I have in mind."

Late that night, Selene came to his bedroom.

"I know you don't like me," she said pettishly, "but Griffin's such a fool and I wanted somebody to talk to. Do you mind? What was it like up there today? Did you see carpets? I wish I had a carpet."

He tried to think about carpets and not the exciting contrast of metallic cloth and flesh.

"I saw one through an open door," he remembered. "It looked odd, but I suppose a person gets used to them. Perhaps I didn't see a very good one. Aren't the good ones very thick?"

"Yes," she said. "Your feet sink into them. I wish I had a *good* carpet and four chairs and a small table as high as my knees to put things on and as many pillows as I wanted. Griffin's such a fool. Do you think I'll ever get those things? I've never caught the eye of a general. Am I pretty enough to get one, do you think?"

He said uneasily: "Of course you're a pretty thing, Selene. But carpets and chairs and pillows—" It made him uncomfortable, like the thought of peering up through binoculars from a parapet.

"I want them," she said unhappily. "I like you very much, but I want so many things and soon I'll be too old even for the eighty-third level, before I've been up higher, and I'll spend the rest of my life tending babies or cooking in the crèche or the refectory."

She stopped abruptly, pulled herself together, and gave him a smile that was somehow ghastly in the half-light.

"You bungler," he said, and she instantly looked at the door with the smile frozen on her face. Reuben took a pistol from under his pillow and demanded, "When do you expect him?"

"What do you mean?" she asked shrilly. "Who are you talking about?"

"My double. Don't be a fool, Selene. May and I—" he savored it— "May and I know all about it. He warned me to beware of a diversion by a woman while the double slipped in and killed me. When do you expect him?"

"I really *do* like you," Selene sobbed. "But Almon promised to take me up there and I *knew* when I was where they'd see me that I'd meet somebody really important. I really do like you, but soon I'll be too old—"

"Selene, listen to me. Listen to me! You'll get your chance. Nobody but you and me will know that the substitution didn't succeed!"

"Then I'll be spying for you on Almon, won't I?" she asked in a choked voice. "All I wanted was a few nice things before I got too old. All right, I was supposed to be in your arms at 2350 hours."

It was 2349. Reuben sprang from bed and stood by the door, his pistol silenced and ready. At 2350 a naked man slipped swiftly into the room, heading for the bed as he raised a ten-centimeter poignard. He stopped in dismay when he realized that the bed was empty.

Reuben killed him with a bullet through the throat.

"But he doesn't look a bit like me," he said in bewilderment, closely examining the face. "Just in a general way."

Selene said dully: "Almon told me people always say that when they see their doubles. It's funny, isn't it? He looks just like you, really."

"How was my body to be disposed of?"

She produced a small flat box. "A shadow suit. You were to be left here and somebody would come tomorrow."

"We won't disappoint him," Reuben pulled the web of the shadow suit over his double and turned on the power. In the half-lit room, it was a perfect disappearance; by daylight it would be less perfect. "They'll ask why the body was shot instead of knifed. Tell them you shot me with the gun from under the pillow. Just say I heard the double come in and you were afraid there might have been a struggle."

She listlessly asked: "How do you know I won't betray you?"

"You won't, Selene." His voice bit. "You're *broken*."

She nodded vaguely, started to say something, and then went out without saying it.

Reuben luxuriously stretched in his narrow bed. Later, his beds would be wider and softer, he thought. He drifted into sleep on a half-formed thought that some day he might vote with other generals on the man to wear the five stars—or even wear them himself, Master of Denv.

He slept healthily through the morning alarm and arrived late at his regular twentieth-level station. He saw his superior, May's man Oscar of the eighty-fifth level, Atomist, ostentatiously take his name. Let him!

Oscar assembled his crew for a grim announcement: "We are going to even the score, and perhaps a little better, with Ellay. At sunset there will be three flights of missiles from Deck One."

There was a joyous murmur and Reuben trotted off on his task.

All forenoon he was occupied with drawing plutonium slugs from hyper-suspicious storekeepers in the great rock-quarried vaults, and seeing them through countless audits and assays all the way to Weapons Assembly. Oscar supervised the scores there who assembled the curved slugs and the explosive lenses into sixty-kilogram warheads.

In mid-afternoon there was an incident. Reuben saw Oscar step aside for a moment to speak to a Maintainer whose guard fell on one of the Assembly Servers, and dragged him away as he pleaded innocence. He had been detected in sabotage. When the warheads were in and the Missilers seated, waiting at their boards, the two Atomists rode up to the eighty-third's refectory.

The news of a near-maximum effort was in the air; it was electric. Reuben heard on all sides in tones of self-congratulation: "We'll clobber them tonight!"

"That Server you caught," he said to Oscar. "What was he up to?"

His commander stared. "Are you trying to learn my job? Don't try it, I warn you. If my black marks against you aren't enough, I could always arrange for some fissionable material in your custody to go astray."

"No, no! I was just wondering why people do something like that."

Oscar sniffed doubtfully. "He's probably insane, like all the Angelos. I've heard the climate does it to them. You're not a Maintainer or a Controller. Why worry about it?"

"They'll brainburn him, I suppose?"

"I suppose. *Listen!*"

Deck One was firing. One, two, three, four, five, six. One, two, three, four, five, six. One, two, three, four, five, six.

People turned to one another and shook hands, laughed and slapped shoulders heartily. Eighteen missiles were racing through the stratosphere, soon to tumble on Ellay. With any luck, one or two would slip through the first wall of interceptors and blast close enough to smash windows and topple walls in the crazy city by the ocean. It would serve the lunatics right.

Five minutes later an exultant voice filled most of Denv.

"Recon missile report," it said. "Eighteen launched, eighteen perfect trajectories. Fifteen shot down by Ellay first-line interceptors, three shot down by Ellay second-line interceptors. Extensive blast damage observed in Griffith Park area of Ellay!"

There were cheers.

And eight Full Maintainers marched into the refectory silently, and marched out with Reuben.

He knew better than to struggle or ask futile questions. Any question you asked of a Maintainer was futile. But he goggled when they marched him onto an upward-bound stairway.

They rode past the eighty-ninth level and Reuben lost count, seeing only the marvels of the upper reaches of Denv. He saw carpets that ran the entire length of corridors, and intricate fountains, and mosaic walls, stained-glass windows, more wonders than he could recognize, things for which he had no name.

He was marched at last into a wood-paneled room with a great polished desk and a map behind it. He saw May, and another man who must have been a general—Rudolph?—but sitting at the desk was a frail old man who wore a circlet of stars on each khaki shoulder.

The old man said to Reuben: "You are an Ellay spy and saboteur."

Reuben looked at May. Did one speak directly to the man who wore the stars, even in reply to such an accusation?

"Answer him, Reuben," May said kindly.

"I am May's man Reuben, of the eighty-third level, an Atomist," he said.

"Explain," said the other general heavily, "if you can, why all eighteen of the warheads you procured today failed to fire."

"But they did!" gasped Reuben. "The Recon missile report said there was blast damage from the three that got through and it didn't say anything about the others failing to fire."

The other general suddenly looked sick and May looked even kindlier. The man who wore the stars turned inquiringly to the chief of the Maintainers, who nodded and said: "That was the Recon missile report, sir."

The general snapped: "What I said was that he would *attempt* to sabotage the attack. Evidently he failed. I also said he is a faulty double, somehow slipped with great ease into my good friend May's organization. You will find that his left thumb print is a clumsy forgery of the real Reuben's thumb print and that his hair has been artificially darkened."

The old man nodded at the chief of the Maintainers, who said: "We have his card, sir."

Reuben abruptly found himself being fingerprinted and deprived of some hair.

"The f.p.s check, sir," one Maintainer said. "He's Reuben."

"Hair's natural, sir," said another.

The general began a rearguard action: "My information about his hair seems to have been inaccurate. But the fingerprint means only that Ellay spies substituted his prints for Reuben's prints in the files—"

"Enough, sir," said the old man with the stars. "Dismissed. All of you. Rudolph, I am surprised. All of you, go."

Reuben found himself in a vast apartment with May, who was bubbling and chuckling uncontrollably until he popped three of the green capsules into his mouth hurriedly.

"This means the eclipse for years of my good friend Rudolph," he crowed. "His game was to have your double sabotage the attack warheads and so make it appear that my organization is rotten with spies. The double must have been under post-hypnotic, primed to admit everything. Rudolph was so sure of himself that he made his accusations before the attack, the fool!"

He fumbled out the green capsules again.

"Sir," said Reuben, alarmed.

"Only temporary," May muttered, and swallowed a fourth. "But you're right. You leave them alone. There are big things to be done in your time, not in mine. I told you I needed a young man who could claw his way to the top. Rudolph's a fool. He doesn't need the capsules because he doesn't ask questions. Funny, I thought a coup like the double affair would hit me hard, but I don't feel a thing. It's not like the old days. I used to plan and plan, and when the trap went *snap* it was better than this stuff. But now I don't feel a thing."

He leaned forward from his chair; the pupils of his eyes were black bullets.

"Do you want to *work?*" he demanded. "Do you want your world stood on its head and your brains to crack and do the only worthwhile job there is to do? Answer me!"

"Sir, I am a loyal May's man. I want to obey your orders and use my ability to the full."

"Good enough," said the general. "You've got brains, you've got push. I'll do the spade work. I won't last long enough to push it through. You'll have to follow. Ever been outside of Denv?"

Reuben stiffened.

"I'm not accusing you of being a spy. It's really all right to go outside of Denv. I've been outside. There isn't much to see at first—a lot of ground pocked and torn up by shorts and overs from Ellay and us. Farther out, especially east, it's different. Grass, trees, flowers. Places where you could grow food.

"When I went outside, it troubled me. It made me ask questions. I wanted to know how we started. Yes—started. *It wasn't always like this.* Somebody built Denv. Am I getting the idea across to you? *It wasn't always like this!*

"Somebody set up the reactors to breed uranium and make plutonium. Somebody tooled us up for the missiles. Somebody wired the boards to control them. Somebody started the hydroponics tanks.

"I've dug through the archives. Maybe I found something. I saw mountains of strength reports, ration reports, supply reports, and yet I never got back to the beginning. I found a piece of paper and maybe I understood it and maybe I didn't. It was about the water of the Colorado River and who should get how much of it. How can you divide water in a river? But it could have been the start of Denv, Ellay, and the missile attacks."

The general shook his head, puzzled, and went on: "I don't see clearly what's ahead. I want to make peace between Denv and Ellay, but I don't know how to start or what it will be like. I think it must mean not firing, not even making any more weapons. Maybe it means that some of us, or a lot of us, will go out of Denv and live a different kind of life. That's why I've clawed my way up. That's why I need a young man who can claw with the best of them. Tell me what you think."

"I think," said Reuben measuredly, "it's magnificent—the salvation of Denv. I'll back you to my dying breath if you'll let me."

May smiled tiredly and leaned back in the chair as Reuben tiptoed out.

What luck, Reuben thought—what unbelievable luck to be at a fulcrum of history like this!

He searched the level for Rudolph's apartment and gained admission.

To the general, he said: "Sir, I have to report that your friend May is insane. He has just been raving to me, advocating the destruction of civilization as we know it, and urging me to follow in his footsteps. I pretended to agree—since I can be of greater service to you if I'm in May's confidence."

"So?" said Rudolph thoughtfully. "Tell me about the double. How did that go wrong?"

"The bunglers were Selene and Almon. Selene because she alarmed me instead of distracting me. Almon because he failed to recognize her incompetence."

"They shall be brainburned. That leaves an eighty-ninth-level vacancy in my organization, doesn't it?"

"You're very kind, sir, but I think I should remain a May's man—outwardly. If I earn any rewards, I can wait for them. I presume that May will be elected to wear the five stars. He won't live more than two years after that, at the rate he is taking drugs."

"We can shorten it," grinned Rudolph. "I have pharmacists who can see that his drugs are more than normal strength."

"That would be excellent, sir. When he is too enfeebled to discharge his duties, there may be an attempt to rake up the affair of the double to discredit you. I could then testify that I was your man all along and that May coerced me."

They put their heads together, the two saviors of civilization as they knew it, and conspired ingeniously long into the endless night.

The Silly Season

WHEN World War II was over, Cyril Kornbluth went to the University of Chicago on the G.I. Bill, in an accelerated program aiming at a master's degree. What kept him from making it was that our mutual friend Richard Wilson was also in Chicago, working as Bureau Manager for a news-wire service called Trans-Radio Press. He offered Cyril a chance to make a few bucks now and then as a stringer and then got him full-time on the staff; when Dick Wilson moved on to bigger things Cyril inherited the job as Chicago bureau chief. Many sf writers have used reporters as viewpoint characters in their stories. Cyril *was* a reporter. It makes a difference.

IT WAS a hot summer afternoon in the Omaha bureau of the World Wireless Press Service, and the control bureau in New York kept nagging me for copy. But since it was a hot summer afternoon, there was no copy. A wrapup of local baseball had cleared about an hour ago, and that was that. Nothing but baseball happens in the summer. During the dog days, politicians are in the Maine woods fishing and boozing, burglars are too tired to burgle, and wives think it over and decide not to decapitate their husbands.

I pawed through some press releases. One sloppy stencil-duplicated sheet began: "Did you know that the lemonade way to summer comfort and health has been endorsed by leading physio-therapists from Maine to California? The Federated Lemon-Growers Association revealed today that a survey of 2,500 physiotherapists in 57 cities of more than 25,000 population disclosed that 87 per cent of them drink lemonade at least once a day between June and September, and that another 72 per cent not only drink the cooling and healthful beverage but actually prescribe it—"

Another note tapped out on the news circuit printer from New York: "960M-HW KICKER? ND SNST-NY"

That was New York saying they needed a bright and sparkling little news item immediately—"soonest." I went to the eastbound printer and punched out: "96NY-UPCMNG FU MINS-OM"

The lemonade handout was hopeless; I dug into the stack again. The State University summer course was inviting the governor to attend its summer conference on aims and approaches in adult secondary education. The Agricultural College wanted me to warn farmers that white-skinned hogs should be kept from the direct rays of the summer sun. The manager of a fifth-rate local pug sent a writeup of his boy and a couple of working press passes to his next bout in the Omaha Arena. The Schwartz and White Bandage Company contributed a glossy eight-by-ten of a blonde in a bathing suit improvised from two S. & W. Redi-Dressings.

Accompanying text: "Pert starlet Miff McCoy is ready for any seaside emergency. That's not only a darling swim suit she has on—it's two standard all-purpose Redi-Dressing bandages made by the Schwartz and White Bandage Company of Omaha. If a broken rib results from too-strenuous beach athletics, Miff's dress can supply the dressing." Yeah. The rest of the stack wasn't even that good. I dumped them all in the circular file, and began to wrack my brains in spite of the heat.

I'd have to fake one, I decided. Unfortunately, there had been no big running silly season story so far this summer—no flying saucers, or monsters in the Florida Everglades, or chloroform bandits terrifying the city. If there had, I could have hopped on and faked a "with." As it was, I'd have to fake a "lead," which is harder and riskier.

The flying saucers? I couldn't revive them; they'd been forgotten for years, except by newsmen. The giant turtle of Lake Huron had been quiet for years, too. If I started a chloroform bandit scare, every old maid in the state would back me up by swearing she heard the bandit trying to break in and smelled chloroform—but the cops wouldn't like it. Strange messages from space received at the State University's radar lab? That might do it. I put a sheet of copy paper in the typewriter and sat, glaring at it and hating the silly season.

There was a slight reprieve—the Western Union tie-line printer by the desk dinged at me and its sickly-yellow bulb lit up. I tapped out:

"ww GA PLS," and the machine began to eject yellow, gummed tape which told me this:

"WU CO62-DPR COLLECT—FT HICKS ARK AUG 22 105P—WORLDWIRELESS OMAHA—TOWN MARSHAL PINKNEY CRAWLES DIED MYSTERIOUS CIRCUMSTANCES FISHTRIPPING OZARK HAMLET RUSH CITY TODAY. RUSHERS PHONED HICKSERS 'BURNED DEATH SHINING DOMES APPEARED YESTERWEEK.' JEEPING BODY HICKSWARD. QUERIED RUSH CONSTABLE P.C. ALLENBY LEARNING 'SEVEN GLASSY DOMES EACH HOUSESIZE CLEARING MILE SOUTH TOWN. RUSHERS UNTOUCHED, UNAPPROACHED. CRAWLES WARNED BUT TOUCHED AND DIED BURNS.' NOTE DESK—RUSH FONECALL 1.85. SHALL I UPFOLLOW?—BENSON—FISHTRIPPING RUSHERS HICKSERS YESTERWEEK JEEPING HICKSWARD HOUSESIZE 1.85 428P CLR . . ."

It was just what the doctor ordered. I typed an acknowledgment for the message and pounded out a story, fast. I punched it and started the tape wiggling through the eastbound transmitter before New York could send any more irked notes. The news circuit printer from New York clucked and began relaying my story immediately:

"ww72 (KICKER)

FORT HICKS, ARKANSAS, AUG 22—(WW)—MYSTERIOUS DEATH TODAY STRUCK DOWN A LAW ENFORCEMENT OFFICER IN A TINY OZARK MOUNTAIN HAMLET. MARSHAL PINKNEY CRAWLES OF FORT HICKS, ARKANSAS, DIED OF BURNS WHILE ON A FISHING TRIP TO THE LITTLE VILLAGE OF RUSH CITY. TERRIFIED NATIVES OF RUSH CITY BLAMED THE TRAGEDY ON WHAT THEY CALLED 'SHINING DOMES.' THEY SAID THE SO-CALLED DOMES APPEARED IN A CLEARING LAST WEEK ONE MILE SOUTH OF TOWN. THERE ARE SEVEN OF THE MYSTERIOUS OBJECTS —EACH ONE THE SIZE OF A HOUSE. THE INHABITANTS OF RUSH CITY DID NOT DARE APPROACH THEM. THEY WARNED THE VISITING MARSHAL CRAWLES—BUT HE DID NOT HEED THEIR WARNING. RUSH CITY'S CONSTABLE P.C. ALLENBY WAS A WITNESS TO THE TRAGEDY. SAID HE:— "THERE ISN'T MUCH TO TELL. MARSHAL CRAWLES JUST WALKED UP TO ONE OF THE DOMES AND PUT HIS HAND ON IT. THERE WAS A BIG FLASH, AND WHEN I COULD SEE AGAIN, HE WAS BURNED TO DEATH.' CONSTABLE ALLENBY IS RETURNING THE BODY OF MARSHAL CRAWLES TO FORT HICKS. 602P220M"

That, I thought, should hold them for a while. I remembered Benson's "note desk" and put through a long distance call to Fort Hicks, person to person. The Omaha operator asked for Fort Hicks information, but there wasn't any. The Fort Hicks operator asked whom she wanted. Omaha finally admitted that we wanted to talk to Mr. Edwin C. Benson. Fort Hicks figured out loud and then decided that Ed was probably at the police station if he hadn't gone home for supper yet. She connected us with the police station, and I got Benson. He had a pleasant voice, not particularly backwoods Arkansas. I gave him some of the old oil about a fine dispatch, and a good, conscientious job, and so on. He took it with plenty of dry reserve, which was odd. Our rural stringers always ate that kind of stuff up. Where, I asked him, was he from?

"Fort Hicks," he told me, "but I've moved around. I did the courthouse beat in Little Rock—" I nearly laughed out loud at that, but the laugh died out as he went on—"rewrite for the A.P. in New Orleans, got to be bureau chief there but I didn't like wire service work. Got an opening on the Chicago Trib desk. That didn't last—they sent me to head up their Washington bureau. There I switched to the New York Times. They made me a war correspondent and I got hurt—back to Fort Hicks. I do some magazine writing now. Did you want a follow-up on the Rush City story?"

"Sure," I told him weakly. "Give it a real ride—use your own judgment. Do you think it's a fake?"

"I saw Pink's body a little while ago at the undertaker's parlor, and I had a talk with Allenby, from Rush City. Pink got burned all right, and Allenby didn't make his story up. Maybe somebody else did—he's pretty dumb—but as far as I can tell, this is the real thing. I'll keep the copy coming. Don't forget about that dollar eighty-five phone call, will you?"

I told him I wouldn't, and hung up. Mr. Edwin C. Benson had handed me quite a jolt. I wondered how badly he had been hurt, that he had been forced to abandon a brilliant news career and bury himself in the Ozarks.

Then there came a call from God, the board chairman of World Wireless. He was fishing in Canada, as all good board chairmen do during the silly season, but he had caught a news broadcast which used my Rush City story. He had a mobile phone in his trailer, and it was but the work of a moment to ring Omaha and louse up my carefully planned vacation schedules and rotation of night shifts. He wanted me to go down to Rush City and cover the story personally. I said yes and began trying to round up the rest of the staff. My night editor was sobered up by his wife and delivered to the bureau in fair shape. A telegrapher on vacation was reached at his summer resort and talked into checking out. I got a taxi company on the phone and told them to have a cross-country cab on the roof in an hour. I specified their best driver, and told them to give him maps of Arkansas.

Meanwhile, two "with domes" dispatches arrived from Benson and got moved on the wire. I monitored a couple of newscasts; the second one carried a story by another wire service on the domes—a pickup of our stuff, but they'd have their own men on the scene fast enough. I filled in the night editor, and went up to the roof for the cab.

The driver took off in the teeth of a gathering thunderstorm. We had to rise above it, and by the time we could get down to sight-pilotage altitude, we were lost. We circled most of the night until the driver picked up a beacon he had on his charts at about 3:30 A.M. We landed at Fort Hicks as day was breaking, not on speaking terms.

Fort Hicks' field clerk told me where Benson lived, and I walked there. It was a white, frame house. A quiet, middle-aged woman let me in. She was his widowed sister, Mrs. McHenry. She got me some coffee and told me she had been up all night waiting for Edwin to come back from Rush City. He had started out about 8:00 P.M., and it was only a two-hour trip by car. She was worried. I tried to pump her about her brother, but she'd only say that he was the bright one of the family. She didn't want to talk about his work as war correspondent. She did show me some of his magazine stuff—boy-and-girl stories in national weeklies. He seemed to sell one every couple of months.

We had arrived at a conversational stalemate when her brother walked in, and I discovered why his news career had been interrupted. He was blind. Aside from a long, puckered brown scar that ran from his left temple back over his ear and onto the nape of his neck, he was a pleasant-looking fellow in his mid-forties.

"Who is it, Vera?" he asked.

"It's Mr. Williams, the gentleman who called you from Omaha today—I mean yesterday."

"How do you do, Williams. Don't get up," he added—hearing, I suppose, the chair squeak as I leaned forward to rise.

"You were so *long,* Edwin," his sister said with relief and reproach.

"That young jackass Howie—my chauffeur for the night—" he added an aside to me—"got lost going there and coming back. But I did spend more time than I'd planned at Rush City." He sat down, facing me. "Williams, there is some difference of opinion about the shining domes. The Rush City people say that they exist, and I say they don't."

His sister brought him a cup of coffee.

"What happened, exactly?" I asked.

"That Allenby took me and a few other hardy citizens to see them. They told me just what they looked like. Seven hemispheres in a big clearing, glassy, looming up like houses, reflecting the gleam of the headlights. But they weren't there. Not to me, and not to any blind man. I know when I'm standing in front of a house or anything else that big. I can feel a little tension on the skin of my face. It works unconsciously, but the mechanism is thoroughly understood.

"The blind get—because they have to—an aural picture of the world. We hear a little hiss of air that means we're at the corner of a building, we hear and feel big, turbulent air currents that mean we're coming to a busy street. Some of the boys can thread their way through an obstacle course and never touch a single obstruction. I'm not that good, maybe because I haven't been blind as long as they have, but by hell, I know when there are seven objects the size of houses in front of me, and there just were no such things in the clearing at Rush City."

"Well," I shrugged, "there goes a fine piece of silly-season journalism. What kind of a gag are the Rush City people trying to pull, and why?"

"No kind of gag. My driver saw the domes, too—and don't forget the late marshal. Pink not only saw them but touched them. All I know is that people see them and I don't. If they exist, they have a kind of existence like nothing else I've ever met."

"I'll go up there myself," I decided.

"Best thing," said Benson. "I don't know what to make of it. You can take our car." He gave me directions and I gave him a schedule of deadlines. We wanted the coroner's verdict, due today, an eyewitness story—his driver would do for that—some background stuff on the area and a few statements from local officials.

I took his car and got to Rush City in two hours. It was an un-painted collection of dog-trot homes, set down in the big pine forest that covers all that rolling Ozark country. There was a general store that had the place's only phone. I suspected it had been kept busy by the wire services and a few enterprising newspapers. A state trooper in a flashy uniform was lounging against a fly-specked tobacco counter when I got there.

"I'm Sam Williams, from World Wireless," I said. "You come to have a look at the domes?"

"World Wireless broke that story, didn't they?" he asked me, with a look I couldn't figure out.

"We did. Our Fort Hicks stringer wired it to us."

The phone rang, and the trooper answered it. It seemed to have been a call to the Governor's office he had placed.

"No, sir," he said over the phone. "No, sir. They're all sticking to the story, but I didn't see anything. I mean, they don't see them any more, but they say they *were* there, and now they aren't any more." A couple more "No, sirs" and he hung up.

"When did that happen?" I asked.

"About a half-hour ago. I just came from there on my bike to re-port."

The phone rang again, and I grabbed it. It was Benson, asking for me. I told him to phone a flash and bulletin to Omaha on the disap-pearance and then took off to find Constable Allenby. He was a stage reuben with a nickel-plated badge and a six-shooter. He cheerfully climbed into the car and guided me to the clearing.

There was a definite little path worn between Rush City and the clearing by now, but there was a disappointment at the end of it. The clearing was empty. A few small boys sticking carefully to its fringes told wildly contradictory stories about the disappearance of the domes, and I jotted down some kind of dispatch out of the most spectacular versions. I remember it involved flashes of blue fire and a smell like sulphur candles. That was all there was to it.

I drove Allenby back. By then a mobile unit from a TV network had arrived. I said hello, waited for an A.P. man to finish a dispatch on the phone, and then dictated my lead direct to Omaha. The ham-let was beginning to fill up with newsmen from the wire services, the big papers, the radio and TV nets and the newsreels. Much good they'd get out of it. The story was over—I thought. I had some coffee at the general store's two-table restaurant corner and drove back to Fort Hicks.

Benson was tirelessly interviewing by phone and firing off copy to Omaha. I told him he could begin to ease off, thanked him for his fine work, paid him for his gas, said goodbye and picked up my taxi at the field. Quite a bill for waiting had been run up.

I listened to the radio as we were flying back to Omaha, and wasn't at all surprised. After baseball, the shining domes were the top news. Shining domes had been seen in twelve states. Some vibrated with a strange sound. They came in all colors and sizes. One had strange writing on it. One was transparent, and there were big green men and women inside. I caught a women's mid-morning quiz show, and the M.C. kept gagging about the domes. One crack I remember was a switch on the "pointed-head" joke. He made it "dome-shaped head," and the ladies in the audience laughed until they nearly burst.

We stopped in Little Rock for gas, and I picked up a couple of afternoon papers. The domes got banner heads on both of them. One carried the World Wireless lead, and had slapped in the bulletin on the disappearance of the domes. The other paper wasn't a World Wireless client, but between its other services and "special correspondents"—phone calls to the general store at Rush City—it had kept practically abreast of us. Both papers had shining dome cartoons on their editorial pages, hastily drawn and slapped in. One paper, anti-administration, showed the President cautiously reaching out a finger to touch the dome of the Capitol, which was rendered as a shining dome and labeled: "SHINING DOME OF CONGRESSIONAL IMMUNITY TO EXECUTIVE DICTATORSHIP." A little man labeled "Mr. and Mrs. Plain, Self-Respecting Citizens of The United States of America" was in one corner of the cartoon saying: "CAREFUL, MR. PRESIDENT! REMEMBER WHAT HAPPENED TO PINKNEY CRAWLES!!"

The other paper, pro-administration, showed a shining dome that had the President's face. A band of fat little men in Prince Albert coats, string ties, and broad-brimmed hats labeled "CONGRESSIONAL SMEAR ARTISTS AND HATCHETMEN" were creeping up on the dome with the President's face, their hands reached out as if to strangle. Above the cartoon a cutline said: "WHO'S GOING TO GET HURT?"

We landed at Omaha, and I checked into the office. Things were clicking right along. The clients were happily gobbling up our dome copy and sending wires asking for more. I dug into the morgue for the "Flying Disc" folder, and the "Huron Turtle" and the "Bayou Vampire" and a few others even further back. I spread out the old clippings and tried to shuffle and arrange them into some kind of underlying sense. I picked up the latest dispatch to come out of the tie-line printer from Western Union. It was from our man in Owosso, Michigan, and told how Mrs. Lettie Overholtzer, age 61, saw a shining dome in her own kitchen at midnight. It grew like a soap bubble until it was as big as her refrigerator, and then disappeared.

I went over to the desk man and told him: "Let's have a downhold on stuff like Lettie Overholtzer. We can move a sprinkling of it, but I don't want to run this into the ground. Those things might turn up again, and then we wouldn't have any room left to play around with them. We'll have everybody's credulity used up."

He looked mildly surprised. "You mean," he asked, "there really *was* something there?"

"I don't know. Maybe. I didn't see anything myself, and the only man down there I trust can't make up his mind. Anyhow, hold it down as far as the clients let us."

I went home to get some sleep. When I went back to work, I found the clients hadn't let us work the downhold after all. Nobody at the other wire services seemed to believe seriously that there had been anything out of the ordinary at Rush City, so they merrily pumped out solemn stories like the Lettie Overholtzer item, and wirefoto maps of locations where domes were reported, and tabulations of number of domes reported.

We had to string along. Our Washington bureau badgered the Pentagon and the A.E.C. into issuing statements, and there was a race between a Navy and an Air Force investigating mission to see who could get to Rush City first. After they got there there was a race to see who could get the first report out. The Air Force won that contest. Before the week was out, "Domies" had appeared. They were hats for juveniles—shining-dome skull caps molded from a transparent plastic. We had to ride with it. I'd started the mania, but it was out of hand and a long time dying down.

The World Series, the best in years, finally killed off the domes. By an unspoken agreement among the services, we simply stopped running stories every time a hysterical woman thought she saw a dome or wanted to get her name in the paper. And, of course, when there was no longer publicity to be had for the asking, people stopped seeing domes. There was no percentage in it. Brooklyn won the Series, international tension climbed as the thermometer dropped, burglars began burgling again, and a bulky folder labeled "DOMES, SHINING," went into our morgue. The shining domes were history, and earnest graduate students in psychology would shortly begin to bother us with requests to borrow that folder.

The only thing that had come of it, I thought, was that we had somehow got through another summer without too much idle wire time, and that Ed Benson and I had struck up a casual correspondence.

A newsman's strange and weary year wore on. Baseball gave way to football. An off-year election kept us on the run. Christmas loomed ahead, with its feature stories and its kickers about Santa Claus, Indiana. Christmas passed, and we began to clear jolly stories about New Year hangovers, and tabulate the great news stories of the year. New Year's day, a ghastly ratrace of covering 103 bowl games. Record snowfalls in the Great Plains and Rockies. Spring floods in Ohio and the Columbia River Valley. Twenty-one tasty Lenten menus, and Holy Week around the world. Baseball again, Daylight Saving Time, Mother's Day, Derby Day, the Preakness and the Belmont Stakes.

It was about then that a disturbing letter arrived from Benson. I was concerned not about its subject matter but because I thought no sane man would write such a thing. It seemed to me that Benson was slipping his trolley. All he said was that he expected a repeat performance of the domes, or of something like the domes. He said "they" probably found the tryout a smashing success and would continue according to plan. I replied cautiously, which amused him.

He wrote back: "I wouldn't put myself out on a limb like this if I had anything to lose by it, but you know my station in life. It was just an intelligent guess, based on a study of power politics and Aesop's fables. And if it does happen, you'll find it a trifle harder to put over, won't you?"

I guessed he was kidding me, but I wasn't certain. When people begin to talk about "them" and what "they" are doing, it's a bad sign. But, guess or not, something pretty much like the domes did turn up in late July, during a crushing heat wave.

This time it was big black spheres rolling across the countryside.

The spheres were seen by a Baptist congregation in central Kansas which had met in a prairie to pray for rain. About eighty Baptists took their Bible oaths that they saw large black spheres some ten feet high, rolling along the prairie. They had passed within five yards of one man. The rest had run from them as soon as they could take in the fact that they really were there.

World Wireless didn't break that story, but we got on it fast enough as soon as we were tipped. Being now the recognized silly season authority in the W.W. Central Division, I took off for Kansas.

It was much the way it had been in Arkansas. The Baptists really thought they had seen the things—with one exception. The exception was an old gentleman with a patriarchal beard. He had been the one man who hadn't run, the man the objects passed nearest to. He was blind. He told me with a great deal of heat that he would have known all about it, blind or not, if any large spheres had rolled within five yards of him, or twenty-five for that matter.

Old Mr. Emerson didn't go into the matter of air currents and turbulence, as Benson had. With him, it was all well below the surface. He took the position that the Lord had removed his sight, and in return had given him another sense which would do for emergency use.

"You just try me out, son!" he piped angrily. "You come stand over here, wait a while and put your hand up in front of my face. I'll tell you when you do it, no matter how quiet you are!" He did it, too, three times, and then took me out into the main street of his little prairie town. There were several wagons drawn up before the grain elevator, and he put on a show for me by threading his way around and between them without touching once.

That—and Benson—seemed to prove that whatever the things were, they had some connection with the domes. I filed a thoughtful dispatch on the blind-man angle, and got back to Omaha to find that it had been cleared through our desk but killed in New York before relay.

We tried to give the black spheres the usual ride, but it didn't last as long. The political cartoonists tired of it sooner, and fewer old maids saw them. People got to jeering at them as newspaper hysteria, and a couple of highbrow magazines ran articles on "the irresponsible press." Only the radio comedians tried to milk the new mania as usual, but they were disconcerted to find their ratings fall. A network edict went out to kill all sphere gags. People were getting sick of them.

"It makes sense," Benson wrote to me. "An occasional exercise of the sense of wonder is refreshing, but it can't last forever. That plus the ingrained American cynicism toward all sources of public information has worked against the black spheres being greeted with the same naïve delight with which the domes were received. Nevertheless, I predict—and I'll thank you to remember that my predictions have been right so far 100 per cent of the time—that next summer will see another mystery comparable to the domes and the black things. And I also predict that the new phenomenon will be imperceptible to any blind person in the immediate vicinity, if there should be any."

If, of course, he was wrong this time, it would only cut his average down to fifty per cent. I managed to wait out the year—the same interminable round I felt I could do in my sleep. Staffers got ulcers and resigned, staffers got tired and were fired, libel suits were filed and settled, one of our desk men got a Nieman Fellowship and went to Harvard, one of our telegraphers got his working hand mashed in a car door and jumped from a bridge but lived with a broken back.

In mid-August, when the weather bureau had been correctly predicting "fair and warmer" for sixteen straight days, it turned up. It wasn't anything on whose nature a blind man could provide a negative check, but it had what I had come to think of as "their" trademark.

A summer seminar was meeting outdoors, because of the frightful heat, at our own State University. Twelve trained school teachers testified that a series of perfectly circular pits opened up in the grass before them, one directly under the education professor teaching the seminar. They testified further that the professor, with an astonished look and a heart-rending cry, plummeted down into that perfectly circular pit. They testified further that the pits remained there for some thirty seconds and then suddenly were there no longer. The scorched summer grass was back where it had been, the pits were gone, and so was the professor.

I interviewed every one of them. They weren't yokels, but grown men and women, all with Masters' degrees, working toward their doctorates during the summers. They agreed closely on their stories as I would expect trained and capable persons to do.

The police, however, did not expect agreement, being used to dealing with the lower-I.Q. brackets. They arrested the twelve on some technical charge—"obstructing peace officers in the performance of their duties," I believe—and were going to beat the living hell out of them when an attorney arrived with twelve writs of habeas corpus. The cops' unvoiced suspicion was that the teachers had conspired to murder their professor, but nobody ever tried to explain why they'd do a thing like that.

The cops' reaction was typical of the way the public took it. Newspapers—which had reveled wildly in the shining domes story and less so in the black spheres story—were cautious. Some went overboard and gave the black pits a ride, in the old style, but they didn't pick up any sales that way. People declared that the press was insulting their intelligence, and also they were bored with marvels.

The few papers who played up the pits were soundly spanked in very dignified editorials printed by other sheets which played down the pits.

At World Wireless, we sent out a memo to all stringers: "File no more enterpriser dispatches on black pit story. Mail queries should be sent to regional desk if a new angle breaks in your territory." We got about ten mail queries, mostly from journalism students acting as string men, and we turned them all down. All the older hands got the pitch, and didn't bother to file it to us when the town drunk or the village old maid loudly reported that she saw a pit open up on High Street across from the drug store. They knew it was probably untrue, and that furthermore nobody cared.

I wrote Benson about all this, and humbly asked him what his prediction for next summer was. He replied, obviously having the time of his life, that there would be at least one more summer phenomenon like the last three, and possibly two more—but none after that.

It's so easy now to reconstruct, with our bitterly earned knowledge!

Any youngster could whisper now of Benson: "Why, the damned fool! Couldn't anybody with the brains of a louse see that they wouldn't keep it up for two years?" One did whisper that to me the other day, when I told this story to him. And I whispered back that, far from being a damned fool, Benson was the one person on the face of the earth, as far as I know, who had bridged with logic the widely separated phenomena with which this reminiscence deals.

Another year passed. I gained three pounds, drank too much, rowed incessantly with my staff, and got a tidy raise. A telegrapher took a swing at me midway through the office Christmas party, and I fired him. My wife and the kids didn't arrive in April when I expected them. I phoned Florida, and she gave me some excuse or other about missing the plane. After a few more missed planes and a few more phone calls, she got around to telling me that she didn't *want* to come back. That was okay with me. In my own intuitive way, I knew that the upcoming silly season was more important than who stayed married to whom.

In July, a dispatch arrived by wire while a new man was working the night desk. It was from Hood River, Oregon. Our stringer there reported that more than one hundred "green capsules" about fifty yards long had appeared in and around an apple orchard. The new desk man was not so new that he did not recall the downhold policy on silly-season items. He killed it, but left it on the spike for my amused inspection in the morning. I suppose exactly the same thing happened in every wire service newsroom in the region. I rolled in at 10:30 and riffled through the stuff on the spike. When I saw the "green capsules" dispatch I tried to phone Portland, but couldn't get a connection. Then the phone buzzed and a correspondent of ours in Seattle began to yell at me, but the line went dead.

I shrugged and phoned Benson, in Fort Hicks. He was at the police station, and asked me: "Is this it?"

"It is," I told him. I read him the telegram from Hood River and told him about the line trouble to Seattle.

"So," he said wonderingly, "I called the turn, didn't I?"

"Called what turn?"

"On the invaders. I don't know who they are—but it's the story of the boy who cried wolf. Only this time, the wolves realized—" Then the phone went dead.

But he was right.

The people of the world were the sheep.

We newsmen—radio, TV, press, and wire services—were the boy, who should have been ready to sound the alarm.

But the cunning wolves had tricked us into sounding the alarm so many times that the villagers were weary, and would not come when there was real peril.

The wolves who then were burning their way through the Ozarks, utterly without opposition, the wolves were the Martians under whose yoke and lash we now endure our miserable existences.

The Remorseful

ONE OF THE things that most attracts me to science fiction is its capacity to give what Harlow Shapley calls "the view from a distant star," the perspective on our humanity through the eyes of nonhumans. *The Remorseful* strikes me as a fine example of this, but if I said I remembered it primarily for this quality I would be lying to you. The memory has to do with censorship. When he wrote the story, Cyril had a line in the first paragraph that said "he masturbated incessantly." The editor who published it, after great soul-searching, deferred to the prudery of the time and changed "masturbated" to "brooded." Well, times have changed. If Cyril were alive today and an editor so peremptorily altered his meaning, I think he would punch the clod in the head. I know I would, and so I am pleased here, for the first time in print, to restore Cyril's original language to the story. On the other hand, I know just how the original editor felt when he made the change, because he was me.

IT DOES NOT matter when it happened. This is because he was alone and time had ceased to have any meaning for him. At first he had searched the rubble for other survivors, which kept him busy for a couple of years. Then he wandered across the continent in great, vague quarterings, but the plane one day would not take off and he knew he would never find anybody anyway. He was by then in his forties, and a kind of sexual delirium overcame him. He searched out and pored over pictures of women, preferring leggy, high-breasted types. They haunted his dreams; he masturbated incessantly with closed eyes, tears leaking from them and running down his filthy bearded face. One day that phase ended for no reason and he took up his wanderings again, on foot. North in the summer, south in the winter on weed-grown U.S. 1, with the haversack of pork and beans on his shoulders, usually talking as he trudged, sometimes singing.

It does not matter when it happened. This is because the Visitors were eternal; endless time stretched before them and behind, which mentions only two of the infinities of infinities that their "lives" included. Precisely when they arrived at a particular planetary system was to them the most trivial of irrelevancies. Eternity was theirs; eventually they would have arrived at all of them.

They had won eternity in the only practical way: by outnumbering it. Each of the Visitors was a billion lives as you are a billion lives— the billion lives, that is, of your cells. But your cells have made the mistake of specializing. Some of them can only contract and relax. Some can only strain urea from your blood. Some can only load, carry, and unload oxygen. Some can only transmit minute electrical pulses and others can only manufacture chemicals in a desperate attempt to keep the impossible Rube Goldberg mechanism that you are from breaking down. They never succeed and you always do. Perhaps before you break down some of your specialized cells unite with somebody else's specialized cells and grow into another impossible, doomed contraption.

The Visitors were more sensibly arranged. Their billion lives were not cells but small, unspecialized, insect-like creatures linked by an electromagnetic field subtler than the coarse grapplings that hold you together. Each of the billion creatures that made up a Visitor could live and carry tiny weights, could manipulate tiny power tools, could carry in its small round black head, enough brain cells to feed, mate, breed, and work—and a few million more brain cells that were pooled into the field which made up the Visitor's consciousness.

When one of the insects died there were no rites; it was matter-of-factly pulled to pieces and eaten by its neighboring insects while it was still fresh. It mattered no more to the Visitor than the growing of your hair does to you, and the growing of your hair is accomplished only by the deaths of countless cells.

"Maybe on Mars!" he shouted as he trudged. The haversack jolted a shoulder blade and he arranged a strap without breaking his stride.

Birds screamed and scattered in the dark pine forests as he roared at them: "Well, why not? There must of been ten thousand up there easy. Progress, God damn it! That's *progress,* man! Never thought it'd come in my time. But you'd think they would of sent a ship back by now so a man wouldn't feel so all alone. You know better than that, man. You know God damned good and well it happened up there too. We had Northern Semisphere, they had Southern Semisphere, so you know God damned good and well what happened up there. Semisphere? Hemisphere. Hemi-semi-demisphere."

That was a good one, the best one he'd come across in years. He roared it out as he went stumping along.

When he got tired of it he roared: "You should of been in the *Old* Old Army, man. We didn't go in 'for this Liberty Unlimited crock in the *Old* Old Army. If you wanted to march in step with somebody else you *marched* in step with somebody else, man. None of this crock about you march out of step or twenty lashes from the sergeant for limiting your liberty."

That was a good one too, but it made him a little uneasy. He tried to remember whether he had been in the army or had just heard about it. He realized in time that a storm was blowing up from his depths; unless he headed it off he would soon be sprawled on the broken concrete of U.S. 1, sobbing and beating his head with his fists. He went back hastily to *Sem*-isphere, *Hem*-isphere, *Hem-i-sem-i-dem*-isphere, roaring it at the scared birds as he trudged.

There were four Visitors aboard the ship when it entered the planetary system. One of them was left on a cold outer planet rich in metal outcrops to establish itself in a billion tiny shelters, build a billion tiny forges, and eventually—in a thousand years or a million; it made no difference—construct a space ship, fission into two or more Visitors for company, and go Visiting. The ship had been getting crowded; as more and more information was acquired in its voyaging it was necessary for the swarms to increase in size, breeding more insects to store the new facts.

The three remaining Visitors turned the prow of their ship toward an intermediate planet and made a brief, baffling stop there. It was uninhabited except for about ten thousand entities—far fewer than one would expect, and certainly not enough for an efficient first-contact study. The Visitors made for the next planet sunward after only the sketchiest observation. And yet that sketchy observation of the entities left them figuratively shaking their heads. Since the Visitors had no genitals they were in a sense without emotions—but you would have said a vague air of annoyance hung over the ship nevertheless.

They ruminated the odd facts that the entities had levitated, appeared at the distance of observation to be insubstantial, appeared at the distance of observation to be unaware of the Visitors. When you are a hundred-yard rippling black carpet moving across a strange land, when the dwellers in this land soar aimlessly about you and above you, you expect to surprise, perhaps to frighten at first, and at least to provoke curiosity. You do not expect to be ignored.

They reserved judgment pending analysis of the sunward planet's entities—possibly colonizing entities, which would explain the sparseness of the outer planet's population, though not its indifference.

They landed.

He woke and drank water from a roadside ditch. There had been a time when water was *the* problem. You put three drops of iodine in a canteen. Or you boiled it if you weren't too weak from dysentery. Or you scooped it from the tank of a flush toilet in the isolated farmhouse with the farmer and his wife and their kids downstairs grotesquely staring with their empty eye sockets at the television screen for the long-ago-spoken latest word. Disease or dust or shattering supersonics broadcast from the bullhorn of a low-skimming drone—what did it matter? Safe water was what mattered.

"But hell," he roared, "it's all good now. Hear that? The rain in the ditches, the standing water in the pools, it's all good now. You should have been Lonely Man back when the going was bad, fella, when the bullhorns still came over and the stiffs shook when they did and Lonely Man didn't die but he wished he could . . ."

This time the storm took him unaware and was long in passing. His hands were ragged from flailing the broken concrete and his eyes were so swollen with weeping that he could hardly see to shoulder his sack of cans. He stumbled often that morning. Once he fell and opened an old scar on his forehead, but not even that interrupted his steady, mumbling chant: " 'Tain't no boner, 'tain't no blooper; Corey's Gin brings super stupor. We shall conquer; we will win. Back our boys with Corey's Gin. Wasting time in war is sinful; black out fast with a Corey skinful."

They landed.

Five thousand insects of each "life" heaved on fifteen thousand wires to open the port and let down the landing ramp. While they heaved a few hundred felt the pangs of death on them. They communicated the minute all-they-knew to blank-minded standby youngsters, died, and were eaten. Other hundreds stopped heaving briefly, gave birth, and resumed heaving.

The three Visitors swarmed down the ramp, three living black carpets. For maximum visibility they arranged themselves in three thin black lines which advanced slowly over the rugged terrain. At the tip of each line a few of the insects occasionally strayed too far from their connecting files and dropped out of the "life" field. These staggered in purposeless circles. Some blundered back into the field; some did not and died, leaving a minute hiatus in the "life's" memory—perhaps the shape of the full-stop symbol in the written language of a planet long ago visited, long ago dust. Normally the thin line was not used for exploring any but the smoothest terrain; the fact that they took a small calculated risk was a measure of the Visitors' slightly irked curiosity.

With three billion faceted eyes the Visitors saw immediately that this was no semi-deserted world, and that furthermore it was probably the world which had colonized the puzzling outer planet. Entities were everywhere; the air was thick with them in some places. There were numerous artifacts, all in ruins. Here the entities of the planet clustered, but here the bafflement deepened. The artifacts were all decidedly material and ponderous—but the entities were insubstantial. Coarsely organized observers would not have perceived them consistently. They existed in a field similar to the organization field of the Visitors. Their bodies were constructs of wave trains rather than atoms. It was impossible to imagine them manipulating the materials of which the artifacts were composed.

And as before, the Visitors were ignored.

Deliberately they clustered themselves in three huge black balls, with the object of being as obstreperous as possible and also to mobilize their field strength for a brute-force attempt at communication with the annoying creatures. By this time their attitude approximated: "We'll show these bastards!"

They didn't—not after running up and down every spectrum of thought in which they could project. Their attempt at reception was more successful, and completely horrifying. A few weak, attenuated messages did come through to the Visitors. They revealed the entities of the planet to be dull, whimpering cravens, whining evasively, bleating with self-pity. Though there were only two sexes among them, a situation which leads normally to a rather weak sex drive as such things go in the cosmos, these wispy things vibrated with libido which it was quite impossible for them to discharge.

The Visitors, thoroughly repelled, were rippling back toward their ship when one signaled: *notice and hide.*

The three great black carpets abruptly vanished—that is, each insect found itself a cranny to disappear into, a pebble or leaf to be on the other side of. Some hope flared that the visit might be productive of a more pleasant contact than the last with those aimless, chittering cretins.

The thing stumping across the terrain toward them was like and unlike the wave-train cretins. It had their conformation but was material rather than undulatory in nature a puzzle that could wait. It appeared to have no contact with the wave-train life form. They soared and darted about it as it approached, but it ignored them. It passed once through a group of three who happened to be on the ground in its way.

Tentatively the three Visitors reached out into its mind. The thoughts were comparatively clear and steady.

When the figure had passed the Visitors chorused: *Agreed,* and headed back to their ship. There was nothing there for them. Among other things they had drawn from the figure's mind was the location of a ruined library; a feeble-minded working party of a million was dispatched to it.

Back at the ship they waited, unhappily ruminating the creature's foreground thoughts: "From Corey's Gin you get the charge to tote that bale and lift that barge. That's progress, God damn it. You know better than that, man. Liberty Unlimited for the Lonely Man, but it be nice to see that Mars ship land . . ."

Agreement: *Despite all previous experience it seems that a sentient race is capable of destroying itself.*

When the feeble-minded library detail returned and gratefully re-united itself with its parent "lives" they studied the magnetic tapes it had brought, reading them direct in the cans. They learned the name of the planet and the technical name for the wave-train entities which had inherited it and which would shortly be its sole proprietors. The solid life forms, it seemed, had not been totally unaware of them, though there was some confusion: Far the vaster section of the library denied that they existed at all. But in the cellular minds of the Visitors there could be no doubt that the creatures described in a neglected few of the library's lesser works were the ones they had encountered. Everything tallied. Their non-material quality; their curious reaction to light. And, above all, their dominant personality trait, of remorse, repentance, furious regret. The technical term that the books gave to them was: ghosts.

The Visitors worked ship, knowing that the taste of this world and its colony would soon be out of what passed for their collective mouths, rinsed clean by new experiences and better-organized entities.

But they had never left a solar system so gratefully or so fast.

Gomez

NEW YORK was not always a nightmare city, and
Cyril (as did I) loved to ramble around the
neighborhoods. We rambled a lot of them together, but where my particular turf was Brooklyn
his was uptown Manhattan, including the Spanish-
speaking neighborhoods. He had an observant
eye, and also a listening ear, which he sharpened
up in neighborhood bars. I don't know who Julio
was—barman? delivery boy? numbers runner?—but
I know where Cyril found him: sitting on a stool,
with an elbow on the mahogany, talking about
baseball or why the Mayor of New York was
clearly insane.

NOW THAT I'm a cranky, constipated old man I can afford to say that
the younger generation of scientists makes me sick to my stomach.
Short-order fry cooks of destruction, they hear through the little window the dim order: "Atom bomb rare, with cobalt sixty!" and sing it
back and rattle their stinking skillets and sling the deadly hash—just
what the customer ordered, with never a notion invading their smug,
too-heated havens that there's a small matter of right and wrong that
takes precedence even over their haute cuisine.

There used to be a slew of them who yelled to high heaven about
it. Weiner, Urey, Szilard, Morrison—dead now, and worse. Unfashionable. The greatest of them you have never heard of. Admiral
MacDonald never did clear the story. He was Julio Gomez, and his
story was cleared yesterday by a fellow my Jewish friends call Malach
Hamovis, the Hovering Angel of Death. A black-bordered letter from
Rosa advised me that Malach Hamovis had come in on runway six
with his flaps down and picked up Julio at the age of thirty-nine.
Pneumonia.

"But," Rosa painfully wrote, "Julio would want you to know he died not too unhappy, after a good though short life with much of satisfaction . . ."

I think it will give him some more satisfaction, wherever he is, to know that his story at last is getting told.

It started twenty-two years ago with a routine assignment on a crisp October morning. I had an appointment with Dr. Sugarman, the head of the physics department at the University. It was the umpth anniversary of something or other—first atomic pile, the test A-bomb, Nagasaki—I don't remember what, and the Sunday editor was putting together a page on it. My job was to interview the three or four University people who were Manhattan District grads.

I found Sugarman in his office at the top of the modest physics building's square gothic tower, brooding through a pointed-arch window at the bright autumn sky. He was a tubby, jowly little fellow. I'd been seeing him around for a couple of years at testimonial banquets and press conferences, but I didn't expect him to remember me. He did, though, and even got the name right.

"Mr. Vilchek?" he beamed. "From the *Tribune?*"

"That's right, Dr. Sugarman. How are you?"

"Fine; fine. Sit down, please. Well, what shall we talk about?"

"Well, Dr. Sugarman, I'd like to have your ideas on the really fundamental issues of atomic energy, A-bomb control and so on. What in your opinion is the single most important factor in these problems?"

His eyes twinkled; he was going to surprise me. "Education!" he said, and leaned back waiting for me to register shock.

I registered. "That's certainly a different approach, doctor. How do you mean that, exactly?"

He said impressively: "Education—*technical* education—is the key to the underlying issues of our time. I am deeply concerned over the unawareness of the general public to the meaning and accomplishments of science. People underrate me—underrate *science,* that is —because they do not *understand* science. Let me show you something." He rummaged for a moment through papers on his desk and handed me a sheet of lined tablet paper covered with chicken-track handwriting. "A letter I got," he said. I squinted at the penciled scrawl and read:

October 12

Esteemed Sir:

*Beg to introduce self to you the atomic Scientist as a youth
17 working with diligence to perfect self in Mathematical
Physics. The knowledge of English is imperfect since am in
New-York 1 year only from Puerto Rico and due to Father and
Mother poverty must wash the dishes in the restaurant. So es-
teemed sir excuse imperfect English which will better.*

*I hesitate intruding your valuable Scientist time but hope you
sometime spare minutes for diligents such as I. My difficulty is
with neutron cross-section absorption of boron steel in Reactor
which theory I am working out. Breeder reactors demand*

$$u = \frac{x}{1} + \frac{x^5}{1} + \frac{x^{10}}{1} + \frac{x^{15}}{1} + \dots$$

*for boron steel, compared with neutron cross-section absorp-
tion of*

$$v = \frac{x^{1/6}}{1} + \frac{x}{1} + \frac{x^2}{1} + \frac{x^3}{1} + \dots$$

*for any Concrete with which I familiarize myself. Whence arises
relationship*

$$v^5 = u \frac{1 - 2u + 4u^2 - 3u^2 + u^4}{1 + 3u + 4u^2 + 2u^3 + u^4}$$

*indicating only a fourfold breeder gain. Intuitively I dissatisfy
with this gain and beg to intrude your time to ask wherein I
neglect. With the most sincere thanks.*

J. Gomez
% Porto Bello Lunchroom
124th St. & St. Nicholas Ave.
New-York, New-York

I laughed and told Dr. Sugarman appreciatively: "That's a good
one. I wish our cranks kept in touch with us by mail, but they don't.
In the newspaper business they come in and demand to see the editor. Could I use it, by the way? The readers ought to get a boot out
of it."

He hesitated and said: "All right—if you don't use my name. Just
say 'a prominent physicist.' I didn't think it was too funny myself
though, but I see your point, of course. The boy may be feeble-

minded—and he probably is—but he believes, like too many people, that science is just a bag of tricks that any ordinary person can acquire—"

And so on and so on.

I went back to the office and wrote the interview in twenty minutes. It took me longer than that to talk the Sunday editor into running the Gomez letter in a box on the atom-anniversary page, but he finally saw it my way. I had to retype it. If I'd just sent the letter down to the composing room as was, we would have had a strike on our hands.

On Sunday morning, at a quarter past six, I woke up to the tune of fists thundering on my hotel-room door. I found my slippers and bathrobe and lurched blearily across the room. They didn't wait for me to unlatch. The door opened. I saw one of the hotel clerks, the Sunday editor, a frosty-faced old man, and three hard-faced, hard-eyed young men. The hotel clerk mumbled and retreated and the others moved in. "Chief," I asked the Sunday editor hazily, "what's going—?"

A hard-faced young man was standing with his back to the door; another was standing with his back to the window and the third was blocking the bathroom door. The icy old man interrupted me with a crisp authoritative question snapped at the editor. "You identify this man as Vilchek?"

The editor nodded.

"Search him," snapped the old man. The fellow standing guard at the window slipped up and frisked me for weapons while I sputtered incoherently and the Sunday editor avoided my eye.

When the search was over the frosty-faced old boy said to me: "I am Rear Admiral MacDonald, Mr. Vilchek. I'm here in my capacity as deputy director of the Office of Security and Intelligence, U. S. Atomic Energy Commission. Did you write this?" He thrust a newspaper clipping at my face.

I read, blearily:

What's So Tough About A-Science?
Teenage Pot-Washer Doesn't Know

A letter received recently by a prominent local atomic scientist points up Dr. Sugarman's complaint (see adjoining column) that the public does not appreciate how hard a physicist works. The text, complete with "mathematics" follows:

Esteemed Sir:
Beg to introduce self to you the Atomic Scientist as youth 17 working—

"Yes," I told the admiral. "I wrote it, except for the headline. What about it?"

He snapped: "The letter is purportedly from a New York youth seeking information, yet there is no address for him given. Why is that?"

I said patiently: "I left it off when I copied it for the composing room. That's *Trib* style on readers' letters. *What* is all this about?"

He ignored the question and asked: "Where is the purported original of the letter?"

I thought hard and told him: "I think I stuck it in my pants pocket. I'll get it—" I started for the chair with my suit draped over it.

"Hold it, mister!" said the young man at the bathroom door. I held it and he proceeded to go through the pockets of the suit. He found the Gomez letter in the inside breast pocket of the coat and passed it to the admiral. The old man compared it, word for word, with the clipping and then put them both in his pocket.

"I want to thank you for your cooperation," he said coldly to me and the Sunday editor. "I caution you not to discuss, and above all not to publish, any account of this incident. The national security is involved in the highest degree. Good day."

He and his boys started for the door, and the Sunday editor came to life. "Admiral," he said, "this is going to be on the front page of tomorrow's *Trib.*"

The admiral went white. After a long pause he said: "You are aware that this country may be plunged into global war at any moment. That American boys are dying every day in border skirmishes. Is it to protect civilians like you who won't obey a reasonable request affecting security?"

The Sunday editor took a seat on the edge of my rumpled bed and lit a cigarette. "I know all that, admiral," he said. "I also know that this is a free country and how to keep it that way. Pitiless light on incidents like this of illegal search and seizure."

The admiral said: "I personally assure you, on my honor as an officer, that you would be doing the country a grave disservice by publishing an account of this."

The Sunday editor said mildly: "Your honor as an officer. You broke into this room without a search warrant. Don't you realize that's against the law? And I saw your boy ready to shoot when Vilchek started for that chair." I began to sweat a little at that, but the admiral was sweating harder.

With an effort he said: "I should apologize for the abruptness and discourtesy with which I've treated you. I do apologize. My only excuse is that, as I've said, this is a crash-priority matter. May I have your assurance that you gentlemen will keep silent?"

"On one condition," said the Sunday editor. "I want the *Trib* to have an exclusive on the Gomez story. I want Mr. Vilchek to cover it, with your full cooperation. In return, we'll hold it for your release and submit it to your security censorship."

"It's a deal," said the admiral, sourly. He seemed to realize suddenly that the Sunday editor had been figuring on such a deal all along.

On the plane for New York, the admiral filled me in. He was precise and unhappy, determined to make the best of a bad job. "I was awakened at three this morning by a phone call from the chairman of the Atomic Energy Commission. *He* had been awakened by a call from Dr. Monroe of the Scientific Advisory Committee. Dr. Monroe had been up late working and sent out for the Sunday *Tribune* to read before going to sleep. He saw the Gomez letter and went off like a sixteen-inch rifle. The neutron cross-section absorption relationship expressed in it happens to be, Mr. Vilchek, his own work. It also happens to be one of the nation's most closely guarded—er—atomic secrets. Presumably this Gomez stumbled on it somehow, as a janitor or something of the sort, and is feeding his ego by pretending to be an atomic scientist."

I scratched my unshaved jaw. "Admiral," I said, "you wouldn't kid me? How can three equations be a top atomic secret?"

The admiral hesitated. "All I can tell you," he said slowly, "is that breeder reactors are involved."

"But the letter said that. You mean this Gomez not only swiped the equations but knew what they were about?"

The admiral said grimly: "Somebody has been incredibly lax. It would be worth many divisions to the Soviet for their man Kapitza to see those equations—and realize that they are valid."

He left me to chew that one over for a while as the plane droned over New Jersey. Finally the pilot called back: "E.T.A. five minutes, sir. We have landing priority at Newark."

"Good," said the admiral. "Signal for a civilian-type car to pick us up without loss of time."

"Civilian," I said.

"Of course civilian!" he snapped. "That's the hell of it. Above all we must not arouse suspicion that there is anything special or unusual about this Gomez or his letter. Copies of the *Tribune* are on their way to the Soviet now as a matter of routine—they take all American papers and magazines they can get. If we tried to stop shipment of *Tribunes* that would be an immediate giveaway that there was something of importance going on."

We landed and the five of us got into a late-model car, neither drab nor flashy. One of the admiral's young men relieved the driver, a corporal with Signal Corps insignia. There wasn't much talk during the drive from Newark to Spanish Harlem, New York. Just once the admiral lit a cigarette, but he flicked it through the window after a couple of nervous puffs.

The Porto Bello Lunchroom was a store-front restaurant in the middle of a shabby tenement block. Wide-eyed, graceful, skinny little kids stared as our car parked in front of it and then converged on us purposefully. "Watch your car, mister?" they begged. The admiral surprised them—and me—with a flood of Spanish that sent the little extortionists scattering back to their stickball game in the street and their potsy layouts chalked on the sidewalks.

"Higgins," said the admiral, "see if there's a back exit." One of his boys got out and walked around the block under the dull, incurious eyes of black-shawled women sitting on their stoops. He was back in five minutes, shaking his head.

"Vilchek and I will go in," said the admiral. "Higgins, stand by the restaurant door and tackle anyone who comes flying out. Let's go, reporter. And remember that I do the talking."

The noon-hour crowd at the Porto Bello's ten tables looked up at us when we came in. The admiral said to a woman at a primitive cashier's table: *"Nueva York* Board of Health, *señora."*

"Ah!" she muttered angrily. *"Por favor, no aquí!* In back, understand? Come." She beckoned a pretty waitress to take over at the cash drawer and led us into the steamy little kitchen. It was crowded with us, an old cook, and a young dishwasher. The admiral and the woman began a rapid exchange of Spanish. He played his part well. I myself couldn't keep my eyes off the kid dishwasher who somehow or other had got hold of one of America's top atomic secrets.

Gomez was seventeen, but he looked fifteen. He was small-boned and lean, with skin the color of bright Virginia tobacco in an English cigarette. His hair was straight and glossy-black and a little long. Every so often he wiped his hands on his apron and brushed it back from his damp forehead. He was working like hell, dipping and swabbing and rinsing and drying like a machine, but he didn't look pushed or angry. He wore a half-smile that I later found out was his normal, relaxed expression and his eyes were far away from the kitchen of the Porto Bello Lunchroom. The elderly cook was making it clear by the exaggerated violence of his gesture and a savage frown that he resented these people invading his territory. I don't think Gomez even knew we were there. A sudden, crazy idea came into my head.

The admiral had turned to him. *"Cómo se llama, chico?"*

He started and put down the dish he was wiping. "Julio Gomez, *señor. Porqué, por favor? Qué pasa?"*

He wasn't the least bit scared.

"Nueva York Board of Health," said the admiral. *"Con su permiso—"* He took Gomez's hands in his and looked at them gravely, front and back, making *tsk-tsk* noises. Then, decisively: *"Vamanos, Julio. Siento mucho. Usted esta muy enfermo."* Everybody started talking at once, the woman doubtless objecting to the slur on her restaurant and the cook to losing his dishwasher and Gomez to losing time from the job.

The admiral gave them broadside for broadside and outlasted them. In five minutes we were leading Gomez silently from the restaurant. *"La loteria!"* a woman customer said in a loud whisper. *"O las mutas,"* somebody said back. Arrested for policy or marihuana, they thought. The pretty waitress at the cashier's table looked stricken and said nervously: "Julio?" as we passed, but he didn't notice.

Gomez sat in the car with the half-smile on his lips and his eyes a million miles away as we rolled downtown to Foley Square. The admiral didn't look as though he'd approve of any questions from me. We got out at the Federal Building and Gomez spoke at last. He said in surprise: "This, it is not the hospital!"

Nobody answered. We marched him up the steps and surrounded him in the elevator. It would have made anybody nervous—it would have made *me* nervous—to be herded like that; everybody's got something on his conscience. But the kid didn't even seem to notice. I decided that he must be a half-wit or—there came that crazy notion again.

The glass door said "U. S. Atomic Energy Commission, Office of Security and Intelligence." The people behind it were flabbergasted when the admiral and party walked in. He turned the head man out of his office and sat at his desk, with Gomez getting the caller's chair. The rest of us stationed ourselves uncomfortably around the room.

It started. The admiral produced the letter and asked in English: "Have you ever seen this before?" He made it clear from the way he held it that Gomez wasn't going to get his hands on it.

"*Sí, seguro*. I write it last week. This is funny business. I am not really sick like you say, no?" He seemed relieved.

"No. Where did you get these equations?"

Gomez said proudly: "I work them out."

The admiral gave a disgusted little laugh. "Don't waste my time, boy. Where did you get these equations?"

Gomez was beginning to get upset. "You got no right to call me liar," he said. "I not so smart as the big physicists, *seguro*, and maybe I make mistakes. Maybe I waste the *profesór* Soo-har-man his time but he got no right to have me arrest. I tell him right in letter he don't have to answer if he don't want. I make no crime and you got no right!"

The admiral looked bored. "Tell me how you worked the equations out," he said.

"Okay," said Gomez sulkily. "You know the random paths of neutron is expressed in matrix mechanics by *profesór* Oppenheim five years ago, all okay. I transform his equations from path-prediction domain to cross-section domain and integrate over absorption areas. This gives u series and v series. And from there, the u–v relationship is obvious, no?"

The admiral, still bored, asked: "Got it?"

I noticed that one of his young men had a shorthand pad out. He said: "Yes."

The admiral picked up the phone and said: "This is MacDonald. Get me Dr. Mines out at Brookhaven right away." He told Gomez blandly: "Dr. Mines is the chief of the A.E.C. Theoretical Physics Division. I'm going to ask him what he thinks of the way you worked the equations out. He's going to tell me that you were just spouting a lot of gibberish. And then you're going to tell me where you *really* got them."

Gomez looked mixed up and the admiral turned back to the phone. "Dr. Mines? This is Admiral MacDonald of Security. I want your opinion on the following." He snapped his fingers impatiently and the stenographer passed him his pad. "Somebody has told me that he discovered a certain relationship by taking—" He read carefully. "—by taking the random paths of a neutron expressed in matrix mechanics by Oppenheim, transforming his equations from the path-prediction domain to the cross-section domain and integrating over the absorption areas."

In the silence of the room I could hear the faint buzz of the voice on the other end. And a great red blush spread over the admiral's face from his brow to his neck. The faintly buzzing voice ceased and after a long pause the admiral said slowly and softly: "No, it wasn't Fermi or Szilard. I'm not at liberty to tell you who. Can you come right down to the Federal Building Security Office in New York? I—I need your help. Crash priority." He hung up the phone wearily and muttered to himself: "Crash priority. Crash." And wandered out of the office looking dazed.

His young men stared at one another in frank astonishment. "Five years," said one, "and—"

"*Nix*," said another, looking pointedly at me.

Gomez asked brightly: "What goes on anyhow? This is damn funny business, I think."

"Relax, kid," I told him. "Looks as if you'll make out all—"

"*Nix*," said the nixer again savagely, and I shut up and waited.

After a while somebody came in with coffee and sandwiches and we ate them. After another while the admiral came in with Dr. Mines. Mines was a white-haired, wrinkled Connecticut Yankee. All I knew about him was that he'd been in mild trouble with Congress for stubbornly plugging world government and getting on some of the wrong letterheads. But I learned right away that he was all scientist and didn't have a phony bone in his body.

"Mr. Gomez?" he asked cheerfully. "The admiral tells me that you are either a well-trained Russian spy or a phenomenal self-taught nuclear physicist. He wants me to find out which."

"Russia?" yelled Gomez, outraged. "He crazy! I am American United States citizen!"

"That's as may be," said Dr. Mines. "Now, the admiral tells me you describe the u–v relationship as 'obvious.' I should call it a highly abstruse derivation in the theory of continued fractions and complex multiplication."

Gomez strangled and gargled helplessly trying to talk, and finally asked, his eyes shining: *"Por favor,* could I have piece paper?"

They got him a stack of paper and the party was on.

For two unbroken hours Gomez and Dr. Mines chattered and scribbled. Mines gradually shed his jacket, vest, and tie, completely oblivious to the rest of us. Gomez was even more abstracted. He *didn't* shed his jacket, vest, and tie. He didn't seem to be aware of anything except the rapid-fire exchange of ideas via scribbled formulae and the terse spoken jargon of mathematics. Dr. Mines shifted on his chair and sometimes his voice rose with excitement. Gomez didn't shift or wriggle or cross his legs. He just sat and scribbled and talked in a low, rapid monotone, looking straight at Dr. Mines with his eyes very wide open and lit up like searchlights.

The rest of us just watched and wondered.

Dr. Mines broke at last. He stood up and said: "I can't take any more, Gomez. I've got to think it over—" He began to leave the room, mechanically scooping up his clothes, and then realized that we were still there.

"Well?" asked the admiral grimly.

Dr. Mines smiled apologetically. "He's a physicist, all right," he said. Gomez sat up abruptly and looked astonished.

"Take him into the next office, Higgins," said the admiral. Gomez let himself be led away, like a sleepwalker.

Dr. Mines began to chuckle. "Security!" he said. "Security!"

The admiral rasped: "Don't trouble yourself over my decisions, if you please, Dr. Mines. My job is keeping the Soviets from pirating American science and I'm doing it to the best of my ability. What I want from you is your opinion on the possibility of that young man having worked out the equations as he claimed."

Dr. Mines was abruptly sobered. "Yes," he said. "Unquestionably he did. And will you excuse my remark? I was under some strain in trying to keep up with Gomez."

"Certainly," said the admiral, and managed a frosty smile. "Now if you'll be so good as to tell me how this completely impossible thing can have happened—?"

"It's happened before, admiral," said Dr. Mines. "I don't suppose you ever heard of Ramanujan?"

"No."

"*Srinivasa* Ramanujan?"

"*No!*"

"Oh. Well, Ramanujan was born in 1887 and died in 1920. He was a poor Hindu who failed twice in college and then settled down as a government clerk. With only a single obsolete textbook to go on he made himself a very great mathematician. In 1913 he sent some of his original work to a Cambridge professor. He was immediately recognized and called to England, where he was accepted as a first-rank man, became a member of the Royal Society, a Fellow of Trinity, and so forth."

The admiral shook his head dazedly.

"It happens," Dr. Mines said. "Oh yes, it happens. Ramanujan had only one out-of-date book. But this is New York. Gomez has access to all the mathematics he could hope for and a great mass of unclassified and declassified nuclear data. And—genius. The way he puts things together . . . he seems to have only the vaguest notion of what a proof should be. He *sees* relationships as a whole. A most convenient faculty, which I envy him. Where I have to take, say, a dozen painful steps from one conclusion to the next he achieves it in one grand flying leap. Ramanujan was like that too, by the way—very strong on intuition, weak on what we call 'rigor.' " Dr. Mines noted with a start that he was holding his tie, vest, and coat in one hand and began to put them on. "Was there anything else?" he asked politely.

"One thing," said the admiral. "Would you say he's—he's a better physicist than you are?"

"Yes," said Dr. Mines. "Much better." And he left.

The admiral slumped, uncharacteristically, at the desk for a long time. Finally he said to the air: "Somebody get me the General Manager. No, the Chairman of the Commission." One of his boys grabbed the phone and got to work on the call.

"Admiral," I said, "where do we stand now?"

"Eh? Oh, it's you. The matter's out of my hands now since no security violation is involved. I consider Gomez to be in my custody and I shall turn him over to the Commission so that he may be put to the best use in the nation's interest."

"Like a machine?" I asked, disgusted.

He gave me both barrels of his ice-blue eyes. "Like a weapon," he said evenly.

He was right, of course. Didn't I know there was a war on? Of course I did. Who didn't? Taxes, housing shortage, somebody's cousin killed in Korea, everybody's kid brother sweating out the draft, prices sky high at the supermarket. Uncomfortably I scratched my unshaved chin and walked to the window. Foley Square below was full of Sunday peace, with only a single girl stroller to be seen. She walked the length of the block across the street from the Federal Building and then turned and walked back. Her walk was dragging and hopeless and tragic.

Suddenly I knew her. She was the pretty little waitress from the Porto Bello; she must have hopped a cab and followed the men who were taking her Julio away. Might as well beat it, sister, I told her silently. Julio isn't just a good-looking kid any more; he's a military asset. The Security Office is turning him over to the policy-level boys for disposal. When that happens you might as well give up and go home.

It was as if she'd heard me. Holding a silly little handkerchief to her face she turned and ran blindly for the subway entrance at the end of the block and disappeared into it.

At that moment the telephone rang.

"MacDonald here," said the admiral. "I'm ready to report on the Gomez affair, Mr. Commissioner."

Gomez was a minor, so his parents signed a contract for him. The job description on the contract doesn't matter, but he got a pretty good salary by government standards and a per-diem allowance too.

I signed a contract too—"Information Specialist." I was partly companion, partly historian, and partly a guy they'd rather have their eyes on than not. When somebody tried to cut me out on grounds of economy, Admiral MacDonald frostily reminded him that he had given his word. I stayed, for all the good it did me.

We didn't have any name. We weren't Operation Anything or Project Whoozis or Task Force Dinwiddie. We were just five people in a big fifteen-room house on the outskirts of Milford, New Jersey. There was Gomez, alone on the top floor with a lot of books, technical magazines, and blackboards and a weekly visit from Dr. Mines. There were the three Security men, Higgins, Dalhousie, and Leitzer, sleeping by turns and prowling the grounds. And there was me.

From briefing sessions with Dr. Mines I kept a diary of what went on. Don't think from that that I knew what the score was. War correspondents have told me of the frustrating life they led at some close-mouthed commands. Soandso-many air sorties, the largest number since January fifteenth. Casualties a full fifteen per cent lighter than expected. Determined advance in an active sector against relatively strong enemy opposition. And so on—all adding up to nothing in the way of real information.

That's what it was like in my diary because that's all they told me. Here are some excerpts: "On the recommendation of Dr. Mines, Mr. Gomez today began work on a phase of reactor design theory to be implemented at Brookhaven National Laboratory. The work involves the setting up of thirty-five pairs of partial differential equations . . . Mr. Gomez announced tentatively today that in checking certain theoretical work in progress at the Los Alamos Laboratory of the A.E.C. he discovered a fallacious assumption concerning neutron-spin which invalidates the conclusions reached. This will be communicated to the Laboratory . . . Dr. Mines said today that Mr. Gomez has successfully invoked a hitherto-unexploited aspect of Minkowski's tensor analysis to crack a stubborn obstacle toward the control of thermonuclear reactions . . ."

I protested at one of the briefing sessions with Dr. Mines against this gobbledegook. He didn't mind my protesting. He leaned back in his chair and said calmly: "Vilchek, with all friendliness I assure you that you're getting everything you can understand. Anything more complex than the vague description of what's going on would be over your head. And anything more specific would give away exact engineering information which would be of use to foreign countries."

"This isn't the way they treated Bill Lawrence when he covered the atomic bomb," I said bitterly.

Mines nodded, with a pleased smile. "That's it exactly," he said. "Broad principles were being developed then—interesting things that could be told without any great harm being done. If you tell somebody that a critical mass of U-two thirty-five or Plutonium goes off with a big bang, you really haven't given away a great deal. He still has millions of man-hours of engineering before him to figure out how much is critical mass, to take only one small point."

So I took his word for it, faithfully copied the communiques he gave me and wrote what I could on the human-interest side for release some day.

So I recorded Gomez's progress with English, his taste for chicken pot pie and rice pudding, his habit of doing his own housework on the top floor and his old-maidish neatness. "You live your first fifteen years in a tin shack, Beel," he told me once, "and you find out you like things nice and clean." I've seen Dr. Mines follow Gomez through the top floor as the boy swept and dusted, talking at him in their mathematical jargon.

Gomez worked in forty-eight-hour spells usually, and not eating much. Then for a couple of days he'd live like a human being, grabbing naps, playing catch on the lawn with one or another of the Security people, talking with me about his childhood in Puerto Rico and his youth in New York. He taught me a little Spanish and asked me to catch him up on bad mistakes in English.

"But don't you ever want to get out of here?" I demanded one day.

He grinned: "Why should I, Beel? Here I eat good, I can send money to the parents. Best, I find out what the big professors are up to without I have to wait five–ten years for damn declassifying."

"Don't you have a girl?"

He was embarrassed and changed the subject back to the big professors.

Dr. Mines drove up then with his chauffeur, who looked like a G-man and almost certainly was. As usual, the physicist was toting a bulging briefcase. After a few polite words with me, he and Julio went indoors and upstairs.

They were closeted for five hours—a record. When Dr. Mines came down I expected the usual briefing session. But he begged off. "Nothing serious," he said. "We just sat down and kicked some ideas of his around. I told him to go ahead. We've been—ah—using him very much like a sort of computer, you know. Turning him loose on the problems that were too tough for me and some of the other men. He's got the itch for research now. It would be very interesting if his forte turned out to be creative."

I agreed.

Julio didn't come down for dinner. I woke up in darkness that night when there was a loud bump overhead, and went upstairs in my pyjamas.

Gomez was sprawled, fully dressed, on the floor. He'd tripped over a footstool. And he didn't seem to have noticed. His lips were moving and he stared straight at me without knowing I was there.

"You all right, Julio?" I asked, and started to help him to his feet.

He got up mechanically and said: "—real values of the zeta function vanish."

"How's that?"

He saw me then and asked, puzzled: "How you got in here, Beel? Is dinnertime?"

"Is four a.m., *por dios.* Don't you think you ought to get some sleep?" He looked terrible.

No; he didn't think he ought to get some sleep. He had some work to do. I went downstairs and heard him pacing overhead for an hour until I dozed off.

This splurge of work didn't wear off in forty-eight hours. For a week I brought him meals and sometimes he ate absently, with one hand, as he scribbled on a yellow pad. Sometimes I'd bring him lunch to find his breakfast untouched. He didn't have much beard, but he let it grow for a week—too busy to shave, too busy to talk, too busy to eat, sleeping in chairs when fatigue caught up with him.

I asked Leitzer, badly worried, if we should do anything about it. He had a direct scrambler-phone connection with the New York Security and Intelligence office, but his orders didn't cover anything like a self-induced nervous breakdown of the man he was guarding.

I thought Dr. Mines would do something when he came—call in an M.D., or tell Gomez to take it easy, or take some of the load off by parceling out whatever he had by the tail.

But he didn't. He went upstairs, came down two hours later, and absently tried to walk past me. I headed him off into my room. "What's the word?" I demanded.

He looked me in the eye and said defiantly: "He's doing fine. I don't want to stop him."

Dr. Mines was a good man. Dr. Mines was a humane man. And he wouldn't lift a finger to keep the boy from working himself into nervous prostration. Dr. Mines liked people well enough, but he reserved his love for theoretical physics. "How important can this thing be?"

He shrugged irritably. "It's just the way some scientists work," he said. "Newton was like that. So was Sir William Rowan Hamilton—"

"Hamilton-Schmamilton," I said. "What's the sense of it? *Why* doesn't he sleep or eat?"

Mines said: "*You* don't know what it's like."

"Of course," I said, getting good and sore. "I'm just a dumb newspaper man. Tell me, Mr. Bones, what is it like?"

There was a long pause, and he said mildly: "I'll try. That boy up there is using his brain. A great chess player can put on a blindfold and play a hundred opponents in a hundred games simultaneously, remembering all the positions of his pieces and theirs and keeping a hundred strategies clear in his mind. Well, that stunt simply isn't in the same league with what Julio's doing up there.

"He has in his head some millions of facts concerning theoretical physics. He's scanning them, picking out one here and there, fitting them into new relationships, checking and rejecting when he has to, fitting the new relationships together, turning them upside down and inside out to see what happens, comparing them with known doctrine, holding them in his memory while he repeats the whole process and compares—and all the while he has a goal firmly in mind against which he's measuring all these things." He seemed to be finished.

For a reporter, I felt strangely shy. "What's he driving at?" I asked.

"I think," he said slowly, "he's approaching a unified field theory."

Apparently that was supposed to explain everything. I let Dr. Mines know that it didn't.

He said thoughtfully: "I don't know whether I can get it over to a layman—no offense, Vilchek. Let's put it this way. You know how math comes in waves, and how it's followed by waves of applied science based on the math. There was a big wave of algebra in the middle ages—following it came navigation, gunnery, surveying, and so on.

Then the renaissance and a wave of analysis—what you'd call calculus. That opened up steam power and how to use it, mechanical engineering, electricity. The wave of *modern* mathematics since say eighteen seventy-five gave us atomic energy. That boy upstairs may be starting off the next big wave."

He got up and reached for his hat.

"Just a minute," I said. I was surprised that my voice was steady. "What comes next? Control of gravity? Control of personality? Sending people by radio?"

Dr. Mines wouldn't meet my eye. Suddenly he looked old and shrunken. "Don't worry about the boy," he said.

I let him go.

That evening I brought Gomez chicken pot pie and a nonalcoholic eggnog. He drank the eggnog, said, "Hi, Beel," and continued to cover yellow sheets of paper.

I went downstairs and worried.

Abruptly it ended late the next afternoon. Gomez wandered into the big first-floor kitchen looking like a starved old rickshaw coolie. He pushed his lank hair back from his forehead, said: "Beel, what is to eat—" and pitched forward onto the linoleum. Leitzer came when I yelled, expertly took Gomez's pulse, rolled him onto a blanket, and threw another one over him. "It's just a faint," he said. "Let's get him to bed."

"Aren't you going to call a doctor, man?"

"Doctor couldn't do anything we can't do," he said stolidly. "And I'm here to see that security isn't breached. Give me a hand."

We got him upstairs and put him to bed. He woke up and said something in Spanish, and then, apologetically: "Very sorry, fellows. I ought to taken it easier."

"I'll get you some lunch," I said, and he grinned.

He ate it all, enjoying it heartily, and finally lay back gorged. "Well," he asked me, "what it is new, Beel?"

"What *is* new. And you should tell me. You finish your work?"

"I got it in shape to finish. The hard part it is over." He rolled out of bed.

"Hey!" I said.

"I'm okay now," he grinned. "Don't write this down in your history, Beel. Everybody will think I act like a woman."

I followed him into his work room, where he flopped into an easy chair, his eyes on a blackboard covered with figures. He wasn't grinning any more.

"Dr. Mines says you're up to something big," I said.

"*Sí.* Big."

"Unified field theory, he says."

"That is it," Gomez said.

"Is it good or bad?" I asked, licking my lips. "The application, I mean."

His boyish mouth set suddenly in a grim line. "That, it is not my business," he said. "I am American citizen of the United States." He stared at the blackboard and its maze of notes.

I looked at it too—*really* looked at it for once—and was surprised by what I saw. Mathematics, of course, I don't know. But I had soaked up a very little *about* mathematics. One of the things I had soaked up was that the expressions of higher mathematics tend to be complicated and elaborate, involving English, Greek, and Hebrew letters, plain and fancy brackets, and a great variety of special signs besides the plus and minus of the elementary school.

The things on the blackboard weren't like that at all. The board was covered with variations of a simple expression that consisted of five letters and two symbols: a right-handed pothook and a left-handed pothook.

"What do they mean?" I asked, pointing.

"Somethings I made up," he said nervously. "The word for that one is 'enfields.' The other one is 'is enfielded by.'"

"What's *that* mean?"

His luminous eyes were haunted. He didn't answer.

"It looks like simple stuff. I read somewhere that all the basic stuff is simple once it's been discovered."

"Yes," he said almost inaudibly. "It is simple, Beel. Too damn simple, I think. Better I carry it in my head, I think." He strode to the blackboard and erased it. Instinctively I half-rose to stop him. He gave me a grin that was somehow bitter and unlike him. "Don't worry," he said. "I don't forget it." He tapped his forehead. "I *can't* forget it." I hope I never see again on any face the look that was on his.

"Julio," I said, appalled. "Why don't you get out of here for a while? Why don't you run over to New York and see your folks and have some fun? They can't keep you here against your will."

"They told me I shouldn't—" he said uncertainly. And then he got tough. "You're damn right, Beel. Let's go in together. I get dressed up. Er—You tell Leitzer, hah?" He couldn't quite face up to the hardboiled security man.

I told Leitzer, who hit the ceiling. But all it boiled down to was that he sincerely wished Gomez and I wouldn't leave. We weren't in the Army, we weren't in jail. I got hot at last and yelled back that we were damn well going out and he couldn't stop us. He called New York on his direct wire and apparently New York confirmed it, regretfully.

We got on the 4:05 Jersey Central, with Higgins and Dalhousie tailing us at a respectful distance. Gomez didn't notice them and I didn't tell him. He was having too much fun. He had a shine put on his shoes at Penn Station and worried about the taxi fare as we rode up to Spanish Harlem.

His parents lived in a neat little three-room apartment. A lot of the furniture looked brand-new, and I was pretty sure who had paid for it. The mother and father spoke only Spanish, and mumbled shyly when *"mi amigo Beel"* was introduced. I had a very halting conversation with the father while the mother and Gomez rattled away happily and she poked his ribs to point up the age-old complaint of any mother anywhere that he wasn't eating enough.

The father, of course, thought the boy was a janitor or something in the Pentagon and, as near as I could make out, he was worried about his Julio being grabbed off by a man-hungry government girl. I kept reassuring him that his Julio was a good boy, a very good boy, and he seemed to get some comfort out of it.

There was a little spat when his mother started to set the table. Gomez said reluctantly that we couldn't stay, that we were eating somewhere else. His mother finally dragged from him the admission that we were going to the Porto Bello so he could see Rosa, and everything was smiles again. The father told me that Rosa was a good girl, a very good girl.

Walking down the three flights of stairs with yelling little kids playing tag around us, Gomez asked proudly: "You not think they in America only a little time, hey?"

I yanked him around by the elbow as we went down the brownstone stoop into the street. Otherwise he would have seen our shadows for sure. I didn't want to spoil his fun.

The Porto Bello was full, and the pretty little girl was on duty as cashier at the table. Gomez got a last-minute attack of cold feet at the sight of her. "No table," he said. "We better go someplace else." I practically dragged him in. "We'll get a table in a minute," I said. "Julio," said the girl, when she saw him.

He looked sheepish. "Hello, Rosa. I'm back for a while."

"I'm glad to see you again," she said tremulously.

"I'm glad to see you again too—" I nudged him. "Rosa, this is my good friend Beel. We work together in Washington."

"Pleased to meet you, Rosa. Can you have dinner with us? I'll bet you and Julio have a lot to talk over."

"Well, I'll see . . . look, there's a table for you. I'll see if I can get away."

We sat down and she flagged down the proprietress and got away in a hurry.

All three of us had *arróz con pollo*—rice with chicken and lots of other things. Their shyness wore off and I was dealt out of the conversation, but I didn't mind. They were a nice young couple. I liked the way they smiled at each other, and the things they remembered happily—movies, walks, talks. It made me feel like a benevolent uncle with one foot in the grave. It made me forget for a while the look on Gomez's face when he turned from the blackboard he had covered with too-simple math.

Over dessert I broke in. By then they were unselfconsciously holding hands. "Look," I said, "why don't you two go on and do the town? Julio, I'll be at the Madison Park Hotel." I scribbled the address and gave it to him. "And I'll get a room for you. Have fun and reel in any time." I rapped his knee. He looked down and I slipped him four twenties. I didn't know whether he had money on him or not, but anything extra the boy could use he had coming to him.

"Swell," he said. "Thanks." And looked shame-faced while I looked paternal.

I had been watching a young man who was moodily eating alone in a corner, reading a paper. He was about Julio's height and build and he wore a sports jacket pretty much like Julio's. And the street was pretty dark outside.

The young man got up moodily and headed for the cashier's table. "Gotta go," I said. "Have fun."

I went out of the restaurant right behind the young man and

walked as close behind him as I dared, hoping we were being followed.

After a block and a half of this, he turned on me and snarled: "Wadda you, mister? A wolf? Beat it!"

"Okay," I said mildly, and turned and walked the other way. Higgins and Dalhousie were standing there, flat-footed and open-mouthed. They sprinted back to the Porto Bello, and *I* followed *them*. But Julio and Rosa had already left.

"Tough, fellows," I said to them as they stood in the doorway. They looked as if they wanted to murder me. "He won't get into any trouble," I said. "He's just going out with his girl." Dalhousie made a strangled noise and told Higgins: "Cruise around the neighborhood. See if you can pick them up. I'll follow Vilchek." He wouldn't talk to me. I shrugged and got a cab and went to the Madison Park Hotel, a pleasantly unfashionable old place with big rooms where I stay when business brings me to New York. They had a couple of adjoining singles; I took one in my own name and the other for Gomez.

I wandered around the neighborhood for a while and had a couple of beers in one of the ultra-Irish bars on Third Avenue. After a pleasant argument with a gent who thought the Russians didn't have any atomic bombs and faked their demonstrations and that we ought to blow up their industrial cities tomorrow at dawn, I went back to the hotel.

I didn't get to sleep easily. The citizen who didn't believe Russia could maul the United States pretty badly or at all had started me thinking again—all kinds of ugly thoughts. Dr. Mines, who had turned into a shrunken old man at the mention of applying Gomez's work. The look on the boy's face. My layman's knowledge that present-day "atomic energy" taps only the smallest fragment of the energy locked up in the atom. My layman's knowledge that once genius has broken a trail in science, mediocrity can follow the trail.

But I slept at last, for three hours.

At four-fifteen A.M. according to my watch the telephone rang long and hard. There was some switchboard and long-distance-operator mumbo-jumbo and then Julio's gleeful voice: "Beel! Congratulate us. We got marriage!"

"Married," I said fuzzily. "You got *married,* not marriage. How's that again?"

"We got *married.* Me and Rosa. We get on the train, the taxi driver takes us to justice of peace, we got *married*, we go to hotel here."

"Congratulations," I said, waking up. "Lots of congratulations. But you're under age, there's a waiting period—"

"Not in this state," he chuckled. "Here is no waiting periods and here I have twenty-one years if I say so."

"Well," I said. "Lots of congratulations, Julio. And tell Rosa she's got herself a good boy."

"Thanks, Beel," he said shyly. "I call you so you don't worry when I don't come in tonight. I think I come in with Rosa tomorrow so we tell her mama and my mama and papa. I call you at the hotel, I still have the piece of paper."

"Okay, Julio. All the best. Don't worry about a thing." I hung up, chuckling, and went right back to sleep.

Well, sir, it happened again.

I was shaken out of my sleep by the strong, skinny hand of Admiral MacDonald. It was seven-thirty and a bright New York morning. Dalhousie had pulled a blank canvassing the neighborhood for Gomez, got panicky, and bucked it up to higher headquarters.

"Where is he?" the admiral rasped.

"On his way here with his bride of one night," I said. "He slipped over a couple of state lines and got married."

"By God," the admiral said, "we've got to do something about this. I'm going to have him drafted and assigned to special duty. This is the last time—"

"*Look,*" I said. "You've got to stop treating him like a chesspiece. You've got duty-honor-country on the brain and thank God for that. Somebody has to; it's your profession. But can't you get it through your head that Gomez is a kid and that you're wrecking his life by forcing him to grind out science like a machine? And I'm just a stupe of a layman, but have you professionals worried once about digging too deep and blowing up the whole shebang?"

He gave me a piercing look and said nothing.

I dressed and had breakfast sent up. The admiral, Dalhousie, and I waited grimly until noon, and then Gomez phoned up.

"Come on up, Julio," I said tiredly.

He breezed in with his blushing bride on his arm. The admiral rose automatically as she entered, and immediately began tongue-lashing the boy. He spoke more in sorrow than in anger. He made it clear that Gomez wasn't treating his country right. That he had a great talent and it belonged to the United States. That his behavior had been irresponsible. That Gomez would have to come to heel and realize that his wishes weren't the most important thing in his life. That he could and would be drafted if there were any more such escapades.

"As a starter, Mr. Gomez," the admiral snapped, "I want you to set down, immediately, the enfieldment matrices you have developed. I consider it almost criminal of you to arrogantly and carelessly trust to your memory alone matters of such vital importance. Here!" He thrust pencil and paper at the boy, who stood, drooping and disconsolate. Little Rosa was near crying. She didn't have the ghost of a notion as to what it was about.

Gomez took the pencil and paper and sat down at the writing table silently. I took Rosa by the arm. She was trembling. "It's all right," I said. "They can't do a thing to him." The admiral glared briefly at me and then returned his gaze to Gomez.

The boy made a couple of tentative marks. Then his eyes went wide and he clutched his hair. *"Dios mío!"* he said. *"Está perdido! Olvidado!"*

Which means: "My God, it's lost! Forgotten!"

The admiral turned white beneath his tan. "Now, boy," he said slowly and soothingly. "I didn't mean to scare you. You just relax and collect yourself. Of course you haven't forgotten, not with that memory of yours. Start with something easy. Write down a general biquadratic equation, say."

Gomez just looked at him. After a long pause he said in a strangled voice: *"No puedo.* I can't. It too I forget. I don't think of the math or physics at all since—" He looked at Rosa and turned a little red. She smiled shyly and looked at her shoes.

"That is it," Gomez said hoarsely. "Not since then. Always before in the back of my head is the math, but not since then."

"My God," the admiral said softly. "Can such a thing happen?" He reached for the phone.

He found out that such things can happen.

Julio went back to Spanish Harlem and bought a piece of the Porto Bello with his savings. I went back to the paper and bought a car with *my* savings. MacDonald never cleared the story, so the Sunday editor had the satisfaction of bulldozing an admiral, but didn't get his exclusive.

Julio and Rosa sent me a card eventually announcing the birth of their first-born: a six-pound boy, Francisco, named after Julio's father. I saved the card and when a New York assignment came my way—it was the National Association of Dry Goods Wholesalers; dry goods are important in our town—I dropped up to see them.

Julio was a little more mature and a little more prosperous. Rosa—alas!—was already putting on weight, but she was still a pretty thing and devoted to her man. The baby was a honey-skinned little wiggler. It was nice to see all of them together, happy with their lot.

Julio insisted that he'd cook *arróz con pollo* for me, as on the night I practically threw him into Rosa's arms, but he'd have to shop for the stuff. I went along.

In the corner grocery he ordered the rice, the chicken, the garbanzos, the peppers, and, swept along by the enthusiasm that hits husbands in groceries, about fifty other things that he thought would be nice to have in the pantry.

The creaking old grocer scribbled down the prices on a shopping bag and began painfully to add them up while Julio was telling me how well the Porto Bello was doing and how they were thinking of renting the adjoining store.

"Seventeen dollars, forty-two cents," the grocer said at last.

Julio flicked one glance at the shopping bag and the upside-down figures. "Should be seventeen thirty-nine," he said reprovingly. "Add up again."

The grocer painfully added up again and said, "Is seventeen thirty-nine. Sorry." He began to pack the groceries into the bag.

"Hey," I said.

We didn't discuss it then or ever. Julio just said: "Don't tell, Beel." And winked.

The Advent on Channel Twelve

IN THE mid-50s Cyril's two sons were both very
small, but not so small that they hadn't discovered
television. The Mickey Mouse Club was a visitor
in the Kornbluth home every night, and the two
little kids, and Cyril himself, never missed it. I
don't know what the boys thought of this national
mania (everywhere you went kids were singing the
Mouseketeer song and wearing mouse-ear hats),
but I can tell what Cyril thought of it—and so can
you, from reading *The Advent on Channel
Twelve*.

IT CAME to pass in the third quarter of the fiscal year that the Federal
Reserve Board did raise the rediscount rate and money was tight in
the land. And certain bankers which sate in New York sent to Ben
Graffis in Hollywood a writing which said, Money is tight in the land
so let Poopy Panda up periscope and fire all bow tubes.

Whereupon Ben Graffis made to them this moan:

O ye bankers, Poopy Panda is like unto the child of my flesh and
you have made of him a devouring dragon. Once was I content with
my studio and my animators when we did make twelve Poopy Pandas
a year; cursed be the day when I floated a New York loan. You have
commanded me to make feature-length cartoon epics and I did obey,
and they do open at the Paramount to sensational grosses, and we do
re-release them to the nabes year on year, without end. You have
commanded me to film live adventure shorts and I did obey, and in
the cutting room we do devilishly splice and pull frames and flop neg-
atives so that I and my cameras are become bearers of false witness
and men look upon my live adventure shorts and say lo! these beasts
and birds are like unto us in their laughter, wooing, pranks, and con-
tention. You have commanded that I become a mountebank for that
I did build Poopy Pandaland, whereinto men enter with their chil-

dren, their silver, and their wits, and wherefrom they go out with their children only, sandbagged by a thousand catch-penny engines; even this did I obey. You have commanded that Poopy Panda shill every weekday night on television between five and six for the Poopy Panda Pals, and even this did I obey, though Poopy Panda is like unto the child of my flesh.

But O ye bankers, this last command will I never obey.

Whereupon the bankers which sate in New York sent to him another writing that said, Even so, let Poopy Panda up periscope and fire all bow tubes, and they said, Remember, boy, we hold thy paper.

And Ben Graffis did obey.

He called unto him his animators and directors and cameramen and writers, and his heart was sore but he dissembled and said:

In jest you call one another brainwashers, forasmuch as you addle the heads of children five hours a week that they shall buy our sponsors' wares. You have fulfilled the prophecies, for is it not written in the Book of the Space Merchants that there shall be spherical trusts? And the Poopy Panda Pals plug the Poopy Panda Magazine, and the Poopy Panda Magazine plugs Poopy Pandaland, and Poopy Pandaland plugs the Poopy Panda Pals. You have asked of the Motivational Research boys how we shall hook the little bastards and they have told ye, and ye have done it. You identify the untalented kid viewers with the talented kid performers, you provide in Otto Clodd a bumbling father image to be derided, you furnish in Jackie Whipple an idealized big brother for the boys and a sex-fantasy for the more precocious girls. You flatter the cans off the viewers by ever saying to them that they shall rule the twenty-first century, nor mind that those who shall in good sooth come to power are doing their homework and not watching television programs. You have created a liturgy of opening hymn and closing benediction, and over all hovers the spirit of Poopy Panda urging and coaxing the viewers to buy our sponsors' wares.

And Ben Graffis breathed a great breath and looked them not in the eye and said to them, Were it not a better thing for Poopy Panda to coax and urge no more, but to command as he were a god?

And the animators and directors and cameramen and writers were sore amazed and they said one to the other, This is the bleeding end, and the bankers which sit in New York have flipped their wigs. And one which was an old animator said to Ben Graffis, trembling, O chief, never would I have stolen for thee Poopy Panda from the Winnie the Pooh illustrations back in twenty-nine had I known this was in the cards, and Ben Graffis fired him.

Whereupon another which was a director said to Ben Graffis, O chief, the thing can be done with a two-week buildup, and Ben Graffis put his hands over his face and said, Let it be so.

And it came to pass that on the Friday after the two-week buildup, in the closing quarter-hour of the Poopy Panda Pals, there was a special film combining live and animated action as they were one.

And in the special film did Poopy Panda appear enhaloed, and the talented kid performers did do him worship, and Otto Clodd did trip over his feet whilst kneeling, and Jackie Whipple did urge in manly and sincere wise that all the Poopy Panda Pals out there in televisionland do likewise, and the enhaloed Poopy Panda did say in his lovable growly voice, Poop-poop-poopy.

And adoration ascended from thirty-seven million souls.

And it came to pass that Ben Graffis went into his office with his animators and cameramen and directors and writers after the show and said to them, It was definitely a TV first, and he did go to the bar.

Whereupon one which was a director looked at Who sate behind the desk that was the desk of Ben Graffis and he said to Ben Graffis, O chief, it is a great gag but how did the special effects boys manage the halo?

And Ben Graffis was sore amazed at Who sate behind his desk and he and they all did crowd about and make as if to poke Him, whereupon He in His lovable growly voice did say, Poop-poop-poopy, and they were not.

And certain unclean ones which had gone before turned unbelieving from their monitors and said, Holy Gee, this is awful. And one which was an operator of marionettes turned to his manager and said, Pal, if Graffis gets this off the ground we're dead. Whereat a great and far-off voice was heard, saying, Poop-poop-poopy, and it was even so; and the days of Poopy Panda were long in the land.

Filtered for error,
Jan. 18th 36 P.P.
Synod on Filtration & Infiltration
O. Clodd, P.P.P.
J. Whipple, P.P.P.

The Marching Morons

I DESCRIBED in this book's introduction my special interest in this story and "The Little Black Bag." So, a year or two after both had been published, when Cyril and I were working out a plot for a new novel (it was published as *Search the Sky*), we returned to the "marching morons" for the finale to the novel. We often borrowed from each other's heads, both for collaborations and once in a while for our own individual work, but I think this was the only time we borrowed from already published work.

SOME THINGS had not changed. A potter's wheel was still a potter's wheel and clay was still clay. Efim Hawkins had built his shop near Goose Lake, which had a narrow band of good fat clay and a narrow beach of white sand. He fired three bottle-nosed kilns with willow charcoal from the wood lot. The wood lot was also useful for long walks while the kilns were cooling; if he let himself stay within sight of them, he would open them prematurely, impatient to see how some new shape or glaze had come through the fire, and—*ping!*—the new shape or glaze would be good for nothing but the shard pile back of his slip tanks.

A business conference was in full swing in his shop, a modest cube of brick, tile-roofed, as the Chicago–Los Angeles "rocket" thundered overhead—very noisy, very sweptback, very fiery jets, shaped as sleekly swift-looking as an airborne barracuda.

The buyer from Marshall Fields was turning over a black-glazed one-liter carafe, nodding approval with his massive, handsome head. "This is real pretty," he told Hawkins and his own secretary, Gomez-Laplace. "This has got lots of what ya call real est'etic principles. Yeah, it is real pretty."

"How much?" the secretary asked the potter.

"Seven-fifty in dozen lots," said Hawkins. "I ran up fifteen dozen last month."

"They are real est'etic," repeated the buyer from Fields. "I will take them all."

"I don't think we can do that, doctor," said the secretary. "They'd cost us thirteen fifty. That would leave only five hundred thirty-two dollars in our quarter's budget. And we still have to run down to East Liverpool to pick up some cheap dinner sets."

"Dinner sets?" asked the buyer, his big face full of wonder.

"Dinner sets. The department's been out of them for two months now. Mr. Garvy-Seabright got pretty nasty about it yesterday. Remember?"

"Garvy-Seabright, that meat-headed bluenose," the buyer said contemptuously. "He don't know nothin' about est'etics. Why for don't he lemme run my own department?" His eye fell on a stray copy of *Whambozambo Comix* and he sat down with it. An occasional deep chuckle or grunt of surprise escaped him as he turned the pages.

Uninterrupted, the potter and the buyer's secretary quickly closed a deal for two dozen of the liter carafes. "I wish we could take more," said the secretary, "but you heard what I told him. We've had to turn away customers for ordinary dinnerware because he shot the last quarter's budget on some Mexican piggy banks some equally enthusiastic importer stuck him with. The fifth floor is packed solid with them."

"I'll bet they look mighty est'etic."

"They're painted with purple cacti."

The potter shuddered and caressed the glaze of the sample carafe.

The buyer looked up and rumbled, "Ain't you dummies through yakkin' yet? What good's a seckertary for if'n he don't take the burden of *de*-tail off'n my back, harh?"

"We're all through, doctor. Are you ready to go?"

The buyer grunted peevishly, dropped *Whambozambo Comix* on the floor, and led the way out of the building and down the log corduroy road to the highway. His car was waiting on the concrete. It was, like all contemporary cars, too low-slung to get over the logs. He climbed down into the car and started the motor with a tremendous sparkle and roar.

"Gomez-Laplace," called out the potter under cover of the noise, "did anything come of the radiation program they were working on the last time I was on duty at the Pole?"

"The same old fallacy," said the secretary gloomily. "It stopped us on mutation, it stopped us on culling, it stopped us on segregation, and now it's stopped us on hypnosis."

"Well, I'm scheduled back to the grind in nine days. Time for another firing right now. I've got a new luster to try . . ."

"I'll miss you. I shall be 'vacationing'—running the drafting room of the New Century Engineering Corporation in Denver. They're going to put up a two hundred-story office building, and naturally somebody's got to be on hand."

"Naturally," said Hawkins with a sour smile.

There was an ear-piercingly sweet blast as the buyer leaned on the horn button. Also, a yard-tall jet of what looked like flame spurted up from the car's radiator cap; the car's power plant was a gas turbine, and had no radiator.

"I'm coming, doctor," said the secretary dispiritedly. He climbed down into the car and it whooshed off with much flame and noise.

The potter, depressed, wandered back up the corduroy road and contemplated his cooling kilns. The rustling wind in the boughs was obscuring the creak and mutter of the shrinking refractory brick. Hawkins wondered about the number two kiln—a reduction fire on a load of lusterware mugs. Had the clay chinking excluded the air? Had it been a properly smoky blaze? Would it do any harm if he just took one close—?

Common sense took Hawkins by the scruff of the neck and yanked him over to the tool shed. He got out his pick and resolutely set off on a prospecting jaunt to a hummocky field that might yield some oxides. He was especially low on coppers.

The long walk left him sweating hard, with his lust for a peek into the kiln quiet in his breast. He swung his pick almost at random into one of the hummocks; it clanged on a stone which he excavated. A largely obliterated inscription said:

> ERSITY OF CHIC
> OGICAL LABO
> ELOVED MEMORY OF
> KILLED IN ACT

The potter swore mildly. He had hoped the field would turn out to be a cemetery, preferably a once-fashionable cemetery full of once-massive bronze caskets moldered into oxides of tin and copper.

Well, hell, maybe there was some around anyway.

He headed lackadaisically for the second largest hillock and sliced into it with his pick. There was a stone to undercut and topple into a trench, and then the potter was very glad he'd stuck at it. His nostrils were filled with the bitter smell and the dirt was tinged with the exciting blue of copper salts. The pick went *clang!*

Hawkins, puffing, pried up a stainless steel plate that was quite badly stained and was also marked with incised letters. It seemed to have pulled loose from rotting bronze; there were rivets on the back that brought up flakes of green patina. The potter wiped off the surface dirt with his sleeve, turned it to catch the sunlight obliquely, and read:

HONEST JOHN BARLOW

"Honest John," famed in university annals, represents a challenge which medical science has not yet answered: revival of a human being accidentally thrown into a state of suspended animation.

In 1988 Mr. Barlow, a leading Evanston real estate dealer, visited his dentist for treatment of an impacted wisdom tooth. His dentist requested and received permission to use the experimental anesthetic Cycloparadimethanol-B-7, developed at the University.

After administration of the anesthetic, the dentist resorted to his drill. By freakish mischance, a short circuit in his machine delivered 220 volts of 60-cycle current into the patient. (In a damage suit instituted by Mrs. Barlow against the dentist, the University and the makers of the drill, a jury found for the defendants.) Mr. Barlow never got up from the dentist's chair and was assumed to have died of poisoning, electrocution, or both.

Morticians preparing him for embalming discovered, however, that their subject was—though certainly not living—just as certainly not dead. The University was notified and a series of exhaustive tests was begun, including attempts to duplicate the trance state on volunteers. After a bad run of seven cases that ended fatally, the attempts were abandoned.

Honest John was long an exhibit at the University museum,

and livened many a football game as mascot of the University's Blue Crushers. The bounds of taste were overstepped, however, when a pledge to Sigma Delta Chi was ordered in '03 to "kidnap" Honest John from his loosely guarded glass museum case and introduce him into the Rachel Swanson Memorial Girls' Gymnasium shower room.

On May 22, 2003, the University Board of Regents issued the following order: "By unanimous vote, it is directed that the remains of Honest John Barlow be removed from the University museum and conveyed to the University's Lieutenant James Scott III Memorial Biological Laboratories and there be securely locked in a specially prepared vault. It is further directed that all possible measures for the preservation of these remains be taken by the Laboratory administration and that access to these remains be denied to all persons except qualified scholars authorized in writing by the Board. The Board reluctantly takes this action in view of recent notices and photographs in the nation's press which, to say the least, reflect but small credit upon the University."

It was far from his field, but Hawkins understood what had happened—an early and accidental blundering onto the bare bones of the Levantman shock anesthesia, which had since been replaced by other methods. To bring subjects out of Levantman shock, you let them have a squirt of simple saline in the trigeminal nerve. Interesting. And now about that bronze—

He heaved the pick into the rotting green salts, expecting no resistance, and almost fractured his wrist. *Something* down there was *solid.* He began to flake off the oxides.

A half-hour of work brought him down to phosphor bronze, a huge casting of the almost incorruptible metal. It had weakened structurally over the centuries; he could fit the point of his pick under a corroded boss and pry off great creaking and grumbling striae of the stuff.

Hawkins wished he had an archeologist with him, but didn't dream of returning to his shop and calling one to take over the find. He was an all-around man: by choice and in his free time, an artist in clay and glaze; by necessity, an automotive, electronics, and atomic engineer who could also swing a project in traffic control, individual and group psychology, architecture or tool design. He didn't yell for a specialist every time something out of his line came up; there were so few with so much to do . . .

He trenched around his find, discovering that it was a great brick-shaped bronze mass with an excitingly hollow sound. A long strip of moldering metal from one of the long vertical faces pulled away, exposing red rust that went *whoosh* and was sucked into the interior of the mass.

It had been de-aired, thought Hawkins, and there must have been an inner jacket of glass which had crystallized through the centuries and quietly crumbled at the first clang of his pick. He didn't know what a vacuum would do to a subject of Levantman shock, but he had hopes, nor did he quite understand what a real estate dealer was, but it might have something to do with pottery. And *anything* might have a bearing on Topic Number One.

He flung his pick out of the trench, climbed out, and set off at a dogtrot for his shop. A little rummaging turned up a hypo and there was a plasticontainer of salt in the kitchen.

Back at his dig, he chipped for another half hour to expose the juncture of lid and body. The hinges were hopeless; he smashed them off.

Hawkins extended the telescopic handle of the pick for the best leverage, fitted its point into a deep pit, set its built-in fulcrum, and heaved. Five more heaves and he could see, inside the vault, what looked like a dusty marble statue. Ten more and he could see that it was the naked body of Honest John Barlow, Evanston real estate dealer, uncorrupted by time.

The potter found the apex of the trigeminal nerve with his needle's point and gave him 60 cc.

In an hour Barlow's chest began to pump.

In another hour, he rasped, "Did it work?"

"*Did* it!" muttered Hawkins.

Barlow opened his eyes and stirred, looked down, turned his hands before his eyes—

"I'll sue!" he screamed. "My clothes! My fingernails!" A horrid suspicion came over his face and he clapped his hands to his hairless scalp. "My hair!" he wailed. "I'll sue you for every penny you've got! That release won't mean a damned thing in court—I didn't sign away my hair and clothes and fingernails!"

"They'll grow back," said Hawkins casually. "Also your epidermis. Those parts of you weren't alive, you know, so they weren't preserved like the rest of you. I'm afraid the clothes are gone, though."

"What is this—the University hospital?" demanded Barlow. "I want a phone. No, you phone. Tell my wife I'm all right and tell Sam Immerman—he's my lawyer—to get over here right away. Greenleaf seven, four oh two two. Ow!" He had tried to sit up, and a portion of his pink skin rubbed against the inner surface of the casket, which was powdered by the ancient crystallized glass. "What the hell did you guys do, boil me alive? Oh, you're going to pay for this!"

"You're all right," said Hawkins, wishing now he had a reference book to clear up several obscure terms. "Your epidermis will start growing immediately. You're not in the hospital. Look here."

He handed Barlow the stainless steel plate that had labeled the casket. After a suspicious glance, the man started to read. Finishing, he laid the plate carefully on the edge of the vault and was silent for a spell.

"Poor Verna," he said at last. "It doesn't say whether she was stuck with the court costs. Do you happen to know—"

"No," said the potter. "All I know is what was on the plate, and how to revive you. The dentist accidentally gave you a dose of what we call Levantman shock anesthesia. We haven't used it for centuries; it was powerful, but too dangerous."

"Centuries . . ." brooded the man. "Centuries . . . I'll bet Sam swindled her out of her eyeteeth. Poor Verna. How long ago was it? What year is this?"

Hawkins shrugged. "We call it 7-B-936. That's no help to you. It takes a long time for these metals to oxidize."

"Like that movie," Barlow muttered. "Who would have thought it? Poor Verna!" He blubbered and sniffled, reminding Hawkins powerfully of the fact that he had been found under a flat rock.

Almost angrily, the potter demanded, "How many children did you have?"

"None yet," sniffed Barlow. "My first wife didn't want them. But Verna wants one—wanted one—but we're going to wait until—we *were* going to wait until—"

"Of course," said the potter, feeling a savage desire to tell him off, blast him to hell and gone for his work. But he choked it down. There was The Problem to think of; there was always The Problem to think of, and this poor blubberer might unexpectedly supply a clue. Hawkins would have to pass him on.

"Come along," Hawkins said. "My time is short."

Barlow looked up, outraged. "How can you be so unfeeling? I'm a human being like—"

The Los Angeles–Chicago "rocket" thundered overhead and Barlow broke off in mid-complaint. "Beautiful!" he breathed, following it with his eyes. "Beautiful!"

He climbed out of the vault, too interested to be pained by its roughness against his infantile skin. "After all," he said briskly, "this should have its sunny side. I never was much for reading, but this is just like one of those stories. And I ought to make some money out of it, shouldn't I?" He gave Hawkins a shrewd glance.

"You want money?" asked the potter. "Here." He handed over a fistful of change and bills. "You'd better put my shoes on. It'll be about a quarter-mile. Oh, and you're—uh, modest?—yes, that was the word. Here." Hawkins gave him his pants, but Barlow was excitedly counting the money.

"Eighty-five, eighty-six—and it's dollars, too! I thought it'd be credits or whatever they call them. 'E Pluribus Unum' and 'Liberty'—just different faces. Say, is there a catch to this? Are these real, genuine, honest twenty-two-cent dollars like we had or just wallpaper?"

"They're quite all right, I assure you," said the potter. "I wish you'd come along. I'm in a hurry."

The man babbled as they stumped toward the shop. "Where are we going—The Council of Scientists, the World Coordinator, or something like that?"

"Who? Oh, no. We call them 'President' and 'Congress.' No, that wouldn't do any good at all. I'm just taking you to see some people."

"I ought to make plenty out of this. *Plenty!* I could write books. Get some smart young fellow to put it into words for me and I'll bet I could turn out a best-seller. What's the setup on things like that?"

"It's about like that. Smart young fellows. But there aren't any best-sellers any more. People don't read much nowadays. We'll find something equally profitable for you to do."

Back in the shop, Hawkins gave Barlow a suit of clothes, deposited him in the waiting room, and called Central in Chicago. "Take him away," he pleaded. "I have time for one more firing and he blathers and blathers. I haven't told him anything. Perhaps we should just turn him loose and let him find his own level, but there's a chance—"

"The Problem," agreed Central. "Yes, there's a chance."

The potter delighted Barlow by making him a cup of coffee with a cube that not only dissolved in cold water but heated the water to boiling point. Killing time, Hawkins chatted about the "rocket" Barlow had admired, and had to haul himself up short; he had almost told the real estate man what its top speed really was—almost, indeed, revealed that it was not a rocket.

He regretted, too, that he had so casually handed Barlow a couple of hundred dollars. The man seemed obsessed with fear that they were worthless since Hawkins refused to take a note or I.O.U. or even a definite promise of repayment. But Hawkins couldn't go into details, and was very glad when a stranger arrived from Central.

"Tinny-Peete, from Algeciras," the stranger told him swiftly as the two of them met at the door. "Psychist for Poprob. Polasigned special overtake Barlow."

"Thank Heaven," said Hawkins. "Barlow," he told the man from the past, "this is Tinny-Peete. He's going to take care of you and help you make lots of money."

The psychist stayed for a cup of the coffee whose preparation had delighted Barlow, and then conducted the real estate man down the corduroy road to his car, leaving the potter to speculate on whether he could at last crack his kilns.

Hawkins, abruptly dismissing Barlow and the Problem, happily picked the chinking from around the door of the number two kiln, prying it open a trifle. A blast of heat and the heady, smoky scent of the reduction fire delighted him. He peered and saw a corner of a shelf glowing cherry-red, becoming obscured by wavering black areas as it lost heat through the opened door. He slipped a charred wood paddle under a mug on the shelf and pulled it out as a sample, the hairs on the back of his hand curling and scorching. The mug crackled and pinged and Hawkins sighed happily.

The bismuth resinate luster had fired to perfection, a haunting film of silvery-black metal with strange bluish lights in it as it turned before the eyes, and the Problem of Population seemed very far away to Hawkins then.

Barlow and Tinny-Peete arrived at the concrete highway where the psychist's car was parked in a safety bay.

"What—a—*boat!*" gasped the man from the past.

"Boat? No, that's my car."

Barlow surveyed it with awe. Swept-back lines, deep-drawn compound curves, kilograms of chrome. He ran his hands futilely over the door—or was it the door?—in a futile search for a handle, and asked respectfully, "How fast does it go?"

The psychist gave him a keen look and said slowly, "Two hundred and fifty. You can tell by the speedometer."

"Wow! My old Chevvy could hit a hundred on a straightaway, but you're out of my class, mister!"

Tinny-Peete somehow got a huge, low door open and Barlow descended three steps into immense cushions, floundering over to the right. He was too fascinated to pay serious attention to his flayed dermis. The dashboard was a lovely wilderness of dials, plugs, indicators, lights, scales, and switches.

The psychist climbed down into the driver's seat and did something with his feet. The motor started like lighting a blowtorch as big as a silo. Wallowing around in the cushions, Barlow saw through a rear-view mirror a tremendous exhaust filled with brilliant white sparkles.

"Do you like it?" yelled the psychist.

"It's terrific!" Barlow yelled back. "It's—"

He was shut up as the car pulled out from the bay into the road with a great *voo-ooo-ooom!* A gale roared past Barlow's head, though the windows seemed to be closed; the impression of speed was terrific. He located the speedometer on the dashboard and saw it climb past 90, 100, 150, 200.

"Fast enough for me," yelled the psychist, noting that Barlow's face fell in response. "Radio?"

He passed over a surprisingly light object like a football helmet, with no trailing wires, and pointed to a row of buttons. Barlow put on the helmet, glad to have the roar of air stilled, and pushed a pushbutton. It lit up satisfyingly and Barlow settled back even farther for a sample of the brave new world's super-modern taste in ingenious entertainment.

"TAKE IT AND STICK IT!" a voice roared in his ears.

He snatched off the helmet and gave the psychist an injured look. Tinny-Peete grinned and turned a dial associated with the pushbutton layout. The man from the past donned the helmet again and found the voice had lowered to normal.

"The show of shows! The supershow! The super-duper show! The quiz of quizzes! *Take it and stick it!*"

There were shrieks of laughter in the background.

"Here we got the contes-tants all ready to go. You know how we work it. I hand a contes-tant a triangle-shaped cutout and like that down the line. Now we got these here boards, they got cut-out places the same shape as the triangles and things, only they're all different shapes, and the first contes-tant that sticks the cutouts into the board, he wins.

"Now I'm gonna innaview the first contes-tant. Right here, honey. What's your name?"

"Name? Uh—"

"Hoddaya like that, folks? She don't remember her name! Hah? *Would you buy that for a quarter?*" The question was spoken with arch significance, and the audience shrieked, howled, and whistled its appreciation.

It was dull listening when you didn't know the punch lines and catch lines. Barlow pushed another button, with his free hand ready at the volume control.

"—latest from Washington. It's about Senator Hull-Mendoza. He is still attacking the Bureau of Fisheries. The North California Syndicalist says he got affidavits that John Kingsley-Schultz is a bluenose from way back. He didn't publistat the affydavits, but he says they say that Kingsley-Schultz was saw at bluenose meetings in Oregon State College and later at Florida University. Kingsley-Schultz says he gotta confess he did major in fly-casting at Oregon and got his Ph.D. in game-fish at Florida.

"And here is a quote from Kingsley-Schultz: 'Hull-Mendoza don't know what he's talking about. He should drop dead.' Unquote. Hull-Mendoza says he won't publistat the affydavits to pertect his sources. He says they was sworn by three former employes of the Bureau which was fired for in-competence and in-com-pat-ibility by Kingsley-Schultz.

"Elsewhere they was the usual run of traffic accidents. A three-way pileup of cars on Route 66 going outta Chicago took twelve lives. The Chicago–Los Angeles morning rocket crashed and exploded in the Mo-have—Mo-javvy—whatever-you-call-it Desert. All the 94 people aboard got killed. A Civil Aeronautics Authority investigator on the scene says that the pilot was buzzing herds of sheep and didn't pull out in time.

"Hey! Here's a hot one from New York! A Diesel tug run wild in the harbor while the crew was below and shoved in the port bow of the luck-shury liner *S. S. Placentia*. It says the ship filled and sank, taking the lives of an es-ti-mated 180 passengers and 50 crew members. Six divers was sent down to study the wreckage, but they died, too, when their suits turned out to be fulla little holes.

"And here is a bulletin I just got from Denver. It seems—"

Barlow took off the headset uncomprehendingly. "He seemed so callous," he yelled at the driver. "I was listening to a newscast—"

Tinny-Peete shook his head and pointed at his ears. The roar of air was deafening. Barlow frowned baffledly and stared out of the window.

A glowing sign said:

MOOGS!
WOULD YOU BUY IT
FOR A QUARTER?

He didn't know what Moogs was or were; the illustration showed an incredibly proportioned girl, 99.9 per cent naked, writhing passionately in animated full color.

The roadside jingle was still with him, but with a new feature. Radar or something spotted the car and alerted the lines of the jingle. Each in turn sped along a roadside track, even with the car, so it could be read before the next line was alerted.

IF THERE'S A GIRL
YOU WANT TO GET
DEFLOCCULIZE
UNROMANTIC SWEAT.
"A*R*M*P*I*T*T*O"

Another animated job, in two panels, the familiar "Before and After." The first said, "Just Any Cigar?" and was illustrated with a two-person domestic tragedy of a wife holding her nose while her coarse and red-faced husband puffed a slimy-looking rope. The second panel glowed, "Or a VUELTA ABAJO?" and was illustrated with—

Barlow blushed and looked at his feet until they had passed the sign.

"Coming into Chicago!" bawled Tinny-Peete.

Other cars were showing up, all of them dreamboats.

Watching them, Barlow began to wonder if he knew what a kilometer was, exactly. They seemed to be traveling so slowly, if you ignored the roaring air past your ears and didn't let the speedy lines of the dreamboats fool you. He would have sworn they were really crawling along at twenty-five, with occasional spurts up to thirty. How much was a kilometer, anyway?

The city loomed ahead, and it was just what it ought to be: towering skyscrapers, overhead ramps, landing platforms for helicopters—

He clutched at the cushions. Those two 'copters. They were going to—they were going to—they—

He didn't see what happened because their apparent collision courses took them behind a giant building.

Screamingly sweet blasts of sound surrounded them as they stopped for a red light. "What the hell is going on here?" said Barlow in a shrill, frightened voice, because the braking time was just about zero, and he wasn't hurled against the dashboard. "Who's kidding who?"

"Why, what's the matter?" demanded the driver.

The light changed to green and he started the pickup. Barlow stiffened as he realized that the rush of air past his ears began just a brief, unreal split-second before the car was actually moving. He grabbed for the door handle on his side.

The city grew on them slowly: scattered buildings, denser buildings, taller buildings, and a red light ahead. The car rolled to a stop in zero braking time, the rush of air cut off an instant after it stopped, and Barlow was out of the car and running frenziedly down a sidewalk one instant after that.

They'll track me down, he thought, panting. *It's a secret police thing. They'll get you—mind-reading machines, television eyes everywhere, afraid you'll tell their slaves about freedom and stuff. They don't let anybody cross them, like that story I once read.*

Winded, he slowed to a walk and congratulated himself that he had guts enough not to turn around. That was what they always watched for. Walking, he was just another business-suited back among hundreds. He would be safe, he would be safe—

A hand gripped his shoulder and words tumbled from a large coarse, handsome face thrust close to his: "Wassamatta bumpinninna people likeya owna sidewalk gotta miner slamya inna mushya bassar!" It was neither the mad potter nor the mad driver.

"Excuse me," said Barlow. "What did you say?"

"Oh, yeah?" yelled the stranger dangerously, and waited for an answer.

Barlow, with the feeling that he had somehow been suckered into the short end of an intricate land-title deal heard himself reply belligerently, "Yeah!"

The stranger let go of his shoulder and snarled, "Oh, yeah?"

"Yeah!" said Barlow, yanking his jacket back into shape.

"Aaah!" snarled the stranger, with more contempt and disgust than ferocity. He added an obscenity current in Barlow's time, a standard but physiologically impossible directive, and strutted off hulking his shoulders and balling his fists.

Barlow walked on, trembling. Evidently he had handled it well enough. He stopped at a red light while the long, low dreamboats roared before him and pedestrians in the sidewalk flow with him threaded their ways through the stream of cars. Brakes screamed, fenders clanged and dented, hoarse cries flew back and forth between drivers and walkers. He leaped backward frantically as one car swerved over an arc of sidewalk to miss another.

The signal changed to green, the cars kept on coming for about thirty seconds and then dwindled to an occasional light-runner. Barlow crossed warily and leaned against a vending machine, blowing big breaths.

Look natural, he told himself. *Do something normal. Buy something from the machine.*

He fumbled out some change, got a newspaper for a dime, a handkerchief for a quarter, and a candy bar for another quarter.

The faint chocolate smell made him ravenous suddenly. He clawed at the glassy wrapper printed *"CRIGGLIES"* quite futilely for a few seconds, and then it divided neatly by itself. The bar made three good bites, and he bought two more and gobbled them down.

Thirsty, he drew a carbonated orange drink in another one of the glassy wrappers from the machine for another dime. When he fumbled with it, it divided neatly and spilled all over his knees. Barlow decided he had been there long enough and walked on.

The shop windows were—shop windows. People still wore and bought clothes, still smoked and bought tobacco, still ate and bought food. And they still went to the movies, he saw with pleased surprise as he passed and then returned to a glittering place whose sign said it was THE BIJOU.

The place seemed to be showing a quintuple feature, *Babies Are Terrible, Don't Have Children,* and *The Canali Kid.*

It was irresistible; he paid a dollar and went in.

He caught the tail end of *The Canali Kid* in three-dimensional, full-color, full-scent production. It appeared to be an interplanetary saga winding up with a chase scene and a reconciliation between estranged hero and heroine. *Babies Are Terrible* and *Don't Have Children* were fantastic arguments against parenthood—the grotesquely exaggerated dangers of painfully graphic childbirth, vicious children, old parents beaten and starved by their sadistic offspring. The audience, Barlow astoundedly noted, was placidly chomping sweets and showing no particular signs of revulsion.

The *Coming Attractions* drove him into the lobby. The fanfares were shattering, the blazing colors blinding, and the added scents stomach-heaving.

When his eyes again became accustomed to the moderate lighting of the lobby, he groped his way to a bench and opened the newspaper he had bought. It turned out to be *The Racing Sheet,* which afflicted him with a crushing sense of loss. The familiar boxed index in the lower left-hand corner of the front page showed almost unbearably that Churchill Downs and Empire City were still in business—

Blinking back tears, he turned to the Past Performances at Churchill. They weren't using abbreviations any more, and the pages because of that were single-column instead of double. But it was all the same—or was it?

He squinted at the first race, a three-quarter-mile maiden claimer for thirteen hundred dollars. Incredibly, the track record was two minutes, ten and three-fifths seconds. Any beetle in his time could have knocked off the three-quarter in one-fifteen. It was the same for the other distances, much worse for route events.

What the hell had happened to everything?

He studied the form of a five-year-old brown mare in the second and couldn't make head or tail of it. She'd won and lost and placed and showed and lost and placed without rhyme or reason. She looked like a front-runner for a couple of races and then she looked like a no-good pig and then she looked like a mudder but the next time it rained she wasn't and then she was a stayer and then she was a pig again. In a good five-thousand-dollar allowances event, too!

Barlow looked at the other entries and it slowly dawned on him that they were all like the five-year-old brown mare. Not a single damned horse running had the slightest trace of class.

Somebody sat down beside him and said, "That's the story."

Barlow whirled to his feet and saw it was Tinny-Peete, his driver.

"I was in doubts about telling you," said the psychist, "but I see you have some growing suspicions of the truth. Please don't get excited. It's all right, I tell you."

"So you've got me," said Barlow.

"*Got* you?"

"Don't pretend. I can put two and two together. You're the secret police. You and the rest of the aristocrats live in luxury on the sweat of these oppressed slaves. You're afraid of me because you have to keep them ignorant."

There was a bellow of bright laughter from the psychist that got them blank looks from other patrons of the lobby. The laughter didn't sound at all sinister.

"Let's get out of here," said Tinny-Peete, still chuckling. "You couldn't possibly have it more wrong." He engaged Barlow's arm and led him to the street. "The actual truth is that the millions of workers live in luxury on the sweat of the handful of aristocrats. I shall probably die before my time of overwork unless—" He gave Barlow a speculative look. "You may be able to help us."

"I know that gag," sneered Barlow. "I made money in my time and to make money you have to get people on your side. Go ahead and shoot me if you want, but you're not going to make a fool out of me."

"You nasty little ingrate!" snapped the psychist, with a kaleidoscopic change of mood. "This damned mess is all your fault and the fault of people like you! Now come along and no more of your nonsense."

He yanked Barlow into an office building lobby and an elevator that, disconcertingly, went *whoosh* loudly as it rose. The real estate man's knees were wobbly as the psychist pushed him from the elevator, down a corridor, and into an office.

A hawk-faced man rose from a plain chair as the door closed behind them. After an angry look at Barlow, he asked the psychist, "Was I called from the Pole to inspect this—this—?"

"Unget updandered. I've dee-probed etfind quasichance exhim Poprobattackline," said the psychist soothingly.

"Doubt," grunted the hawk-faced man.

"Try," suggested Tinny-Peete.

"Very well. Mr. Barlow, I understand you and your lamented had no children."

"What of it?"

"This of it. You were a blind, selfish stupid ass to tolerate economic and social conditions which penalized child-bearing by the prudent and foresighted. You made us what we are today, and I want you to know that we are far from satisfied. Damn-fool rockets! Damn-fool automobiles! Damn-fool cities with overhead ramps!"

"As far as I can see," said Barlow, "you're running down the best features of your time. Are you crazy?"

"The rockets aren't rockets. They're turbo-jets—good turbo-jets, but the fancy shell around them makes for a bad drag. The automobiles have a top speed of one hundred kilometers per hour—a kilometer is, if I recall my paleolinguistics, three-fifths of a mile—and the speedometers are all rigged accordingly so the drivers will think they're going two hundred and fifty. The cities are ridiculous, expensive, unsanitary, wasteful conglomerations of people who'd be better off and more productive if they were spread over the countryside.

"We need the rockets and trick speedometers and cities because, while you and your kind were being prudent and foresighted and not having children, the migrant workers, slum dwellers, and tenant farmers were shiftlessly and short-sightedly having children—breeding, breeding. My God, how they bred!"

"Wait a minute," objected Barlow. "There were lots of people in our crowd who had two or three children."

"The attrition of accidents, illness, wars, and such took care of that. Your intelligence was bred out. It is gone. Children that should have been born never were. The just-average, they'll-get-along majority took over the population. The average IQ now is forty-five."

"But that's far in the future—"

"So are you," grunted the hawk-faced man sourly.

"But who are *you* people?"

"Just people—real people. Some generations ago, the geneticists realized at last that nobody was going to pay any attention to what they said, so they abandoned words for deeds. Specifically, they formed and recruited for a closed corporation intended to maintain and improve the breed. We are their descendants, about three million of us. There are five billion of the others, so we are their slaves.

"During the past couple of years I've designed a skyscraper, kept Billings Memorial Hospital here in Chicago running, headed off war with Mexico, and directed traffic at LaGuardia Field in New York."

"I don't understand! Why don't you let them go to hell in their own way?"

The man grimaced. "We tried it once for three months. We holed up at the South Pole and waited. They didn't notice it. Some drafting-room people were missing, some chief nurses didn't show up, minor government people on the non-policy level couldn't be located. It didn't seem to matter.

"In a week there was hunger. In two weeks there were famine and plague, in three weeks war and anarchy. We called off the experiment; it took us most of the next generation to get things squared away again."

"But why *didn't* you let them kill each other off?"

"Five billion corpses mean about five hundred million tons of rotting flesh."

Barlow had another idea. "Why don't you sterilize them?"

"Two and one-half billion operations is a lot of operations. Because they breed continuously, the job would never be done."

"I see. Like the marching Chinese!"

"Who the devil are they?"

"It was a—uh—paradox of my time. Somebody figured out that if all the Chinese in the world were to line up four abreast, I think it was, and start marching past a given point, they'd never stop because of the babies that would be born and grow up before they passed the point."

"That's right. Only instead of 'a given point,' make it 'the largest conceivable number of operating rooms that we could build and staff.' There could never be enough."

"Say!" said Barlow. "Those movies about babies—was that your propaganda?"

"It was. It doesn't seem to mean a thing to them. We have abandoned the idea of attempting propaganda contrary to a biological drive."

"So if you work *with* a biological drive—?"

"I know of none consistent with inhibition of fertility."

Barlow's face went poker-blank, the result of years of careful discipline. "You don't, huh? You're the great brains and you can't think of any?"

"Why, no," said the psychist innocently. "Can you?"

"That depends. I sold ten thousand acres of Siberian tundra—through a dummy firm, of course—after the partition of Russia. The buyers thought they were getting improved building lots on the outskirts of Kiev. I'd say that was a lot tougher than this job."

"How so?" asked the hawk-faced man.

"Those were normal, suspicious customers and these are morons, born suckers. You just figure out a con they'll fall for; they won't know enough to do any smart checking."

The psychist and the hawk-faced man had also had training; they kept themselves from looking with sudden hope at each other.

"You seem to have something in mind," said the psychist.

Barlow's poker face went blanker still. "Maybe I have. I haven't heard any offer yet."

"There's the satisfaction of knowing that you've prevented Earth's resources from being so plundered," the hawk-faced man pointed out, "that the race will soon become extinct."

"I don't know that," Barlow said bluntly. "All I have is your word."

"If you really have a method, I don't think any price would be too great," the psychist offered.

"Money," said Barlow.

"All you want."

"More than you want," the hawk-faced man corrected.

"Prestige," added Barlow. "Plenty of publicity. My picture and my name in the papers and over TV every day, statues to me, parks and cities and streets and other things named after me. A whole chapter in the history books."

The psychist made a facial sign to the hawk-faced man that meant, "Oh, brother!"

The hawk-faced man signaled back. "Steady, boy!"

"It's not too much to ask," the psychist agreed.

Barlow, sensing a seller's market, said, "Power!"

"Power?" the hawk-faced man repeated puzzledly. "Your own hydro station or nuclear pile?"

"I mean a world dictatorship with me as dictator!"

"Well, now—" said the psychist, but the hawk-faced man interrupted, "It would take a special emergency act of Congress but the situation warrants it. I think that can be guaranteed."

"Could you give us some indication of your plan?" the psychist asked.

"Ever hear of lemmings?"

"No."

"They are—were, I guess, since you haven't heard of them—little animals in Norway, and every few years they'd swarm to the coast and swim out to sea until they drowned. I figure on putting some lemming urge into the population."

"How?"

"I'll save that till I get the right signatures on the deal."

The hawk-faced man said, "I'd like to work with you on it, Barlow. My name's Ryan-Ngana." He put out his hand.

Barlow looked closely at the hand, then at the man's face. "Ryan what?"

"Ngana."

"That sounds like an African name."

"It is. My mother's father was a Watusi."

Barlow didn't take the hand. "I thought you looked pretty dark. I don't want to hurt your feelings, but I don't think I'd be at my best working with you. There must be somebody else just as well qualified, I'm sure."

The psychist made a facial sign to Ryan-Ngana that meant, "Steady *yourself,* boy!"

"Very well," Ryan-Ngana told Barlow. "We'll see what arrangement can be made."

"It's not that I'm prejudiced, you understand. Some of my best friends—"

"Mr. Barlow, don't give it another thought. Anybody who could pick on the lemming analogy is going to be useful to us."

And so he would, thought Ryan-Ngana, alone in the office after Tinny-Peete had taken Barlow up to the helicopter stage. So he would. Poprob had exhausted every rational attempt and the new Poprobattacklines would have to be irrational or sub-rational. This creature from the past with his lemming legends and his improved building lots would be a fountain of precious vicious self-interest.

Ryan-Ngana sighed and stretched. He had to go and run the San Francisco subway. Summoned early from the Pole to study Barlow, he'd left unfinished a nice little theorem. Between interruptions, he was slowly constructing an n-dimensional geometry whose foundations and superstructure owed no debt whatsoever to intuition.

Upstairs, waiting for a helicopter, Barlow was explaining to Tinny-Peete that he had nothing against Negroes, and Tinny-Peete wished he had some of Ryan-Ngana's imperturbability and humor for the ordeal.

The helicopter took them to International Airport, where, Tinny-Peete explained, Barlow would leave for the Pole.

The man from the past wasn't sure he'd like a dreary waste of ice and cold.

"It's all right," said the psychist. "A civilized layout. Warm, pleasant. You'll be able to work more efficiently there. All the facts at your fingertips, a good secretary—"

"I'll need a pretty big staff," said Barlow, who had learned from thousands of deals never to take the first offer.

"I meant a private, confidential one," said Tinny-Peete readily, "but you can have as many as you want. You'll naturally have top-primary-top priority if you really have a workable plan."

"Let's not forget this dictatorship angle," said Barlow.

He didn't know that the psychist would just as readily have promised him deification to get him happily on the "rocket" for the Pole. Tinny-Peete had no wish to be torn limb from limb; he knew very well that it would end that way if the population learned from this anachronism that there was a small elite which considered itself head, shoulders, trunk, and groin above the rest. The fact that this assumption was perfectly true and the fact that the elite was condemned by its superiority to a life of the most grinding toil would not be considered; the difference would.

The psychist finally put Barlow aboard the "rocket" with some thirty people—real people—headed for the Pole.

Barlow was airsick all the way because of a post-hypnotic suggestion Tinny-Peete had planted in him. One idea was to make him as averse as possible to a return trip, and another idea was to spare the other passengers from his aggressive, talkative company.

Barlow during the first day at the Pole was reminded of his first day in the Army. It was the same now-where-the-hell-are-we-going-to-put-*you?* business until he took a firm line with them. Then instead of acting like supply sergeants they acted like hotel clerks.

It was a wonderful, wonderfully calculated buildup, and one that he failed to suspect. After all, in his time a visitor from the past would have been lionized.

At day's end he reclined in a snug underground billet with the sixty-mile gales roaring yards overhead, and tried to put two and two together.

It was like old times, he thought—like a coup in real estate where you had the competition by the throat, like a fifty-percent rent boost when you knew damned well there was no place for the tenants to move, like smiling when you read over the breakfast orange juice that the city council had decided to build a school on the ground you had acquired by a deal with the city council. And it was simple: He would just sell tundra building lots to eagerly suicidal lemmings, and that was absolutely all there was to solving the Problem that had these double-domes spinning.

They'd have to work out most of the details, naturally, but what the hell, that was what subordinates were for. He'd need specialists in advertising, engineering, communications—did they know anything about hypnotism? That might be helpful. If not, there'd have to be a lot of bribery done, but he'd make sure—damned sure—there were unlimited funds.

Just selling building lots to lemmings . . .

He wished, as he fell asleep, that poor Verna could have been in on this. It was his biggest, most stupendous deal. Verna—that sharp shyster Sam Immerman must have swindled her . . .

It began the next day with people coming to visit him. He knew the approach. They merely wanted to be helpful to their illustrious visitor from the past and would he help fill them in about his era, which unfortunately was somewhat obscure historically, and what did he think could be done about the Problem? He told them he was too old to be roped any more, and they wouldn't get any information out of him until he got a letter of intent from at least the Polar President, and a session of the Polar Congress empowered to make him dictator.

He got the letter and the session. He presented his program, was asked whether his conscience didn't revolt at its callousness, explained succinctly that a deal was a deal and anybody who wasn't smart enough to protect himself didn't deserve protection—"Caveat emptor," he threw in for scholarship, and had to translate it to "Let the buyer beware." He didn't, he stated, give a damn about either the morons or their intelligent slaves; he'd told them his price and that was all he was interested in.

Would they meet it or wouldn't they?

The Polar President offered to resign in his favor, with certain temporary emergency powers that the Polar Congress would vote him if he thought them necessary. Barlow demanded the title of World Dictator, complete control of world finances, salary to be decided by himself, and the publicity campaign and historical writeup to begin at once.

"As for the emergency powers," he added, "they are neither to be temporary nor limited."

Somebody wanted the floor to discuss the matter, with the declared hope that perhaps Barlow would modify his demands.

"You've got the proposition," Barlow said. "I'm not knocking off even ten percent."

"But what if the Congress refuses, sir?" the President asked.

"Then you can stay up here at the Pole and try to work it out yourselves. I'll get what I want from the morons. A shrewd operator like me doesn't have to compromise; I haven't got a single competitor in this whole cockeyed moronic era."

Congress waived debate and voted by show of hands. Barlow won unanimously.

"You don't know how close you came to losing me," he said in his first official address to the joint Houses. "I'm not the boy to haggle; either I get what I ask, or I go elsewhere. The first thing I want is to see designs for a new palace for me—nothing *un*ostentatious, either— and your best painters and sculptors to start working on my portraits and statues. Meanwhile, I'll get my staff together."

He dismissed the Polar President and the Polar Congress, telling them that he'd let them know when the next meeting would be.

A week later, the program started with North America the first target.

Mrs. Garvy was resting after dinner before the ordeal of turning on the dishwasher. The TV, of course, was on and it said: "Oooh!"— long, shuddery and ecstatic, the cue for the *Parfum Assault Criminale* spot commercial. "Girls," said the announcer hoarsely, "do you want your man? It's easy to get him—easy as a trip to Venus."

"Huh?" said Mrs. Garvy.

"Wassamatter?" snorted her husband, starting out of a doze.

"Ja hear that?"

"Wha'?"

"He said 'easy like a trip to Venus.' "

"So?"

"Well, I thought ya couldn't get to Venus. I thought they just had that one rocket thing that crashed on the Moon."

"Aah, women don't keep up with the news," said Garvy righteously, subsiding again.

"Oh," said his wife uncertainly.

And the next day, on *Henry's Other Mistress*, there was a new character who had just breezed in: Buzz Rentshaw, Master Rocket Pilot of the Venus run. On *Henry's Other Mistress*, "the broadcast drama about you and your neighbors, *folksy* people, *ordinary* people, *real* people!" Mrs. Garvy listened with amazement over a cooling cup of coffee as Buzz made hay of her hazy convictions.

MONA: Darling, it's so good to see you again!

BUZZ: You don't know how I've missed you on that dreary Venus run.

SOUND: *Venetian blind run down, key turned in door lock.*

MONA: Was it *very* dull, dearest?

BUZZ: Let's not talk about my humdrum job, darling. Let's talk about us.

SOUND: *Creaking bed.*

Well, the program was back to normal at last. That evening Mrs. Garvy tried to ask again whether her husband was sure about those rockets, but he was dozing right through *Take It and Stick It*, so she watched the screen and forgot the puzzle.

She was still rocking with laughter at the gag line, "Would you buy it for a quarter?" when the commercial went on for the detergent powder she always faithfully loaded her dishwasher with on the first of every month.

The announcer displayed mountains of suds from a tiny piece of the stuff and coyly added: "Of course, Cleano don't lay around for you to pick up like the soap root on Venus, but it's pretty cheap and it's almost pretty near just as good. So for us plain folks who ain't lucky enough to live up there on Venus, Cleano is the real cleaning stuff!"

Then the chorus went into their "Cleano-is-the-stuff" jingle, but Mrs. Garvy didn't hear it. She was a stubborn woman, but it occurred to her that she was very sick indeed. She didn't want to worry her husband. The next day she quietly made an appointment with her family freud.

In the waiting room she picked up a fresh new copy of *Readers Pablum* and put it down with a faint palpitation. The lead article, according to the table of contents on the cover, was titled "The Most Memorable Venusian I Ever Met."

"The freud will see you now," said the nurse, and Mrs. Garvy tottered into his office.

His traditional glasses and whiskers were reassuring. She choked out the ritual: "Freud, forgive me, for I have neuroses."

He chanted the antiphonal: "Tut, my dear girl, what seems to be the trouble?"

"I got like a hole in the head," she quavered. "I seem to forget all kinds of things. Things like everybody seems to know and I don't."

"Well, that happens to everybody occasionally, my dear. I suggest a vacation on Venus."

The freud stared, open-mouthed, at the empty chair. His nurse came in and demanded, "Hey, you see how she scrammed? What was the matter with *her?*"

He took off his glasses and whiskers meditatively. "You can search me. I told her she should maybe try a vacation on Venus." A momentary bafflement came into his face and he dug through his desk drawers until he found a copy of the four-color, profusely illustrated journal of his profession. It had come that morning and he had lip-read it, though looking mostly at the pictures. He leafed to the article *Advantages of the Planet Venus in Rest Cures.*

"It's right there," he said.

The nurse looked. "It sure is," she agreed. "Why shouldn't it be?"

"The trouble with these here neurotics," decided the freud, "is that they all the time got to fight reality. Show in the next twitch."

He put on his glasses and whiskers again and forgot Mrs. Garvy and her strange behavior.

"Freud, forgive me, for I have neuroses."

"Tut, my dear girl, what seems to be the trouble?"

Like many cures of mental disorders, Mrs. Garvy's was achieved largely by self-treatment. She disciplined herself sternly out of the crazy notion that there had been only one rocket ship and that one a failure. She could join without wincing, eventually, in any conversation on the desirability of Venus as a place to retire, on its fabulous floral profusion. Finally she went to Venus.

All her friends were trying to book passage with the Evening Star Travel and Real Estate Corporation, but naturally the demand was crushing. She considered herself lucky to get a seat at last for the two-week summer cruise. The space ship took off from a place called Los Alamos, New Mexico. It looked just like all the spaceships on television and in the picture magazines, but was more comfortable than you would expect.

Mrs. Garvy was delighted with the fifty or so fellow-passengers assembled before takeoff. They were from all over the country and she had a distinct impression that they were on the brainy side. The captain, a tall, hawk-faced, impressive fellow named Ryan-Something or other, welcomed them aboard and trusted that their trip would be a memorable one. He regretted that there would be nothing to see because, "due to the meteorite season," the ports would be dogged down. It was disappointing, yet reassuring that the line was taking no chances.

There was the expected momentary discomfort at takeoff and then two monotonous days of droning travel through space to be whiled away in the lounge at cards or craps. The landing was a routine bump and the voyagers were issued tablets to swallow to immunize them against any minor ailments.

When the tablets took effect, the lock was opened, and Venus was theirs.

It looked much like a tropical island on Earth, except for a blanket of cloud overhead. But it had a heady, otherworldly quality that was intoxicating and glamorous.

The ten days of the vacation were suffused with a hazy magic. The soap root, as advertised, was free and sudsy. The fruits, mostly tropical varieties transplanted from Earth, were delightful. The simple shelters provided by the travel company were more than adequate for the balmy days and nights.

It was with sincere regret that the voyagers filed again into the ship, and swallowed more tablets doled out to counteract and sterilize any Venus illnesses they might unwittingly communicate to Earth.

Vacationing was one thing. Power politics was another.

At the Pole, a small man was in a soundproof room, his face deathly pale and his body limp in a straight chair.

In the American Senate Chamber, Senator Hull-Mendoza (Synd., N. Cal.) was saying: "Mr. President and gentlemen, I would be remiss in my duty as a legislature if'n I didn't bring to the attention of the au-gust body I see here a perilous situation which is fraught with peril. As is well known to members of this au-gust body, the perfection of space flight has brought with it a situation I can only describe as fraught with peril. Mr. President and gentlemen, now that swift American rockets now traverse the trackless void of space between this planet and our nearest planetarial neighbor in space—and, gentlemen, I refer to Venus, the star of dawn, the brightest jewel in fair Vulcan's diadome—now, I say, I want to inquire what steps are being taken to colonize Venus with a vanguard of patriotic citizens like those minutemen of yore.

"Mr. President and gentlemen! There are in this world nations, envious nations—I do not name Mexico—who by fair means or foul may seek to wrest from Columbia's grasp the torch of freedom of space; nations whose low living standards and innate depravity give them an unfair advantage over the citizens of our fair republic.

"This is my program: I suggest that a city of more than a hundred thousand population be selected by lot. The citizens of the fortunate city are to be awarded choice lands on Venus free and clear, to have and to hold and convey to their descendants. And the national government shall provide free transportation to Venus for these citizens. And this program shall continue, city by city, until there has been deposited on Venus a sufficient vanguard of citizens to protect our manifest rights in that planet.

"Objections will be raised, for carping critics we have always with us. They will say there isn't enough steel. They will call it a cheap giveaway. I say there *is* enough steel for *one* city's population to be transferred to Venus, and that is all that is needed. For when the time comes for the second city to be transferred, the first, emptied city can be wrecked for the needed steel! And is it a giveaway? Yes! It is the most glorious giveaway in the history of mankind! Mr. President and gentlemen, there is no time to waste—Venus must be American!"

Black-Kupperman, at the Pole, opened his eyes and said feebly, "The style was a little uneven. Do you think anybody'll notice?"

"You did fine, boy; just fine," Barlow reassured him.

Hull-Mendoza's bill became law.

Drafting machines at the South Pole were busy around the clock and the Pittsburgh steel mills spewed millions of plates into the Los Alamos spaceport of the Evening Star Travel and Real Estate Corporation. It was going to be Los Angeles, for logistic reasons, and the three most accomplished psycho-kineticists went to Washington and mingled in the crowd at the drawing to make certain that the Los Angeles capsule slithered into the fingers of the blindfolded Senator.

Los Angeles loved the idea and a forest of spaceships began to blossom in the desert. They weren't very good spaceships, but they didn't have to be.

A team at the Pole worked at Barlow's direction on a mail setup. There would have to be letters to and from Venus to keep the slightest taint of suspicion from arising. Luckily Barlow remembered that the problem had been solved once before—by Hitler. Relatives of persons incinerated in the furnaces of Lublin or Majdanek continued to get cheery postal cards.

The Los Angeles flight went off on schedule, under tremendous press, newsreel, and television coverage. The world cheered the gallant Angelenos who were setting off on their patriotic voyage to the land of milk and honey. The forest of spaceships thundered up, and up, and out of sight without untoward incident. Billions envied the Angelenos, cramped and on short rations though they were.

Wreckers from San Francisco, whose capsule came up second, moved immediately into the city of the angels for the scrap steel their own flight would require. Senator Hull-Mendoza's constituents could do no less.

The president of Mexico, hypnotically alarmed at this extension of *yanqui imperialismo* beyond the stratosphere, launched his own Venus-colony program.

Across the water it was England versus Ireland, France versus Germany, China versus Russia, India versus Indonesia. Ancient hatreds grew into the flames that were rocket ships assailing the air by hundreds daily.

Dear Ed,
   how are you? Sam and I are fine and hope you are fine. Is it nice up there like they say with food and close grone on trees? I drove by Springfield yesterday and it sure looked funny all the buildings down but of coarse it is worth it we have to keep the greasers in their place. Do you have any truble with them on Venus? Drop me a line some time. Your loving sister,
                                                                Alma
Dear Alma,
   I am fine and hope you are fine. It is a fine place here fine climate and easy living. The doctor told me today that I seem to be ten years younger. He thinks there is something in the air here keeps people young. We do not have much trouble with the greasers here they keep to theirselves it is just a question of us outnumbering them and staking out the best places for the Americans. In South Bay I know a nice little island that I have been saving for you and Sam with lots of blanket trees and ham bushes. Hoping to see you and Sam soon, your loving brother,
                                                                Ed

Sam and Alma were on their way shortly.

Poprob got a dividend in every nation after the emigration had passed the halfway mark. The lonesome stay-at-homes were unable to bear the melancholy of a low population density; their conditioning had been to swarms of their kin. After that point it was possible to foist off the crudest stripped-down accommodations on would-be emigrants; they didn't care.

Black-Kupperman did a final job on President Hull-Mendoza, the last job that genius of hypnotics would ever do on any moron, important or otherwise.

Hull-Mendoza, panic-stricken by his presidency over an emptying nation, joined his constituents. The *Independence,* aboard which traveled the national government of America, was the most elaborate of all the spaceships—bigger, more comfortable, with a lounge that was handsome, though cramped, and cloakrooms for Senators and Representatives. It went, however, to the same place as the others and Black-Kupperman killed himself, leaving a note that stated he "couldn't live with my conscience."

The day after the American President departed, Barlow flew into a rage. Across his specially built desk were supposed to flow all Poprob high-level documents and this thing—this outrageous thing—called Poprob*term* apparently had got into the executive stage before he had even had a glimpse of it!

He buzzed for Rogge-Smith, his statistician. Rogge-Smith seemed to be at the bottom of it. Poprobterm seemed to be about first and second and third derivatives, whatever they were. Barlow had a deep distrust of anything more complex than what he called an "average."

While Rogge-Smith was still at the door, Barlow snapped, "What's the meaning of this? Why haven't I been consulted? How far have you people got and why have you been working on something I haven't authorized?"

"Didn't want to bother you, Chief," said Rogge-Smith. "It was really a technical matter, kind of a final cleanup. Want to come and see the work?"

Mollified, Barlow followed his statistician down the corridor.

"You still shouldn't have gone ahead without my okay," he grumbled. "Where the hell would you people have been without me?"

"That's right, Chief. We couldn't have swung it ourselves; our minds just don't work that way. And all that stuff you knew from Hitler—it wouldn't have occurred to us. Like poor Black-Kupperman."

They were in a fair-sized machine shop at the end of a slight upward incline. It was cold. Rogge-Smith pushed a button that started a motor, and a flood of arctic light poured in as the roof parted slowly. It showed a small spaceship with the door open.

Barlow gaped as Rogge-Smith took him by the elbow and his other boys appeared: Swenson-Swenson, the engineer; Tsutsugimushi-Duncan, his propellants man; Kalb-French, advertising.

"In you go, Chief," said Tsutsugimushi-Duncan. "This is Poprobterm."

"But I'm the world Dictator!"

"You bet, Chief. You'll be in history, all right—but this is necessary, I'm afraid."

The door was closed. Acceleration slammed Barlow cruelly to the metal floor. Something broke and warm, wet stuff, salty-tasting, ran from his mouth to his chin. Arctic sunlight through a port suddenly became a fierce lancet stabbing at his eyes; he was out of the atmosphere.

Lying twisted and broken under the acceleration, Barlow realized that some things had not changed, that Jack Ketch was never asked to dinner however many shillings you paid him to do your dirty work, that murder will out, that crime pays only temporarily.

The last thing he learned was that death is the end of pain.

The Last Man Left in the Bar

AROUND 1956, bars were full of new-fangled television sets, and television was full of tanktown
prizefighters and musical programs. I remember
discussing *The Hit Parade* with Cyril, and con-
fessing to him that I loved Giselle Mackenzie with
a pure and permanent passion. I suspect that, in
one of the fragments of bar talk, with a slight
change of name, I am quoted.

YOU KNOW HIM, Joe—or Sam, Mike, Tony, Ben, whatever your de-
ceitful, cheaply genial name may be. And do not lie to yourself, Gentle Reader; you know him too.

A loner, he was.

You did not notice him when he slipped in; you only knew by his
aggrieved air when he (finally) caught your eye and self-consciously
said "Shot of Red Top and a beer" that he'd ruffle your working day.
(Six at night until two in the morning is a day? But ah, the horrible
alternative is to work for a living.)

Shot of Red Top and a beer at 8:35.

And unbeknownst to him, Gentle Reader, in the garage up the
street the two contrivers of his dilemma conspired; the breaths of tall
dark stooped cadaverous Galardo and the mouse-eyed lassie mingled.

"Hyü shall be a religion-isst," he instructed her.

"I know the role," she squeaked and quoted: " 'Woe to the day on
which I was born into the world! Woe to the womb which bare me!
Woe to the bowels which admitted me! Woe to the breasts which
suckled me! Woe to the feet upon which I sat and rested! Woe to the
hands which carried me and reared me until I grew! Woe to my
tongue and my lips which have brought forth and spoken vanity, de-
traction, falsehood, ignorance, derision, idle tales, craft and hypoc-
risy! Woe to mine eyes which have looked upon scandalous things!
Woe to mine ears which have delighted in the words of slanderers!

Woe to my hands which have seized what did not of right belong to them! Woe to my belly and my bowels which have lusted after food unlawful to be eaten! Woe to my throat which like a fire has consumed all that it found!' "

He sobbed with the beauty of it and nodded at last, tears hanging in his eyes: "Yess, that religion. It iss one of my fave-o-ritts."

She was carried away. "I can do others. Oh, I can do others. I can do Mithras, and Isis, and Marduk, and Eddyism and Billsword and Pealing and Uranium, both orthodox and reformed."

"Mithras, Isis, and Marduk are long gone and the resst are ss-till tü come. Listen tü your master, dü not chat-ter, and we shall an art-work make of which there will be talk under the green sky until all food is eaten."

Meanwhile, Gentle Reader, the loner listened. To his left strong si-lent sinewy men in fellowship, the builders, the doers, the darers: "So I told the foreman where he should put his Bullard. I told him I run a Warner and Swasey, I run a Warner and Swasey good, I never even *seen* a Bullard up close in my life, and where he should put it. I know how to run a Warner and Swasey and why should he take me off a Warner and Swasey I know how to run and put me on a Bullard and where he should put it ain't I right?"

"Absolutely."

To his right the clear-eyed virtuous matrons, the steadfast, the true-seeing, the loving-kind: "Oh, I don't know what I want, what do you want? I'm a Scotch drinker really but I don't feel like Scotch but if I come home with Muscatel on my breath Eddie calls me a wino and laughs his head off. I don't know what I want. What do you want?"

In the box above the bar the rollicking raster raced.

VIDEO	AUDIO
Gampa smashes bottle over the head of *Bibby*.	*Gampa:* Young whippersnapper!
Bibby spits out water.	*Bibby:* Next time put some fla-voring in it, Gramps!
Gampa picks up sugar bowl and smashes it over *Bibby's* head. *Bibby* licks sugar from face.	*Bibby:* My, that's better! But what of Naughty Roger and his attempted kidnapping of Sis to extort the secret of the Q-bomb?

cut to
Limbo Shot of Reel-Rye bottle.   *Announcer*: Yes, kiddies! What
of Roger?
But first a word from the makers
of Reel-Rye, that happy syrup
that gives your milk grown-up flavor! YES! Grown-up flavor!

Shot of Red Top and a beer. At 8:50.

In his own un-secret heart: Steady, boy. You've got to think this
out. Nothing impossible about it, no reason to settle for a stalemate;
just a little time to think it out. Galardo said the Black Chapter
would accept a token submission, let me return the Seal, and that
would be that. But I mustn't count on that as a datum; he lied to me
about the Serpentists. Token submission *sounds* right; they go in big
for symbolism. Maybe because they're so stone-broke, like the Japs.
Drinking a cup of tea, they gussie it all up until it's a religion; that's
the way you squeeze nourishment out of poverty—

Skip the Japs. Think. He lied to me about the Serpentists. The big
thing to remember is, I have the Chapter Seal and they need it back,
or think they do. All you need's a little time to think things through,
place where he won't dare jump you and grab the Seal. And this is it.

"Joe. Sam, Mike, Tony, Ben, whoever you are. Hit me again."

Joe—Sam, Mike, Tony, Ben?—tilts the amber bottle quietly; the
liquid's level rises and crowns the little glass with a convex meniscus.
He turns off the stream with an easy roll of the wrist. The suntan line
of neon tubing at the bar back twinkles off the curve of surface tension, the placid whiskey, the frothy beer. At 9:05.

To his left: "So Finkelstein finally meets Goldberg in the garment
center and he grabs him like this by the lapel, and he yells, 'You
louse, you rat, you no-good, what's this about you running around
with my wife? I ought to—I ought to—say, you call *this* a *button-
hole?*' "

Restrained and apprehensive laughter; Catholic, Protestant, Jew
(choice of one), what's the difference I always say.

Did they have a Jewish Question still, or was all smoothed and
troweled and interfaithed and brotherhoodooed—

Wait. Your formulation implies that they're in the future, and you
have no proof of that. Think straighter; you don't know *where* they
are, or *when* they are, or *who* they are. You *do* know that you

walked into Big Maggie's resonance chamber to change the target, experimental iridium for old reliable zinc
and
"Bartender," in a controlled and formal voice. Shot of Red Top and a beer at 9:09, the hand vibrating with remembrance of a dirty-green el Greco sky which *might* be Brookhaven's heavens a million years either way from now, or one second sideways, or (bow to Method and formally exhaust the possibilities) a hallucination. The Seal snatched from the greenlit rock altar could be a blank washer, a wheel from a toy truck, or the screw top from a jar of shaving cream but for the fact that it wasn't. It was the Seal.

So: they began seeping through after that. The Chapter wanted it back. The Serpentists wanted it, period. Galardo had started by bargaining and wound up by threatening, but how could you do anything but laugh at his best offer, a rusty five-pound spur gear with a worn keyway and three teeth missing? His threats were richer than his bribes; they culminated with The Century of Flame. "Faith, father, it doesn't scare me at all, at all; sure, no man could stand it." Subjective–objective (How you used to sling *them* around!), and Master Newton's billiard-table similes dissolve into sense impressions of pointer readings as you learn your trade, but Galardo had scared hell out of you, or into you, with The Century of Flame.

But you had the Seal of the Chapter and you had time to think, while on the screen above the bar:

VIDEO	AUDIO
Long shot down steep, cobble-stoned French village street. *Pierre* darts out of alley in middle distance, looks wildly around, and runs toward camera, pistol in hand. *Annette* and *Paul* appear from same alley and dash after him.	*Paul:* Stop, you fool!
Cut to *Cu* of *Pierre's* face; beard stubble and sweat.	*Pierre:* A fool, am I?
Cut to long shot; *Pierre* aims and fires; *Paul* grabs his left shoulder and falls.	*Annette:* Darling!

Cut to two-shot, *Annette* and *Paul.*

Paul: Don't mind me. Take my gun—after him. He's a mad dog, I tell you!

Dolly back. *Annette* takes his pistol.

Annette: This, my dear, is as good a time as any to drop my little masquerade. Are you American agents really so stupid that you never thought I might be—a plant, as you call it?

Annette stands; we see her aim down at *Paul,* out of the picture. Then we dolly in to a *Cu* of her head; she is smiling triumphantly.

Sound: click of cocking pistol.

A hand holding a pistol enters the *Cu;* the pistol muzzle touches *Annette's* neck.

Harkrider: Drop it, Madame Golkov.

Dolly back to middle shot. *Harkrider* stands behind *Annette* as *Paul* gets up briskly and takes the pistol from her hand.

Paul: No, Madame Golkov; we American agents were not really so stupid. Wish I could say the same for—your people. Pierre Tourneur *was* a plant, I am glad to say; otherwise he would not have missed me. He is one of the best pistol shots in Counterintelligence.

Cut to long shot of street, *Harkrider* and *Paul* walk away from the camera, *Annette* between them. Fadeout.

Harkrider: Come along, Madame Golkov.

Music: theme up and out.

To his right: "It ain't reasonable. All that shooting and yelling and falling down and not one person sticks his head out of a window to see what's going on. They should of had a few people looking out to see what's going on, otherwise it ain't reasonable."

"Yeah, who's fighting tonight?"

"Rocky Mausoleum against Rocky Mazzarella. From Toledo."

"Rocky Mazzarella beat Rocky Granatino, didn't he?"

"Ah, that was Rocky Bolderoni, and he whipped Rocky Capacola."

Them and their neatly packaged problems, them and their neatly packaged shows with beginning middle and end. The rite of the low-budget shot-in-Europe spy series, the rite of pugilism, the rite of the dog walk after dinner and the beer at the bar with cocelebrant worshippers at the high altar of Nothing.

9:30. Shot of Red Top and a beer, positively the last one until you get this figured out; you're beginning to buzz like a transformer.

Do they have transformers? Do they have vitamins? Do they have anything but that glaring green sky, and the rock altar and treasures like the Seal and the rusty gear with three broken teeth? "All smelling of iodoform. And all quite bald." But Galardo looked as if he were dying of tuberculosis, and the letter from the Serpentists was in a sick and straggling hand. Relics of medieval barbarism.

To his left—

"*Galardo!*" he screamed.

The bartender scurried over—Joe, Sam, Mike, Tony, Ben?—scowling. "What's the matter, mister?"

"I'm sorry. I got a stitch in my side. A cramp."

Bullyboy scowled competently and turned. "What'll you have, mister?"

Galardo said cadaverously: "Wodeffer my vriend hyere iss havfing."

"Shot of Red Top and a beer, right?"

"*What are you doing here?*"

"Drink-ing beferachiss . . . havf hyü de-site-it hwat tü dü?"

The bartender rapped down the shot glass and tilted the bottle over it, looking at Galardo. Some of the whiskey slopped over. The bartender started, went to the tap and carefully drew a glass of beer, slicing the collar twice.

"My vriend hyere will pay."

He got out a half dollar, fumbling, and put it on the wet wood. The bartender, old-fashioned, rapped it twice on the bar to show he wasn't stealing it even though you weren't watching; he rang it up double virtuous on the cash register, the absent owner's fishy eye.

"What are you doing here?" again, in a low, reasonable, almost amused voice to show him you have the whip hand.

"Drink-ing beferachiss . . . it iss so cle-an hyere." Galardo's sunken face, unbelievably, looked wistful as he surveyed the barroom, his head swiveling slowly from extreme left to extreme right. "Clean. Well. Isn't it clean there?"

"Sheh, not!" Galardo said mournfully. "Sheh, not! Hyere it iss so cle-an . . . hwai did yü outreach tü us? Hag-rid us, wretch-it, hagrid us?" There were tears hanging in his eyes. "Haff yü de-site-it hwat tü dü?"

Expansively: "I don't pretend to understand the situation *fully,* Galardo. But you know and I know that I've got something you people [think you] need. Now there doesn't seem to be any body of law covering artifacts that appear [*plink!*] in a magnetron on accidental overload, and I just have your word that it's yours."

"Ah, that iss how yü re-member it now," said sorrowful Galardo.

"Well, it's the way it [but wasn't something green? I think of spired Toledo and three angled crosses toppling] happened. I don't want anything silly, like a million dollars in small unmarked bills, and I don't want to be bullied, to be bullied, no, I mean not by you, not by anybody. Just, just tell me who you are, what all this is about. This is nonsense, you see, and we can't have nonsense. I'm afraid I'm not expressing myself very well—"

And a confident smile and turn away from him, which shows that you aren't afraid, you can turn your back and dare him to make something of it. In public, in the bar? It is laughable; you have him in the palm of your hand. "Shot of Red Top and a beer, please, Sam." At 9:48.

The bartender draws the beer and pours the whiskey. He pauses before he picks up the dollar bill fished from the pants pocket, pauses almost timidly and works his face into a friend's grimace. But you can read him; he is making amends for his suspicion that you were going to start a drunken brawl when Galardo merely surprised you a bit. You can read him because your mind is tensed to concert pitch tonight, ready for Galardo, ready for the Serpentists, ready to crack this thing wide open; strange!

But you weren't ready for the words he spoke from his fake apologetic friend's grimace as you delicately raised the heavy amber-filled glass to your lips: "Where'd your friend go?"

You slopped the whiskey as you turned and looked.

Galardo gone.

You smiled and shrugged; he comes and goes as he pleases, you know. Irresponsible, no manners at all—but *loyal.* A prince among men when you get to know him, a prince, I tell you. All this in your smile and shrug—why, you could have been an actor! The worry, the faint neurotic worry, didn't show at all, and indeed there is no reason why it should. You have the whip hand; you have the Seal; Galardo will come crawling back and explain everything. As for example:

"You may wonder why I've asked all of you to assemble in the libr'reh."

or

"For goodness' sake, Gracie, I wasn't going to go to Cuba! When you heard me on the extension phone I was just ordering a dozen Havana *cigars!*"

or

"In your notation, we are from 19,276 A.D. Our basic mathematic is a quite comprehensible subsumption of your contemporary statistical analysis and topology which I shall now proceed to explain to you."

And that was all.

With sorrow, Gentle Reader, you will have noticed that the marble did not remark: "I am chiseled," the lumber "I am sawn," the paint "I am applied to canvas," the tea leaf "I am whisked about in an exquisite Korean bowl to brew while the celebrants of *cha no yu* squeeze this nourishment out of their poverty." Vain victim, relax and play your hunches; subconscious integration does it. Stick with your lit-tle old subconscious integration and all will go *swimmingly,* if only it weren't so damned noisy in here. But it was dark on the street and conceivably things could happen there; stick with crowds and stick with witnesses, but if only it weren't so . . .

To his left they were settling down; it was the hour of confidences, and man to man they told the secret of their success: "In the needle trade, I'm in the needle trade, I don't sell anybody a crooked needle, my father told me that. Albert, he said to me, don't never sell nobody nothing but a straight needle. And today I have four shops."

To his right they were settling down; freed of the cares of the day they invited their souls, explored the spiritual realm, theologized with exquisite distinctions: "Now *wait* a minute, I didn't say I was a *good* Mormon, I said I was a Mormon and that's what I am, a Mormon. I *never* said I was a *good* Mormon, I just said I was a Mormon, my mother was a Mormon and my father was a Mormon, and that makes me a Mormon but I *never* said I was a *good* Mormon—"

Distinguo, rolled the canonical thunder; *distinguo.*

Demurely a bonneted lassie shook her small-change tambourine beneath his chin and whispered, snarling: "Galardo lied."

Admit it; you were startled. But what need for the bartender to come running with raised hand, what need for needle-trader to your left to shrink away, the L.D.S. to cower?

"Mister, that's twice you let out a yell, we run a quiet place, if you can't be good, begone."

Begob.

"I ash-assure you, bartender, it was—unintenable."

Greed vies with hate; greed wins; greed always wins: "Just keep it quiet, mister, this ain't the Bowery, this is a family place." Then, relenting: "The same?"

"Yes, please." At 10:15 the patient lassie jingled silver on the parchment palm outstretched. He placed a quarter on the tambourine and asked politely: "Did you say something to me before, Miss?"

"God bless you, sir. Yes, sir, I did say something. I said Galardo lied; the Seal is holy to the Serpent, sir, and to his humble emissaries. If you'll only hand it over, sir, the Serpent will somewhat mitigate the fearsome torments which are rightly yours for snatching the Seal from the Altar, sir."

[Snatchings from Altars? *Ma foi,* the wench is mad!]

"Listen, lady. That's only talk. What annoys me about you people is, you won't talk sense. I want to know who you are, what this is about, maybe just a little hint about your mathematics, and I'll do the rest and you can have the blooming Seal. I'm a passable physicist even if I'm only a technician. I bet there's something you didn't know. I bet you didn't know the tech shortage is tighter than the scientist shortage. You get a guy can tune a magnetron, he writes his own ticket. So I'm weak on quantum mechanics, the theory side, I'm still a good all-around man and be-*lieve* me, the Ph.D.'s would kiss my ever-loving *feet* if I told them I got an offer from Argonne—

"So listen, you Janissary emissary. I'm happy right here in this necessary commissary and here I *stay.*"

But she was looking at him with bright frightened mouse's eyes and slipped on down the line when he paused for breath, putting out the parchment palm to others but not ceasing to watch him.

Coins tapped the tambour. "God bless you. God bless you. God bless you."

The raving-maniacal ghost of G. Washington Hill descended then into a girdled sibyl; she screamed from the screen: "It's *Hit Parade!*"

"I like them production numbers."

"I like that Pigalle Mackintosh."

"I like them production numbers. Lotsa pretty girls, pretty clothes, something to take your mind off your troubles."

"I like that Pigalle Mackintosh. She don't just sing, mind you, she plays the saxophone. Talent."

"I like them production numbers. They show you just what the song is all about. Like last week they did *Sadist Calypso* with this mad scientist cutting up the girls, and then Pigalle comes in and whips him to death at the last verse, you see just what the song's all about, something to take your mind off your troubles."

"I like that Pigalle Mackintosh. She don't just sing, mind you, she plays the saxophone and cracks a blacksnake whip, like last week in *Sadist Calypso—*"

"Yeah. Something to take your mind off your troubles."

Irritably he felt in his pocket for the Seal and moved, stumbling a little, to one of the tables against the knotty pine wall. His head slipped forward on the polished wood and he sank into the sea of myth.

Galardo came to him in his dream and spoke under a storm-green sky: "Take your mind off your troubles, Edward. It was stolen like the first penny, like the quiz answers, like the pity for your bereavement." His hand, a tambourine, was out.

"Never shall I yield," he declaimed to the miserable wretch. "By the *honneur* of a Gascon, I stole it fair and square; 'tis mine, knave! *En garde!*"

Galardo quailed and ran, melting into the sky, the altar, the tambourine.

A ham-hand manhandled him. "Light-up time," said Sam. "I let you sleep because you got it here, but I got to close up now."

"Sam," he says uncertainly.

"One for the road, mister. On the house. *Up-sy*-daisy!" meaty hooks under his armpits heaving him to the bar.

The lights are out behind the bar, the jolly neons, glittering off how many gems of amber rye and the tan crystals of beer? A meager bulb above the register is the oasis in the desert of inky night.

"Sam," groggily, "you don't understand. I mean I never explained it—"

"Drink up, mister," a pale free drink, soda bubbles lightly tinged with tawny rye. A small sip to gain time.

"Sam, there are some people after me—"

"You'll feel better in the morning, mister. Drink up, I got to close up, hurry up."

"These people, Sam [it's cold in here and scary as a noise in the attic; the bottles stand accusingly, the chrome globes that top them eye you] these people, they've got a thing, The Century of—"

"Sure, mister, I let you sleep because you got it here, but we close up now, drink up your drink."

"Sam, let me go home with you, will you? It isn't anything like that, don't misunderstand, I just can't be alone. These people—look, I've got money—"

He spreads out what he dug from his pocket.

"Sure, mister, you got lots of money, two dollars and thirty-eight cents. Now you take your money and get out of the store because I got to lock up and clean out the register—"

"Listen, bartender, I'm not drunk, maybe I don't have much money on me but I'm an important man! Important! They couldn't run Big Maggie at Brookhaven without me, I may not have a degree but what I get from these people if you'll only let me stay here—"

The bartender takes the pale one on the house you only sipped and dumps it in the sink; his hands are iron on you and you float while he chants:

> *"Decent man. Decent place.*
> *Hold their liquor. Got it here.*
> *Try be nice. Drunken bum.*
> *Don't—come—back."*

The crash of your coccyx on the concrete and the slam of the door are one.

Run!

Down the black street stumbling over cans, cats, orts, to the pool of light in the night, safe corner where a standard sprouts and sprays radiance.

The tall black figure that steps between is Galardo.

The short one has a tambourine.

"*Take it!*" He thrust out the Seal on his shaking palm. "If you won't tell me anything, you won't. Take it and go away!"

Galardo inspects it and sadly says: "Thiss appearss to be a blank wash-er."

"Mistake," he slobbers. "Minute." He claws in his pockets, ripping. "Here! Here!"

The lassie squeaks: "The wheel of a toy truck. It will not do at all, sir." Her glittereyes.

"Then this! This is it! This must be it!"

Their heads shake slowly. Unable to look his fingers feel the rim and rolled threading of the jar cap.

They nod together, sad and glitter-eyed, and The Century of Flame begins.

The Mindworm

WHAT'S the difference between science fiction and
fantasy? Easy, you say: fantasy is about fairies
and vampires and werewolves, while science fiction is about Mars and the year 8000 A.D. But it's
not a very satisfactory answer, because there have
been first-rate stories about werewolves, say (for
instance, James Blish's "There Shall Be No Darkness") that are clearly science fiction. The difference is that in a science fiction story you are willing
to believe, for the duration of the story at least,
that it *might* under certain circumstances be true—
somewhere else, or at some future time—while in
fantasy you don't think for a moment it's true, but
are just enjoying the gooseflesh or the romp. And
then you come across something like *The Mindworm* . . .

THE HANDSOME j. g. and the pretty nurse held out against it as long
as they reasonably could, but blue Pacific water, languid tropical
nights, the low atoll dreaming on the horizon—and the complete absence of any other nice young people for company on the small, uncomfortable parts boat—did their work. On June 30th they watched
through dark glasses as the dazzling thing burst over the fleet and the
atoll. Her manicured hand gripped his arm in excitement and terror.
Unfelt radiation sleeted through their loins.

A storekeeper-third-class named Bielaski watched the young couple with more interest than he showed in Test Able. After all, he had
twenty-five dollars riding on the nurse. That night he lost it to a chief
bosun's mate who had backed the j. g.

In the course of time, the careless nurse was discharged under conditions other than honorable. The j. g., who didn't like to put things
in writing, phoned her all the way from Manila to say it was a

damned shame. When her gratitude gave way to specific inquiry, their overseas connection went bad and he had to hang up.

She had a child, a boy, turned it over to a foundling home, and vanished from his life into a series of good jobs and finally marriage.

The boy grew up stupid, puny and stubborn, greedy and miserable. To the home's hilarious young athletics director he suddenly said: "You hate me. You think I make the rest of the boys look bad."

The athletics director blustered and laughed, and later told the doctor over coffee: "I watch myself around the kids. They're sharp—they catch a look or a gesture and it's like a blow in the face to them, I know that, so I watch myself. So how did he know?"

The doctor told the boy: "Three pounds more this month isn't bad, but how about you pitch in and clean up your plate *every* day? Can't live on meat and water; those vegetables make you big and strong."

The boy said: "What's 'neurasthenic' mean?"

The doctor later said to the director: "It made my flesh creep. I was looking at his little spindling body and dishing out the old pep talk about growing big and strong, and inside my head I was thinking 'we'd call him neurasthenic in the old days' and then out he popped with it. What should we do? Should we do anything? Maybe it'll go away. I don't know anything about these things. I don't know whether anybody does."

"Reads minds, does he?" asked the director. *Be damned if he's going to read my mind about Schultz Meat Market's ten percent.* "Doctor, I think I'm going to take my vacation a little early this year. Has anybody shown any interest in adopting the child?"

"Not him. He wasn't a baby doll when we got him, and at present he's an exceptionally unattractive-looking kid. You know how people don't give a damn about anything but their looks."

"*Some* couples would take anything, or so they tell me."

"Unapproved for foster-parenthood, you mean?"

"Red tape and arbitrary classifications sometimes limit us too severely in our adoptions."

"If you're going to wish him on some screwball couple that the courts turned down as unfit, I want no part of it."

"You don't have to have any part of it, doctor. By the way, which dorm does he sleep in?"

"West," grunted the doctor, leaving the office.

The director called a few friends—a judge, a couple the judge referred him to, a court clerk. Then he left by way of the east wing of the building.

The boy survived three months with the Berrymans. Hard-drinking Mimi alternately caressed and shrieked at him; Edward W. tried to be a good scout and just gradually lost interest, looking clean through him. He hit the road in June and got by with it for a while. He wore a Boy Scout uniform, and Boy Scouts can turn up anywhere, any time. The money he had taken with him lasted a month. When the last penny of the last dollar was three days spent, he was adrift on a Nebraska prairie. He had walked out of the last small town because the constable was beginning to wonder what on earth he was hanging around for and who he belonged to. The town was miles behind on the two-lane highway; the infrequent cars did not stop.

One of Nebraska's "rivers", a dry bed at this time of year, lay ahead, spanned by a railroad culvert. There were some men in its shade, and he was hungry.

They were ugly, dirty men, and their thoughts were muddled and stupid. They called him "Shorty" and gave him a little dirty bread and some stinking sardines from a can. The thoughts of one of them became less muddled and uglier. He talked to the rest out of the boy's hearing, and they whooped with laughter. The boy got ready to run, but his legs wouldn't hold him up.

He could read the thoughts of the men quite clearly as they headed for him. Outrage, fear, and disgust blended in him and somehow turned inside-out and one of the men was dead on the dry ground, grasshoppers vaulting onto his flannel shirt, the others backing away, frightened now, not frightening.

He wasn't hungry any more; he felt quite comfortable and satisfied. He got up and headed for the other men, who ran. The rearmost of them was thinking *Jeez he folded up the evil eye we was only gonna—*

Again the boy let the thoughts flow into his head and again he flipped his own thoughts around them; it was quite easy to do. It was different—this man's terror from the other's lustful anticipation. But both had their points . . .

At his leisure, he robbed the bodies of three dollars and twenty-four cents.

Thereafter his fame preceded him like a death wind. Two years on the road and he had his growth and his fill of the dull and stupid minds he met there. He moved to northern cities, a year here, a year there, quiet, unobtrusive, prudent, an epicure.

Sebastian Long woke suddenly, with something on his mind. As night fog cleared away he remembered, happily. Today he started the Demeter Bowl! At last there was time, at last there was money—six hundred and twenty-three dollars in the bank. He had packed and shipped the three dozen cocktail glasses last night, engraved with Mrs. Klausman's initials—his last commercial order for as many months as the Bowl would take.

He shifted from nightshirt to denims, gulped coffee, boiled an egg but was too excited to eat it. He went to the front of his shop-workroom-apartment, checked the lock, waved at neighbors' children on their way to school, and ceremoniously set a sign in the cluttered window.

It said: "NO COMMERCIAL ORDERS TAKEN UNTIL FUR-THER NOTICE."

From a closet he tenderly carried a shrouded object that made a double armful and laid it on his workbench. Unshrouded, it was a glass bowl—*what* a glass bowl! The clearest Swedish lead glass, the purest lines he had ever seen, his secret treasure since the crazy day he had bought it, long ago, for six months' earnings. His wife had given him hell for that until the day she died. From the closet he brought a portfolio filled with sketches and designs dating back to the day he had bought the bowl. He smiled over the first, excitedly scrawled—a florid, rococo conception, unsuited to the classicism of the lines and the serenity of the perfect glass.

Through many years and hundreds of sketches he had refined his conception to the point where it was, he humbly felt, not unsuited to the medium. A strongly-molded Demeter was to dominate the piece, a matron as serene as the glass, and all the fruits of the earth would flow from her gravely outstretched arms.

Suddenly and surely, he began to work. With a candle he thinly smoked an oval area on the outside of the bowl. Two steady fingers clipped the Demeter drawing against the carbon black; a hair-fine needle in his other hand traced her lines. When the transfer of the design was done, Sebastian Long readied his lathe. He fitted a small copper wheel, slightly worn as he liked them, into the chuck and with his fingers charged it with the finest rouge from Rouen. He took an ashtray cracked in delivery and held it against the spinning disk. It bit in smoothly, with the *wiping* feel to it that was exactly right.

Holding out his hands, seeing that the fingers did not tremble with excitement, he eased the great bowl to the lathe and was about to make the first tiny cut of the millions that would go into the masterpiece.

Somebody knocked on his door and rattled the doorknob.

Sebastian Long did not move or look toward the door. Soon the busybody would read the sign and go away. But the pounding and the rattling of the knob went on. He eased down the bowl and angrily went to the window, picked up the sign, and shook it at whoever it was—he couldn't make out the face very well. But the idiot wouldn't go away.

The engraver unlocked the door, opened it a bit, and snapped: "The shop is closed. I shall not be taking any orders for several months. Please don't bother me now."

"It's about the Demeter Bowl," said the intruder.

Sebastian Long stared at him. "What the devil do you know about my Demeter Bowl?" He saw the man was a stranger, undersized by a little, middle-aged . . .

"Just let me in please," urged the man. "It's important. Please!"

"I don't know what you're talking about," said the engraver. "But what do you know about my Demeter Bowl?" He hooked his thumbs pugnaciously over the waistband of his denims and glowered at the stranger. The stranger promptly took advantage of his hand being removed from the door and glided in.

Sebastian Long thought briefly that it might be a nightmare as the man darted quickly about his shop, picking up a graver and throwing it down, picking up a wire scratch-wheel and throwing it down. "Here, you!" he roared, as the stranger picked up a crescent wrench which he did not throw down.

As Long started for him, the stranger darted to the workbench and brought the crescent wrench down shatteringly on the bowl.

Sebastian Long's heart was bursting with sorrow and rage; such a storm of emotions as he never had known thundered through him. Paralyzed, he saw the stranger smile with anticipation.

The engraver's legs folded under him and he fell to the floor, drained and dead.

The Mindworm, locked in the bedroom of his brownstone front, smiled again, reminiscently.

Smiling, he checked the day on a wall calendar.

"Dolores!" yelled her mother in Spanish. "Are you going to pass the whole day in there?"

She had been practicing low-lidded, sexy half-smiles like Lauren Bacall in the bathroom mirror. She stormed out and yelled in English: "I don't know how many times I tell you not to call me that Spick name no more!"

"Dolly!" sneered her mother. "Dah-lee! When was there a Saint Dah-lee that you call yourself after, eh?"

The girl snarled a Spanish obscenity at her mother and ran down the tenement stairs. Jeez, she was gonna be late for sure!

Held up by a stream of traffic between her and her streetcar, she danced with impatience. Then the miracle happened. Just like in the movies, a big convertible pulled up before her and its lounging driver said, opening the door: "You seem to be in a hurry. Could I drop you somewhere?"

Dazed at the sudden realization of a hundred daydreams, she did not fail to give the driver a low-lidded, sexy smile as she said: "Why, *thanks!*" and climbed in. He wasn't no Cary Grant, but he had all his hair . . . kind of small, but so was she . . . and jeez, the convertible had *leopard-skin seat covers!*

The car was in the stream of traffic, purring down the avenue. "It's a lovely day," she said. "Really too nice to work."

The driver smiled shyly, kind of like Jimmy Stewart but of course not so tall, and said: "I feel like playing hooky myself. How would you like a spin down Long Island?"

"Be wonderful!" The convertible cut left on an odd-numbered street.

"Play hooky, you said. What do you do?"

"Advertising."

"*Advertising!*" Dolly wanted to kick herself for ever having doubted, for ever having thought in low, self-loathing moments that it wouldn't work out, that she'd marry a grocer or a mechanic and live forever after in a smelly tenement and grow old and sick and stooped. She felt vaguely in her happy daze that it might have been cuter, she might have accidentally pushed him into a pond or something, but this was cute enough. An advertising man, leopard-skin seat covers . . . what more could a girl with a sexy smile and a nice little figure want?

Speeding down the South Shore she learned that his name was Michael Brent, exactly as it ought to be. She wished she could tell him she was Jennifer Brown or one of those real cute names they had nowadays, but was reassured when he told her he thought Dolly Gonzalez was a beautiful name. He didn't, and she noticed the omission, add: "It's the most beautiful name I ever heard!" That, she comfortably thought as she settled herself against the cushions, would come later.

They stopped at Medford for lunch, a wonderful lunch in a little restaurant where you went down some steps and there were candles on the table. She called him "Michael" and he called her "Dolly." She learned that he liked dark girls and thought the stories in *True Story* really were true, and that he thought she was just tall enough, and that Greer Garson was wonderful, but not the way she was, and that he thought her dress was just wonderful.

They drove slowly after Medford, and Michael Brent did most of the talking. He had traveled all over the world. He had been in the war and wounded—just a flesh wound. He was thirty-eight, and had been married once, but she died. There were no children. He was alone in the world. He had nobody to share his town house in the 50's, his country place in Westchester, his lodge in the Maine woods. Every word sent the girl floating higher and higher on a tide of happiness; the signs were unmistakable.

When they reached Montauk Point, the last sandy bit of the continent before blue water and Europe, it was sunset, with a great wrinkled sheet of purple and rose stretching half across the sky and the first stars appearing above the dark horizon of the water.

The two of them walked from the parked car out onto the sand, alone, bathed in glorious Technicolor. Her heart was nearly bursting with joy as she heard Michael Brent say, his arms tightening around her: "Darling, will you marry me?"

"Oh, *yes*, Michael!" she breathed, dying.

The Mindworm, drowsing, suddenly felt the sharp sting of danger. He cast out through the great city, dragging tentacles of thought:

". . . die if she don't let me . . ."

". . . six an' six is twelve an' carry one an' three is four. . ."

". . . gobblegobble madre de dios pero soy gobblegobble . . ."

". . . parlay Domino an' Missab and shoot the roll on Duchess Peg in the feature . . ."

". . . melt resin add the silver chloride and dissolve in oil of lavender stand and decant and fire to cone zero twelve give you shimmering streaks of luster down the walls . . ."

". . . moiderin' square-headed gobblegobble tried ta poke his eye out wassamatta witta ref . . ."

". . . O God I am most heartily sorry I have offended thee in . . ."

". . . talk like a commie . . ."

". . . gobblegobblegobble two dolla twenny-fi' sense gobble . . ."

". . . just a nip and fill it up with water and brush my teeth . . ."

". . . really know I'm God but fear to confess their sins . . ."

". . . dirty lousy rock-headed claw-handed paddle-footed goggle-eyed snot-nosed hunch-backed feeble-minded pot-bellied son of . . ."

". . . write on the wall alfie is a stunkur and then . . ."

". . . thinks I believe it's a television set but I know he's got a bomb in there but who can I tell who can help so alone . . ."

". . . gabble was ich weiss nicht gabble geh bei Broadvay gabble . . ."

". . . habt mein daughter Rosie such a fella gobblegobble . . ."

". . . wonder if that's one didn't look back . . ."

". . . seen with her in the Medford restaurant . . ."

The Mindworm struck into that thought.

". . . not a mark on her but the M. E.'s have been wrong before and heart failure don't mean a thing anyway try to talk to her old lady authorize an autopsy get Pancho little guy talks Spanish be best . . ."

The Mindworm knew he would have to be moving again—soon. He was sorry; some of the thoughts he had tapped indicated good . . . hunting?

Regretfully, he again dragged his net:

". . . with chartreuse drinks I mean drapes could use a drink come to think of it . . ."

". . . reep-beep-reep-beep reepiddy-beepiddy-beep bop man wadda beat . . ."

" $\sum_{r=i+1}^{n} \varphi(a_r, a_r) - \sum_{s=i}^{i} \varphi(a_r, a_s)$, *What the Hell was that?*"

The Mindworm withdrew, in frantic haste. The intelligence was massive, its overtones those of a vigorous adult. He had learned from certain dangerous children that there was peril of a leveling flow. Shaken and scared, he contemplated traveling. He would need more than that wretched girl had supplied, and it would not be epicurean. There would be no time to find individuals at a ripe emotional crisis, or goad them to one. It would be plain—munching. The Mindworm drank a glass of water, also necessary to his metabolism.

EIGHT FOUND DEAD
IN UPTOWN MOVIE;
"MOLESTER" SOUGHT

Eight persons, including three women, were found dead Wednesday night of unknown causes in widely separated seats in the balcony of the Odeon Theater at 117th St. and Broadway. Police are seeking a man described by the balcony usher, Michael Fenelly, 18, as "acting like a woman-molester."

Fenelly discovered the first of the fatalities after seeing the man "moving from one empty seat to another several times." He went to ask a woman in a seat next to one the man had just vacated whether he had annoyed her. She was dead.

Almost at once, a scream rang out. In another part of the balcony Mrs. Sadie Rabinowitz, 40, uttered the cry when another victim toppled from his seat next to her.

Theater manager I. J. Marcusohn stopped the show and turned on the house lights. He tried to instruct his staff to keep the audience from leaving before the police arrived. He failed to get word to them in time, however, and most of the audience was gone when a detail from the 24th Pct. and an ambulance from Harlem hospital took over at the scene of the tragedy.

The Medical Examiner's office has not yet made a report as to the causes of death. A spokesman said the victims showed no signs of poisoning or violence. He added that it "was inconceivable that it could be a coincidence."

Lt. John Braidwood of the 24th Pct. said of the alleged

molester: "We got a fair description of him and naturally we will try to bring him in for questioning."

Clickety-click, clickety-click, clickety-click sang the rails as the Mindworm drowsed in his coach seat.

Some people were walking forward from the diner. One was thinking: "Different-looking fellow. (a) he's aberrant. (b) he's nonaberrant and ill. Cancel (b)—respiration normal, skin smooth and healthy, no tremor of limbs, well-groomed. Is aberrant (1) trivially. (2) significantly. Cancel (1)—displayed no involuntary interest when . . . odd! *Running* for the washroom! Unexpected because (a) neat grooming indicates amour propre inconsistent with amusing others; (b) evident health inconsistent with . . ." It had taken one second, was fully detailed.

The Mindworm, locked in the toilet of the coach, wondered what the next stop was. He was getting off at it—not frightened, just careful. Dodge them, keep dodging them and everything would be all right. Send out no mental taps until the train was far away and everything would be all right.

He got off at a West Virginia coal and iron town surrounded by ruined mountains and filled with the offscourings of Eastern Europe. Serbs, Albanians, Croats, Hungarians, Slovenes, Bulgarians, and all possible combinations and permutations thereof. He walked slowly from the smoke-stained, brownstone passenger station. The train had roared on its way.

". . . ain' no gemmum that's fo sho', fi-cen' tip fo' a good shine lak ah give um . . ."

". . . dumb bassar don't know how to make out a billa lading yet he ain't never gonna know so fire him get it over with . . ."

". . . gabblegabblegabble . . ." Not a word he recognized in it.

". . . gobblegobble dat tam vooman I brek she nack . . ."

". . . gobble trink visky chin glassabeer gobblegobblegobble . . ."

". . . gabblegabblegabble . . ."

". . . makes me so gobblegobble mad little no-good tramp no she ain' but I don' like no standup from no dame . . ."

A blond, square-headed boy fuming under a street light.

". . . out wit' Casey Oswiak I could kill that dumb bohunk alla time trine ta paw her . . ."

It was a possibility. The Mindworm drew near.

". . . stand me up for that gobblegobble bohunk I oughtta slap her inna mush like my ole man says . . ."

"Hello," said the Mindworm.

"Waddaya wan'?"

"Casey Oswiak told me to tell you not to wait up for your girl. He's taking her out tonight."

The blond boy's rage boiled into his face and shot from his eyes. He was about to swing when the Mindworm began to feed. It was like pheasant after chicken, venison after beef. The coarseness of the environment, or the ancient strain? The Mindworm wondered as he strolled down the street. A girl passed him:

". . . oh but he's gonna be mad like last time wish I came right away so jealous kinda nice but he might bust me one some day be nice to him tonight there he is lam'post leaning on it looks kinda funny gawd I hope he ain't drunk looks kinda funny sleeping sick or bozhe moi gabblegabblegabble . . ."

Her thoughts trailed into a foreign language of which the Mindworm knew not a word. After hysteria had gone she recalled, in the foreign language, that she had passed him.

The Mindworm, stimulated by the unfamiliar quality of the last feeding, determined to stay for some days. He checked in at a Main Street hotel.

Musing, he dragged his net:

". . . gobblegobblewhompyeargobblecheskygobblegabblechy-esh . . ."

". . . take him down cellar beat the can off the damn chesky thief put the fear of god into him teach him can't bust into no boxcars in *mah* parta the caounty . . ."

". . . gabblegabble . . ."

". . . phone ole Mister Ryan in She-cawgo and he'll tell them three-card monte grifters who got the horse-room rights in this necka the woods by damn don't pay protection money for no protection . . ."

The Mindworm followed that one further; it sounded as though it could lead to some money if he wanted to stay in the town long enough.

The Eastern Europeans of the town, he mistakenly thought, were like the tramps and bums he had known and fed on during his years on the road—stupid and safe, safe and stupid, quite the same thing.

In the morning he found no mention of the square-headed boy's death in the town's paper and thought it had gone practically unnoticed. It had—by the paper, which was of, by, and for the coal and iron company and its native-American bosses and straw bosses. The other town, the one without a charter or police force, with only an imported weekly newspaper or two from the nearest city, noticed it. The other town had roots more than two thousand years deep, which are hard to pull up. But the Mindworm didn't know it was there.

He fed again that night, on a giddy young streetwalker in her room. He had astounded and delighted her with a fistful of ten-dollar bills before he began to gorge. Again the delightful difference from city-bred folk was there. . . .

Again in the morning he had been unnoticed, he thought. The chartered town, unwilling to admit that there were streetwalkers or that they were found dead, wiped the slate clean; its only member who really cared was the native-American cop on the beat who had collected weekly from the dead girl.

The other town, unknown to the Mindworm, buzzed with it. A delegation went to the other town's only public officer. Unfortunately he was young, American-trained, perhaps even ignorant about some important things. For what he told them was: "My children, that is foolish superstition. Go home."

The Mindworm, through the day, roiled the surface of the town proper by allowing himself to be roped into a poker game in a parlor of the hotel. He wasn't good at it, he didn't like it, and he quit with relief when he had cleaned six shifty-eyed, hard-drinking loafers out of about three hundred dollars. One of them went straight to the police station and accused the unknown of being a sharper. A humorous sergeant, the Mindworm was pleased to note, joshed the loafer out of his temper.

Nightfall again, hunger again . . .

He walked the streets of the town and found them empty. It was strange. The native-American citizens were out, tending bar, walking their beats, locking up their newspaper on the stones, collecting their rents, managing their movies—but where were the others? He cast his net:

". . . gobblegobblegobble whomp year gobble . . ."

". . . crazy old pollack mama of mine try to lock me in with Errol

Flynn at the Majestic never know the difference if I sneak out the back . . ."

That was near. He crossed the street and it was nearer. He homed on the thought:

". . . jeez he's a hunka man like Stanley but he never looks at me that Vera Kowalik I'd like to kick her just once in the gobblegobble-gobble crazy old mama won't be American so ashamed . . ."

It was half a block, no more, down a side street. Brick houses, two stories, with back yards on an alley. She was going out the back way.

How strangely quiet it was in the alley.

". . . ea-sy down them steps fix that damn board that's how she caught me last time what the hell are they all so scared of went to see Father Drugas won't talk bet somebody got it again that Vera Kowalik and her big . . ."

". . . gobble bozhe gobble whomp year gobble . . ."

She was closer; she was closer.

"All think I'm a kid show them who's a kid bet if Stanley caught me all alone out here in the alley dark and all he wouldn't think I was a kid that damn Vera Kowalik her folks don't think she's a kid . . ."

For all her bravado she was stark terrified when he said: "Hello."

"Who—who—who—?" she stammered.

Quick, before she screamed. Her terror was delightful.

Not too replete to be alert, he cast about, questing.

". . . gobblegobblegobble whomp year."

The countless eyes of the other town, with more than two thousand years of experience in such things, had been following him. What he had sensed as a meaningless hash of noise was actually an impassioned outburst in a nearby darkened house.

"Fools! fools! Now he has taken a virgin! I said not to wait. What will we say to her mother?"

An old man with handlebar mustache and, in spite of the heat, his shirt sleeves decently rolled down and buttoned at the cuffs, evenly replied: "My heart in me died with hers, Casimir, but one must be sure. It would be a terrible thing to make a mistake in such an affair."

The weight of conservative elder opinion was with him. Other old men with mustaches, some perhaps remembering mistakes long ago, nodded and said: "A terrible thing. A terrible thing."

The Mindworm strolled back to his hotel and napped on the made bed briefly. A tingle of danger awakened him. Instantly he cast out:

". . . gobblegobble whompyear."

". . . whampyir."

"WAMPYIR!"

Close! Close and deadly!

The door of his room burst open, and mustached old men with their shirt sleeves rolled down and decently buttoned at the cuffs unhesitatingly marched in, their thoughts a turmoil of alien noises, foreign gibberish that he could not wrap his mind around, disconcerting, from every direction.

The sharpened stake was through his heart and the scythe blade through his throat before he could realize that he had not been the first of his kind; and that what clever people have not yet learned, some quite ordinary people have not yet entirely forgotten.

With These Hands

WHEN Cyril Kornbluth married, it was to a young femmefan from Ohio named Mary G. Byers. Mary was (and is) a sculptor and ceramicist, and the furnishings of their home included a potter's wheel and a kiln, both regularly in use. From Mary Cyril got an understanding of the joys and difficulties of urging shapeless matter to become art. For years I had one of his own ceramics (to be catalogued, he said, as "the Pohl bowl"), until some forgotten guest decided it was an ashtray, and decided to put it on the floor next to his chair and got up in too much of a hurry to notice where he was putting his feet. And from Mary Cyril also got the raw material for *With These Hands*.

I

HALVORSEN WAITED in the Chancery office while Monsignor Reedy disposed of three persons who had preceded him. He was a little dizzy with hunger and noticed only vaguely that the prelate's secretary was beckoning to him. He started to his feet when the secretary pointedly opened the door to Monsignor Reedy's inner office and stood waiting beside it.

The artist crossed the floor, forgetting that he had leaned his portfolio against his chair, remembered at the door and went back for it, flushing. The secretary looked patient.

"Thanks," Halvorsen murmured to him as the door closed.

There was something wrong with the prelate's manner.

"I've brought the designs for the Stations, Padre," he said, opening the portfolio on the desk.

"Bad news, Roald," said the monsignor. "I know how you've been looking forward to the commission—"

"Somebody else get it?" asked the artist faintly, leaning against the desk. "I thought his eminence definitely decided I had the—"

"It's not that," said the monsignor. "But the Sacred Congregation of Rites this week made a pronouncement on images of devotion. Stereopantograph is to be licit within a diocese at the discretion of the bishop. And his eminence—"

"S.P.G.—slimy imitations," protested Halvorsen. "Real as a plastic eye. No texture. No guts. *You* know that, Padre!" he said accusingly.

"I'm sorry, Roald," said the monsignor. "Your work is better than we'll get from a stereopantograph—to my eyes, at least. But there are other considerations."

"Money!" spat the artist.

"Yes, money," the prelate admitted. "His eminence wants to see the St. Xavier U. building program through before he dies. Is that wrong, Roald? And there are our schools, our charities, our Venus mission. S.P.G. will mean a considerable saving on procurement and maintenance of devotional images. Even if I could, I would not disagree with his eminence on adopting it as a matter of diocesan policy."

The prelate's eyes fell on the detailed drawings of the Stations of the Cross and lingered.

"Your St. Veronica," he said abstractedly. "Very fine. It suggests one of Caravaggio's careworn saints to me. I would have liked to see her in the bronze."

"So would I," said Halvorsen hoarsely. "Keep the drawings, Padre." He started for the door.

"But I can't—"

"That's all right."

The artist walked past the secretary blindly and out of the Chancery into Fifth Avenue's spring sunlight. He hoped Monsignor Reedy was enjoying the drawings and was ashamed of himself and sorry for Halvorsen. And he was glad he didn't have to carry the heavy portfolio any more. Everything was heavy lately—chisels, hammer, wooden palette. Maybe the padre would send him something and pretend it was for expenses or an advance, as he had in the past.

Halvorsen's feet carried him up the Avenue. No, there wouldn't be any advances any more. The last steady trickle of income had just been dried up, by an announcement in *Osservatore Romano*. Religious conservatism had carried the church as far as it would go in its ancient role of art patron.

When all Europe was writing on the wonderful new vellum, the church stuck to good old papyrus. When all Europe was writing on the wonderful new paper, the church stuck to good old vellum. When all architects and municipal monument committees and portrait bust clients were patronizing the stereopantograph, the church stuck to good old expensive sculpture. But not any more.

He was passing an S.P.G. salon now, where one of his Tuesday night pupils worked: one of the few men in the classes. Mostly they consisted of lazy, moody, irritable girls. Halvorsen, surprised at himself, entered the salon, walking between asthenic semi-nude stereos executed in transparent plastic that made the skin of his neck and shoulders prickle with gooseflesh.

Slime! he thought. *How can they—*

"May I help—oh, hello, Roald. What brings you here?"

He knew suddenly what had brought him there. "Could you make a little advance on next month's tuition, Lewis? I'm strapped." He took a nervous look around the chamber of horrors, avoiding the man's condescending face.

"I guess so, Roald. Would ten dollars be any help? That'll carry us through to the twenty-fifth, right?"

"Fine, right, sure," he said, while he was being unwillingly towed around the place.

"I know you don't think much of S.P.G., but it's quiet now, so this is a good chance to see how we work. I don't say it's Art with a capital A, but you've got to admit it's *an* art, something people like at a price they can afford to pay. Here's where we sit them. Then you run out the feelers to the reference points on the face. You know what they are?"

He heard himself say dryly: "I know what they are. The Egyptian sculptors used them when they carved statues of the pharaohs."

"Yes? I never knew that. There's nothing new under the Sun, is there? But *this* is the heart of the S.P.G." The youngster proudly swung open the door of an electronic device in the wall of the portrait booth. Tubes winked sullenly at Halvorsen.

"The esthetikon?" he asked indifferently. He did not feel indifferent, but it would be absurd to show anger, no matter how much he felt it, against a mindless aggregation of circuits that could calculate layouts, criticize and correct pictures for a desired effect— and that had put the artist of design out of a job.

"Yes. The lenses take sixteen profiles, you know, and we set the esthetikon for whatever we want—cute, rugged, sexy, spiritual, brainy, or a combination. It fairs curves from profile to profile to give us just what we want, distorts the profiles themselves within limits if it has to, and there's your portrait stored in the memory tank waiting to be taped. You set your ratio for any enlargement or reduction you want and play it back. I wish we were reproducing today; it's fascinating to watch. You just pour in your cold-set plastic, the nozzles ooze out a core and start crawling over to scan—a drop here, a worm there, and it begins to take shape.

"We mostly do portrait busts here, the Avenue trade, but Wilgus, the foreman, used to work in a monument shop in Brooklyn. He did that heroic-size war memorial on the East River Drive—hired Garda Bouchette, the TV girl, for the central figure. And what a figure! He told me he set the esthetikon plates for three-quarters sexy, one-quarter spiritual. Here's something interesting—standing figurine of Orin Ryerson, the banker. He ordered twelve. Figurines are coming in. The girls like them because they can show their shapes. You'd be surprised at some of the poses they want to try—"

Somehow, Halvorsen got out with the ten dollars, walked to Sixth Avenue, and sat down hard in a cheap restaurant. He had coffee and dozed a little, waking with a guilty start at a racket across the street. There was a building going up. For a while he watched the great machines pour walls and floors, the workmen rolling here and there on their little chariots to weld on a wall panel, stripe on an electric circuit of conductive ink, or spray plastic finish over the "wired" wall, all without leaving the saddles of their little mechanical chariots.

Halvorsen felt more determined. He bought a paper from a vending machine by the restaurant door, drew another cup of coffee, and turned to the help-wanted ads.

The tricky trade-school ads urged him to learn construction work and make big money. Be a plumbing-machine setup man. Be a house-wiring machine tender. Be a servotruck driver. Be a lumber-stacker operator. Learn pouring-machine maintenance.

Make big money!

A sort of panic overcame him. He ran to the phone booth and dialed a Passaic number. He heard the *ring-ring-ring* and strained to hear old Mr. Krehbeil's stumping footsteps growing louder as he neared the phone, even though he knew he would hear nothing until the receiver was picked up.

Ring-ring-ring. "Hello?" grunted the old man's voice, and his face appeared on the little screen. "Hello, Mr. Halvorsen. What can I do for you?"

Halvorsen was tongue-tied. He couldn't possibly say: I just wanted to see if you were still there. I was afraid you weren't there any more. He choked and improvised: "Hello, Mr. Krehbeil. It's about the banister on the stairs in my place. I noticed it's pretty shaky. Could you come over sometime and fix it for me?"

Krehbeil peered suspiciously out of the screen. "I could do that," he said slowly. "I don't have much work nowadays. But you can carpenter as good as me, Mr. Halvorsen, and frankly you're very slow pay and I like cabinet work better. I'm not a young man and climbing around on ladders takes it out of me. If you can't find anybody else, I'll take the work, but I got to have some of the money first, just for the materials. It isn't easy to get good wood any more."

"All right," said Halvorsen. "Thanks, Mr. Krehbeil. I'll call you if I can't get anybody else."

He hung up and went back to his table and newspaper. His face was burning with anger at the old man's reluctance and his own foolish panic. Krehbeil didn't realize they were both in the same leaky boat. Krehbeil, who didn't get a job in a month, still thought with senile pride that he was a journeyman carpenter and cabinet-maker who could make his solid way anywhere with his toolbox and his skill, and that he could afford to look down on anything as disreputable as an artist—even an artist who could carpenter as well as he did himself.

Labuerre had made Halvorsen learn carpentry, and Labuerre had been right. You build a scaffold so you can sculp up high, not so it will collapse and you break a leg. You build your platforms so they hold the rock steady, not so it wobbles and chatters at every blow of the chisel. You build your armatures so they hold the plasticine you slam onto them.

But the help-wanted ads wanted no builders of scaffolds, platforms, and armatures. The factories were calling for setup men and maintenance men for the production and assembly machines.

From upstate, General Vegetables had sent a recruiting team for farm help—harvest setup and maintenance men, a few openings for experienced operators of tankcaulking machinery. Under "office and professional" the demand was heavy for computer men, for girls who could run the I.B.M. Letteriter, esp. familiar sales and collections corresp., for office machinery maintenance and repair men. A job printing house wanted an esthetikon operator for letterhead layouts and the like. A.T. & T. wanted trainees to earn while learning telephone maintenance. A direct-mail advertising outfit wanted an artist —no, they wanted a sales-executive who could scrawl picture ideas that would be subjected to the criticism and correction of the esthetikon.

Halvorsen leafed tiredly through the rest of the paper. He knew he wouldn't get a job, and if he did he wouldn't hold it. He knew it was a terrible thing to admit to yourself that you might starve to death because you were bored by anything except art, but he admitted it.

It had happened often enough in the past—artists undergoing preposterous hardships, not, as people thought, because they were devoted to art, but because nothing else was interesting. If there were only some impressive, sonorous word that summed up the aching, oppressive futility that overcame him when he tried to get out of art— only there wasn't.

He thought he could tell which of the photos in the tabloid had been corrected by the esthetikon.

There was a shot of Jink Ditsy, who was to star in a remake of *Peter Pan*. Her ears had been made to look not pointed but pointy, her upper lip had been lengthened a trifle, her nose had been pugged a little and tilted quite a lot, her freckles were cuter than cute, her brows were innocently arched, and her lower lip and eyes were nothing less than pornography.

There was a shot, apparently uncorrected, of the last Venus ship coming in at LaGuardia and the average-looking explorers grinning. Caption: "Austin Malone and crew smile relief on safe arrival. Malone says Venus colonies need men, machines. See story on p. 2."

Petulantly, Halvorsen threw the paper under the table and walked out. What had space travel to do with him? Vacations on the Moon and expeditions to Venus and Mars were part of the deadly encroachment on his livelihood and no more.

II

He took the subway to Passaic and walked down a long-still traffic beltway to his studio, almost the only building alive in the slums near the rusting railroad freightyard.

A sign that had once said "F. Labuerre, Sculptor—Portraits and Architectural Commissions" now said "Roald Halvorsen; Art Classes —Reasonable Fees." It was a grimy two-story frame building with a shopfront in which were mounted some of his students' charcoal figure studies and oil still-lifes. He lived upstairs, taught downstairs front, and did his own work downstairs, back behind dirty, ceiling-high drapes.

Going in, he noticed that he had forgotten to lock the door again. He slammed it bitterly. At the noise, somebody called from behind the drapes: "Who's that?"

"Halvorsen!" he yelled in a sudden fury. "I live here. I own this place. Come out of there! What do you want?"

There was a fumbling at the drapes and a girl stepped between them, shrinking from their dirt.

"Your door was open," she said firmly, "and it's a shop. I've just been here a couple of minutes. I came to ask about classes, but I don't think I'm interested if you're this bad-tempered."

A pupil. Pupils were never to be abused, especially not now.

"I'm terribly sorry," he said. "I had a trying day in the city." Now turn it on. "I wouldn't tell everybody a terrible secret like this, but I've lost a commission. You understand? I thought so. Anybody who'd traipse out here to my dingy abode would be *simpatica*. Won't you sit down? No, not there—humor an artist and sit over there. The warm background of that still-life brings out your color—quite good color. Have you ever been painted? You've a very interesting face, you know. Some day I'd like to—but you mentioned classes.

"We have figure classes, male and female models alternating, on Tuesday nights. For that I have to be very stern and ask you to sign up for an entire course of twelve lessons at sixty dollars. It's the models' fees—they're exorbitant. Saturday afternoons we have still-life classes for beginners in oils. That's only two dollars a class, but you might sign up for a series of six and pay ten dollars in advance, which saves you two whole dollars. I also give private instructions to a few talented amateurs."

The price was open on that one—whatever the traffic would bear. It had been a year since he'd had a private pupil and she'd taken only six lessons at five dollars an hour.

"The still-life sounds interesting," said the girl, holding her head self-consciously the way they all did when he gave them the patter. It was a good head, carried well up. The muscles clung close, not yet slacked into geotropic loops and lumps. The line of youth is heliotropic, he confusedly thought. "I saw some interesting things back there. Was that your own work?"

She rose, obviously with the expectation of being taken into the studio. Her body was one of those long-lined, small-breasted, coltish jobs that the pre-Raphaelites loved to draw.

"Well—" said Halvorsen. A deliberate show of reluctance and then a bright smile of confidence. "*You'll* understand," he said positively and drew aside the curtains.

"What a curious place!" She wandered about, inspecting the drums of plaster, clay, and plasticine, the racks of tools, the stands, the stones, the chisels, the forge, the kiln, the lumber, the glaze bench.

"I *like* this," she said determinedly, picking up a figure a half-meter tall, a Venus he had cast in bronze while studying under Labuerre some years ago. "How much is it?"

An honest answer would scare her off, and there was no chance in the world that she'd buy. "I hardly ever put my things up for sale," he told her lightly. "That was just a little study. I do work on commission only nowadays."

Her eyes flicked about the dingy room, seeming to take in its scaling plaster and warped floor and see through the wall to the abandoned slum in which it was set. There was amusement in her glance.

I am not being honest, she thinks. She thinks that is funny. Very well, I will be honest. "Six hundred dollars," he said flatly.

The girl set the figurine on its stand with a rap and said, half angry and half amused: "I don't understand it. That's more than a month's pay for me. I could get an S.P.G. statuette just as pretty as this for ten dollars. Who do you artists think you are, anyway?"

Halvorsen debated with himself about what he could say in reply:

An S.P.G. operator spends a week learning his skill and I spend a lifetime learning mine.

An S.P.G. operator makes a mechanical copy of a human form distorted by formulae mechanically arrived at from psychotests of population samples. I take full responsibility for my work; it is mine, though I use what I see fit from Egypt, Greece, Rome, the Middle

Ages, the Renaissance, the Augustan and Romantic and Modern Eras.

An S.P.G. operator works in soft, homogeneous plastic; I work in bronze that is more complicated than you dream, that is cast and acid-dipped today so it will slowly take on rich and subtle coloring many years from today.

An S.P.G. operator could not make an Orpheus Fountain—

He mumbled, "Orpheus," and keeled over.

Halvorsen awoke in his bed on the second floor of the building. His fingers and toes buzzed electrically and he felt very clear-headed. The girl and a man, unmistakably a doctor, were watching him.

"You don't seem to belong to any Medical Plans, Halvorsen," the doctor said irritably. "There weren't any cards on you at all. No Red, no Blue, no Green, no Brown."

"I used to be on the Green Plan, but I let it lapse," the artist said defensively.

"And look what happened!"

"Stop nagging him!" the girl said. "I'll pay you your fee."

"It's supposed to come through a Plan," the doctor fretted.

"We won't tell anybody," the girl promised. "Here's five dollars. Just stop nagging him."

"Malnutrition," said the doctor. "Normally I'd send him to a hospital, but I don't see how I could manage it. He isn't on any Plan at all. Look, I'll take the money and leave some vitamins. That's what he needs—vitamins. And food."

"I'll see that he eats," the girl said, and the doctor left.

"How long since you've had anything?" she asked Halvorsen.

"I had some coffee today," he answered, thinking back. "I'd been working on detail drawings for a commission and it fell through. I told you that. It was a shock."

"I'm Lucretia Grumman," she said, and went out.

He dozed until she came back with an armful of groceries.

"It's hard to get around down here," she complained.

"It was Labuerre's studio," he told her defiantly. "He left it to me when he died. Things weren't so rundown in his time. I studied under him; he was one of the last. He had a joke—'They don't really want my stuff, but they're ashamed to let me starve.' He warned me that they wouldn't be ashamed to let *me* starve, but I insisted and he took me in."

Halvorsen drank some milk and ate some bread. He thought of the change from the ten dollars in his pocket and decided not to mention it. Then he remembered that the doctor had gone through his pockets.

"I can pay you for this," he said. "It's very kind of you, but you mustn't think I'm penniless. I've just been too preoccupied to take care of myself."

"Sure," said the girl. "But we can call this an advance. I want to sign up for some classes."

"Be happy to have you."

"Am I bothering you?" asked the girl. "You said something odd when you fainted—'Orpheus.'"

"Did I say that? I must have been thinking of Milles's Orpheus Fountain in Copenhagen. I've seen photos, but I've never been there."

"Germany? But there's nothing left of Germany."

"Copenhagen's in Denmark. There's quite a lot of Denmark left. It was only on the fringes. Heavily radiated, but still there."

"I want to travel too," she said. "I work at LaGuardia and I've never been off, except for an orbiting excursion. I want to go to the Moon on my vacation. They give us a bonus in travel vouchers. It must be wonderful dancing under the low gravity."

Spaceport? Off? Low gravity? Terms belonging to the detested electronic world of the stereopantograph in which he had no place.

"Be very interesting," he said, closing his eyes to conceal disgust.

"I *am* bothering you. I'll go away now, but I'll be back Tuesday night for the class. What time do I come and what should I bring?"

"Eight. It's charcoal—I sell you the sticks and paper. Just bring a smock."

"All right. And I want to take the oils class too. And I want to bring some people I know to see your work. I'm sure they'll see something they like. Austin Malone's in from Venus—he's a special friend of mine."

"Lucretia," he said. "Or do some people call you Lucy?"

"Lucy."

"Will you take that little bronze you liked? As a thank you?"

"I can't do that!"

"Please. I'd feel much better about this. I really mean it."

She nodded abruptly, flushing, and almost ran from the room.

Now why did I do that? he asked himself. He hoped it was because he liked Lucy Grumman very much. He hoped it wasn't a cold-blooded investment of a piece of sculpture that would never be sold, anyway, just to make sure she'd be back with class fees and more groceries.

III

She was back on Tuesday, a half-hour early and carrying a smock. He introduced her formally to the others as they arrived: a dozen or so bored young women who, he suspected, talked a great deal about their art lessons outside, but in class used any excuse to stop sketching.

He didn't dare show Lucy any particular consideration. There were fierce little miniature cliques in the class. Halvorsen knew they laughed at him and his line among themselves, and yet, strangely, were fiercely jealous of their seniority and right to individual attention.

The lesson was an ordeal, as usual. The model, a muscle-bound young graduate of the barbell gyms and figure-photography studios, was stupid and argumentative about ten-minute poses. Two of the girls came near a hair-pulling brawl over the rights to a preferred sketching location. A third girl had discovered Picasso's cubist period during the past week and proudly announced that she didn't *feel* perspective.

But the two interminable hours finally ticked by. He nagged them into cleaning up—not as bad as the Saturdays with oils—and stood by the open door. Otherwise they would have stayed all night, cackling about absent students and snarling sulkily among themselves. His well-laid plans went sour, though. A large and flashy car drove up as the girls were leaving.

"That's Austin Malone," said Lucy. "He came to pick me up and look at your work."

That was all the wedge her fellow-pupils needed.

"*Aus-*tin Ma-*lone! Well!*"

"Lucy, darling, I'd love to meet a real *spaceman*."

"Roald, darling, would you mind very much if I stayed a moment?"

"I'm certainly not going to miss this and I don't care if you mind or not, Roald, darling!"

Malone was an impressive figure. Halvorsen thought: he looks as though he's been run through an esthetikon set for "brawny" and "determined." Lucy made a hash of the introductions and the spaceman didn't rise to conversational bait dangled enticingly by the girls.

In a clear voice, he said to Halvorsen: "I don't want to take up too much of your time. Lucy tells me you have some things for sale. Is there any place we can look at them where it's quiet?"

The students made sulky exits.

"Back here," said the artist.

The girl and Malone followed him through the curtains. The spaceman made a slow circuit of the studio, seeming to repel questions.

He sat down at last and said: "I don't know what to think, Halvorsen. This place stuns me. Do you *know* you're in the Dark Ages?"

People who never have given a thought to Chartres and Mont St. Michel usually call it the Dark Ages, Halvorsen thought wryly. He asked, "Technologically, you mean? No, not at all. My plaster's better, my colors are better, my metal is better—tool metal, not casting metal, that is."

"I mean *hand* work," said the spaceman. "Actually working by *hand.*"

The artist shrugged. "There have been crazes for the techniques of the boiler works and the machine shop," he admitted. "Some interesting things were done, but they didn't stand up well. Is there anything here that takes your eye?"

"I like those dolphins," said the spaceman, pointing to a perforated terra-cotta relief on the wall. They had been commissioned by an architect, then later refused for reasons of economy when the house had run way over estimate. "They'd look bully over the fireplace in my town apartment. Like them, Lucy?"

"I think they're wonderful," said the girl.

Roald saw the spaceman go rigid with the effort not to turn and stare at her. He loved her and he was jealous.

Roald told the story of the dolphins and said: "The price that the architect thought was too high was three hundred and sixty dollars."

Malone grunted. "Doesn't seem unreasonable—if you set a high store on inspiration."

"I don't know about inspiration," the artist said evenly. "But I was awake for two days and two nights shoveling coal and adjusting drafts to fire that thing in my kiln."

The spaceman looked contemptuous. "I'll take it," he said. "Be something to talk about during those awkward pauses. Tell me, Halvorsen, how's Lucy's work? Do you think she ought to stick with it?"

"Austin," objected the girl, "don't be so blunt. How can he possibly know after one day?"

"She can't draw yet," the artist said cautiously. "It's all coordination, you know—thousands of hours of practice, training your eye and hand to work together until you can put a line on paper where you want it. Lucy, if you're really interested in it, you'll learn to draw well. I don't think any of the other students will. They're in it because of boredom or snobbery, and they'll stop before they have their eye–hand coordination."

"I *am* interested," she said firmly.

Malone's determined restraint broke. "Damned right you are. In—" He recovered himself and demanded of Halvorsen: "I understand your point about coordination. But thousands of hours when you can buy a camera? It's absurd."

"I was talking about drawing, not art," replied Halvorsen. "Drawing is putting a line on paper where you want it, I said." He took a deep breath and hoped the great distinction wouldn't sound ludicrous and trivial. "So let's say that art is knowing how to put the line in the right place."

"Be practical. There isn't any art. Not any more. I get around quite a bit and I never see anything but photos and S.P.G.s. A few heirlooms, yes, but nobody's painting or carving any more."

"There's some art, Malone. My students—a couple of them in the still-life class—are quite good. There are more across the country. Art for occupational therapy, or a hobby, or something to do with the hands. There's trade in their work. They sell them to each other, they give them to their friends, they hang them on their walls. There are even some sculptors like that. Sculpture is prescribed by doctors. The occupational therapists say it's even better than drawing and painting, so some of these people work in plasticine and soft stone, and some of them get to be good."

"Maybe so. I'm an engineer, Halvorsen. We glory in doing things the easy way. Doing things the easy way got me to Mars and Venus and it's going to get me to Ganymede. You're doing things the hard way, and your inefficiency has no place in this world. Look at you! You've lost a fingertip—some accident, I suppose."

"I never noticed—" said Lucy, and then let out a faint, "Oh!"

Halvorsen curled the middle finger of his left hand into the palm, where he usually carried it to hide the missing first joint.

"Accidents are a sign of inadequate mastery of material and equipment," said Malone sententiously. "While you stick to your methods and I stick to mine, *you can't compete with me.*"

His tone made it clear that he was talking about more than engineering.

"Shall we go now, Lucy? Here's my card, Halvorsen. Send those dolphins along and I'll mail you a check."

IV

The artist walked the half-dozen blocks to Mr. Krehbeil's place the next day. He found the old man in the basement shop of his fussy house, hunched over his bench with a powerful light overhead. He was trying to file a saw.

"Mr. Krehbeil!" Halvorsen called over the shriek of metal.

The carpenter turned around and peered with watery eyes. "I can't see like I used to," he said querulously. "I go over the same teeth on this damn saw, I skip teeth, I can't see the light shine off it when I got one set. The glare." He banged down his three-cornered file petulantly. "Well, what can I do for you?"

"I need some crating stock. Anything. I'll trade you a couple of my maple four-by-fours."

The old face became cunning. "And will you set my saw? My *saws*, I mean. It's nothing to you—an hour's work. You have the eyes."

Halvorsen said bitterly, "All right." The old man had to drive his bargain, even though he might never use his saws again. And then the artist promptly repented of his bitterness, offering up a quick prayer that his own failure to conform didn't make him as much of a nuisance to the world as Krehbeil was.

The carpenter was pleased as they went through his small stock of wood and chose boards to crate the dolphin relief. He was pleased enough to give Halvorsen coffee and cake before the artist buckled down to filing the saws.

Over the kitchen table, Halvorsen tried to probe. "Things pretty slow now?"

It would be hard to spoil Krehbeil's day now. "People are always fools. They don't know good hand work. Some day," he said apocalyptically, "I laugh on the other side of my face when their foolish machine-buildings go falling down in a strong wind, all of them, all over the country. Even my boy—I used to beat him good, almost every day—he works a foolish concrete machine and his house should fall on his head like the rest."

Halvorsen knew it was Krehbeil's son who supported him by mail, and changed the subject. "You get some cabinet work?"

"Stupid women! What they call antiques—they don't know Meissen, they don't know Biedermeier. They bring me trash to repair sometimes. I make them pay; I swindle them good."

"I wonder if things would be different if there were anything left over in Europe . . ."

"People will still be fools, Mr. Halvorsen," said the carpenter positively. "Didn't you say you were going to file those saws today?"

So the artist spent two noisy hours filing before he carried his crating stock to the studio.

Lucy was there. She had brought some things to eat. He dumped the lumber with a bang and demanded: "Why aren't you at work?"

"We get days off," she said vaguely. "Austin thought he'd give me the cash for the terra-cotta and I could give it to you."

She held out an envelope while he studied her silently. The farce was beginning again. But this time he dreaded it.

It would not be the first time that a lonesome, discontented girl chose to see him as a combination of romantic rebel and lost pup, with the consequences you'd expect.

He knew from books, experience, and Labuerre's conversation in the old days that there was nothing novel about the comedy—that there had even been artists, lots of them, who had counted on endless repetitions of it for their livelihood.

The girl drops in with groceries and the artist is pleasantly surprised; the girl admires this little thing or that after payday and buys it and the artist is pleasantly surprised; the girl brings her friends to take lessons or make little purchases and the artist is pleasantly surprised. The girl may be seduced by the artist or vice versa, which shortens the comedy, or they may get married, which lengthens it somewhat.

It had been three years since Halvorsen had last played out the farce with a manic-depressive divorcée from Elmira: three years during which he had crossed the mid-point between thirty and forty; three more years to get beaten down by being unwanted and working too much and eating too little.

Also, he knew, he was in love with this girl.

He took the envelope, counted three hundred and twenty dollars, and crammed it into his pocket. "That was your idea," he said. "Thanks. Now get out, will you? I've got work to do."

She stood there, shocked.

"I said get out. I have work to do."

"Austin was right," she told him miserably. "You don't care how people feel. You just want to get things out of them."

She ran from the studio, and Halvorsen fought with himself not to run after her.

He walked slowly into his workshop and studied his array of tools, though he paid little attention to his finished pieces. It would be nice to spend about half of this money on open-hearth steel rod and bar stock to forge into chisels; he thought he knew where he could get some—but she would be back, or he would break and go to her and be forgiven and the comedy would be played out, after all.

He couldn't let that happen.

V

Aalesund, on the Atlantic side of the Dourefeld Mountains of Norway, was in the lee of the blasted continent. One more archeologist there made no difference, as long as he had the sense to recognize the propellor-like international signposts that said with their three blades, *Radiation Hazard,* and knew what every schoolboy knew about protective clothing and reading a personal Geiger counter.

The car Halvorsen rented was for a brief trip over the mountains to study contaminated Oslo. Well muffled, he could make it and back in a dozen hours and no harm done.

But he took the car past Oslo, Wennersborg, and Goteborg, along the Kattegat coast to Helsingborg, and abandoned it there, among the three-bladed polyglot signs, crossing to Denmark. Danes were as unlike Prussians as they could be, but their unfortunate little peninsula was a sprout off Prussia that radio-cobalt dust couldn't tell from the real thing. The three-bladed signs were most specific.

With a long way to walk along the rubble-littered highways, he stripped off the impregnated coveralls and boots. He had long since shed the noisy counter and the uncomfortable gloves and mask.

The silence was eerie as he limped into Copenhagen at noon. He didn't know whether the radiation was getting to him or whether he was tired and hungry and no more. As though thinking of a stranger, he liked what he was doing.

I'll be my own audience, he thought. *God knows I learned there isn't any other, not any more. You have to know when to stop. Rodin, the dirty old, wonderful old man, knew that. He taught us not to slick it and polish it and smooth it until it looked like liquid instead of bronze and stone. Van Gogh was crazy as a loon, but he knew when to stop and varnish it, and he didn't care if the paint looked like paint instead of looking like sunset clouds or moonbeams. Up in Hartford, Browne and Sharpe stop when they've got a turret lathe; they don't put caryatids on it. I'll stop while my life is a life, before it becomes a thing with distracting embellishments such as a wife who will come to despise me, a succession of gradually less worthwhile pieces that nobody will look at.*

Blame nobody, he told himself, lightheadedly.

And then it was in front of him, terminating a vista of weeds and bomb rubble—Milles's Orpheus Fountain.

It took a man, he thought. Esthetikon circuits couldn't do it. There was a gross mixture of styles, a calculated flaw that the esthetikon couldn't be set to make. Orpheus and the souls were classic or later; the three-headed dog was archaic. That was to tell you about the antiquity and invincibility of Hell, and that Cerberus knows Orpheus will never go back into life with his bride.

There was the heroic, tragic central figure that looked mighty enough to battle with the gods, but battle wasn't any good against the grinning, knowing, hateful three-headed dog it stood on. You don't battle the pavement where you walk or the floor of the house you're in; you can't. So Orpheus, his face a mask of controlled and suffering fury, crashes a great chord from his lyre that moved trees and stones. Around him the naked souls in Hell start at the chord, each in its own way: the young lovers down in death; the mother down in death; the musician, deaf and down in death, straining to hear.

Halvorsen, walking uncertainly toward the fountain, felt something break inside him, and a heaviness in his lungs. As he pitched forward among the weeds, he didn't care that the three-headed dog was grinning its knowing, hateful grin down at him. He had heard the chord from the lyre.

Shark Ship

DOWN NEAR Union Square in New York City there used to be a store that specialized in whip-&-chain items, mostly photographs of girls in high-heeled boots and black-leather bras tying up other girls in white. There was never a hint of overt sex. Nothing was visible on any of the girls that was not visible on any bathing beach. This kept the proprietors out of jail on pornography charges (this was a *long* time ago). The place fascinated Cyril. He never came to H. L. (*Galaxy*) Gold's place on East Fourteenth Street without stopping in for their latest catalogue on the way. I always assumed that somewhere, somewhen, he would make use of all this . . . and after his death, halfway through "Shark Ship," I came across the sequence involving the decimation of land-based mankind and let out a whoop of recognition.

IT WAS THE SPRING SWARMING of the plankton; every man and woman and most of the children aboard Grenville's Convoy had a job to do. As the seventy-five gigantic sailing ships plowed their two degrees of the South Atlantic, the fluid that foamed beneath their cutwaters seethed also with life. In the few weeks of the swarming, in the few meters of surface water where sunlight penetrated in sufficient strength to trigger photosynthesis, microscopic spores burst into microscopic plants, were devoured by minute animals which in turn were swept into the maws of barely visible sea monsters almost a tenth of an inch from head to tail; these in turn were fiercely pursued and gobbled in shoals by the fierce little brit, the tiny herring and shrimp that could turn a hundred miles of green water to molten silver before your eyes.

Through the silver ocean of the swarming the Convoy scudded and tacked in great controlled zigs and zags, reaping the silver of the sea in the endlessly reeling bronze nets each ship payed out behind.

The Commodore on *Grenville* did not sleep during the swarming; he and his staff dispatched cutters to scout the swarms, hung on the meteorologists' words, digested the endless reports from the scout vessels, and toiled through the night to prepare the dawn signal. The mainmast flags might tell the captains "Convoy course five degrees right," or "Two degrees left," or only "Convoy course: no change." On those dawn signals depended the life for the next six months of the million and a quarter souls of the Convoy. It had not happened often, but it had happened that a succession of blunders reduced a Convoy's harvest below the minimum necessary to sustain life. Derelicts were sometimes sighted and salvaged from such convoys; strong-stomached men and women were needed for the first boarding and clearing away of human debris. Cannibalism occurred, an obscene thing one had nightmares about.

The seventy-five captains had their own particular purgatory to endure throughout the harvest, the Sail-Seine Equation. It was their job to balance the push on the sails and the drag of the ballooning seines so that push exceeded drag by just the number of pounds that would keep the ship on course and in station, given every conceivable variation of wind force and direction, temperature of water, consistency of brit, and smoothness of hull. Once the catch was salted down it was customary for the captains to converge on *Grenville* for a roaring feast by way of letdown.

Rank had its privileges. There was no such relief for the captains' Net Officers or their underlings in Operations and Maintenance, or for their Food Officers, under whom served the Processing and Stowage people. They merely worked, streaming the nets twenty-four hours a day, keeping them bellied out with lines from mast and outriding gigs, keeping them spooling over the great drum amidships, tending the blades that had to scrape the brit from the nets without damaging the nets, repairing the damage when it did occur; and without interruption of the harvest, flash-cooking the part of the harvest to be cooked, drying the part to be dried, pressing oil from the harvest as required, and stowing what was cooked and dried and pressed where it would not spoil, where it would not alter the trim of the ship, where it would not be pilfered by children. This went on for weeks after the silver had gone thin and patchy against the green, and after the silver had altogether vanished.

The routines of many were not changed at all by the swarming season. The blacksmiths, the sailmakers, the carpenters, the watertenders, to a degree the storekeepers, functioned as before, tending to the fabric of the ship, renewing, replacing, reworking. The ships were things of brass, bronze, and unrusting steel. Phosphor-bronze strands were woven into net, lines, and cables; cordage, masts, and hull were metal; all were inspected daily by the First Officer and his men and women for the smallest pinhead of corrosion. The smallest pinhead of corrosion could spread; it could send a ship to the bottom before it had done spreading, as the chaplains were fond of reminding worshippers when the ships rigged for church on Sundays. To keep the hellish red of iron rust and the sinister blue of copper rust from invading, the squads of oilers were always on the move, with oil distilled from the catch. The sails and the clothes alone could not be preserved; they wore out. It was for this that the felting machines down below chopped wornout sails and clothing into new fibers and twisted and rolled them with kelp and with glue from the catch into new felt for new sails and clothing.

While the plankton continued to swarm twice a year, Grenville's Convoy could continue to sail the South Atlantic, from ten-mile limit to ten-mile limit. Not one of the seventy-five ships in the Convoy had an anchor.

The Captain's Party that followed the end of Swarming 283 was slow getting underway. McBee, whose ship was Port Squadron 19, said to Salter of Starboard Squadron 30: "To be frank, I'm too damned exhausted to care whether I ever go to another party, but I didn't want to disappoint the Old Man."

The Commodore, trim /and bronzed, not showing his eighty years, was across the great cabin from them greeting new arrivals.

Salter said: "You'll feel differently after a good sleep. It was a great harvest, wasn't it? Enough weather to make it tricky and interesting. Remember 276? *That* was the one that wore me out. A grind, going by the book. But this time, on the fifteenth day my fore-topsail was going to go about noon, big rip in her, but I needed her for my S-S balance. What to do? I broke out a balloon spinnaker—now wait a minute, let me tell it first before you throw the book at me—and pumped my fore trim tank out. Presto! No trouble; fore-topsail replaced in fifteen minutes."

McBee was horrified. "You could have lost your net!"

"My weatherman absolutely ruled out any sudden squalls."

"Weatherman. You could have lost your net!"

Salter studied him. "Saying that once was thoughtless, McBee. Saying it twice is insulting. Do you think I'd gamble with twenty thousand lives?"

McBee passed his hands over his tired face. "I'm sorry," he said. "I told you I was exhausted. Of course under special circumstances it can be a safe maneuver." He walked to a porthole for a glance at his own ship, the nineteenth in the long echelon behind *Grenville*. Salter stared after him. "Losing one's net" was a phrase that occurred in several proverbs; it stood for abysmal folly. In actuality a ship that lost its phosphor-bronze wire mesh was doomed, and quickly. One could improvise with sails or try to jury-rig a net out of the remaining rigging, but not well enough to feed twenty thousand hands, and no fewer than that were needed for maintenance. Grenville's Convoy had met a derelict which lost its net back before 240; children still told horror stories about it, how the remnants of port and starboard watches, mad to a man, were at war, a war of vicious night forays with knives and clubs.

Salter went to the bar and accepted from the Commodore's steward his first drink of the evening, a steel tumbler of colorless fluid distilled from a fermented mash of sargassum weed. It was about forty per cent alcohol and tasted pleasantly of iodides.

He looked up from his sip and his eyes widened. There was a man in captain's uniform talking with the Commodore and he did not recognize his face. But there had been no promotions lately!

The Commodore saw him looking and beckoned him over. He saluted and then accepted the old man's hand-clasp. "Captain Salter," the Commodore said, "my youngest and rashest, and my best harvester. Salter, this is Captain Degerand of the White Fleet."

Salter frankly gawked. He knew perfectly well that Grenville's Convoy was far from sailing alone upon the seas. On watch he had beheld distant sails from time to time. He was aware that cruising the two-degree belt north of theirs was another convoy and that in the belt south of theirs was still another, in fact that the seaborne population of the world was a constant one billion, eighty million.

But never had he expected to meet face to face any of them except the one and a quarter million who sailed under Grenville's flag.

Degerand was younger than he, all deeply tanned skin and flashing pointed teeth. His uniform was perfectly ordinary and very queer. He understood Salter's puzzled look. "It's woven cloth," he said. "The White Fleet was launched several decades after Grenville's. By then they had machinery to reconstitute fibers suitable for spinning and they equipped us with it. It's six of one and half a dozen of the other. I think our sails may last longer than yours, but the looms require a lot of skilled labor when they break down."

The Commodore had left them.

"Are we very different from you?" Salter asked.

Degerand said: "Our differences are nothing. Against the dirt men we are brothers—blood brothers."

The term "dirt men" was discomforting; the juxtaposition with "blood" more so. Apparently he was referring to whoever it was that lived on the continents and islands—a shocking breach of manners, of honor, of faith. The words of the Charter circled through Salter's head. ". . . return for the sea and its bounty . . . renounce and ab-jure the land from which we . . ." Salter had been ten years old be-fore he knew that there *were* continents and islands. His dismay must have shown on his face.

"They have doomed us," the foreign captain said. "We cannot refit. They have sent us out, each upon our two degrees of ocean in larger or smaller convoys as the richness of the brit dictated, and they have cut us off. To each of us will come the catastrophic storm, the bad harvest, the lost net, and death."

It was Salter's impression that Degerand had said the same words many times before, usually to large audiences.

The Commodore's talker boomed out: "Now hear this!" His huge voice filled the stateroom easily; his usual job was to roar through a megaphone across a league of ocean, supplementing flag and lamp signals. "Now hear this!" he boomed. "There's tuna on the table—big fish for big sailors!"

A grinning steward whisked a felt from the sideboard, and there by Heaven it lay! A great baked fish as long as your leg, smoking hot and trimmed with kelp! A hungry roar greeted it; the captains made for the stack of trays and began to file past the steward, busy with knife and steel.

Salter marveled to Degerand: "I didn't dream there were any left that size. When you think of the tons of brit that old-timer must have gobbled!"

The foreigner said darkly: "We slew the whales, the sharks, the perch, the cod, the herring—everything that used the sea but us. They fed on brit and one another and concentrated it in firm savory flesh like that, but we were jealous of the energy squandered in the long food chain; we decreed that the chain would stop with the link brit-to-man."

Salter by then had filled a tray. "Brit's more reliable," he said. "A Convoy can't take chances on fisherman's luck." He happily bolted a steaming mouthful.

"Safety is not everything," Degerand said. He ate, more slowly than Salter. "Your Commodore said you were a rash seaman."

"He was joking. If he believed that, he would have to remove me from command."

The Commodore walked up to them, patting his mouth with a handkerchief and beaming. "Surprised, eh?" he demanded. "Glasgow's lookout spotted that big fellow yesterday half a kilometer away. He signaled me and I told him to lower and row for him. The boat crew sneaked up while he was browsing and gaffed him clean. Very virtuous of us. By killing him we economize on brit and provide a fitting celebration for my captains. Eat hearty! It may be the last we'll ever see."

Degerand rudely contradicted his senior officer. "They can't be wiped out clean, Commodore, not exterminated. The sea is deep. Its genetic potential cannot be destroyed. We merely make temporary alterations of the feeding balance."

"Seen any sperm whale lately?" the Commodore asked, raising his white eyebrows. "Go get yourself another helping, captain, before it's gone." It was a dismissal; the foreigner bowed and went to the buffet.

The Commodore asked: "What do you think of him?"

"He has some extreme ideas," Salter said.

"The White Fleet appears to have gone bad," the old man said. "That fellow showed up on a cutter last week in the middle of harvest wanting my immediate, personal attention. He's on the staff of the White Fleet Commodore. I gather they're all like him. They've got slack; maybe rust has got ahead of them, maybe they're overbreeding. A ship lost its net and they didn't let it go. They cannibalized rigging from the whole fleet to make a net foɪ it."

"But—"

"But—but—but. Of course it was the wrong thing and now they're all suffering. Now they haven't the stomach to draw lots and cut their losses." He lowered his voice. "Their idea is some sort of raid on the Western Continent, that America thing, for steel and bronze and whatever else they find not welded to the deck. It's nonsense, of course, spawned by a few silly-clever people on the staff. The crews will never go along with it. Degerand was sent to invite us in!"

Salter said nothing for a while and then: "I certainly hope we'll have nothing to do with it."

"I'm sending him back at dawn with my compliments, and a negative, and my sincere advice to his Commodore that he drop the whole thing before his own crew hears of it and has him bowspritted." The Commodore gave him a wintry smile. "Such a reply is easy to make, of course, just after concluding an excellent harvest. It might be more difficult to signal a negative if we had a couple of ships unnetted and only enough catch in salt to feed sixty percent of the hands. Do you think you could give the hard answer under those circumstances?"

"I think so, sir."

The Commodore walked away, his face enigmatic. Salter thought he knew what was going on. He had been given one small foretaste of top command. Perhaps he was being groomed for Commodore—not to succeed the old man, surely, but his successor.

McBee approached, full of big fish and drink. "Foolish thing I said," he stammered. "Let's have drink, forget about it, eh?"

He was glad to.

"Damn fine seaman!" McBee yelled after a couple more drinks. "Best little captain in the Convoy! Not a scared old crock like poor old McBee, 'fraid of every puff of wind!"

And then he had to cheer up McBee until the party began to thin out. McBee fell asleep at last and Salter saw him to his gig before boarding his own for the long row to the bobbing masthead lights of his ship.

Starboard Squadron Thirty was at rest in the night. Only the slowly moving oil lamps of the women on their ceaseless rust patrol were alive. The brit catch, dried, came to some seven thousand tons. It was a comfortable margin over the 5,670 tons needed for six months' full rations before the autumnal swarming and harvest. The trim tanks along the keel had been pumped almost dry by the ship's current prison population as the cooked and dried and salted cubes were stored in the glass-lined warehouse tier; the gigantic vessel rode easily on a swelling sea before a Force One westerly breeze.

Salter was exhausted. He thought briefly of having his cox'n whistle for a bosun's chair so that he might be hauled at his ease up the fifty-yard cliff that was the hull before them, and dismissed the idea with regret. Rank hath its privileges and also its obligations. He stood up in the gig, jumped for the ladder and began the long climb. As he passed the portholes of the cabin tiers he virtuously kept eyes front, on the bronze plates of the hull inches from his nose. Many couples in the privacy of their double cabins would be celebrating the end of the back-breaking, night-and-day toil. One valued privacy aboard the ship; one's own 648 cubic feet of cabin, one's own porthole, acquired an almost religious meaning, particularly after the weeks of swarming cooperative labor.

Taking care not to pant, he finished the climb with a flourish, springing onto the flush deck. There was no audience. Feeling a little ridiculous and forsaken, he walked aft in the dark with only the wind and the creak of the rigging in his ears. The five great basket masts strained silently behind their breeze-filled sails; he paused a moment beside Wednesday mast, huge as a redwood, and put his hands on it to feel the power that vibrated in its steel latticework.

Six intent women went past, their hand lamps sweeping the deck; he jumped, though they never noticed him. They were in something like a trance state while on their tour of duty. Normal courtesies were suspended for them; with their work began the job of survival. One thousand women, five per cent of the ship's company, inspected night and day for corrosion. Sea water is a vicious solvent and the ship had to live in it; fanaticism was the answer.

His stateroom above the rudder waited; the hatchway to it glowed a hundred feet down the deck with the light of a wasteful lantern. After harvest, when the tanks brimmed with oil, one type acted as though the tanks would brim forever. The captain wearily walked around and over a dozen stay-ropes to the hatchway and blew out the lamp. Before descending he took a mechanical look around the deck; all was well—

Except for a patch of paleness at the fantail.

"Will this day never end?" he asked the darkened lantern and went to the fantail. The patch was a little girl in a night dress wandering aimlessly over the deck, her thumb in her mouth. She seemed to be about two years old, and was more than half asleep. She could have gone over the railing in a moment; a small wail, a small splash—

He picked her up like a feather. "Who's your daddy, princess?" he asked.

"Dunno," she grinned. The devil she didn't! It was too dark to read her ID necklace and he was too tired to light the lantern. He trudged down the deck to the crew of inspectors. He said to their chief: "One of you get this child back to her parents' cabin," and held her out.

The chief was indignant. "Sir, we are on watch!"

"File a grievance with the Commodore if you wish. Take the child."

One of the rounder women did, and made cooing noises while her chief glared. "Bye-bye, princess," the captain said. "You ought to be keel-hauled for this, but I'll give you another chance."

"Bye-bye," the little girl said, waving, and the captain went yawning down the hatchway to bed.

His stateroom was luxurious by the austere standards of the ship. It was equal to six of the standard nine-by-nine cabins in volume, or to three of the double cabins for couples. These, however, had something he did not. Officers above the rank of lieutenant were celibate. Experience had shown that this was the only answer to nepotism, and nepotism was a luxury which no convoy could afford. It meant, sooner or later, inefficient command. Inefficient command meant, sooner or later, death.

Because he thought he would not sleep, he did not.

Marriage. Parenthood. What a strange business it must be! To share a bed with a wife, a cabin with two children decently behind their screen for sixteen years . . . what did one talk about in bed? His last mistress had hardly talked at all, except with her eyes. When these showed signs that she was falling in love with him, Heaven knew why, he broke with her as quietly as possible and since then irritably rejected the thought of acquiring a successor. That had been two years ago, when he was thirty-eight, and already beginning to feel like a cabin-crawler fit only to be dropped over the fantail into the wake. An old lecher, a roué, a *user* of women. Of course she had talked a little; what did they have in common to talk about? With a wife ripening beside him, with children to share, it would have been different. That pale, tall quiet girl deserved better than he could give; he hoped she was decently married now in a double cabin, perhaps already heavy with the first of her two children.

A whistle squeaked above his head; somebody was blowing into one of the dozen speaking tubes clustered against the bulkhead. Then a push-wire popped open the steel lid of Tube Seven, Signals. He resignedly picked up the flexible reply tube and said into it: "This is the captain. Go ahead."

"*Grenville* signals Force Three squall approaching from astern, sir."

"Force Three squall from astern. Turn out the fore-starboard watch. Have them reef sail to Condition Charlie."

"Fore-starboard watch, reef sail to Condition Charlie, aye-aye."

"Execute."

"Aye-aye, sir." The lid of Tube Seven, Signals, popped shut. At once he heard the distant, penetrating shrill of the pipe, the faint vibration as one sixth of the deck crew began to stir in their cabins, awaken, hit the deck bleary-eyed, begin to trample through the corridors and up the hatchways to the deck. He got up himself and pulled on clothes, yawning. Reefing from Condition Fox to Condition Charlie was no serious matter, not even in the dark, and Walters on watch was a good officer. But he'd better have a look.

Being flush-decked, the ship offered him no bridge. He conned her from the "first top" of Friday mast, the rearmost of her five. The "first top" was a glorified crow's nest fifty feet up the steel basketwork of that great tower; it afforded him a view of all masts and spars in one glance.

He climbed to his command post too far gone for fatigue. A full moon now lit the scene, good. That much less chance of a green topman stepping on a ratline that would prove to be a shadow and hurtling two hundred feet to the deck. That much more snap in the reefing; that much sooner it would be over. Suddenly he was sure he would be able to sleep if he ever got back to bed again.

He turned for a look at the bronze, moonlit heaps of the great net on the fantail. Within a week it would be cleaned and oiled; within two weeks stowed below in the cable tier, safe from wind and weather.

The regiments of the fore-starboard watch swarmed up the masts from Monday to Friday, swarmed out along the spars as bosun's whistles squealed out the drill—

The squall struck.

Wind screamed and tore at him; the captain flung his arms around a stanchion. Rain pounded down upon his head and the ship reeled in a vast, slow curtsy, port to starboard. Behind him there was a metal sound as the bronze net shifted inches sideways, back.

The sudden clouds had blotted out the moon; he could not see the men who swarmed along the yards but with sudden terrible clarity he felt through the soles of his feet what they were doing. They were clawing their way through the sail-reefing drill, blinded and deafened by sleety rain and wind. They were out of phase by now; they were no longer trying to shorten sail equally on each mast; they were trying to get the thing done and descend. The wind screamed in his face as he turned and clung. Now they were ahead of the job on Monday and Tuesday masts, behind the job on Thursday and Friday masts.

So the ship was going to pitch. The wind would catch it unequally and it would kneel in prayer, the cutwater plunging with a great, deep stately obeisance down into the fathoms of ocean, the stern soaring slowly, ponderously, into the air until the topmost rudder-trunnion streamed a hundred-foot cascade into the boiling froth of the wake.

That was half the pitch. It happened, and the captain clung, groaning aloud. He heard above the screaming wind loose gear rattling on the deck, clashing forward in an avalanche. He heard a heavy clink at the stern and bit his lower lip until it ran with blood that the tearing cold rain flooded from his chin.

The pitch reached its maximum and the second half began, after interminable moments when she seemed frozen at a five-degree angle forever. The cutwater rose, rose, rose, the bowsprit blocked out horizon stars, the loose gear countercharged astern in a crushing tide of bales, windlass cranks, water-breakers, stilling coils, steel sun reflectors, lashing tails of bronze rigging—

Into the heaped piles of the net, straining at its retainers on the two great bollards that took root in the keel itself four hundred feet below. The energy of the pitch hurled the belly of the net open crashing, into the sea. The bollards held for a moment.

A retainer cable screamed and snapped like a man's back, and then the second cable broke. The roaring slither of the bronze links thundering over the fantail shook the ship.

The squall ended as it had come; the clouds scudded on and the moon bared itself, to shine on a deck scrubbed clean. The net was lost.

Captain Salter looked down the fifty feet from the rim of the crow's nest and thought: I should jump. It would be quicker that way.

But he did not. He slowly began to climb down the ladder to the bare deck.

Having no electrical equipment, the ship was necessarily a representative republic rather than a democracy. Twenty thousand people can discuss and decide only with the aid of microphones, loudspeakers, and rapid calculators to balance the ayes and noes. With lungpower the only means of communication and an abacus in a clerk's hands the only tallying device, certainly no more than fifty people can talk together and make sense, and there are pessimists who say the number is closer to five than fifty. The Ship's Council that met at dawn on the fantail numbered fifty.

It was a beautiful dawn; it lifted the heart to see salmon sky, iridescent sea, spread white sails of the Convoy ranged in a great slanting line across sixty miles of oceanic blue.

It was the kind of dawn for which one lived—a full catch salted down, the water-butts filled, the evaporators trickling from their thousand tubes nine gallons each sunrise to sunset, wind enough for easy steerageway and a pretty spread of sail. These were the rewards. One hundred and forty-one years ago Grenville's Convoy had been launched at Newport News, Virginia, to claim them.

Oh, the high adventure of the launching! The men and women who had gone aboard thought themselves heroes, conquerors of nature, self-sacrificers for the glory of NEMET! But NEMET meant only Northeastern Metropolitan Area, one dense warren that stretched from Boston to Newport, built up and dug down, sprawling westward, gulping Pittsburgh without a pause, beginning to peter out past Cincinnati.

The first generation asea clung and sighed for the culture of NEMET, consoled itself with its patriotic sacrifice; any relief was better than none at all, and Grenville's Convoy had drained one and a quarter million population from the huddle. They were immigrants into the sea; like all immigrants they longed for the Old Country. Then the second generation. Like all second generations they had no patience with the old people or their tales. *This* was real, this sea, this gale, this rope! Then the third generation. Like all third generations it felt a sudden desperate hollowness and lack of identity. What was real? Who are we? What is NEMET which we have lost? But by then grandfather and grandmother could only mumble vaguely; the cultural heritage was gone, squandered in three generations, spent forever. As always, the fourth generation did not care.

And those who sat in counsel on the fantail were members of the fifth and sixth generations. They knew all there was to know about life. Life was the hull and masts, the sail and rigging, the net and the evaporators. Nothing more. *Nothing less.* Without masts there was no life. Nor was there life without the net.

The Ship's Council did not command; command was reserved to the captain and his officers. The Council governed, and on occasion tried criminal cases. During the black Winter Without Harvest eighty years before it had decreed euthanasia for all persons over sixty-three years of age and for one out of twenty of the other adults aboard. It had rendered bloody judgment on the ringleaders of Peale's Mutiny. It had sent them into the wake and Peale himself had been bowspritted, given the maritime equivalent of crucifixion. Since then no megalomaniacs had decided to make life interesting for their shipmates, so Peale's long agony had served its purpose.

The fifty of them represented every department of the ship and every age group. If there was wisdom aboard, it was concentrated there on the fantail. But there was little to say.

The eldest of them, Retired Sailmaker Hodgins, presided. Venerably bearded, still strong of voice, he told them:

"Shipmates, our accident has come. We are dead men. Decency demands that we do not spin out the struggle and sink into—unlawful eatings. Reason tells us that we cannot survive. What I propose is an honorable voluntary death for us all, and the legacy of our ship's fabric to be divided among the remainder of the Convoy at the discretion of the Commodore."

He had little hope of his old man's viewpoint prevailing. The Chief Inspector rose at once. She had only three words to say: *"Not my children."*

Women's heads nodded grimly, and men's with resignation. Decency and duty and common sense were all very well until you ran up against that steel bulkhead. *Not my children.*

A brilliant young chaplain asked: "Has the question even been raised as to whether a collection among the fleet might not provide cordage enough to improvise a net?"

Captain Salter should have answered that, but he, murderer of the twenty thousand souls in his care, could not speak. He nodded jerkily at his signals officer.

Lieutenant Zwingli temporized by taking out his signals slate and pretending to refresh his memory. He said: "At 0035 today a lamp signal was made to *Grenville* advising that our net was lost. *Grenville* replied as follows: 'Effective now, your ship no longer part of Convoy. Have no recommendations. Personal sympathy and regrets. Signed, Commodore.'"

Captain Salter found his voice. "I've sent a couple of other messages to *Grenville* and to our neighboring vessels. They do not reply. This is as it should be. We are no longer part of the Convoy. Through our own—lapse—we have become a drag on the Convoy. We cannot look to it for help. I have no word of condemnation for anybody. This is how life is."

The chaplain folded his hands and began to pray inaudibly.

And then a council member spoke whom Captain Salter knew in another role. It was Jewel Flyte, the tall, pale girl who had been his mistress two years ago. She must be serving as an alternate, he thought, looking at her with new eyes. He did not know she was even that; he had avoided her since then. And no, she was not married; she wore no ring. And neither was her hair drawn back in the semi-official style of the semi-official voluntary celibates, the super-patriots (or simply sex-shy people, or dislikers of children) who surrendered their right to reproduce for the good of the ship (or their own convenience). She was simply a girl in the uniform of a—a what? He had to think hard before he could match the badge over her breast to a department. She was Ship's Archivist with her crossed key and quill, an obscure clerk and shelf-duster under—far under!—the Chief of Yeomen Writers. She must have been elected alternate by the Yeomen in a spasm of sympathy for her blind-alley career.

"My job," she said in her calm steady voice, "is chiefly to search for precedents in the Log when unusual events must be recorded and nobody recollects offhand the form in which they should be recorded. It is one of those provoking jobs which must be done by someone but which cannot absorb the full time of a person. I have therefore had many free hours of actual working time. I have also remained unmarried and am not inclined to sports or games. I tell you this so you may believe me when I say that during the past two years I have read the Ship's Log in its entirety."

There was a little buzz. Truly an astonishing, and an astonishingly pointless, thing to do! Wind and weather, storms and calms, messages and meetings and censuses, crimes, trials and punishments of a hundred and forty-one years; what a bore!

"Something I read," she went on, "may have some bearing on our dilemma." She took a slate from her pocket and read: "Extract from the Log dated June 30th, Convoy Year 72. 'The Shakespeare-Joyce-Melville Party returned after dark in the gig. They had not accomplished any part of their mission. Six were dead of wounds; all bodies were recovered. The remaining six were mentally shaken but responded to our last ataractics. They spoke of a new religion ashore and its consequences on population. I am persuaded that we seabornes can no longer relate to the continentals. The clandestine shore trips will cease.' The entry is signed 'Scolley, Captain'."

A man named Scolley smiled for a brief proud moment. His ancestor! And then like the others he waited for the extract to make sense. Like the others he found that it would not do so.

Captain Salter wanted to speak, and wondered how to address her. She had been "Jewel" and they all knew it; could he call her "Yeoman Flyte" without looking like, being, a fool? Well, if he was fool enough to lose his net he was fool enough to be formal with an ex-mistress. "Yeoman Flyte," he said, "where does the extract leave us?"

In her calm voice she told them all: "Penetrating the few obscure words, it appears to mean that until Convoy Year 72 the Charter was regularly violated, with the connivance of successive captains. I suggest that we consider violating it once more, to survive."

The Charter. It was a sort of groundswell of their ethical life, learned early, paid homage every Sunday when they were rigged for church. It was inscribed in phosphor-bronze plates on the Monday mast of every ship at sea, and the wording was always the same.

IN RETURN FOR THE SEA AND ITS BOUNTY WE RENOUNCE AND ABJURE FOR OURSELVES AND OUR DESCENDANTS THE LAND FROM WHICH WE SPRUNG: FOR THE COMMON GOOD OF MAN WE SET SAIL FOREVER.

At least half of them were unconsciously murmuring the words.

Retired Sailmaker Hodgins rose, shaking. "Blasphemy!" he said. "The woman should be bowspritted!"

The chaplain said thoughtfully: "I know a little more about what constitutes blasphemy than Sailmaker Hodgins, I believe, and assure you that he is mistaken. It is a superstitious error to believe that there is any religious sanction for the Charter. It is no ordinance of God but a contract between men."

"It is a Revelation!" Hodgins shouted. "A Revelation! It is the newest testament! It is God's finger pointing the way to the clean hard life at sea, away from the grubbing and filth, from the overbreeding and the sickness!"

That was a common view.

"*What about my children?*" demanded the Chief Inspector. "Does God want them to starve or be—be—" She could not finish the question, but the last unspoken word of it rang in all their minds.

Eaten.

Aboard some ships with an accidental preponderance of the elderly, aboard other ships where some blazing personality generations back had raised the Charter to a powerful cult, suicide might have been voted. Aboard other ships where nothing extraordinary had happened in six generations, where things had been easy and the knack and tradition of hard decision-making had been lost, there might have been confusion and inaction and the inevitable degeneration into savagery. Aboard Salter's ship the Council voted to send a small party ashore to investigate. They used every imaginable euphemism to describe the action, took six hours to make up their minds, and sat at last on the fantail cringing a little, as if waiting for a thunderbolt.

The shore party would consist of Salter, Captain; Flyte, Archivist; Pemberton, Junior Chaplain; Graves, Chief Inspector.

Salter climbed to his conning top on Friday mast, consulted a chart from the archives, and gave the order through speaking tube to the tiller gang: "Change course red four degrees."

The repeat came back incredulously.

"Execute," he said. The ship creaked as eighty men heaved the tiller; imperceptibly at first the wake began to curve behind them.

Ship Starboard 30 departed from its ancient station; across a mile of sea the bosun's whistles could be heard from Starboard 31 as she put on sail to close the gap.

"They might have signaled something," Salter thought, dropping his glasses at last on his chest. But the masthead of Starboard 31 remained bare of all but its commission pennant.

He whistled up his signals officer and pointed to their own pennant. "Take that thing down," he said hoarsely, and went below to his cabin.

The new course would find them at last riding off a place the map described as New York City.

Salter issued what he expected would be his last commands to Lieutenant Zwingli; the whaleboat was waiting in its davits; the other three were in it.

"You'll keep your station here as well as you're able," said the captain. "If we live, we'll be back in a couple of months. Should we not return, that would be a potent argument against beaching the ship and attempting to live off the continent—but it will be your problem then and not mine."

They exchanged salutes. Salter sprang into the whaleboat, signaled the deck hands standing by at the ropes, and the long creaking descent began.

Salter, Captain, age 40; unmarried *ex officio;* parents Clayton Salter, master instrument maintenanceman, and Eva Romano, chief dietician; selected from dame school age 10 for A Track training; seamanship school certificate at age 16, navigation certificate at age 20, First Lieutenants School age 24, commissioned ensign age 24; lieutenant at 30, commander at 32; commissioned captain and succeeded to command of Ship Starboard 30 the same year.

Flyte, Archivist, age 25; unmarried; parents Joseph Flyte, entertainer, and Jessie Waggoner, entertainer; completed dame school age 14, B Track training, Yeoman's School certificate at age 16, Advanced Yeoman's School certificate at age 18, Efficiency rating, 3.5.

Pemberton, Chaplain, age 30; married to Riva Shields, nurse; no children by choice; parents Will Pemberton, master distiller-water-tender, and Agnes Hunt, felter-machinist's mate; completed dame school age 12, B Track training, Divinity School Certificate at age 20; mid-starboard watch curate, later fore-starboard chaplain.

Graves, chief inspector, age 34, married to George Omany, blacksmith third class; two children; completed dame school age 15, Inspectors School Certificate at age 16; inspector third class, second class, first class, master inspector, then chief. Efficiency rating, 4.0; three commendations.

Versus the Continent of North America.

They all rowed for an hour; then a shoreward breeze came up and Salter stepped the mast. "Ship your oars," he said, and then wished he dared countermand the order. Now they would have time to think of what they were doing.

The very water they sailed was different in color from the deep water they knew, and different in its way of moving. The life in it—

"Great God!" Mrs. Graves cried, pointing astern.

It was a huge fish, half the size of their boat. It surfaced lazily and slipped beneath the water in an uninterrupted arc. They had seen steel-gray skin, not scales, and a great slit of a mouth.

Salter said, shaken: "Unbelievable. Still, I suppose in the unfished offshore waters a few of the large forms survive. And the intermediate sizes to feed them—" And foot-long smaller sizes to feed *them,* and—

Was it mere arrogant presumption that Man had permanently changed the life of the sea?

The afternoon sun slanted down and the tip of Monday mast sank below the horizon's curve astern; the breeze that filled their sail bowled them toward a mist which wrapped vague concretions they feared to study too closely. A shadowed figure huge as a mast with one arm upraised; behind it blocks and blocks of something solid.

"This is the end of the sea," said the captain.

Mrs. Graves said what she would have said if a silly under-inspector had reported to her blue rust on steel: "Nonsense!" Then, stammering: "I beg your pardon, Captain. Of course you are correct."

"But it sounded strange," Chaplain Pemberton said helpfully. "I wonder where they all are?"

Jewel Flyte said in her quiet way: "We should have passed over the discharge from waste tubes before now. They used to pump their waste through tubes under the sea and discharge it several miles out. It colored the water and it stank. During the first voyaging years the captains knew it was time to tack away from land by the color and the bad smell."

"They must have improved their disposal system by now," Salter said. "It's been centuries."

His last word hung in the air.

The chaplain studied the mist from the bow. It was impossible to deny it; the huge thing was an Idol. Rising from the bay of a great city, an Idol, and a female one—the worst kind! "I thought they had them only in High Places," he muttered, discouraged.

Jewel Flyte understood. "I think it has no religious significance," she said. "It's a sort of—huge piece of scrimshaw."

Mrs. Graves studied the vast thing and saw in her mind the glyphic arts as practiced at sea: compacted kelp shaved and whittled into little heirloom boxes, miniature portrait busts of children. She decided that Yeoman Flyte had a dangerously wild imagination. Scrimshaw! Tall as a mast!

There should be some commerce, thought the captain. Boats going to and fro. The Place ahead was plainly an island, plainly inhabited; goods and people should be going to it and coming from it. Gigs and cutters and whaleboats should be plying this bay and those two rivers; at that narrow bit they should be lined up impatiently waiting, tacking and riding under sea anchors and furled sails. There was nothing but a few white birds that shrilled nervously at their solitary boat.

The blocky concretions were emerging from the haze; they were sunset-red cubes with regular black eyes dotting them; they were huge dice laid down side by side, each as large as a ship, each therefore capable of holding twenty thousand persons.

Where were they all?

The breeze and the tide drove them swiftly through the neck of water where a hundred boats should be waiting. "Furl the sail," said Salter. "Out oars."

With no sounds but the whisper of the oarlocks, the cries of the white birds, and the slapping of the wavelets they rowed under the shadow of the great red dice to a dock, one of a hundred teeth projecting from the island's rim.

"Easy the starboard oars," said Salter; "handsomely the port oars. Up oars. Chaplain, the boat hook." He had brought them to a steel ladder; Mrs. Graves gasped at the red rust thick on it. Salter tied the painter to a corroded brass ring. "Come along," he said, and began to climb.

When the four of them stood on the iron-plated dock Pemberton, naturally, prayed. Mrs. Graves followed the prayer with half her attention or less; the rest she could not divert from the shocking slovenliness of the prospect—rust, dust, litter, neglect. What went on in the mind of Jewel Flyte her calm face did not betray. And the captain scanned those black windows a hundred yards inboard—no; inland!—and waited and wondered.

They began to walk to them at last, Salter leading. The sensation underfoot was strange and dead, tiring to the arches and the thighs.

The huge red dice were not as insane close up as they had appeared from a distance. They were thousand-foot cubes of brick, the stuff that lined ovens. They were set back within squares of green, cracked surfacing which Jewel Flyte named "cement" or "concrete" from some queer corner of her erudition.

There was an entrance, and written over it: THE HERBERT BROWNELL JR. MEMORIAL HOUSES. A bronze plaque shot a pang of guilt through them all as they thought of The Compact, but its words were different and ignoble.

NOTICE TO ALL TENANTS

A project Apartment is a Privilege and not a Right. Daily Inspection is the Cornerstone of the Project. Attendance at Least Once a Week at the Church or Synagogue of your Choice is Required for Families wishing to remain in Good Standing; Proof of Attendance must be presented on Demand. Possession of Tobacco or Alcohol will be considered Prima Facie Evidence of Undesirability. Excessive Water Use, Excessive Energy Use and Food Waste will be Grounds for Desirability Review. The speaking of Languages other than American by persons over the Age of Six will be considered Prima Facie Evidence of Nonassimilability, though this shall not be construed to prohibit Religious Ritual in Languages other than American.

Below it stood another plaque in paler bronze, an afterthought:

None of the foregoing shall be construed to condone the Practice of Depravity under the Guise of Religion by Whatever Name, and all Tenants are warned that any Failure to report the

Practice of Depravity will result in summary Eviction and De-nunciation.

Around this later plaque some hand had painted with crude strokes of a tar brush a sort of anatomical frame at which they stared in won-dering disgust.

At last Pemberton said: "They were a devout people." Nobody noticed the past tense, it sounded so right.

"Very sensible," said Mrs. Graves. "No nonsense about them."

Captain Salter privately disagreed. A ship run with such dour coer-cion would founder in a month; could land people be that much different?

Jewel Flyte said nothing, but her eyes were wet. Perhaps she was thinking of scared little human rats dodging and twisting through the inhuman maze of great fears and minute rewards.

"After all," said Mrs. Graves, "it's nothing but a Cabin Tier. We have cabins and so had they. Captain, might we have a look?"

"This *is* a reconnaissance," Salter shrugged. They went into a lit-tered lobby and easily recognized an elevator which had long ago ceased to operate; there were many hand-run dumbwaiters at sea.

A gust of air flapped a sheet of printed paper across the chaplain's ankles; he stooped to pick it up with a kind of instinctive outrage—leaving paper unsecured, perhaps to blow overboard and be lost for-ever to the ship's economy! Then he flushed at his silliness. "So much to unlearn," he said, and spread the paper to look at it. A moment later he crumpled it in a ball and hurled it from him as hard and as far as he could, and wiped his hands with loathing on his jacket. His face was utterly shocked.

The others stared. It was Mrs. Graves who went for the paper.

"Don't look at it," said the chaplain.

"I think she'd better," Salter said.

The maintenancewoman spread the paper, studied it and said: "Just some nonsense. Captain, what do you make of it?"

It was a large page torn from a book, and on it were simple polychrome drawings and some lines of verse in the style of a child's first reader. Salter repressed a shocked guffaw. The picture was of a little boy and a little girl quaintly dressed and locked in murderous combat, using teeth and nails. *"Jack and Jill went up the hill,"* said the text, *"to fetch a pail of water. She threw Jack down and broke his crown; it was a lovely slaughter."*

Jewel Flyte took the page from his hands. All she said was, after a long pause: "I suppose they couldn't start them too young." She dropped the page and she too wiped her hands.

"Come along," the captain said. "We'll try the stairs."

The stairs were dust, rat dung, cobwebs, and two human skeletons. Murderous knuckledusters fitted loosely the bones of the two right hands. Salter hardened himself to pick up one of the weapons, but could not bring himself to try it on. Jewel Flyte said apologetically: "Please be careful, Captain. It might be poisoned. That seems to be the way they were."

Salter froze. By God, but the girl was right! Delicately, handling the spiked steel thing by its edges, he held it up. Yes; stains—it *would* be stained, and perhaps with poison also. He dropped it into the thoracic cage of one skeleton and said: "Come on." They climbed in quest of a dusty light from above; it was a doorway onto a corridor of many doors. There was evidence of fire and violence. A barricade of queer pudgy chairs and divans had been built to block the corridor, and had been breached. Behind it were sprawled three more heaps of bones.

"They have no heads," the chaplain said hoarsely. "Captain Salter, this is not a place for human beings. We must go back to the ship, even if it means honorable death. This is not a place for human beings."

"Thank you, chaplain," said Salter. "You've cast your vote. Is anybody with you?"

"Kill your own children, chaplain," said Mrs. Graves. "Not mine."

Jewel Flyte gave the chaplain a sympathetic shrug and said: "No."

One door stood open, its lock shattered by blows of a fire axe. Salter said: "We'll try that one." They entered into the home of an ordinary middle-class death-worshipping family as it had been a century ago, in the one hundred and thirty-first year of Merdeka the Chosen.

Merdeka the Chosen, the All-Foreigner, the Ur-Alien, had never intended any of it. He began as a retail mail-order vendor of movie and television stills, eight-by-ten glossies for the fan trade. It was a hard dollar; you had to keep an immense stock to cater to a tottery Mae Bush admirer, to the pony-tailed screamer over Rip Torn, and to everybody in between. He would have no truck with pinups. "Dirty, lascivious pictures!" he snarled when broadly hinting letters arrived. "Filth! Men and women kissing, ogling, pawing each other! Orgies! Bah!" Merdeka kept a neutered dog, a spayed cat, and a crumpled uncomplaining housekeeper who was technically his wife. He was poor; he was very poor. Yet he never neglected his charitable duties, contributing every year to the Planned Parenthood Federation and the Midtown Hysterectomy Clinic.

They knew him in the Third Avenue saloons where he talked every night, arguing with Irishmen, sometimes getting asked outside to be knocked down. He let them knock him down, and sneered from the pavement. Was *this* their argument? *He* could argue. He spewed facts and figures and clichés in unanswerable profusion. Hell, man, the Russians'll have a bomb base on the moon in two years and in two years the Army and the Air Force will still be beating each other over the head with pigs' bladders. Just a minute, let me tell you: the goddammycin's making idiots of us all; do you know of any children born in the past two years that're healthy? And: 'flu be go to hell; it's our own germ warfare from Camp Crowder right outside Baltimore that got out of hand, and it happened the week of the twenty-fourth. And: the human animal's obsolete; they've proved at M.I.T., Steinwitz and Kohlmann *proved* that the human animal cannot survive the current radiation levels. And: enjoy your lung cancer, friend; for every automobile and its stinking exhaust there will be two-point-seven-oh-three cases of lung cancer, and we've got to have our automobiles, don't we? And: delinquency my foot; they're insane and it's got to the point where the economy cannot support mass insanity; they've got to be castrated; it's the only way. And: they should dig up the body of Metchnikoff and throw it to the dogs; he's the degenerate who invented venereal prophylaxis and since then vice without punishment has run hogwild through the world; what we need on the streets is a few of those old-time locomotor ataxia cases limping and drooling to show the kids where vice leads.

He didn't know where he came from. The delicate New York way of establishing origins is to ask: "Merdeka, hah? What kind of a name is that now?" And to this he would reply that he wasn't a lying Englishman or a loudmouthed Irishman or a perverted Frenchman or a chiseling Jew or a barbarian Russian or a toadying German or a thickheaded Scandihoovian, and if his listener didn't like it, what did he have to say in reply?

He was from an orphanage, and the legend at the orphanage was that a policeman had found him, two hours old, in a garbage can co-incident with the death by hemorrhage on a trolley car of a luetic young woman whose name appeared to be Merdeka and who had certainly been recently delivered of a child. No other facts were es-tablished, but for generation after generation of orphanage inmates there was great solace in having one of their number who indis-putably had got off to a worse start than they.

A watershed of his career occurred when he noticed that he was, for the seventh time that year, reordering prints of scenes from Mr. Howard Hughes's production *The Outlaw*. These were not the off-the-bust stills of Miss Jane Russell, surprisingly, but were group scenes of Miss Russell suspended by her wrists and about to be whipped. Merdeka studied the scene, growled, "Give it to the bitch!" and doubled the order. It sold out. He canvassed his files for other whipping and torture stills from *Desert Song*-type movies, made up a special assortment, and it sold out within a week. Then he knew.

The man and the opportunity had come together, for perhaps the fiftieth time in history. He hired a model and took the first specially posed pictures himself. They showed her cringing from a whip, tied to a chair with a clothesline, and herself brandishing the whip.

Within two months Merdeka had cleared six thousand dollars and he put every cent of it back into more photographs and direct-mail advertising. Within a year he was big enough to attract the post office obscenity people. He went to Washington and screamed in their faces: "My stuff isn't obscene and I'll sue you if you bother me, you stinking bureaucrats! You show me one breast, you show me one behind, you show me one human being touching another in my pic-tures! You can't and you know you can't! I don't believe in sex and I don't push sex, so you leave me the hell alone! Life is pain and suffering and being scared, so people like to look at my pictures; my pictures are about *them,* the scared little jerks! You're just a bunch of goddam perverts if you think there's anything dirty about my pic-tures!"

He had them there; Merdeka's girls always wore at least full pan-ties, bras, and stockings; he had them there. The post office obscenity people were vaguely positive that there was *something* wrong with pictures of beautiful women tied down to be whipped or burned with hot irons, but what?

The next year they tried to get him on his income tax; those deductions for the Planned Parenthood Federation and the Midtown Hysterectomy Clinic were preposterous, but he proved them with canceled checks to the last nickel. "In fact," he indignantly told them, "I spend a lot of time at the Clinic and sometimes they let me watch the operations. *That's* how highly they think of me at the Clinic."

The next year he started *DEATH: the Weekly Picture Magazine* with the aid of a half-dozen bright young grads from the new Harvard School of Communicationeering. As *DEATH's* Communicator in Chief (only yesterday he would have been its Publisher, and only fifty years before he would have been its Editor) he slumped biliously in a pigskin-paneled office, peering suspiciously at the closed-circuit TV screen which had a hundred wired eyes throughout *DEATH's* offices, sometimes growling over the voice circuit: "You! What's your name? Boland? You're through, Boland. Pick up your time at the paymaster." For any reason; for no reason. He was a living legend in his narrow-lapel charcoal flannel suit and stringy bullfighter neckties; the bright young men in their Victorian Revival frock coats and pearl-pinned cravats wondered at his—not "obstinacy"; not when there might be a mike even in the corner saloon; say, his "timelessness."

The bright young men became bright young-old men, and the magazine which had been conceived as a vehicle for deadheading house ads of the mail order picture business went into the black. On the cover of every issue of *DEATH* was a pictured execution-of-the-week, and no price for one was ever too high. A fifty-thousand-dollar donation to a mosque had purchased the right to secretly snap the Bread Ordeal by which perished a Yemenite suspected of tapping an oil pipeline. An interminable illustrated History of Flagellation was a staple of the reading matter, and the Medical Section (in color) was tremendously popular. So too was the weekly Traffic Report.

When the last of the Compact Ships was launched into the Pacific the event made *DEATH* because of the several fatal accidents which accompanied the launching; otherwise Merdeka ignored the ships. It was strange that he who had unorthodoxies about everything had no opinion at all about the Compact Ships and their crews. Perhaps it was that he really knew he was the greatest manslayer who ever lived, and even so could not face commanding total extinction, including that of the seaborne leaven. The more articulate Sokei-an, who in the name of Rinzei Zen Buddhism was at that time depopulating the immense area dominated by China, made no bones about it: "Even I in my Hate may err; let the celestial vessels be." The opinions of Dr. Spät, European member of the trio, are forever beyond recovery due to his advocacy of the "one-generation" plan.

With advancing years Merdeka's wits cooled and gelled. There came a time when he needed a theory and was forced to stab the button of the intercom for his young-old Managing Communicator and growl at him: "Give me a theory!" And the M.C. reeled out: "The structural intermesh of *DEATH: the Weekly Picture Magazine* with Western culture is no random point-event but a rising world-line. Predecessor attitudes such as the Hollywood dogma 'No breasts—blood!' and the tabloid press's exploitation of violence were floundering and empirical. It was Merdeka who sigma-ized the convergent traits of our times and asymptotically congruentizes with them publication-wise. Wrestling and the roller-derby as blood sports, the routinization of femicide in the detective tale, the standardization at one million per year of traffic fatalities, the wholesome interest of our youth in gang rumbles, all point toward the Age of Hate and Death. The ethic of Love and Life is obsolescent, and who is to say that Man is the loser thereby? Life and Death compete in the marketplace of ideas for the Mind of Man—"

Merdeka growled something and snapped off the set. Merdeka leaned back. Two billion circulation this week, and the auto ads were beginning to Tip. Last year only the suggestion of a dropped shopping basket as the Dynajetic 16 roared across the page, this year a hand, limp on the pictured pavement. Next year, blood. In February the Sylphella Salon chain ads had Tipped, with a crash. "—and the free optional judo course for slenderized Madame or Mademoiselle: learn how to kill a man with your lovely bare hands, with or without mess as desired." Applications had risen twenty-eight percent. By *God* there was a structural intermesh for you!

It was too slow; it was still too slow. He picked up a direct-line phone and screamed into it: "Too slow! What am I paying you people for? The world is wallowing in filth! Movies are dirtier than ever! Kissing! Pawing! Ogling! Men and women together—obscene! Clean up the magazine covers! Clean up the ads!"

The person at the other end of the direct line was Executive Secretary of the Society for Purity in Communications; Merdeka had no need to announce himself to him, for Merdeka was S.P.C.'s principal underwriter. He began to rattle off at once: "We've got the Mothers' March on Washington this week, sir, and a mass dummy pornographic mailing addressed to every Middle Atlantic State female between the ages of six and twelve next week, sir; I believe this one-two punch will put the Federal Censorship Commission over the goal line before recess—"

Merdeka hung up. "Lewd communications," he snarled. "Breeding, breeding, breeding, like maggots in a garbage can. Burning and breeding. But we will make them clean."

He did not need a Theory to tell him that he could not take away Love without providing a substitute.

He walked down Sixth Avenue that night, for the first time in years. In this saloon he had argued; outside that saloon he had been punched in the nose. Well, he was winning the argument, all the arguments. A mother and daughter walked past uneasily, eyes on the shadows. The mother was dressed Square; she wore a sheath dress that showed her neck and clavicles at the top and her legs from mid-shin at the bottom. In some parts of town she'd be spat on, but the daughter, never. The girl was Hip; she was covered from neck to ankles by a loose, unbelted sack-culotte. Her mother's hair floated; hers was hidden by a cloche. Nevertheless the both of them were abruptly yanked into one of those shadows they prudently had eyed, for they had not watched the well-lit sidewalk for waiting nooses.

The familiar sounds of a Working Over came from the shadows as Merdeka strolled on. "I mean cool!" an ecstatic young voice—boy's, girl's, what did it matter?—breathed between crunching blows.

That year the Federal Censorship Commission was created, and the next year the old Internment Camps in the southwest were filled to capacity by violators, and the next year the First Church of Merdeka was founded in Chicago. Merdeka died of an aortal aneurism five years after that, but his soul went marching on.

"The Family that Prays together Slays together," was the wall motto in the apartment, but there was no evidence that the implied injunction had been observed. The bedroom of the mother and the father were secured by steel doors and terrific locks, but Junior had got them all the same; somehow he had burned through the steel.

"Thermite?" Jewel Flyte asked herself softly, trying to remember.

First he had got the father, quickly and quietly with a wire garotte as he lay sleeping, so as not to alarm his mother. To her he had taken her own spiked knobkerry and got in a mortal stroke, but not before she reached under her pillow for a pistol. Junior's teenage bones testified by their arrangement to the violence of that leaden blow.

Incredulously they looked at the family library of comic books, published in a series called "The Merdekan Five-Foot Shelf of Classics." Jewel Flyte leafed slowly through one called *Moby Dick* and found that it consisted of a near-braining in a bedroom, agonizingly depicted deaths at sea, and for a climax the eating alive of one Ahab by a monster. "Surely there must have been more," she whispered.

Chaplain Pemberton put down *Hamlet* quickly and held onto a wall. He was quite sure that he felt his sanity slipping palpably away, that he would gibber in a moment. He prayed and after a while felt better; he rigorously kept his eyes away from the Classics after that.

Mrs. Graves snorted at the waste of it all, at the picture of the ugly, pop-eyed, busted-nose man labeled MERDEKA THE CHOSEN, THE PURE, THE PURIFIER. There were *two* tables, which was a folly. Who needed two tables? Then she looked closer, saw that one of them was really a bloodstained flogging bench and felt slightly ill. Its nameplate said *Correctional Furniture Corp. Size 6, Ages 10–14.* She had, God knew, slapped her children more than once when they deviated from her standard of perfection, but when she saw those stains she felt a stirring of warmth for the parricidal bones in the next room.

Captain Salter said: "Let's get organized. Does anybody think there are any of them left?"

"I think not," said Mrs. Graves. "People like that can't survive. The world must have been swept clean. They, ah, killed one another but that's not the important point. This couple had one child, age ten to fourteen. This cabin of theirs seems to be built for one child. We should look at a few more cabins to learn whether a one-child family is—was—normal. If we find out that it was, we can suspect that they are—gone. Or nearly so." She coined a happy phrase: "By race suicide."

"The arithmetic of it is quite plausible," Salter said. "If no factors work except the single-child factor, in one century of five generations a population of two billion will have bred itself down to a hundred and twenty-five million. In another century, the population is just

under four million. In another, a hundred and twenty-two thousand
. . . by the thirty-second generation the last couple descended from
the original two billion will breed one child, and that's the end. And
there are the other factors. Besides those who do not breed by choice"
—his eyes avoided Jewel Flyte—"there are the things we have seen on
the stairs, and in the corridor, and in these compartments."

"Then there's our answer," said Mrs. Graves. She smacked the obscene table with her hand, forgetting what it was. "We beach the ship
and march the ship's company onto dry land. We clean up, we learn
what we have to to get along—" Her words trailed off. She shook her
head. "Sorry," she said gloomily. "I'm talking nonsense."

The chaplain understood her, but he said: "The land is merely another of the many mansions. Surely they could learn!"

"It's not politically feasible," Salter said. "Not in its present form."
He thought of presenting the proposal to the Ship's Council in the
shadow of the mast that bore the Compact, and twitched his head in
an involuntary negative.

"There is a formula possible," Jewel Flyte said.

The Brownells burst in on them then, all eighteen of the Brownells.
They had been stalking the shore party since its landing. Nine sack-
culotted women in cloches and nine men in penitential black, they
streamed through the gaping door and surrounded the sea people
with a ring of spears. Other factors had indeed operated, but this was
not yet the thirty-second generation of extinction.

The leader of the Brownells, a male, said with satisfaction: "Just
when we needed—new blood." Salter understood that he was not
speaking in genetic terms.

The females, more verbal types, said critically: "Evil-doers, obviously. Displaying their limbs without shame, brazenly flaunting the
rotted pillars of the temple of lust. Come from the accursed sea itself,
abode of infamy, to seduce us from our decent and regular lives."

"We know what to do with the women," said the male leader. The
rest took up the antiphon.

"We'll knock them down."

"And roll them on their backs."

"And pull one arm out and tie it fast."

"And pull the other arm out and tie it fast."

"And pull one limb out and tie it fast."

"And pull the other limb out and tie it fast."

"And then—"

"We'll beat them to death and Merdeka will smile."

Chaplain Pemberton stared incredulously. "You must look into your hearts," he told them in a reasonable voice. "You must look deeper than you have, and you will find that you have been deluded. This is not the way for human beings to act. Somebody has misled you dreadfully. Let me explain—"

"Blasphemy," the leader of the females said, and put her spear expertly into the chaplain's intestines. The shock of the broad, cold blade pulsed through him and felled him. Jewel Flyte knelt beside him instantly, checking heart beat and breathing. He was alive.

"Get up," the male leader said. "Displaying and offering yourself to such as we is useless. We are pure in heart."

A male child ran to the door. "Wagners!" he screamed. "Twenty Wagners coming up the stairs!"

His father roared at him: "Stand straight and don't mumble!" and slashed out with the butt of his spear, catching him hard in the ribs. The child grinned, but only after the pure-hearted eighteen had run to the stairs.

Then he blasted a whistle down the corridor while the sea people stared with what attention they could divert from the bleeding chaplain. Six doors popped open at the whistle and men and women emerged from them to launch spears into the backs of the Brownells clustered to defend the stairs. "Thanks, Pop!" the boy kept screaming while the pure-hearted Wagners swarmed over the remnants of the pure-hearted Brownells; at last his screaming bothered one of the Wagners and the boy was himself speared.

Jewel Flyte said: "I've had enough of this. Captain, please pick the chaplain up and come along."

"They'll kill us."

"You'll have the chaplain," said Mrs. Graves. "One moment." She darted into a bedroom and came back hefting the spiked knobkerry.

"Well, perhaps," the girl said. She began undoing the long row of buttons down the front of her coveralls and shrugged out of the garment, then unfastened and stepped out of her underwear. With the clothes over her arm she walked into the corridor and to the stairs, the stupefied captain and inspector following.

To the pure-hearted Merdekans she was not Prynne winning her case; she was Evil incarnate. They screamed, broke and ran wildly, dropping their weapons. That a human being could do such a thing was beyond their comprehension; Merdeka alone knew what kind of monster this was that drew them strangely and horribly, in violation of all sanity. They ran as she had hoped they would; the other side of the coin was spearing even more swift and thorough than would have been accorded to her fully clothed. But they ran, gibbering with fright and covering their eyes, into apartments and corners of the corridor, their backs turned on the awful thing.

The sea people picked their way over the shambles at the stairway and went unopposed down the stairs and to the dock. It was a troublesome piece of work for Salter to pass the chaplain down to Mrs. Graves in the boat, but in ten minutes they had cast off, rowed out a little, and set sail to catch the land breeze generated by the differential twilight cooling of water and brick. After playing her part in stepping the mast, Jewel Flyte dressed.

"It won't always be that easy," she said when the last button was fastened. Mrs. Graves had been thinking the same thing, but had not said it to avoid the appearance of envying that superb young body.

Salter was checking the chaplain as well as he knew how. "I think he'll be all right," he said. "Surgical repair and a long rest. He hasn't lost much blood. This is a strange story we'll have to tell the Ship's Council."

Mrs. Graves said, "They've no choice. We've lost our net and the land is there waiting for us. A few maniacs oppose us—what of it?"

Again a huge fish lazily surfaced; Salter regarded it thoughtfully. He said: "They'll propose scavenging bronze ashore and fashioning another net and going on just as if nothing had happened. And really, we could do that, you know."

Jewel Flyte said: "No. Not forever. This time it was the net, at the end of harvest. What if it were three masts in midwinter, in mid-Atlantic?"

"Or," said the captain, "the rudder—any time. Anywhere. But can you imagine telling the Council they've got to walk off the ship onto land, take up quarters in those brick cabins, change *everything?* And fight maniacs, and learn to *farm?*"

"There must be a way," said Jewel Flyte. "Just as Merdeka, whatever it was, was a way. There were too many people, and Merdeka was the answer to too many people. There's always an answer. Man is a land mammal in spite of brief excursions at sea. We were seed stock put aside, waiting for the land to be cleared so we could return. Just as these offshore fish are waiting very patiently for us to stop harvesting twice a year so they can return to deep water and multiply. What's the way, Captain?"

He thought hard. "We could," he said slowly, "begin by simply sailing in close and fishing the offshore waters for big stuff. Then tie up and build a sort of bridge from the ship to the shore. We'd continue to live aboard the ship but we'd go out during daylight to try farming."

"It sounds right."

"And keep improving the bridge, making it more and more solid, until before they notice it it's really a solid part of the ship and a solid part of the shore. It might take . . . mmm . . . ten years?"

"Time enough for the old shellbacks to make up their minds," Mrs. Graves unexpectedly snorted.

"And we'd relax the one-to-one reproduction rule, and some young adults will simply be crowded over the bridge to live on the land—" His face suddenly fell. "And then the whole damned farce starts all over again, I suppose. I pointed out that it takes thirty-two generations bearing one child apiece to run a population of two billion into zero. Well, I should have mentioned that it takes thirty-two generations bearing four children apiece to run a population of two into two billion. Oh, what's the use, Jewel?"

She chuckled. "There was an answer last time," she said. "There will be an answer the next time."

"It won't be the same answer as Merdeka," he vowed. "We grew up a little at sea. This time we can do it with brains and not with nightmares and superstition."

"I don't know," she said. "Our ship will be the first, and then the other ships will have their accidents one by one and come and tie up and build their bridges, hating every minute of it for the first two generations and then not hating it, just living it . . . and who will be the greatest man who ever lived?"

The captain looked horrified.

"Yes, you! Salter, the Builder of the Bridge; Tommy, do you know an old word for 'bridge-builder'? *Pontifex.*"

"Oh, my God!" Tommy Salter said in despair.

A flicker of consciousness was passing through the wounded chaplain; he heard the words and was pleased that somebody aboard was praying.

Friend to Man

KORNBLUTH'S WRITING concerned mostly the foibles of human beings, and so he seldom gave us an alien being as a character. But there are exceptions, and "Friend to Man" is one.

CALL HIM, if anything, Smith. He had answered to that and to other names in the past. Occupation, fugitive. His flight, it is true, had days before slowed to a walk and then to a crawl, but still he moved, a speck of gray, across the vast and featureless red plain of a planet not his own.

Nobody was following Smith, he sometimes realized, and then he would rest for a while, but not long. After a minute or an hour the posse of his mind would reform and spur behind him; reason would cry no and still he would heave himself to his feet and begin again to inch across the sand.

The posse, imaginary and terrible, faded from front to rear. Perhaps in the very last rank of pursuers was a dim shadow of a schoolmate. Smith had never been one to fight fair. More solid were the images of his first commercial venture, the hijacking job. A truck driver with his chest burned out namelessly pursued; by his side a faceless cop. The ranks of the posse grew crowded then, for Smith had been a sort of organizer after that, but never an organizer too proud to demonstrate his skill. An immemorially old-fashioned garroting-wire trailed inches from the nape of Winkle's neck, for Winkle had nearly sung to the police.

"Squealer!" shrieked Smith abruptly, startling himself. Shaking, he closed his eyes and still Winkle plodded after him, the tails of wire bobbing with every step, stiffly.

A solid, businesslike patrolman eclipsed him, drilled through the throat; beside him was the miraculously resurrected shade of Henderson.

The twelve-man crew of a pirated lighter marched, as you would expect, in military formation, but they bled ceaselessly from their ears and eyes as people do when shot into space without helmets.

These he could bear, but, somehow, Smith did not like to look at the leader of the posse. It was odd, but he did not like to look at her. She had no business there! If they were ghosts why was she there? He hadn't killed her, and, as far as he knew, Amy was alive and doing business in the Open Quarter at Portsmouth. It wasn't fair, Smith wearily thought. He inched across the featureless plain and Amy followed with her eyes.

Let us! Let us! We have waited so long!
Wait longer, little ones. Wait longer.

Smith, arriving at the planet, had gravitated to the Open Quarter and found, of course, that his reputation had preceded him. Little, sharp-faced men had sidled up to pay their respects, and they happened to know of a job waiting for the right touch—

He brushed them off.

Smith found the virginal, gray-eyed Amy punching tapes for the Transport Company, tepidly engaged to a junior executive. The daughter of the Board Chairman, she fancied herself daring to work in the rough office at the port.

First was the child's play of banishing her young man. A minor operation, it was managed with the smoothness and dispatch one learns after years of such things. Young Square-Jaw had been quite willing to be seduced by a talented young woman from the Open Quarter, and had been so comically astonished when the photographs appeared on the office bulletin board!

He had left by the next freighter, sweltering in a bunk by the tube butts, and the forlorn gray eyes were wet for him.

But how much longer must we wait?
Much longer, little ones. It is weak—too weak.

The posse, Smith thought vaguely, was closing in. That meant, he supposed, that he was dying. It would not be too bad to be dead, quickly and cleanly. He had a horror of filth.

Really, he thought, this was too bad! The posse was in front of him—

It was not the posse; it was a spindly, complicated creature that, after a minute of bleary staring, he recognized as a native of the planet.

Smith thought and thought as he stared and could think of nothing to do about it. The problem was one of the few that he had never considered and debated within himself. If it had been a cop he would have acted; if it had been any human being he would have acted, but this—

He could think of nothing more logical to do than to lie down, pull the hood across his face, and go to sleep.

He woke in an underground chamber big enough for half a dozen men. It was egg-shaped and cool, illuminated by sunlight red-filtered through the top half. He touched the red-lit surface and found it to be composed of glass marbles cemented together with a translucent plastic. The marbles he knew; the red desert was full of them, wind-polished against each other for millennia, rarely perfectly round, as all of these were. They had been most carefully collected. The bottom half of the egg-shaped cave was a mosaic of flatter, opaque pebbles, cemented with the same plastic.

Smith found himself thinking clear, dry, level thoughts. The posse was gone and he was sane and there had been a native and this must be the native's burrow. He had been cached there as food, of course, so he would kill the native and possibly drink its body fluids, for his canteen had been empty for a long time. He drew a knife and wondered how to kill, his eyes on the dark circle which led from the burrow to the surface.

Silently the dark circle was filled with the tangled appendages of the creature, and in the midst of the appendages was, insanely, a Standard Transport Corporation five-liter can.

The STC monogram had been worn down, but was unmistakable. The can had heft to it.

Water? The creature seemed to hold it out. He reached into the tangle and the can was smoothly released to him. The catch flipped up and he drank flat, distilled water in great gulps.

He felt that he bulged with the stuff when he stopped, and knew the first uneasy intimations of inevitable cramp. The native was not moving, but something that could have been an eye turned on him.

"Salt?" asked Smith, his voice thin in the thin air. "I need salt with water."

The thing rubbed two appendages together and he saw a drop of amber exude and spread on them. It was, he realized a moment later, rosining the bow, for the appendages drew across each other and he heard a whining, vibrating cricket-voice say: "S-s-z-z-aw-w?"

"Salt," said Smith.

It did better the next time. The amber drop spread, and—"S-z-aw-t?" was sounded, with a little tap of the bow for the final phoneme.

It vanished, and Smith leaned back with the cramps beginning. His stomach convulsed and he lost the water he had drunk. It seeped without a trace into the floor. He doubled up and groaned—once. The groan had not eased him in body or mind; he would groan no more but let the cramps run their course.

Nothing but what is useful had always been his tacit motto. There had not been a false step in the episode of Amy. When Square-Jaw had been disposed of, Smith had waited until her father, perhaps worldly enough to know his game, certain at all events not to like the way he played it, left on one of his regular inspection trips. He had been formally introduced to her by a mutual friend who owed money to a dangerous man in the Quarter, but who had not yet been found out by the tight little clique that thought it ruled the commercial world of that planet.

With precision he had initiated her into the Open Quarter by such easy stages that at no one point could she ever suddenly realize that she was in it or the gray eyes ever fill with shock. Smith had, unknown to her, disposed of some of her friends, chosen other new ones, stage-managed entire days for her, gently forcing opinions and attitudes, insistent, withdrawing at the slightest token of counter-pressure, always urging again when the counter-pressure relaxed.

The night she had taken Optol had been prepared for by a magazine article—notorious in the profession as a whitewash—a chance conversation in which chance did not figure at all, a televised lecture on addiction, and a trip to an Optol joint at which everybody had been gay and healthy. On the second visit, Amy had pleaded for the stuff—just out of curiosity, of course, and he had reluctantly called the unfrocked medic, who injected the gray eyes with the oil.

It had been worth his minute pains; he had got two hundred feet of film while she staggered and reeled loathsomely. And she had, after the Optol evaporated, described with amazed delight how *different* everything had looked, and how exquisitely she had danced . . .

"S-z-aw-t!" announced the native from the mouth of the burrow. It bowled at him marbles of rock salt from the surface, where rain never fell to dissolve them.

He licked one, then cautiously sipped water. He looked at the native, thought, and put his knife away. It came into the burrow and reclined at the opposite end from Smith.

It knows what a knife is, and water and salt, and something about language, he thought between sips. What's the racket?

But when? But when?
Wait longer, little ones. Wait longer.

"You understand me?" Smith asked abruptly.

The amber drop exuded, and the native played whiningly: *"A-ah-nn-nah-t-ann."*

"Well," said Smith, "thanks."

He never really knew where the water came from, but guessed that it had been distilled in some fashion within the body of the native. He had, certainly, seen the thing shovel indiscriminate loads of crystals into its mouth—calcium carbonate, aluminum hydroxide, anything—and later emit amorphous powders from one vent and water from another. His food, brought on half an STC can, was utterly unrecognizable—a jelly, with bits of crystal embedded in it that he had to spit out.

What it did for a living was never clear. It would lie for hours in torpor, disappear on mysterious errands, bring him food and water, sweep out the burrow with a specialized limb, converse when requested.

It was days before Smith really *saw* the creature. In the middle of a talk with it he recognized it as a fellow organism rather than as a machine, or gadget, or nightmare, or alien monster. It was, for Smith, a vast step to take.

Not easily he compared his own body with the native's, and admitted that, of course, his was inferior. The cunning jointing of the limbs, the marvelously practical detail of the eye, the economy of the external muscle system, were admirable.

Now and then at night the posse would return and crowd about him as he lay dreaming, and he knew that he screamed then, reverberatingly in the burrow. He awoke to find the most humanoid of the native's limbs resting on his brow, soothingly, and he was grateful for the new favor; he had begun to take his food and water for granted.

The conversations with the creature were whimsy as much as anything else. It was, he thought, the rarest of Samaritans, who had no interest in the private life of its wounded wayfarer.

He told it of life in the cities of the planet, and it sawed out politely that the cities were very big indeed. He told it of the pleasures of human beings, and it politely agreed that their pleasures were most pleasant.

Under its cool benevolence he stammered and faltered in his ruthlessness. On the nights when he woke screaming and was comforted by it he would demand to know why it cared to comfort him.

It would saw out: *"S-z-lee-p mm-ah-ee-nn-d s-z-ruhng."* And from that he could conjecture that sound sleep makes the mind strong, or that the mind must be strong for the body to be strong, or whatever else he wished. It was *kindness,* he knew, and he felt shifty and rotted when he thought of, say, Amy.

It will be soon, will it not? Soon?
Quite soon, little ones. Quite, quite soon.

Amy had not fallen; she had been led, slowly, carefully, by the hand. She had gone delightfully down, night after night. He had been amused to note that there was a night not long after the night of Optol when he had urged her to abstain from further indulgence in a certain diversion that had no name that anyone used, an Avernian pleasure the penalties against which were so severe that one would not compromise himself so far as admitting that he knew it existed and was practiced. Smith had urged her to abstain, and had most sincerely this time meant it. She was heading for the inevitable collapse, and her father was due back from his inspection tour. The whole process had taken some fifty days.

Her father, another gray-eyed booby . . . A projection room. "A hoax." "Fifty thousand in small, unmarked . . ." The flickering reel change. "It *can't* be—" "You should know that scar." "I'll kill you first!" "That won't burn the prints." The lights. "The last one—I don't believe . . ." "Fifty thousand." "I'll kill you—"

But he hadn't. He'd killed himself, for no good reason that Smith could understand. Disgustedly, no longer a blackmailer, much out of pocket by this deal that had fizzled, he turned hawker and peddled prints of the film to the sort of person who would buy such things. He almost got his expenses back. After the week of concentration on his sudden mercantile enterprise, he had thought to inquire about Amy.

She had had her smashup, lost her job tape-punching now that her father was dead and her really scandalous behavior could no longer be ignored. She had got an unconventional job in the Open Quarter. She had left it. She appeared, hanging around the shops at Standard Transport, where the watchmen had orders to drive her away. She always came back, and one day, evidently, got what she wanted.

For on the Portsmouth–Jamestown run, which Smith was making to see a man who had a bar with a small theater in what was ostensibly a storeroom, his ship had parted at the seams.

"Dumped me where you found me—mid-desert."

"T-urr-ss-t-ee," sawed the native.

There seemed to be some reproach in the word, and Smith chided himself for imagining that a creature which spoke by stridulation could charge its language with the same emotional overtones as those who used lungs and vocal cords.

But there the note was again: "Ei-m-m-ee—t-urr-ss-t—t-oo."

Amy thirst too. A stridulating moralist. But still . . . one had to admit . . . in his frosty way, Smith was reasoning, but a wash of emotion blurred the diagrams, the cold diagrams by which he had always lived.

It's getting me, he thought—it's getting me at last. He'd seen it happen before, and always admitted that it might happen to him—but it was a shock.

Hesitantly, which was strange for him, he asked if he could somehow find his way across the desert to Portsmouth. The creature ticked approvingly, brought in sand, and with one delicate appendage began to trace what might be a map.

He was going to do it. He was going to be clean again, he who had always had a horror of filth and never until now had seen that his life was viler than maggots, more loathsome than carrion. A warm glow of self-approval filled him while he bent over the map. Yes, he was going to perform the incredible hike and somehow make restitution to her. Who would have thought an inhuman creature like his benefactor could have done this to him? With all the enthusiasm of any convert, he felt young again, with life before him, a life where he could choose between fair and foul. He chuckled with the newness of it.

But to work! Good intentions were not enough. There was the map to memorize, his bearings to establish, some portable food supply to be gathered—

He followed the map with his finger. The tracing appendage of the creature guided him, another quietly lay around him, its tip at the small of his back. He accepted it, though it itched somewhat. Not for an itch would he risk offending the bearer of his new life.

He was going to get Amy to a cure, give her money, bear her abuse—she could not understand all at once that he was another man —turn his undoubted talent to an honest—

Farewell! Farewell!
Farewell, little ones. Farewell.

The map blurred a bit before Smith's eyes. Then the map toppled and slid and became the red-lit ceiling of the burrow. Then Smith tried to move and could not. The itching in his back was a torment.

The screy mother did not look at the prostrate host as she turned and crawled up from the incubator to the surface. Something like fond humor wrinkled the surface of her thoughts as she remembered the little ones and their impatience. Heigh-ho! She had given them the best she could, letting many a smaller host go by until this fine, big host came her way. It had taken feeding and humoring, but it would last many and many a month while the little wrigglers grew and ate and grew within it. Heigh-ho! Life went on, she thought; one did the best one could . . .

The Altar at Midnight

THE THING about Kornbluth's characters, James
Blish once said to me, is that so many of them are
working stiffs, and they *sound* like working stiffs;
and how could a middle-class college-going intel-
lectually oriented youngster like Cyril know so
much about how an ex-railway switchman felt
about the world? I knew the answer. He found out
about it from ex-railway switchmen, and all the
rest of the world's invisible men who hang around
a neighborhood bar until they succeed in taking
aboard enough anesthesia to get through another
night. Cyril was endlessly fascinated by barfly
companions. He drank with them, listened to
them, compared notes on the world with them—
and stored them away, until they emerged again
in the pages of a story like this one.

HE HAD quite a rum-blossom on him for a kid, I thought at first. But
when he moved closer to the light by the cash register to ask the bartender for a match or something, I saw it wasn't that. Not just the
nose. Broken veins on his cheeks, too, and the funny eyes. He must
have seen me look, because he slid back away from the light.

The bartender shook my bottle of ale in front of me like a Swiss
bell-ringer so it foamed inside the green glass.

"You ready for another, sir?" he asked.

I shook my head. Down the bar, he tried it on the kid—he was
drinking Scotch and water or something like that—and found out he
could push him around. He sold him three Scotch and waters in ten
minutes.

When he tried for number four, the kid had his courage up and
said, "I'll tell *you* when I'm ready for another, Jack." But there
wasn't any trouble.

It was almost nine and the place began to fill up. The manager, a real hood type, stationed himself by the door to screen out the high-school kids and give the big hello to conventioneers. The girls came hurrying in too, with their little makeup cases and their fancy hair piled up and their frozen faces with the perfect mouths drawn on them. One of them stopped to say something to the manager, some excuse about something, and he said: "That's aw ri'; getcha assina dressing room."

A three-piece band behind the drapes at the back of the stage began to make warmup noises and there were two bartenders keeping busy. Mostly it was beer—a midweek crowd. I finished my ale and had to wait a couple of minutes before I could get another bottle. The bar filled up from the end near the stage because all the cus-tomers wanted a good, close look at the strippers for their fifty-cent bottles of beer. But I noticed that nobody sat down next to the kid, or, if anybody did, he didn't stay long—you go out for some fun and the bartender pushes you around and nobody wants to sit next to you. I picked up my bottle and glass and went down on the stool to his left.

He turned to me right away and said: "What kind of a place is this, anyway?" The broken veins were all over his face, little ones, but so many, so close, that they made his face look something like marbled rubber. The funny look in his eyes was it—the trick contact lenses. But I tried not to stare and not to look away.

"It's okay," I said. "It's a good show if you don't mind a lot of noise from—"

He stuck a cigarette into his mouth and poked the pack at me. "I'm a spacer," he said, interrupting.

I took one of his cigarettes and said: "Oh."

He snapped a lighter for the cigarettes and said: "Venus."

I was noticing that his pack of cigarettes on the bar had some kind of yellow sticker instead of the blue tax stamp.

"Ain't that a crock?" he asked. "You can't smoke and they give you lighters for a souvenir. But it's a good lighter. On Mars last week, they gave us all some cheap pen-and-pencil sets."

"You get something every trip, hah?" I took a good, long drink of ale and he finished his Scotch and water.

"Shoot. You call a trip a 'shoot.'"

One of the girls was working her way down the bar. She was going to slide onto the empty stool at his right and give him the business, but she looked at him first and decided not to. She curled around me and asked if I'd buy her a li'l ole drink. I said no and she moved on to the next. I could kind of feel the young fellow quivering. When I looked at him, he stood up. I followed him out of the dump. The manager grinned without thinking and said, "G'night, boys," to us.

The kid stopped in the street and said to me: "You don't have to follow me around, Pappy." He sounded like one wrong word and I would get socked in the teeth.

"Take it easy. I know a place where they won't spit in your eye."

He pulled himself together and made a joke of it. "This I have to see," he said. "Near here?"

"A few blocks."

We started walking. It was a nice night.

"I don't know this city at all," he said. "I'm from Covington, Kentucky. You do your drinking at home there. We don't have places like this." He meant the whole Skid Row area.

"It's not so bad," I said. "I spend a lot of time here."

"Is that a fact? I mean, down home a man your age would likely have a wife and children."

"I do. The hell with them."

He laughed like a real youngster and I figured he couldn't even be twenty-five. He didn't have any trouble with the broken curbstones in spite of his Scotch and waters. I asked him about it.

"Sense of balance," he said. "You have to be tops for balance to be a spacer—you spend so much time outside in a suit. People don't know how much. Punctures. And you aren't worth a damn if you lose your point."

"What's that mean?"

"Oh. Well, it's hard to describe. When you're outside and you lose your point, it means you're all mixed up, you don't know which way the can—that's the ship—which way the can is. It's having all that room around you. But if you have a good balance, you feel a little tugging to the ship, or maybe you just *know* which way the ship is without feeling it. Then you have your point and you can get the work done."

"There must be a lot that's hard to describe."

He thought that might be a crack and he clammed up on me.

"You call this Gandytown," I said after a while. "It's where the stove-up old railroad men hang out. This is the place."

It was the second week of the month, before everybody's pension check was all gone. Oswiak's was jumping. The Grandsons of the Pioneers were on the juke singing the *Man from Mars Yodel* and old Paddy Shea was jigging in the middle of the floor. He had a full seidel of beer in his right hand and his empty left sleeve was flapping.

The kid balked at the screen door. "Too damn bright," he said.

I shrugged and went on in and he followed. We sat down at a table. At Oswiak's you can drink at the bar if you want to, but none of the regulars do.

Paddy jigged over and said: "Welcome home, Doc." He's a Liverpool Irishman; they talk like Scots, some say, but they sound like Brooklyn to me.

"Hello, Paddy. I brought somebody uglier than you. Now what do you say?"

Paddy jigged around the kid in a half-circle with his sleeve flapping and then flopped into a chair when the record stopped. He took a big drink from the seidel and said: "Can he do this?" Paddy stretched his face into an awful grin that showed his teeth. He has three of them. The kid laughed and asked me: "What the hell did you drag me into here for?"

"Paddy says he'll buy drinks for the house the day anybody uglier than he is comes in."

Oswiak's wife waddled over for the order and the kid asked us what we'd have. I figured I could start drinking, so it was three double Scotches.

After the second round, Paddy started blowing about how they took his arm off without any anesthetics except a bottle of gin because the red-ball freight he was tangled up in couldn't wait.

That brought some of the other old gimps over to the table with their stories.

Blackie Bauer had been sitting in a boxcar with his legs sticking through the door when the train started with a jerk. Wham, the door closed. Everybody laughed at Blackie for being that dumb in the first place, and he got mad.

Sam Fireman has palsy. This week he was claiming he used to be a watchmaker before he began to shake. The week before, he'd said he was a brain surgeon. A woman I didn't know, a real old Boxcar

Bertha, dragged herself over and began some kind of story about how her sister married a Greek, but she passed out before we found out what happened.

Somebody wanted to know what was wrong with the kid's face— Bauer, I think it was, after he came back to the table.

"Compression and decompression," the kid said. "You're all the time climbing into your suit and out of your suit. Inboard air's thin to start with. You get a few redlines—that's these ruptured blood vessels —and you say the hell with the money; all you'll make is just one more trip. But, God, it's a lot of money for anybody my age! You keep saying that until you can't be anything but a spacer. The eyes are hard-radiation scars."

"You like dot all ofer?" asked Oswiak's wife politely.

"All over, ma'am," the kid told her in a miserable voice. "But I'm going to quit before I get a Bowman Head."

I took a savage gulp at the raw Scotch.

"I don't care," said Maggie Rorty. "I think he's cute."

"Compared with—" Paddy began, but I kicked him under the table.

We sang for a while, and then we told gags and recited limericks for a while, and I noticed that the kid and Maggie had wandered into the back room—the one with the latch on the door.

Oswiak's wife asked me, very puzzled: "Doc, w'y dey do dot flyink by planyets?"

"It's the damn govermint," Sam Fireman said.

"Why not?" I said. "They got the Bowman Drive, why the hell shouldn't they use it? Serves 'em right." I had a double Scotch and added: "Twenty years of it and they found out a few things they didn't know. Redlines are only one of them. Twenty years more, maybe they'll find out a few more things they didn't know. Maybe by the time there's a bathtub in every American home and an alcoholism clinic in every American town, they'll find out a whole *lot* of things they didn't know. And every American boy will be a pop-eyed, blood-raddled wreck, like our friend here, from riding the Bowman Drive."

"It's the damn govermint," Sam Fireman repeated.

"And what the hell did you mean by that remark about alcoholism?" Paddy said, real sore. "Personally, I can take it or leave it alone."

So we got to talking about that and everybody there turned out to be people who could take it or leave it alone.

It was maybe midnight when the kid showed at the table again, looking kind of dazed. I was drunker than I ought to be by midnight, so I said I was going for a walk. He tagged along and we wound up on a bench at Screwball Square. The soap-boxers were still going strong. As I said, it was a nice night. After a while, a pot-bellied old auntie who didn't give a damn about the face sat down and tried to talk the kid into going to see some etchings. The kid didn't get it and I led him over to hear the soap-boxers before there was trouble.

One of the orators was a mush-mouthed evangelist. "And oh, my friends," he said, "when I looked through the porthole of the spaceship and beheld the wonder of the Firmament—"

"You're a stinkin' Yankee liar!" the kid yelled at him. "You say one damn more word about can-shootin' and I'll ram your spaceship down your lyin' throat! Wheah's your redlines if you're such a hot spacer?"

The crowd didn't know what he was talking about, but "wheah's your redlines" sounded good to them, so they heckled mushmouth off his box with it.

I got the kid to a bench. The liquor was working in him all of a sudden. He simmered down after a while and asked: "Doc, should I've given Miz Rorty some money? I asked her afterward and she said she'd admire to have something to remember me by, so I gave her my lighter. She seem' to be real pleased with it. But I was wondering if maybe I embarrassed her by asking her right out. Like I tol' you, back in Covington, Kentucky, we don't have places like that. Or maybe we did and I just didn't know about them. But what do you think I should've done about Miz Rorty?"

"Just what you did," I told him. "If they want money, they ask you for it first. Where you staying?"

"Y.M.C.A.," he said, almost asleep. "Back in Covington, Kentucky, I was a member of the Y and I kept up my membership. They have to let me in because I'm a member. Spacers have all kinds of trouble, Doc. Woman trouble. Hotel trouble. Fam'ly trouble. Religious trouble. I was raised a Southern Baptist, but wheah's Heaven, anyway? I ask' Doctor Chitwood las' time home before the redlines got so thick—Doc, you aren't a minister of the Gospel, are you? I hope I di'n' say anything to offend you."

"No offense, son," I said. "No offense."

I walked him to the avenue and waited for a fleet cab. It was almost five minutes. The independent cabs roll drunks and dent the fenders of fleet cabs if they show up in Skid Row and then the fleet drivers have to make reports on their own time to the company. It keeps them away. But I got one and dumped the kid in.

"The Y Hotel," I told the driver. "Here's five. Help him in when you get there."

When I walked through Screwball Square again, some college kids were yelling "wheah's your redlines" at old Charlie, the last of the Wobblies.

Old Charlie kept roaring: "The hell with your breadlines! I'm talking about atomic bombs. *Right—up—there!*" And he pointed at the Moon.

It was a nice night, but the liquor was dying in me.

There was a joint around the corner, so I went in and had a drink to carry me to the club; I had a bottle there. I got into the first cab that came.

"Athletic Club," I said.

"Inna dawghouse, harh?" the driver said, and he gave me a big personality smile.

I didn't say anything and he started the car.

He was right, of course. I was in everybody's doghouse. Some day I'd scare hell out of Tom and Lise by going home and showing them what their daddy looked like.

Down at the Institute, I was in the doghouse.

"Oh, dear," everybody at the Institute said to everybody, "I'm sure I don't know what ails the man. A lovely wife and two lovely grown children and she had to tell him 'either you go or I go.' And *drinking!* And this is rather subtle, but it's a well-known fact that neurotics seek out low company to compensate for their guilt feelings. The *places* he frequents. Doctor Francis Bowman, the man who made space flight a reality. The man who put the Bomb Base on the Moon! Really, I'm sure I don't know what ails him."

The hell with them all.

Dominoes

TWENTY YEARS AGO I was writing a full-scale history of the Great Depression (one of these days I may finish it). When I completed the chapter on the causes of the 1929 stock market crash I showed it to Cyril. He shook his head. "Too complicated," he said. "I bet there was a simpler explanation." And he went home and wrote "Dominoes."

"MONEY!" his wife screamed at him. "You're killing yourself, Will. Pull out of the market and let's go some place where we can live like human—"

He slammed the apartment door on her reproaches and winced, standing in the carpeted corridor, as an ulcer twinge went through him. The elevator door rolled open and the elevator man said, beaming: "Good morning, Mr. Born. It's a lovely day today."

"I'm glad, Sam," W. J. Born said sourly. "I just had a lovely, lovely breakfast." Sam didn't know how to take it, and compromised by giving him a meager smile.

"How's the market look, Mr. Born?" he hinted as the car stopped on the first floor. "My cousin told me to switch from Lunar Entertainment, he's studying to be a pilot, but the *Journal* has it listed for growth."

W. J. Born grunted: "If I knew I wouldn't tell you. You've got no business in the market. Not if you think you can play it like a craps table."

He fumed all through his taxi ride to the office. Sam, a million Sams, had no business in the market. But they were in, and they had built up the Great Boom of 1975 on which W. J. Born Associates was coasting merrily along. For how long? His ulcer twinged again at the thought.

He arrived at 9:15. Already the office was a maelstrom. The clattering tickers, blinking boards, and racing messengers spelled out the latest, hottest word from markets in London, Paris, Milan, Vienna. Soon New York would chime in, then Chicago, then San Francisco.

Maybe this would be the day. Maybe New York would open on a significant decline in Moon Mining and Smelting. Maybe Chicago would nervously respond with a slump in commodities and San Francisco's Utah Uranium would plummet in sympathy. Maybe panic in the Tokyo Exchange on the heels of the alarming news from the States—panic relayed across Asia with the rising sun to Vienna, Milan, Paris, London, and crashing like a shockwave into the opening New York market again.

Dominoes, W. J. Born thought. A row of dominoes. Flick one and they all topple in a heap. Maybe this would be the day.

Miss Illig had a dozen calls from his personal crash-priority clients penciled in on his desk pad already. He ignored them and said into her good-morning smile: "Get me Mr. Loring on the phone."

Loring's phone rang and rang while W. J. Born boiled inwardly. But the lab was a barn of a place, and when he was hard at work he was deaf and blind to distractions. You had to hand him that. He was screwy, he was insolent, he had an inferiority complex that stuck out a yard, but he was a worker.

Loring's insolent voice said in his ear: "Who's this?"

"Born," he snapped. "How's it going?"

There was a long pause, and Loring said casually: "I worked all night. I think I got it licked."

"What do you mean?"

Very irritated: "I said I think I got it licked. I sent a clock and a cat and a cage of white mice out for two hours. They came back okay."

"You mean—" W. J. Born began hoarsely, and moistened his lips. "How many years?" he asked evenly.

"The mice didn't say, but I think they spent two hours in 1977."

"I'm coming right over," W. J. Born snapped, and hung up. His office staff stared as he strode out.

If the man was lying—! No; he didn't lie. He'd been sopping up money for six months, ever since he bulled his way into Born's office with his time machine project, but he hadn't lied once. With brutal frankness he had admitted his own failures and his doubts that the thing ever would be made to work. But now, W. J. Born rejoiced, it had turned into the smartest gamble of his career. Six months and a quarter of a million dollars—a two-year forecast on the market was worth a billion! Four thousand to one, he gloated; four thousand to one! Two hours to learn when the Great Bull Market of 1975 would collapse and then back to his office armed with the information, ready to buy up to the very crest of the boom and then get out at the peak, wealthy forever, forever beyond the reach of fortune, good or bad!

He stumped upstairs to Loring's loft in the West Seventies.

Loring was badly overplaying the role of casual roughneck. Gangling, redheaded, and unshaved, he grinned at Born and said: "Watcha think of soy futures, W. J.? Hold or switch?"

W. J. Born began automatically: "If I knew I wouldn't—oh, don't be silly. Show me the confounded thing."

Loring showed him. The whining generators were unchanged; the tall Van de Graaf accumulator still looked like something out of a third-rate horror movie. The thirty square feet of haywired vacuum tubes and resistances were still an incomprehensible tangle. But since his last visit a phone booth without a phone had been added. A sheet-copper disk set into its ceiling was connected to the machinery by a ponderous cable. Its floor was a slab of polished glass.

"That's it," Loring said. "I got it at a junkyard and fixed it up pretty. You want to watch a test on the mice?"

"No," W. J. Born said. "I want to try it myself. What do you think I've been paying you for?" He paused. "Do you guarantee its safety?"

"Look, W. J.," Loring said, "I guarantee nothing. I *think* this will send you two years into the future. I *think* if you're back in it at the end of two hours you'll snap back to the present. I'll tell you this, though. If it *does* send you into the future, you had better be back in it at the end of two hours. Otherwise you may snap back into the same space as a strolling pedestrian or a moving car—and an H-bomb will be out of your league."

W. J. Born's ulcer twinged. With difficulty he asked: "Is there anything else I ought to know?"

"Nope," Loring said after considering for a moment. "You're just a paying passenger."

"Then let's go." W. J. Born checked to make sure that he had his memorandum book and smooth-working pen in his pocket and stepped into the telephone booth.

Loring closed the door, grinned, waved, and vanished—literally vanished, while Born was looking at him.

Born yanked the door open and said: "Loring! What the devil—" And then he saw that it was late afternoon instead of early morning. That Loring was nowhere in the loft. That the generators were silent and the tubes dark and cold. That there was a mantle of dust and a faint musty smell.

He rushed from the big room and down the stairs. It was the same street in the West Seventies. Two hours, he thought, and looked at his watch. It said 9:55, but the sun unmistakably said it was late afternoon. Something had happened. He resisted an impulse to grab a passing high-school boy and ask him what year it was. There was a newsstand down the street, and Born went to it faster than he had moved in years. He threw down a quarter and snatched a *Post,* dated —September 11th, 1977. He had done it.

Eagerly he riffled to the *Post's* meager financial page. Moon Mining and Smelting had opened at 27. Uranium at 19. United Com at 24. Catastrophic lows! The crash had come!

He looked at his watch again, in panic. 9:59. It had said 9:55. He'd have to be back in the phone booth by 11:55 or—he shuddered. An H-bomb would be out of his league.

Now to pinpoint the crash. "Cab!" he yelled, waving his paper. It eased to the curb. "Public library," W. J. Born grunted, and leaned back to read the *Post* with glee.

The headline said: 25000 RIOT HERE FOR UPPED JOBLESS DOLE. Naturally; naturally. He gasped as he saw who had won the 1976 presidential election. Lord, what odds he'd be able to get back in 1975 if he wanted to bet on the nomination! NO CRIME WAVE, SAYS COMMISSIONER. Things hadn't changed very much after all. BLONDE MODEL HACKED IN TUB; MYSTERY BOYFRIEND SOUGHT. He read that one all the way through, caught by a two-column photo of the blonde model for a hosiery account. And then he noticed that the cab wasn't moving. It was caught in a rock-solid traffic jam. The time was 10:05.

"Driver," he said.

The man turned around, soothing and scared. A fare was a fare;

there was a depression on. "It's all right, mister. We'll be out of here in a minute. They turn off the Drive and that blocks the avenue for a couple of minutes, that's all. We'll be rolling in a minute."

They were rolling in a minute, but for a few seconds only. The cab inched agonizingly along while W. J. Born twisted the newspaper in his hands. At 10:13 he threw a bill at the driver and jumped from the cab.

Panting, he reached the library at 10:46 by his watch. By the time that the rest of the world was keeping on that day it was quitting-time in the midtown offices. He had bucked a stream of girls in surprisingly short skirts and surprisingly big hats all the way.

He got lost in the marble immensities of the library and his own panic. When he found the newspaper room his watch said 11:03. W. J. Born panted to the girl at the desk: "File of the *Stock Exchange Journal* for 1975, 1976 and 1977."

"We have the microfilms for 1975 and 1976, sir, and loose copies for this year."

"Tell me," he said, "what year for the big crash? That's what I want to look up."

"That's 1975, sir. Shall I get you that?"

"Wait," he said. "Do you happen to remember the month?"

"I think it was March or August or something like that, sir."

"Get me the whole file, please," he said. Nineteen seventy-five. His year—his real year. Would he have a month? A week? Or—?

"Sign this card, mister," the girl was saying patiently. "There's a reading machine, you just go sit there and I'll bring you the spool."

He scribbled his name and went to the machine, the only one vacant in a row of a dozen. The time on his watch was 11:05. He had fifty minutes.

The girl dawdled over cards at her desk and chatted with a good-looking young page with a stack of books while sweat began to pop from Born's brow. At last she disappeared into the stacks behind her desk.

Born waited. And waited. And waited. Eleven-ten. Eleven-fifteen. Eleven-twenty.

An H-bomb would be out of his league.

His ulcer stabbed him as the girl appeared again, daintily carrying a spool of 35-millimeter film between thumb and forefinger, smiling brightly at Born. "Here we are," she said, and inserted the spool in the machine and snapped a switch. Nothing happened.

"Oh, darn," she said. "The light's out. I *told* the electrician."

Born wanted to scream and then to explain, which would have been just as foolish.

"There's a free reader," she pointed down the line. W. J. Born's knees tottered as they walked to it. He looked at his watch—11:27. Twenty-eight minutes to go. The ground-glass screen lit up with a shadow of the familiar format; January 1st, 1975. "You just turn the crank," she said, and showed him. The shadows spun past on the screen at dizzying speed, and she went back to her desk.

Born cranked the film up to April 1975, the month he had left 91 minutes ago, and to the sixteenth day of April, the very day he had left. The shadow on the ground glass was the same paper he had seen that morning: SYNTHETICS SURGE TO NEW VIENNA PEAK.

Trembling he cranked into a vision of the future; the *Stock Exchange Journal* for April 17th, 1975.

Three-inch type screamed: SECURITIES CRASH IN GLOBAL CRISIS: BANKS CLOSE; CLIENTS STORM BROKERAGES!

Suddenly he was calm, knowing the future and safe from its blows. He rose from the reader and strode firmly into the marble halls. Everything was all right now. Twenty-six minutes was time enough to get back to the machine. He'd have a jump of several hours on the market; his own money would be safe as houses; he could get his personal clients off the hook.

He got a cab with miraculous ease and rolled straight to the loft building in the West Seventies without hindrance. At 11:50 by his watch he was closing the door of the phone booth in the dusty, musty-smelling lab.

At 11:54 he noticed an abrupt change in the sunlight that filtered through the dirt-streaked windows and stepped calmly out. It was April 16th, 1975, again. Loring was sound asleep beside a gas hotplate on which coffee simmered. W. J. Born turned off the gas and went downstairs softly. Loring was a screwy, insolent, insecure young man, but by his genius he had enabled W. J. Born to harvest his fortune at the golden moment of perfection.

Back in his office he called his floor broker and said firmly: "Cronin, get this straight. I want you to sell every share of stock and every bond in my personal account immediately, at the market, and to require certified checks in payment."

Cronin asked forthrightly: "Chief, have you gone crazy?"

"I have not. Don't waste a moment, and report regularly to me. Get your boys to work. Drop everything else."

Born had a light, bland lunch sent in and refused to see anybody or take any calls except from the floor broker. Cronin kept reporting that the dumping was going right along, that Mr. Born must be crazy, that the unheard-of demand for certified checks was causing alarm, and finally, at the close, that Mr. Born's wishes were being carried out. Born told him to get the checks to him immediately.

They arrived in an hour, drawn on a dozen New York banks. W. J. Born called in a dozen senior messengers, and dealt out the checks, one bank to a messenger. He told them to withdraw the cash, rent safe-deposit boxes of the necessary sizes in those banks where he did not already have boxes, and deposit the cash.

He then phoned the banks to confirm the weird arrangement. He was on first-name terms with at least one vice president in each bank, which helped enormously.

W. J. Born leaned back, a happy man. Let the smash come. He turned on his flashboard for the first time that day. The New York closing was sharply off. Chicago was worse. San Francisco was shaky —as he watched, the flashing figures on the composite price index at San Francisco began to drop. In five minutes it was a screaming nosedive into the pit. The closing bell stopped it short of catastrophe.

W. J. Born went out to dinner after phoning his wife that he would not be home. He returned to the office and watched a board in one of the outer rooms that carried Tokyo Exchange through the night hours, and congratulated himself as the figures told a tale of panic and ruin. The dominoes were toppling, toppling, toppling.

He went to his club for the night and woke early, eating alone in an almost-deserted breakfast room. The ticker in the lobby sputtered a good morning as he drew on his gloves against the chilly April dawn. He stopped to watch. The ticker began spewing a tale of disaster on the great bourses of Europe, and Mr. Born walked to his office. Brokers a-plenty were arriving early, muttering in little crowds in the lobby and elevators.

"What do you make of it, Born?" one of them asked.

"What goes up must come down," he said. "*I'm* safely out."

"So I hear," the man told him, with a look that Born decided was envious.

Vienna, Milan, Paris, and London were telling their sorry story on the boards in the customers' rooms. There were a few clients silting up the place already, and the night staff had been busy taking orders by phone for the opening. They all were to sell at the market.

W. J. Born grinned at one of the night men and cracked a rare joke: "Want to buy a brokerage house, Willard?"

Willard glanced at the board and said: "No thanks, Mr. Born. But it was nice of you to keep me in mind."

Most of the staff drifted in early; the sense of crisis was heavy in the air. Born instructed his staff to do what they could for his personal clients first, and holed up in his office.

The opening bell was the signal for hell to break loose. The tickers never had the ghost of a chance of keeping up with the crash, unquestionably the biggest and steepest in the history of finance. Born got some pleasure out of the fact that his boys' promptness had cut the losses of his personal clients a little. A very important banker called in midmorning to ask Born into a billion-dollar pool that would shore up the market by a show of confidence. Born said no, knowing that no show of confidence would keep Moon Mining and Smelting from opening at 27 on September 11th, 1977. The banker hung up abruptly.

Miss Illig asked: "Do you want to see Mr. Loring? He's here."

"Send him in."

Loring was deathly pale, with a copy of the *Journal* rolled up in his fist. "I need some money," he said.

W. J. Born shook his head. "You see what's going on," he said. "Money's tight. I've enjoyed our association, Loring, but I think it's time to end it. You've had a quarter of a million dollars clear; I make no claims on your process—"

"It's gone," Loring said hoarsely. "I haven't paid for the damn equipment—not ten cents on the dollar yet. I've been playing the market. I lost a hundred and fifty thousand on soy futures this morning. They'll dismantle my stuff and haul it away. I've got to have some money."

"*No!*" W. J. Born barked. "Absolutely not!"

"They'll come with a truck for the generators this afternoon. I stalled them. My stocks kept going up. And now—all I wanted was enough in reserve to keep working. *I've got to have money."*

"No," said Born. "After all, it's not my fault."

Loring's ugly face was close to his. "Isn't it?" he snarled. And he spread out the paper on the desk.

Born read the headline—again—of the *Stock Exchange Journal* for April 17th, 1975: SECURITIES CRASH IN GLOBAL CRISIS: BANKS CLOSE; CLIENTS STORM BROKERAGES! But this time he was not too rushed to read on: "A world-wide slump in securities has wiped out billions of paper dollars since it started shortly before closing yesterday at the New York Stock Exchange. No end to the catastrophic flood of sell orders is yet in sight. Veteran New York observers agreed that dumping of securities on the New York market late yesterday by W. J. Born of W. J. Born Associates pulled the plug out of the big boom which must now be consigned to memory. Banks have been hard-hit by the—"

"Isn't it?" Loring snarled. "Isn't it?" His eyes were crazy as he reached for Born's thin neck.

Dominoes, W. J. Born thought vaguely through the pain, and managed to hit a button on his desk. Miss Illig came in and screamed and went out again and came back with a couple of husky customers' men, but it was too late.

Two Dooms

JUST BEFORE his death, Cyril finished two major pieces of work. One was the final revision of our last novel in collaboration, *Wolfbane*. The other was this. Cyril's name for the story was "The Doomsman," and it was accepted under that title by *The Magazine of Fantasy and Science Fiction*. But he died before it was published. Under the circumstances, the editor thought that title ghoulish, and so he changed it. There have been any number of sf stories since about what would have happened if the Germans and the Japanese had won World War II, but this was one of the first—and one of the best.

IT WAS MAY, not yet summer by five weeks, but the afternoon heat under the corrugated roofs of Manhattan Engineer District's Los Alamos Laboratory was daily less bearable. Young Dr. Edward Royland had lost fifteen pounds from an already meager frame during his nine-month hitch in the desert. He wondered every day while the thermometer crawled up to its 5:45 peak whether he had made a mistake he would regret the rest of his life in accepting work with the Laboratory rather than letting the local draft board have his carcass and do what they pleased with it. His University of Chicago classmates were glamorously collecting ribbons and wounds from Saipan to Brussels; one of them, a first-rate mathematician named Hatfield, would do no more first-rate mathematics. He had gone down, burning, in an Eighth Air Force Mitchell bomber ambushed over Lille.

"And what, Daddy, did you do in the war?"

"Well, kids, it's a little hard to explain. They had this stupid atomic bomb project that never came to anything, and they tied up a lot of us in a Godforsaken place in New Mexico. We figured and we calcu-

lated and we fooled with uranium and some of us got radiation burns
and then the war was over and they sent us home."

Royland was not amused by this prospect. He had heat rash under
his arms and he was waiting, not patiently, for the Computer Section
to send him his figures on Phase 56c, which was the (god-damn
childish) code designation for Element Assembly Time. Phase 56c
was Royland's own particular baby. He was under Rotschmidt, su-
pervisor of WEAPON DESIGN TRACK III, and Rotschmidt was under
Oppenheimer, who bossed the works. Sometimes a General Groves
came through, a fine figure of a man, and once from a window
Royland had seen the venerable Henry L. Stimson, Secretary of War,
walking slowly down their dusty street, leaning on a cane and surrounded by young staff officers. That's what Royland was seeing of
the war.

Laboratory! It had sounded inviting, cool, bustling but quiet. So
every morning these days he was blasted out of his cot in a barracks
cubicle at seven by "Oppie's whistle," fought for a shower and shave
with thirty-seven other bachelor scientists in eight languages, bolted a
bad cafeteria breakfast, and went through the barbed-wire Restricted
Line to his "office"—another matchboard-walled cubicle, smaller and
hotter and noisier, with talking and typing and clack of adding machines all around him.

Under the circumstances he was doing good work, he supposed.
He wasn't happy about being restricted to his one tiny problem,
Phase 56c, but no doubt he was happier than Hatfield had been when
his Mitchell got it.

Under the circumstances . . . they included a weird haywire arrangement for computing. Instead of a decent differential analyzer
machine they had a human sea of office girls with Burroughs' desk
calculators; the girls screamed "Banzai!" and charged on differential
equations and swamped them by sheer volume; they clicked them to
death with their little adding machines. Royland thought hungrily of
Conant's huge, beautiful analog differentiator up at M.I.T.; it was
probably tied up by whatever the mysterious "Radiation Laboratory"
there was doing. Royland suspected that the "Radiation Laboratory"
had as much to do with radiation as his own "Manhattan Engineer
District" had to do with Manhattan engineering. And the world was
supposed to be trembling on the edge these days of a New Dispen-
sation of Computing that would obsolete even the M.I.T. machine—

tubes, relays, and binary arithmetic at blinding speed instead of the suavely turning cams and the smoothly extruding rods and the elegant scribed curves of Conant's masterpiece. He decided that he wouldn't like that; he would like it even less than he liked the little office girls clacking away, pushing lank hair from their dewed brows with undistracted hands.

He wiped his own brow with a sodden handkerchief and permitted himself a glance at his watch and the thermometer. Five-fifteen and 103 Fahrenheit.

He thought vaguely of getting out, of fouling up just enough to be released from the project and drafted. No; there was the post-war career to think of. But one of the big shots, Teller, had been irrepressible; he had rambled outside of his assigned mission again and again until Oppenheimer let him go; now Teller was working with Lawrence at Berkeley on something that had reputedly gone sour at a reputed quarter of a billion dollars—

A girl in khaki knocked and entered. "Your material from the Computer Section, Dr. Royland. Check them and sign here, please." He counted the dozen sheets, signed the clipboarded form she held out, and plunged into the material for thirty minutes.

When he sat back in his chair, the sweat dripped into his eyes unnoticed. His hands were shaking a little, though he did not know that either. Phase 56c of WEAPON DESIGN TRACK III was finished, over, done, successfully accomplished. The answer to the question "Can U_{235} slugs be assembled into a critical mass within a physically feasible time?" was in. The answer was "Yes."

Royland was a theory man, not a Wheatstone or a Kelvin; he liked the numbers for themselves and had no special passion to grab for wires, mica, and bits of graphite so that what the numbers said might immediately be given flesh in a wonderful new gadget. Nevertheless he could visualize at once a workable atomic bomb assembly within the framework of Phase 56c. You have so many microseconds to assemble your critical mass without it boiling away in vapor; you use them by blowing the subassemblies together with shaped charges; lots of microseconds to spare by that method; practically foolproof. Then comes the Big Bang.

Oppie's whistle blew; it was quitting time. Royland sat still in his cubicle. He should go, of course, to Rotschmidt and tell him; Rotschmidt would probably clap him on the back and pour him a jigger of Bols Geneva from the tall clay bottle he kept in his safe. Then Rotschmidt would go to Oppenheimer. Before sunset the project would be redesigned! TRACK I, TRACK II, TRACK IV, and TRACK V would be shut down and their people crammed into TRACK III, the one with the paydirt! New excitement would boil through the project; it had been torpid and souring for three months. Phase 56c was the first good news in at least that long; it had been one damned blind alley after another. General Groves had looked sour and dubious last time around.

Desk drawers were slamming throughout the corrugated, sun-baked building; doors were slamming shut on cubicles; down the corridor, somebody roared with laughter, strained laughter. Passing Royland's door somebody cried impatiently: *"—aber was kan Man tun?"*

Royland whispered to himself: "You damned fool, what are you thinking of?"

But he knew—he was thinking of the Big Bang, the Big Dirty Bang, and of torture. The judicial torture of the old days, incredibly cruel by today's lights, stretched the whole body, or crushed it, or burned it, or shattered the fingers and legs. But even that old judicial torture carefully avoided the most sensitive parts of the body, the generative organs, though damage to these, or a real threat of damage to these, would have produced quick and copious confessions. You have to be more or less crazy to torture somebody that way; the sane man does not think of it as a possibility.

An M.P. corporal tried Royland's door and looked in. "Quitting time, professor," he said.

"Okay," Royland said. Mechanically he locked his desk drawers and his files, turned his window lock, and set out his waste-paper basket in the corridor. Click the door; another day, another dollar.

Maybe the project *was* breaking up. They did now and then. The huge boner at Berkeley proved that. And Royland's barracks was light two physicists now; their cubicles stood empty since they had been drafted to M.I.T. for some anti-submarine thing. Groves had *not* looked happy last time around; how did a general make up his mind anyway? Give them three months, then the ax? Maybe Stimson would run out of patience and cut the loss, close the District down. Maybe F.D.R. would say at a Cabinet meeting, "By the way, Henry, what ever became of—?" and that would be the end if old Henry could say only that the scientists appear to be optimistic of eventual success, Mr. President, but that as yet there seems to be nothing *concrete—*

He passed through the barbed wire of the Line under scrutiny of an M.P. lieutenant and walked down the barracks-edged company street of the maintenance troops to their motor pool. He wanted a jeep and a trip ticket; he wanted a long desert drive in the twilight; he wanted a dinner of *frijoles* and eggplant with his old friend Charles Miller Nahataspe, the medicine man of the adjoining Hopi reservation. Royland's hobby was anthropology; he wanted to get a little drunk on it—he hoped it would clear his mind.

Nahataspe welcomed him cheerfully to his hut; his million wrinkles all smiled. "You want me to play informant for a while?" he grinned. He had been to Carlisle in the 1880's and had been laughing at the white man ever since; he admitted that physics was funny, but for a real joke give him cultural anthropology every time. "You want some nice unsavory stuff about our institutionalized homosexuality? Should I cook us a dog for dinner? Have a seat on the blanket, Edward."

"What happened to your chairs? And the funny picture of McKinley? And—and everything?" The hut was bare except for cooking pots that simmered on the stone-curbed central hearth.

"I gave the stuff away," Nahataspe said carelessly. "You get tired of things."

Royland thought he knew what that meant. Nahataspe believed he would die quite soon; these particular Indians did not believe in dying encumbered by possessions. Manners, of course, forbade discussing death.

The Indian watched his face and finally said: "Oh, it's all right for *you* to talk about it. Don't be embarrassed."

Royland asked nervously: "Don't you feel well?"

"I feel terrible. There's a snake eating my liver. Pitch in and eat. You feel pretty awful yourself, don't you?"

The hard-learned habit of security caused Royland to evade the question. "You don't mean that literally about the snake, do you Charles?"

"Of course I do," Miller insisted. He scooped a steaming gourd full of stew from the pot and blew on it. "What would an untutored child of nature know about bacteria, viruses, toxins, and neoplasms? What would I know about break-the-sky medicine?"

Royland looked up sharply; the Indian was blandly eating. "Do you hear any talk about break-the-sky medicine?" Royland asked.

"No talk, Edward. I've had a few dreams about it." He pointed with his chin toward the Laboratory. "You fellows over there shouldn't dream so hard; it leaks out."

Royland helped himself to stew without answering. The stew was good, far better than the cafeteria stuff, and he did not *have* to guess the source of the meat in it.

Miller said consolingly: "It's only kid stuff, Edward. Don't get so worked up about it. We have a long dull story about a horned toad who ate some loco-weed and thought he was the Sky God. He got angry and he tried to break the sky but he couldn't so he slunk into his hole ashamed to face all the other animals and died. But they never knew he tried to break the sky at all."

In spite of himself Royland demanded: "Do you have any stories about anybody who did break the sky?" His hands were shaking again and his voice almost hysterical. Oppie and the rest of them were going to break the sky, kick humanity right in the crotch, and unleash a prowling monster that would go up and down by night and day peering in all the windows of all the houses in the world, leaving no sane man ever unterrified for his life and the lives of his kin. Phase 56c, God-damn it to blackest hell, made sure of that! Well done, Royland; you earned your dollar today!

Decisively the old Indian set his gourd aside. He said: "We have a saying that the only good paleface is a dead paleface, but I'll make an exception for you, Edward. I've got some strong stuff from Mexico that will make you feel better. I don't like to see my friends hurting."

"Peyote? I've tried it. Seeing a few colored lights won't make me feel better, but thanks."

"Not peyote, this stuff. It's God Food. I wouldn't take it myself without a month of preparation; otherwise the Gods would scoop me up in a net. That's because my people see clearly, and your eyes are clouded." He was busily rummaging through a clay-chinked wicker box as he spoke; he came up with a covered dish. "You people have your sight cleared just a little by the God Food, so it's safe for you."

Royland thought he knew what the old man was talking about. It was one of Nahataspe's biggest jokes that Hopi children understood

Einstein's relativity as soon as they could talk—and there was some truth to it. The Hopi language—and thought—had no tenses and therefore no concept of time-as-an-entity; it had nothing like the Indo-European speech's subjects and predicates, and therefore no built-in metaphysics of cause and effect. In the Hopi language and mind all things were frozen together forever into one great relationship, a crystalline structure of space–time events that simply were because they were. So much for Nahataspe's people "seeing clearly." But Royland gave himself and any other physicist credit for seeing as clearly when they were working a four-dimensional problem in the X Y Z space variables and the T time variable.

He could have spoiled the old man's joke by pointing that out, but of course he did not. No, no; he'd get a jag and maybe a bellyache from Nahataspe's herb medicine and then go home to his cubicle with his problem unresolved: to kick or not to kick?

The old man began to mumble in Hopi, and drew a tattered cloth across the door frame of his hut; it shut out the last rays of the setting sun, long and slanting on the desert, pink-red against the adobe cubes of the Indian settlement. It took a minute for Royland's eyes to accommodate to the flickering light from the hearth and the indigo square of the ceiling smoke hole. Now Nahataspe was "dancing," doing a crouched shuffle around the hut holding the covered dish before him. Out of the corner of his mouth, without interrupting the rhythm, he said to Royland: "Drink some hot water now." Royland sipped from one of the pots on the hearth; so far it was much like peyote ritual, but he felt calmer.

Nahataspe uttered a loud scream, added apologetically: "Sorry, Edward," and crouched before him whipping the cover off the dish like a headwaiter. So God Food was dried black mushrooms, miserable, wrinkled little things. "You swallow them all and chase them with hot water," Nahataspe said.

Obediently Royland choked them down and gulped from the jug; the old man resumed his dance and chanting.

A little old self-hypnosis, Royland thought bitterly. Grab some imitation sleep and forget about old 56c, as if you could. He could see the big dirty one now, a hell of a fireball, maybe over Munich, or Cologne, or Tokyo, or Nara. Cooked people, fused cathedral stone, the bronze of the big Buddha running like water, perhaps lapping around the ankles of a priest and burning his feet off so he fell prone into the stuff. He couldn't see the gamma radiation, but it would be there, invisible sleet doing the dirty unthinkable thing, coldly burning away the sex of men and women, cutting short so many fans of life at their points of origin. Phase 56c could snuff out a family of Bachs, or five generations of Bernoullis, or see to it that the great Huxley-Darwin cross did not occur.

The fireball loomed, purple and red and fringed with green—

The mushrooms were reaching him, he thought fuzzily. He could really see it. Nahataspe, crouched and treading, moved through the fireball just as he had the last time, and the time before that. Déjà vu, extraordinarily strong, stronger than ever before, gripped him. Royland knew all this had happened to him before, and remembered perfectly what would come next; it was on the very tip of his tongue, as they say—

The fireballs began to dance around him and he felt his strength drain suddenly out; he was lighter than a feather; the breeze would carry him away; he would be blown like a dust mote into the circle that the circling fireballs made. And he knew it was wrong. He croaked with the last of his energy, feeling himself slip out of the world: "Charlie! Help!"

Out of the corner of his mind as he slipped away he sensed that the old man was pulling him now under the arms, trying to tug him out of the hut, crying dimly into his ear: "You should have told me you did not see through smoke! You see clear; I never knew; I nev—"

And then he slipped through into blackness and silence.

Royland awoke sick and fuzzy; it was morning in the hut; there was no sign of Nahataspe. Well. Unless the old man had gotten to a phone and reported to the Laboratory, there were now jeeps scouring the desert in search of him and all hell was breaking loose in Security and Personnel. He would catch some of that hell on his return, and avert it with his news about assembly time.

Then he noticed that the hut had been cleaned of Nahataspe's few remaining possessions, even to the door cloth. A pang went through him; had the old man died in the night? He limped from the hut and looked around for a funeral pyre, a crowd of mourners. They were not there; the adobe cubes stood untenanted in the sunlight, and more weeds grew in the single street than he remembered. And his jeep, parked last night against the hut, was missing.

There were no wheeltracks, and uncrushed weeds grew tall where the jeep had stood.

Nahataspe's God Food had been powerful stuff. Royland's hand crept uncertainly to his face. No; no beard.

He looked about him, looked hard. He made the effort necessary to see details. He did not glance at the hut and because it was approximately the same as it had always been, concluded that it was unchanged, eternal. He looked and saw changes everywhere. Once-sharp adobe corners were rounded; protruding roof beams were bleached bone-white by how many years of desert sun? The wooden framing of the deep fortress-like windows had crumbled; the third building from him had wavering soot stains above its window boles and its beams were charred.

He went to it, numbly thinking: Phase 56c at least is settled. Not old Rip's baby now. They'll know me from fingerprints, I guess. One year? Ten? I *feel* the same.

The burned-out house was a shambles. In one corner were piled dry human bones. Royland leaned dizzily against the doorframe; its charcoal crumbled and streaked his hand. Those skulls were Indian— he was anthropologist enough to know that. Indian men, women and children, slain and piled in a heap. Who kills Indians? There should have been some sign of clothes, burned rags, but there were none. Who strips Indians naked and kills them?

Signs of a dreadful massacre were everywhere in the house. Bullet-pocks in the walls, high and low. Savage nicks left by bayonets—and swords? Dark stains of blood; it had run two inches high and left its mark. Metal glinted in a ribcage across the room. Swaying, he walked to the boneheap and thrust his hand into it. The thing bit him like a razor blade; he did not look at it as he plucked it out and carried it to the dusty street. With his back turned to the burned house he studied his find. It was a piece of swordblade six inches long, hand-honed to a perfect edge with a couple of nicks in it. It had stiffening ribs and the usual blood gutters. It had a perceptible curve that would fit into only one shape: the Samurai sword of Japan.

However long it had taken, the war was obviously over.

He went to the village well and found it choked with dust. It was while he stared into the dry hole that he first became afraid. Suddenly it all was real; he was no more an onlooker but a frightened and very thirsty man. He ransacked the dozen houses of the settlement and

•

found nothing to his purpose—a child's skeleton here, a couple of cartridge cases there.

There was only one thing left, and that was the road, the same earth track it had always been, wide enough for one jeep or the rump-sprung station wagon of the Indian settlement that once had been. Panic invited him to run; he did not yield. He sat on the well curb, took off his shoes to meticulously smooth wrinkles out of his khaki G.I. socks, put the shoes on, and retied the laces loosely enough to allow for swelling, and hesitated a moment. Then he grinned, selected two pebbles carefully from the dust and popped them in his mouth. "Beaver Patrol, forward march," he said, and began to hike.

Yes, he was thirsty; soon he would be hungry and tired; what of it? The dirt road would meet state-maintained blacktop in three miles and then there would be traffic and he'd hitch a ride. Let them argue with his fingerprints if they felt like it. The Japanese had got as far as New Mexico, had they? Then God help their home islands when the counterblow had come. Americans were a ferocious people when trespassed on. Conceivably, there was not a Japanese left alive . . .

He began to construct his story as he hiked. In large parts it was a repeated "I don't know." He would tell them: "I don't expect you to believe this, so my feelings won't be hurt when you don't. Just listen to what I say and hold everything until the F.B.I. has checked my fingerprints. My name is—" And so on.

It was midmorning then, and he would be on the highway soon. His nostrils, sharpened by hunger, picked up a dozen scents on the desert breeze: the spice of sage, a whiff of acetylene stink from a rattler dozing on the shaded side of a rock, the throat-tightening reek of tar suggested for a moment on the air. That would be the highway, perhaps a recent hotpatch on a chuckhole. Then a startling tang of sulfur dioxide drowned them out and passed on, leaving him stung and sniffling and groping for a handkerchief that was not there. What in God's name had that been, and where from? Without ceasing to trudge he studied the horizon slowly and found a smoke pall to the far west dimly smudging the sky. It looked like a small city's, or a fair-sized factory's, pollution. A city or a factory where "in his time" —he formed the thought reluctantly—there had been none.

Then he was at the highway. It had been improved; it was a two-laner still, but it was nicely graded now, built up by perhaps three

•

inches of gravel and tar beyond its old level, and lavishly ditched on either side.

If he had a coin he would have tossed it, but you went for weeks without spending a cent at Los Alamos Laboratory; Uncle took care of everything, from cigarettes to tombstones. He turned left and began to walk westward toward that sky smudge.

I am a reasonable animal, he was telling himself, and I will accept whatever comes in a spirit of reason. I will control what I can and try to understand the rest—

A faint siren scream began behind him and built up fast. The reasonable animal jumped for the ditch and hugged it for dear life. The siren howled closer, and motors roared. At the ear-splitting climax Royland put his head up for one glimpse, then fell back into the ditch as if a grenade had exploded in his middle.

The convoy roared on, down the *center* of the two-lane highway, straddling the white line. First the three little recon cars with the twin-mount machine guns, each filled brimful with three helmeted Japanese soldiers. Then the high-profiled, armored car of state, six-wheeled, with a probably ceremonial gun turret astern—nickel-plated gunbarrels are impractical—and the Japanese admiral in the fore-and-aft hat taking his lordly ease beside a rawboned, hatchet-faced SS officer in gleaming black. Then, diminuendo, two more little recon jobs . . .

"We've lost," Royland said in his ditch meditatively. "Ceremonial tanks with glass windows—we lost a *long* time ago." Had there been a Rising Sun insignia or was he now imagining that?

He climbed out and continued to trudge westward on the improved blacktop. You couldn't say "I reject the universe," not when you were as thirsty as he was.

He didn't even turn when the put-putting of a westbound vehicle grew loud behind him and then very loud when it stopped at his side.

"Zeegail," a curious voice said. "What are you doing here?"

The vehicle was just as odd in its own way as the ceremonial tank. It was minimum motor transportation, a kid's sled on wheels, powered by a noisy little air-cooled outboard motor. The driver sat with no more comfort than a cleat to back his coccyx against, and behind him were two twenty-five pound flour sacks that took up all the remaining room the little buckboard provided. The driver had the leathery Southwestern look; he wore a baggy blue outfit that was obviously a uniform and obviously unmilitary. He had a nametape on his breast above an incomprehensible row of dull ribbons: MART-FIELD, E., 1218824, P/7 NQOTD43. He saw Royland's eyes on the tape and said kindly: "My name is Martfield—Paymaster Seventh, but there's no need to use my rank here. Are you all right, my man?"

"Thirsty," Royland said. "What's the NQOTD43 for?"

"You can read!" Martfield said, astounded. "Those clothes—"

"Something to drink, please," Royland said. For the moment nothing else mattered in the world. He sat down on the buckboard like a puppet with cut strings.

"See here, fellow!" Martfield snapped in a curious, strangled way, forcing the words through his throat with a stagy, conventional effect of controlled anger. "You can stand until I invite you to sit!"

"Have you any water?" Royland asked dully.

With the same bark: "Who do you think you are?"

"I happen to be a theoretical physicist—" tiredly arguing with a dim seventh-carbon-copy imitation of a drill sergeant.

"Oh-*hoh!*" Martfield suddenly laughed. His stiffness vanished; he actually reached into his baggy tunic and brought out a pint canteen that gurgled. He then forgot all about the canteen in his hand, roguishly dug Royland in the ribs and said: "I should have suspected. You scientists! Somebody was supposed to pick you up—but he was another scientist, eh? Ah-hah-hah-hah!"

Royland took the canteen from his hand and sipped. So a scientist was supposed to be an idiot-savant, eh? Never mind now; drink. People said you were not supposed to fill your stomach with water after great thirst; it sounded to him like one of those puritanical rules people make up out of nothing because they sound reasonable. He finished the canteen while Martfield, Paymaster Seventh, looked alarmed, and wished only that there were three or four more of them.

"Got any food?" he demanded.

Martfield cringed briefly. "Doctor, I regret extremely that I have nothing with me. However if you would do me the honor of riding with me to my quarters—"

"Let's go," Royland said. He squatted on the flour sacks and away they chugged at a good thirty miles an hour; it was a fair little engine. The Paymaster Seventh continued deferential, apologizing over his shoulder because there was no windscreen, later dropped his cringing entirely to explain that Royland was seated on flour—"*white* flour, understand?" An over-the-shoulder wink. He had a friend in the bakery at Los Alamos. Several buckboards passed the other way as they traveled. At each encounter there was a peering examination of insignia to decide who saluted. Once they met a sketchily enclosed vehicle that furnished its driver with a low seat instead of obliging him to sit with legs straight out, and Paymaster Seventh Martfield almost dislocated his shoulder saluting first. The driver of that one was a Japanese in a kimono. A long curved sword lay across his lap.

Mile after mile the smell of sulfur and sulfides increased; finally there rose before them the towers of a Frasch Process layout. It looked like an oilfield, but instead of ground-laid pipelines and bass-drum storage tanks there were foothills of yellow sulfur. They drove between them—more salutes from baggily uniformed workers with shovels and yard-long Stilson wrenches. Off to the right were things that might have been Solvay Process towers for sulfuric acid, and a glittering horror of a neo-Roman administration-and-labs building. The Rising Sun banner fluttered from its central flagstaff.

Music surged as they drove deeper into the area; first it was a welcome counterirritant to the pop-pop of the two-cycle buckboard engine, and then a nuisance by itself. Royland looked, annoyed, for the loudspeakers, and saw them everywhere—on power poles, buildings, gateposts. Schmaltzy Strauss waltzes bathed them like smog, made thinking just a little harder, made communication just a little more blurry even after you had learned to live with the noise.

"I miss music in the wilderness," Martfield confided over his shoulder. He throttled down the buckboard until they were just rolling; they had passed some line unrecognized by Royland beyond which one did not salute everybody—just the occasional Japanese walking by in business suit with blueprint-roll and slide rule, or in kimono with sword. It was a German who nailed Royland, however: a classic jack-booted German in black broadcloth, black leather, and plenty of silver trim. He watched them roll for a moment after exchanging salutes with Martfield, made up his mind, and said: "Halt."

The Paymaster Seventh slapped on the brake, killed the engine, and popped to attention beside the buckboard. Royland more or less imitated him. The German said, stiffly but without accent: "Whom have you brought here, Paymaster?"

"A scientist, sir. I picked him up on the road returning from Los Alamos with personal supplies. He appears to be a minerals prospector who missed a rendezvous, but naturally I have not questioned the Doctor."

The German turned to Royland contemplatively. "So, Doctor. Your name and specialty."

"Dr. Edward Royland," he said. "I do nuclear power research." If there was no bomb he'd be damned if he'd invent it now for these people.

"So? That is very interesting, considering that there is no such thing as nuclear power research. Which camp are you from?" The German threw an aside to the Paymaster Seventh, who was literally shaking with fear at the turn things had taken. "You may go, Paymaster. Of course you will report yourself for harboring a fugitive."

"At once, sir," Martfield said in a sick voice. He moved slowly away pushing the little buckboard before him. The Strauss waltz oom-pah'd its last chord and instantly the loudspeakers struck up a hoppity-hoppity folk dance, heavy on the brass.

"Come with me," the German said, and walked off, not even looking behind to see whether Royland was obeying. This itself demonstrated how unlikely any disobedience was to succeed. Royland followed at his heels, which of course were garnished with silver spurs. Royland had not seen a horse so far that day.

A Japanese stopped them politely inside the administration building, a rimless-glasses, office-manager type in a gray suit. "How nice to see you again, Major Kappel! Is there anything I might do to help you?"

The German stiffened. "I didn't want to bother your people, Mr. Ito. This fellow appears to be a fugitive from one of our camps; I was going to turn him over to our liaison group for examination and return."

Mr. Ito looked at Royland and slapped his face hard. Royland, by the insanity of sheer reflex, cocked his fist as a red-blooded boy should, but the German's reflexes operated also. He had a pistol in his hand and pressed against Royland's ribs before he could throw the punch.

"All right," Royland said, and put down his hand.

Mr. Ito laughed. "You are at least partly right, Major Kappel; he certainly is not from one of *our* camps! But do not let me delay you further. May I hope for a report on the outcome of this?"

"Of course, Mr. Ito," said the German. He holstered his pistol and walked on, trailed by the scientist. Royland heard him grumble something that sounded like "Damned extraterritoriality!"

They descended to a basement level where all the door signs were in German, and in an office labeled WISSENSCHAFT-SLICHESICHERHEITSLIAISON Royland finally told his story. His audience was the major, a fat officer deferentially addressed as Colonel Biederman, and a bearded old civilian, a Dr. Piqueron, called in from another office. Royland suppressed only the matter of bomb research, and did it easily with the old security habit. His improvised cover story made the Los Alamos Laboratory a research center only for the generation of electricity.

The three heard him out in silence. Finally, in an amused voice, the colonel asked: "Who was this Hitler you mentioned?"

For that Royland was not prepared. His jaw dropped.

Major Kappel said: "Oddly enough, he struck on a name which does figure, somewhat infamously, in the annals of the Third Reich. One Adolf Hitler was an early Party agitator, but as I recall it he intrigued against the Leader during the War of Triumph and was executed."

"An ingenious madman," the colonel said. "Sterilized, of course?"

"Why, I don't know. I suppose so. Doctor, would you—?"

Dr. Piqueron quickly examined Royland and found him all there, which astonished them. Then they thought of looking for his camp tattoo number on the left bicep, and found none. Then, thoroughly upset, they discovered that he had no birth number above his left nipple either.

"And," Dr. Piqueron stammered, "his shoes are odd, sir—I just noticed. Sir, how long since you've seen sewn shoes and braided laces?"

"You must be hungry," the colonel suddenly said. "Doctor, have my aide get something to eat for—for the doctor."

"Major," said Royland, "I hope no harm will come to the fellow who picked me up. You told him to report himself."

"Have no fear, er, doctor," said the major. "Such humanity! You are of German blood?"

"Not that I know of; it may be."

"It *must* be!" said the colonel.

A platter of hash and a glass of beer arrived on a tray. Royland postponed everything. At last he demanded: "Now. Do you believe me? There must be fingerprints to prove my story still in existence."

"I feel like a fool," the major said. "You still could be hoaxing us. Dr. Piqueron, did not a German scientist establish that nuclear power is a theoretical and practical impossibility, that one always must put more into it than one can take out?"

Piqueron nodded and said reverently: "Heisenberg. Nineteen fifty-three, during the War of Triumph. His group was then assigned to electrical weapons research and produced the blinding bomb. But this fact does not invalidate the doctor's story; he says only that his group was *attempting* to produce nuclear power."

"We've got to research this," said the colonel. "Dr. Piqueron, entertain this man, whatever he is, in your laboratory."

Piqueron's laboratory down the hall was a place of astounding simplicity, even crudeness. The sinks, reagents, and balance were capable only of simple qualitative and quantitative analyses; various works in progress testified that they were not even strained to their modest limits. Samples of sulfur and its compounds were analyzed here. It hardly seemed to call for a "doctor" of anything, and hardly even for a human being. Machinery should be continuously testing the products as they flowed out; variations should be scribed mechanically on a moving tape; automatic controls should at least stop the processes and signal an alarm when variation went beyond limits; at most it might correct whatever was going wrong. But here sat Piqueron every day, titrating, precipitating, and weighing, entering results by hand in a ledger and telephoning them to the works!

Piqueron looked about proudly. "As a physicist you wouldn't understand all this, of course," he said. "Shall I explain?"

"Perhaps later, doctor, if you'd be good enough. If you'd first help me orient myself—"

So Piqueron told him about the War of Triumph (1940–1955) and what came after.

In 1940 the realm of der Fuehrer (Herr Goebbels, of course—that strapping blond fellow with the heroic jaw and eagle's eye whom you can see in the picture there) was simultaneously and treacherously invaded by the misguided French, the sub-human Slavs, and the perfidious British. The attack, for which the shocked Germans coined the name *blitzkrieg,* was timed to coincide with an internal eruption of sabotage, well-poisoning, and assassination by the *Zigeunerjuden,* or Jewpsies, of whom little is now known; there seem to be none left.

By Nature's ineluctable law, the Germans had necessarily to be tested to the utmost so that they might fully respond. Therefore Germany was overrun from East and West, and Holy Berlin itself was taken; but Goebbels and his court withdrew like Barbarossa into the mountain fastnesses to await their day. It came unexpectedly soon. The deluded Americans launched a million-man amphibious attack on the homeland of the Japanese in 1945. The Japanese resisted with almost Teutonic courage. Not one American in twenty reached shore alive, and not one in a hundred got a mile inland. Particularly lethal were the women and children, who lay in camouflaged pits hugging artillery shells and aircraft bombs, which they detonated when enough invaders drew near to make it worthwhile.

The second invasion attempt, a month later, was made up of second-line troops scraped up from everywhere, including occupation duty in Germany.

"Literally," Piqueron said, "the Japanese did not know how to surrender, so they did not. They could not conquer, but they could and did continue suicidal resistance, consuming manpower of the allies and their own womanpower and childpower—a shrewd bargain for the Japanese! The Russians refused to become involved in the Japanese war; they watched with apish delight while two future enemies, as they supposed, were engaged in mutual destruction.

"A third assault wave broke on Kyushu and gained the island at last. What lay ahead? Only another assault on Honshu, the main island, home of the Emperor and the principal shrines. It was 1946; the volatile, child-like Americans were war-weary and mutinous; the best of them were gone by then. In desperation the Anglo-American leaders offered the Russians an economic sphere embracing the China coast and Japan as the price of participation."

The Russians grinned and assented; they would take that—at *least* that. They mounted a huge assault for the spring of 1947; they would take Korea and leap off from there for northern Honshu while the Anglo-American forces struck in the south. Surely this would provide at last a symbol before which the Japanese might without shame bow down and admit defeat!

And then, from the mountain fastnesses, came the radio voice: "Germans! Your Leader calls upon you again!" Followed the Hundred Days of Glory during which the German Army reconstituted itself and expelled the occupation troops—by then, children without combat experience, and leavened by not-quite-disabled veterans. Followed the seizure of the airfields; the Luftwaffe in business again. Followed the drive, almost a dress parade, to the Channel Coast, gobbling up immense munition dumps awaiting shipment to the Pacific Theater, millions of warm uniforms, good boots, mountains of rations, piles of shells and explosives that lined the French roads for scores of miles, thousands of two-and-a-half-ton trucks, and lakes of gasoline to fuel them. The shipyards of Europe, from Hamburg to Toulon, had been turning out, furiously, invasion barges for the Pacific. In April of 1947 they sailed against England in their thousands.

Halfway around the world, the British Navy was pounding Tokyo, Nagasaki, Kobe, Hiroshima, Nara. Three quarters of the way across Asia the Russian Army marched stolidly on; let the decadent British pickle their own fish; the glorious motherland at last was gaining her long-sought, long-denied, warm-water seacoast. The British, tired women without their men, children fatherless these eight years, old folks deathly weary, deathly worried about their sons, were brave but they were not insane. They accepted honorable peace terms; they capitulated.

With the Western front secure for the first time in history, the ancient Drive to the East was resumed; the immemorial struggle of Teuton against Slav went on.

His spectacles glittering with rapture, Dr. Piqueron said: "We were worthy in those days of the Teutonic Knights who seized Prussia from the sub-men! On the ever-glorious Twenty-first of May, Moscow was ours!"

Moscow and the monolithic state machinery it controlled, and all the roads and rail lines and communication wires which led only to—and from—Moscow. Detroit-built tanks and trucks sped along those roads in the fine, bracing spring weather; the Red Army turned one hundred and eighty degrees at last and countermarched halfway across the Eurasian landmass, and at Kazan it broke exhausted against the Frederik Line.

Europe at last was One and German. Beyond Europe lay the dark and swarming masses of Asia, mysterious and repulsive folk whom it would be better to handle through the non-German, but chivalrous, Japanese. The Japanese were reinforced with shipping from Birkenhead, artillery from the Putilov Works, jet fighters from Châteauroux, steel from the Ruhr, rice from the Po valley, herring from Norway, timber from Sweden, oil from Romania, laborers from India. The American forces were driven from Kyushu in the winter of 1948, and bloodily back across their chain of island steppingstones that followed.

Surrender they would not; it was a monstrous affront that shield-shaped North America dared to lie there between the German Atlantic and the Japanese Pacific threatening both. The affront was wiped out in 1955.

For one hundred and fifty years now the Germans and the Japanese had uneasily eyed each other across the banks of the Mississippi. Their orators were fond of referring to that river as a vast frontier unblemished by a single fortification. There was even some interpenetration; a Japanese colony fished out of Nova Scotia on the very rim of German America; a sulfur mine which was part of the Farben system lay in New Mexico, the very heart of Japanese America—this was where Dr. Edward Royland found himself, being lectured to by Dr. Piqueron, Dr. Gaston Pierre Piqueron, true-blue German.

"Here, of course," Dr. Piqueron said gloomily, "we are so damned provincial. Little ceremony and less manners. Well, it would be too much to expect them to assign *German* Germans to this dreary outpost, so we French Germans must endure it somehow."

"You're all French?" Royland asked, startled.

"French *Germans,*" Piqueron stiffly corrected him. "Colonel Biederman happens to be a French German also; Major Kappel is—hrrmph—an Italian German." He sniffed to show what he thought of that.

The Italian German entered at that point, not in time to shut off the question: "And you all come from Europe?"

They looked at him in bafflement. "My grandfather did," Dr. Piqueron said. Royland remembered; so Roman legions used to guard their empire—Romans born and raised in Britain, or on the Danube, Romans who would never in their lives see Italy or Rome.

Major Kappel said affably: "Well, this needn't concern us. I'm afraid, my dear fellow, that your little hoax has not succeeded." He clapped Royland merrily on the back. "I admit you've tricked us all nicely; now may we have the facts?"

Piqueron said, surprised: "His story is false? The shoes? The missing *geburtsnummer?* And he appears to understand some chemistry!"

"Ah-h-h—but he said his specialty was *physics,* doctor! Suspicious in itself!"

"Quite so. A discrepancy. But the rest—?"

"As to his birth number, who knows? As to his shoes, who cares? I took some inconspicuous notes while he was entertaining us and have checked thoroughly. There *was* no Manhattan Engineering District. There *was* no Dr. Oppenheimer, or Fermi, or Bohr. There *is* no theory of relativity, or equivalence of mass and energy. Uranium has one use only—coloring glass a pretty orange. There is such a thing as an isotope but it has nothing to do with chemistry; it is the name used in Race Science for a permissible variation within a subrace. And what have you to say to *that,* my dear fellow?"

Royland wondered first, such was the positiveness with which Major Kappel spoke, whether he had slipped into a universe of different physical properties and history entirely, one in which Julius Caesar discovered Peru and the oxygen molecule was lighter than the hydrogen atom. He managed to speak. "How did you find all that out, major?"

"Oh, don't think I did a skimpy job," Kappel smiled. "I looked it all up in the *big* encyclopedia."

Dr. Piqueron, chemist, nodded grave approval of the major's diligence and thorough grasp of the scientific method.

"You still don't want to tell us?" Major Kappel asked coaxingly.

"I can only stand by what I said."

Kappel shrugged. "It's not my job to persuade you; I wouldn't know how to begin. But I can and will ship you off forthwith to a work camp."

"What—is a work camp?" Royland unsteadily asked.

"Good heavens, man, a camp where one works! You're obviously an *ungleichgeschaltling* and you've got to be *gleichgeschaltet.*" He did not speak these words as if they were foreign; they were obviously part of the everyday American working vocabulary. *Gleichgeschaltet* meant to Royland something like "coordinated, brought into tune with." So he would be brought into tune—with what, and how?

The Major went on: "You'll get your clothes and your bunk and your chow, and you'll work, and eventually your irregular vagabondish habits will disappear and you'll be turned loose on the labor market. And you'll be damned glad we took the trouble with you." His face fell. "By the way, I was too late with your friend the Paymaster. I'm sorry. I sent a messenger to Disciplinary Control with a stop order. After all, if you took us in for an hour, why should you not have fooled a Pay-Seventh?"

"Too late? He's *dead?* For picking up a *hitchhiker?*"

"I don't know what that last word means," said the Major. "If it's dialect for 'vagabond,' the answer is ordinarily 'yes.' The man, after all, was a Pay-Seventh; he could read. Either you're keeping up your hoax with remarkable fidelity or you've been living in isolation. Could that be it? Is there a tribe of you somewhere? Well, the interrogators will find out; that's their job."

"The Dogpatch legend!" Dr. Piqueron burst out, thunderstruck. "He may be an Abnerite!"

"By Heaven," Major Kappel said slowly, "that might be it. What a feather in my cap to find a living Abnerite."

"*Whose* cap?" demanded Dr. Piqueron coldly.

"I think I'll look the Dogpatch legend up," said Kappel, heading for the door and probably the big encyclopedia.

"So will I," Dr. Piqueron announced firmly. The last Royland saw of them they were racing down the corridor, neck and neck.

Very funny. And they had killed simple-minded Paymaster Martfield for picking up a hitchhiker. The Nazis always had been pretty funny—fat Hermann pretending he was young Seigfried. As blond as Hitler, as slim as Goering, and as tall as Goebbels. Immature guttersnipes who hadn't been able to hang a convincing frame on Dimitrov for the Reichstag fire; the world had roared at their bungling. Huge, corny party rallies with let's-play-detectives nonsense like touching the local flags to that hallowed banner on which the martyred Horst Wessel had had a nosebleed. And they had rolled over Europe, and they killed people . . .

One thing was certain: life in the work camp would at least bore him to death. He was supposed to be an illiterate simpleton, so things were excused him which were not excused an exalted Pay-Seventh. He poked through a closet in the corner of the laboratory—he and Piqueron were the same size—

He found a natty change of uniform and what must be a civilian suit: somewhat baggy pants and a sort of tunic with the neat, sensible Russian collar. Obviously it would be all right to wear it because here it was; just as obviously, it was all wrong for him to be dressed in chinos and a flannel shirt. He did not know exactly what this made him, but Martfield had been done to death for picking up a man in chinos and a flannel shirt. Royland changed into the civilian suit, stuffed his own shirt and pants far back on the top shelf of the closet; this was probably concealment enough from those murderous clowns. He walked out, and up the stairs, and through the busy lobby, and into the industrial complex. Nobody saluted him and he saluted nobody. He knew where he was going—to a good, sound Japanese laboratory where there were no Germans.

Royland had known Japanese students at the University and admired them beyond words. Their brains, frugality, doggedness, and good humor made them, as far as he was concerned, the most sensible people he had ever known. Tojo and his warlords were not, as far as Royland was concerned, essentially Japanese but just more damnfool soldiers and politicians. The real Japanese would courteously listen to him, calmly check against available facts—

He rubbed his cheek and remembered Mr. Ito and his slap in the face. Well, presumably Mr. Ito was a damnfool soldier and politician —and demonstrating for the German's benefit in a touchy border area full of jurisdictional questions.

At any rate, he would *not* go to a labor camp and bust rocks or refinish furniture until those imbeciles decided he was *gleichgeschaltet;* he would go mad in a month.

Royland walked to the Solvay towers and followed the glass pipes containing their output of sulfuric acid along the ground until he came to a bottling shed where beetle-browed men worked silently filling great wicker-basketed carboys and heaving them outside. He followed other men who levered them up onto hand trucks and rolled them in one door of a storage shed. Out the door at the other end more men loaded them onto enclosed trucks which were driven up from time to time.

Royland settled himself in a corner of the storage shed behind a barricade of carboys and listened to the truck dispatcher swear at his drivers and the carboy handlers swear at their carboys.

"Get the god-damn Frisco shipment *loaded,* stupid! I don't *care* if you gotta go, we gotta get it out by *midnight!*"

So a few hours after dark Royland was riding west, without much air, and in the dangerous company of one thousand gallons of acid. He hoped he had a careful driver.

A night, a day, and another night on the road. The truck never stopped except to gas up; the drivers took turns and ate sandwiches at the wheel and dozed off shift. It rained the second night. Royland, craftily and perhaps a little crazily, licked the drops that ran down the tarpaulin flap covering the rear. At the first crack of dawn, hunched between two wicker carcasses, he saw they were rolling through irrigated vegetable fields, and the water in the ditches was too much for him. He heard the transmission shift down to slow for a curve, swarmed over the tailgate, and dropped to the road. He was weak and limp enough to hit like a sack.

He got up, ignoring his bruises, and hobbled to one of the brimming five-foot ditches; he drank, and drank, and drank. This time puritanical folklore proved right; he lost it all immediately, or what had not been greedily absorbed by his shriveled stomach. He did not mind; it was bliss enough to *stretch*.

The field crop was tomatoes, almost dead ripe. He was starved for them; as he saw the rosy beauties he knew that tomatoes were the only thing in the world he craved. He gobbled one so that the juice ran down his chin; he ate the next two delicately, letting his teeth break the crispness of their skin and the beautiful taste ravish his tongue. There were tomatoes as far as the eye could see, on either side of the road, the green of the vines and the red dots of the ripe fruit graphed by the checkerboard of silvery ditches that caught the first light. Nevertheless, he filled his pockets with them before he walked on.

Royland was happy.

Farewell to the Germans and their sordid hash and murderous ways. *Look* at these beautiful fields! The Japanese are an innately artistic people who bring beauty to every detail of daily life. And they make damn good physicists, too. Confined in their stony home, cramped as he had been in the truck, they grew twisted and painful; why should they not have reached out for more room to grow, and what other way is there to reach but to make war? He could be very understanding about any people who had planted these beautiful tomatoes for him.

A dark blemish the size of a man attracted his attention. It lay on the margin of one of the swirling five-foot ditches out there to his right. And then it rolled slowly into the ditch with a splash, floundered a little, and proceeded to drown.

In a hobbling run Royland broke from the road and across the field. He did not know whether he was limber enough to swim. As he stood panting on the edge of the ditch, peering into the water, a head of hair surfaced near him. He flung himself down, stretched wildly, and grabbed the hair—and yet had detachment enough to feel a pang when the tomatoes in his tunic pocket smashed.

"Steady," he muttered to himself, yanked the head toward him, took hold with his other hand and lifted. A surprised face confronted him and then went blank and unconscious.

For half an hour Royland, weak as he was, struggled, cursed feebly, and sweated to get that body out of the water. At last he plunged in himself, found it only chest-deep, and shoved the carcass over the mudslick bank. He did not know by then whether the man was alive or dead or much care. He knew only that he couldn't walk away and leave the job half finished.

The body was that of a fat, middle-aged Oriental, surely Chinese rather than Japanese, though Royland could not say why he thought so. His clothes were soaked rags except for a leather wallet the size of a cigar box which he wore on a wide cloth belt. Its sole content was a handsome blue-glazed porcelain bottle. Royland sniffed at it and reeled. Some kind of super-gin! He sniffed again, and then took a conservative gulp of the stuff. While he was still coughing he felt the bottle being removed from his hand. When he looked he saw the Chinese, eyes still closed, accurately guiding the neck of the bottle to his mouth. The Chinese drank and drank and drank, then returned the bottle to the wallet and finally opened his eyes.

"Honorable sir," said the Chinese in flat, California American speech, "you have deigned to save my unworthy life. May I supplicate your honorable name?"

"Ah, Royland. Look, take it easy. Don't try to get up; you shouldn't even talk."

Somebody screamed behind Royland: "There has been thieving of tomatoes! There has been smasheeng and deestruction of thee vines! Chil-dren you, will bee weet-ness be-fore the Jappa-neese!"

Christ, now what?

Now a skinny black man, not a Negro, in a dirty loincloth, and beside him like a pan-pipes five skinny black loinclothed offspring in descending order. All were capering, pointing, and threatening. The Chinese groaned, fished in his tattered robes with one hand, and pulled out a soggy wad of bills. He peeled one off, held it out, and said: "Begone, pestilential barbarians from beyond Tian-Shang. My master and I give you alms, not tribute."

The Dravidian, or whatever he was, grabbed the bill and keened: "Een-suffee-cient for the terrible dommage! The Jappa-neese—"

The Chinese waved them away boredly. He said: "If my master will condescend to help me arise?"

Royland uncertainly helped him up. The man was wobbly, whether from the near-drowning or the terrific belt of alcohol he'd taken there was no knowing. They proceeded to the road, followed by shrieks to be careful about stepping on the vines.

On the road, the Chinese said: "My unworthy name is Li Po. Will my master deign to indicate in which direction we are to travel?"

"What's this master business?" Royland demanded. "If you're grateful, swell, but I don't *own* you."

"My master is pleased to jest," said Li Po. Politely, face-saving and third-personing Royland until hell wouldn't have it, he explained that Royland, having meddled with the Celestial decree that Li Po should, while drunk, roll into the irrigation ditch and drown, now had Li Po on his hands, for the Celestial Ones had washed theirs of him. "As my master of course will recollect in a moment or two." Understandingly, he expressed his sympathy with Royland's misfortune in acquiring him as an obligation, especially since he had a hearty appetite, was known to be dishonest, and suffered from fainting fits and spasms when confronted with work.

"I don't *know* about all this," Royland said fretfully. "Wasn't there another Li Po? A poet?"

"Your servant prefers to venerate his namesake as one of the greatest drunkards the Flowery Kingdom has ever known," the Chinese observed. And a moment later he bent over, clipped Royland behind the knees so that he toppled forward and bumped his head, and performed the same obeisance himself, more gracefully. A vehicle went sputtering and popping by on the road as they kowtowed.

Li Po said reproachfully: "I humbly observe that my master is unaware of the etiquette our noble overlords exact. Such negligence cost the head of my insignificant elder brother in his twelfth year. Would my master be pleased to explain how he can have reached his honorable years without learning what babes in their cradles are taught?"

Royland answered with the whole truth. Li Po politely begged clarification from time to time, and a sketch of his mental horizons emerged from his questioning. That "magic" had whisked Royland forward a century or more he did not doubt for an instant, but he found it difficult to understand why the proper *fung shui* precautions had not been taken to avert a disastrous outcome to the God Food experiment. He suspected, from a description of Nahataspe's hut, that a simple wall at right angles to the door would have kept all really important demons out. When Royland described his escape from German territory to Japanese, and why he had effected it, he was very bland and blank. Royland judged that Li Po privately thought him not very bright for having left *any* place to come here.

And Royland hoped he was not right. "Tell me what it's like," he said.

"This realm," said Li Po, "under our benevolent and noble overlords, is the haven of all whose skin is not the bleached-bone hue which indicates the undying curse of the Celestial Ones. Hither flock men of Han like my unworthy self, and the sons of Hind beyond the Tian-Shang that we may till new soil and raise up sons, and sons of sons to venerate us when we ascend."

"What was that bit," Royland demanded, "about the bleached bones? Do they shoot, ah, white men on sight here, or do they not?"

Li Po said evasively: "We are approaching the village where I unworthily serve as fortune teller, doctor of *fung shui*, occasional poet and storyteller. Let my master have no fear about his color. This humble one will roughen his master's skin, tell a circumstantial and artistic lie or two, and pass his master off as merely a leper."

After a week in Li Po's village Royland knew that life was good there. The place was a wattle-and-clay settlement of about two hundred souls on the bank of an irrigation ditch large enough to be dignified by the name of "canal." It was situated nobody knew just where; Royland thought it must be the San Fernando Valley. The soil was thick and rich and bore furiously the year round. A huge kind of radish was the principal crop. It was too coarse to be eaten by man; the villagers understood that it was feed for chickens somewhere up north. At any rate they harvested the stuff, fed it through a great hand-powered shredder, and shade-cured the shreds. Every few days a Japanese of low caste would come by in a truck, they would load tons of the stuff onto it, and wave their giant radish goodbye forever. Presumably the chickens ate it, and the Japanese then ate the chickens.

The villagers ate chicken too, but only at weddings and funerals. The rest of the time they ate vegetables which they cultivated, a quarter-acre to a family, the way other craftsmen facet diamonds. A single cabbage might receive, during its ninety days from planting to maturity, one hundred work hours from grandmother, grandfather, son, daughter, eldest grandchild, and on down to the smallest toddler. Theoretically the entire family line should have starved to death, for there are not one hundred energy hours in a cabbage; somehow they did not. They merely stayed thin and cheerful and hard-working and fecund.

They spoke English by Imperial decree; the reasoning seemed to be that they were as unworthy to speak Japanese as to paint the Imperial Chrysanthemum Seal on their houses, and that to let them cling to their old languages and dialects would have been politically unwise.

They were a mixed lot of Chinese, Hindus, Dravidians, and, to Royland's surprise, low-caste and outcaste Japanese; he had not known there were such things. Village tradition had it that a *samurai* named Ugetsu long ago said, pointing at the drunk tank of a Hong Kong jail, "I'll have that lot," and "that lot" had been the ancestors of these villagers transported to America in a foul hold practically as ballast and settled here by the canal with orders to start making their radish quota. The place was at any rate called The Ugetsu Village, and if some of the descendants were teetotallers, others like Li Po gave color to the legend of their starting point.

After a week the cheerful pretense that he was a sufferer from Housen's disease evaporated and he could wash the mud off his face. He had merely to avoid the upper-caste Japanese and especially the *samurai*. This was not exactly a stigma; in general it was a good idea for *everybody* to avoid the *samurai*.

In the village Royland found his first love and his first religion both false.

He had settled down; he was getting used to the Oriental work rhythm of slow, repeated, incessant effort; it did not surprise him any longer that he could count his ribs. When he ate a bowl of artfully arranged vegetables, the red of pimiento played off against the yellow of parsnip, a slice of pickled beet adding visual and olfactory tang to the picture, he felt full enough; he *was* full enough for the next day's feeble work in the field. It was pleasant enough to play slowly with a wooden mattock in the rich soil; did not people once buy sand so their children might do exactly what he did, and envy their innocent absorption? Royland was innocently absorbed, then, and the radish truck had collected six times since his arrival, when he began to feel stirrings of lust. On the edge of starvation (but who knew this? For everybody was) his mind was dulled, but not his loins. They burned, and he looked about him in the fields, and the first girl he saw who was not repulsive he fell abysmally in love with.

Bewildered, he told Li Po, who was also Ugetsu Village's go-between. The storyteller was delighted; he waddled off to seek information and returned. "My master's choice is wise. The slave on whom his lordly eye deigned to rest is known as Vashti, daughter of Hari Bose, the distiller. She is his seventh child and so no great dowry can be expected (I shall ask for fifteen kegs toddy, but would settle for seven), but all this humble village knows that she is a skilled and willing worker in the hut as in the fields. I fear she has the customary lamentable Hindu talent for concocting curries, but a dozen good beatings at the most should cause her to reserve it to appropriate occasions, such as visits from her mother and sisters."

So, according to the sensible custom of Ugetsu, Vashti came that night to the hut which Royland shared with Li Po, and Li Po visited with cronies by his master's puzzling request. He begged humbly to point out that it would be dark in the hut, so this talk of lacking privacy was inexplicable to say the least. Royland made it an order, and Li Po did not really object, so he obeyed it.

It was a damnably strange night during which Royland learned all about India's national sport and most highly developed art form. Vashti, if she found him weak on the theory side, made no complaints. On the contrary, when Royland woke she was doing something or other to his feet.

"More?" he thought incredulously. "With *feet?*" He asked what she was doing. Submissively she replied: "Worshipping my lord husband-to-be's big toe. I am a pious and old-fashioned woman."

So she painted his toe with red paint and prayed to it, and then she fixed breakfast—curry, and excellent. She watched him eat, and then modestly licked his leavings from the bowl. She handed him his clothes, which she had washed while he still slept, and helped him into them after she helped him wash. Royland thought incredulously: "It's not possible! It must be a show, to sell me on marrying her—as if I had to be sold!" His heart turned to custard as he saw her, without a moment's pause, turn from dressing him to polishing his wooden rake. He asked that day in the field, roundabout fashion, and learned that this was the kind of service he could look forward to for the rest of his life after marriage. If the woman got lazy he'd have to beat her, but this seldom happened more than every year or so. We have good girls here in Ugetsu Village.

So an Ugetsu Village peasant was in some ways better off than anybody from "his time" who was less than a millionaire!

His starved dullness was such that he did not realize this was true for only half the Ugetsu Village peasants.

Religion sneaked up on him in similar fashion. He went to the part-time Taoist priest because he was a little bored with Li Po's current after-dinner saga. He could have sat like all the others and listened passively to the interminable tale of the glorious Yellow Emperor, and the beautiful but wicked Princess Emerald, and the virtuous but plain Princess Moon Blossom; it just happened that he went to the priest of Tao and got hooked hard.

The kindly old man, a toolmaker by day, dropped a few pearls of wisdom which, in his foggy starvation-daze, Royland did not perceive to be pearls of undemonstrable nonsense, and showed Royland how to meditate. It worked the first time. Royland bunged right smack through into a two-hundred-proof state of *samadhi*—the Eastern version of self-hypnotized Enlightenment—that made him feel wonderful and all-knowing and left him without a hangover when it wore off. He had despised, in college, the type of people who took psychology courses and so had taken none himself; he did not know a thing about self-hypnosis except as just demonstrated by this very nice old gentleman. For several days he was offensively religious and kept trying to talk to Li Po about the Eightfold Way, and Li Po kept changing the subject.

It took murder to bring him out of love and religion.

At twilight they were all sitting and listening to the storyteller as usual. Royland had been there just one month and for all he knew would be there forever. He soon would have his bride officially; he knew he had discovered The Truth About the Universe by way of Tao meditation; why should he change? Changing demanded a furious outburst of energy, and he did not have energy on that scale. He metered out his energy day and night; one had to save so much for tonight's love play, and then one had to save so much for tomorrow's planting. He was a poor man; he could not afford to change.

Li Po had reached a rather interesting bit where the Yellow Emperor was declaiming hotly: "Then she shall die! Whoever dare transgress Our divine will—"

A flashlight began to play over their faces. They perceived that it was in the hand of a *samurai* with kimono and sword. Everybody hastily kowtowed, but the *samurai* shouted irritably (all *samurai* were irritable, all the time): "Sit up, you fools! I want to see your stupid faces. I hear there's a peculiar one in this flea-bitten dungheap you call a village."

Well, by now Royland knew his duty. He rose and with downcast eyes asked: "Is the noble protector in search of my unworthy self?"

"Ha!" the *samurai* roared. "It's true! A big nose!" He hurled the flashlight away (all *samurai* were nobly contemptuous of the merely material), held his scabbard in his left hand, and swept out the long curved sword with his right.

Li Po stepped forward and said in his most enchanting voice: "If the Heaven-born would only deign to heed a word from this humble—" What he must have known would happen happened. With a contemptuous backhand sweep of the blade the *samurai* beheaded him and Li Po's debt was paid.

The trunk of the storyteller stood for a moment and then fell stiffly forward. The *samurai* stooped to wipe his blade clean on Li Po's ragged robes.

Royland had forgotten much, but not everything. With the villagers scattering before him he plunged forward and tackled the *samurai* low and hard. No doubt the *samurai* was a Brown Belt judo master; if so he had nobody but himself to blame for turning his back. Royland, not remembering that he was barefoot, tried to kick the *samurai's* face in. He broke his worshipful big toe, but its untrimmed horny nail removed the left eye of the warrior and after that it was no contest. He never let the *samurai* get up off the ground; he took out his other eye with the handle of a rake and then killed him an inch at a time with his hands, his feet, and the clownish rustic's traditional weapon, a flail. It took easily half an hour, and for the final twenty minutes the *samurai* was screaming for his mother. He died when the last light left the western sky, and in darkness Royland stood quite alone with the two corpses. The villagers were gone.

He assumed, or pretended, that they were within earshot and yelled at them brokenly: "I'm sorry, Vashti. I'm sorry, all of you. I'm going. Can I make you understand?

"Listen. You aren't living. This isn't life. You're not making anything but babies, you're not changing, you're not growing up. That's not enough! You've got to read and write. You can't pass on anything but baby stories like the Yellow Emperor by word of mouth. The village is growing. Soon your fields will touch the fields of Sukoshi Village to the west, and then what happens? You won't know what to do, so you'll fight with Sukoshi Village.

"Religion. No! It's just getting drunk the way you do it. You're set up for it by being half-starved and then you go into *samadhi* and you feel better so you think you understand everything. No! You've got to *do* things. If you don't grow up, you die. All of you.

"Women. *That's* wrong. It's good for the men, but it's wrong. Half of you are slaves, do you understand? Women are people too, but you use them like animals and you've convinced them it's right for them to be old at thirty and discarded for the next girl. For God's sake, can't you try to think of yourselves in their place?

"The breeding, the crazy breeding—it's got to stop. You frugal Orientals! But you aren't frugal; you're crazy drunken sailors. You're squandering the whole world. Every mouth you breed has got to be fed by the land, and the land isn't infinite.

"I hope some of you understood. Li Po would have, a little, but he's dead.

"I'm going away now. You've been kind to me and all I've done is make trouble. I'm sorry."

He fumbled on the ground and found the *samurai's* flashlight. With it he hunted the village's outskirts until he found the Japanese's buckboard car. He started the motor with its crank and noisily rolled down the dirt track from the village to the highway.

Royland drove all night, still westward. His knowledge of southern California's geography was inexact, but he hoped to hit Los Angeles.

There might be a chance of losing himself in a great city. He had abandoned hope of finding present-day counterparts of his old classmates like Jimmy Ichimura; obviously they had lost out. Why shouldn't they have lost? The soldier-politicians had won the war by happenstance, so all power to the soldier-politicians! Reasoning under the great natural law *post hoc ergo propter hoc,* Tojo and his crowd had decided: fanatic feudalism won the war; therefore fanatic feudalism is a good thing, and it necessarily follows that the more fanatical and feudal it is, the better a thing it is. So you had Sukoshi Village, and Ugetsu Village; Ichi Village, Ni Village, San Village, Shi Village, dotting that part of Great Japan formerly known as North America, breeding with the good old fanatic feudalism and so feudally averse to new thought and innovations that it made you want to scream at them—which he had.

The single weak headlight of his buckboard passed few others on the road; a decent feudal village is self-contained.

Damn them and their suicidal cheerfulness! It was a pleasant trait; it was a fool in a canoe approaching the rapids saying: "Chin up! Everything's going to be all right if we just keep smiling."

The car ran out of gas when false dawn first began to pale the sky behind him. He pushed it into the roadside ditch and walked on; by full light he was in a tumble-down, planless, evil-smelling, paper-and-galvanized-iron city whose name he did not know. There was no likelihood of him being noticed as a "white" man by anyone not specifically looking for him. A month of outdoor labor had browned him, and a month of artistically composed vegetable plates had left him gaunt.

The city was carpeted with awakening humanity. Its narrow streets were paved with sprawled-out men, women, and children beginning to stir and hawk up phlegm and rub their rheumy eyes. An open sewer-latrine running down the center of each street was casually used, ostrich-fashion—the users hid their own eyes while in action.

Every mangled variety of English rang in Royland's ears as he trod between bodies.

There had to be something more, he told himself. This was the shabby industrial outskirts, the lowest marginal-labor area. Somewhere in the city there was beauty, science, learning!

He walked aimlessly plodding until noon, and found nothing of the sort. These people in the cities were food-handlers, food-traders, food-transporters. They took in one another's washing and sold one another chop suey. They made automobiles (Yes! There were one-family automobile factories which probably made six buckboards a year, filing all metal parts by hand out of bar stock!) and orange crates and baskets and coffins; abacuses, nails, and boots.

The Mysterious East has done it again, he thought bitterly. The Indians-Chinese-Japanese won themselves a nice sparse area. They could have laid things out neatly and made it pleasant for everybody instead of for a minute speck of aristocracy which he was unable even to detect in this human soup . . . but they had done it again. They had bred irresponsibly just as fast as they could until the land was *full*. Only famines and pestilence could "help" them now.

He found exactly one building which owned some clear space around it and which would survive an earthquake or a flicked cigarette butt. It was the German Consulate.

I'll give them the Bomb, he said to himself. Why not? None of this is mine. And for the Bomb I'll exact a price of some comfort and dignity for as long as I live. *Let* them blow one another up! He climbed the consulate steps.

To the black-uniformed guard at the swastika-trimmed bronze doors he said: *"Wenn die Lichtstärke der von einer Fläche kommenden Strahlung dem Cosinus des Winkels zwischen Strahlrichtung und Flächennormalen proportional ist, so nennen wir die Fläche eine volkommen streunde Fläche."* Lambert's Law, Optics I. All the Goethe he remembered happened to rhyme, which might have made the guard suspicious.

Naturally the German came to attention and said apologetically: "I don't speak German. What is it, sir?"

"You may take me to the consul," Royland said, affecting boredom.

"Yes, sir. At once, sir. Er, you're an *agent* of course, sir?"

Royland said witheringly: *"Sicherheit, bitte!"*

"Yessir. This way, sir!"

The consul was a considerate, understanding gentleman. He was somewhat surprised by Royland's true tale, but said from time to time: "I see; I see. Not impossible. Please go on."

Royland concluded: "Those people at the sulfur mine were, I hope, unrepresentative. One of them at least complained that it was a dreary sort of backwoods assignment. I am simply gambling that there is intelligence in your Reich. I ask you to get me a real physicist for twenty minutes of conversation. You, Mr. Consul, will not regret it. I am in a position to turn over considerable information on—atomic power." So he had not been able to say it after all; the Bomb was still an obscene kick below the belt.

"This has been very interesting, Dr. Royland," said the consul gravely. "You referred to your enterprise as a gamble. I too shall gamble. What have I to lose by putting you *en rapport* with a scientist of ours if you prove to be a plausible lunatic?" He smiled to soften it. "Very little indeed. On the other hand, what have I to gain if your extraordinary story is quite true? A great deal. I will go along with you, doctor. Have you eaten?"

The relief was tremendous. He had lunch in a basement kitchen with the Consulate guards—a huge lunch, a rather nasty lunch of stewed *lungen* with a floured gravy, and cup after cup of coffee. Finally one of the guards lit up an ugly little spindle-shaped cigar, the kind Royland had only seen before in the caricatures of George Grosz, and as an afterthought offered one to him.

He drank in the rank smoke and managed not to cough. It stung his mouth and cut the greasy aftertaste of the stew unsatisfactorily. One of the blessings of the Third Reich, one of its gross pleasures. They were just people, after all—a certain censorious, busybody type of person with altogether too much power, but they were human. By which he meant, he supposed, members of Western Industrial Culture like him.

After lunch he was taken by truck from the city to an airfield by one of the guards. The plane was somewhat bigger than a B-29 he had once seen, and lacked propellers. He presumed it was one of the "jets" Dr. Piqueron had mentioned. His guard gave his dossier to a Luftwaffe sergeant at the foot of the ramp and said cheerfully: "Happy landings, fellow. It's all going to be all right."

"Thanks," he said. "I'll remember you, Corporal Collins. You've been very helpful." Collins turned away.

Royland climbed the ramp into the barrel of the plane. A bucket-seat job, and most of the seats were filled. He dropped into one on the very narrow aisle. His neighbor was in rags; his face showed signs of an old beating. When Royland addressed him he simply cringed away and began to sob.

The Luftwaffe sergeant came up, entered, and slammed the door. The "jets" began to wind up, making an unbelievable racket; further conversation was impossible. While the plane taxied, Royland peered through the windowless gloom at his fellow-passengers. They all looked poor and poorly.

God, were they so quickly and quietly airborne? They were. Even in the bucket seat, Royland fell asleep.

He was awakened, he did not know how much later, by the sergeant. The man was shaking his shoulder and asking him: "Any joolery hid away? Watches? Got some nice fresh water to sell to people that wanna buy it."

Royland had nothing, and would not take part in the miserable little racket if he had. He shook his head indignantly and the man moved on with a grin. He would not last long!—petty chiselers were leaks in the efficient dictatorship; they were rapidly detected and stopped up. Mussolini made the trains run on time, after all. (But naggingly Royland recalled mentioning this to a Northwestern University English professor, one Bevans. Bevans had coldly informed him that from 1931 to 1936 he had lived under Mussolini as a student and tourist guide, and therefore had extraordinary opportunities for observing whether the trains ran on time or not, and could definitely state that they did not; that railway timetables under Mussolini were best regarded as humorous fiction.)

And another thought nagged at him, a thought connected with a pale, scarred face named Bloom. Bloom was a young refugee physical chemist working on WEAPONS DEVELOPMENT TRACK I, and he was somewhat crazy, perhaps. Royland, on TRACK III, used to see little of him and could have done with even less. You couldn't say hello to the man without it turning into a lecture on the horrors of Nazism. He had wild stories about "gas chambers" and crematoria which no reasonable man could believe, and was a blanket slanderer of the German medical profession. He claimed that trained doctors, certified men, used human beings in experiments which terminated fatally. Once, to try and bring Bloom to reason, he asked what sort of experiments these were, but the monomaniac had heard that worked out: piffling nonsense about reviving mortally frozen men by putting naked women into bed with them! The man was probably sexually deranged to believe that; he naively added that one variable in the series of experiments was to use women immediately after sexual intercourse, one hour after sexual intercourse, et cetera. Royland had blushed for him and violently changed the subject.

But that was not what he was groping for. Neither was Bloom's crazy story about the woman who made lampshades from the tattooed skin of concentration camp prisoners; there were people capable of such things, of course, but under no regime whatever do they rise to positions of authority; they simply can't do the work required in positions of authority because their insanity gets in the way.

"Know your enemy," of course—but making up pointless lies? At least Bloom was not the conscious prevaricator. He got letters in Yiddish from friends and relations in Palestine, and these were laden with the latest wild rumors supposed to be based on the latest word from "escapees."

Now he remembered. In the cafeteria about three months ago Bloom had been sipping tea with somewhat shaking hand and rereading a letter. Royland tried to pass him with only a nod, but the skinny hand shot out and held him.

Bloom looked up with tears in his eyes: "It's cruel, I'm tellink you, Royland, it's cruel. They're not givink them the right to scream, to strike a futile blow, to sayink prayers *Kiddush ha Shem* like a Jew should when he is dyink for Consecration of the Name! They trick them, they say they go to farm settlements, to labor camps, so four-five of the stinkink bastards can handle a whole trainload Jews. They trick the clothes off of them at the camps, they sayink they delouse them. They trick them into room says showerbath over the door and then is too late to sayink prayers; *then goes on the gas*."

Bloom had let go of him and put his head on the table between his hands. Royland had mumbled something, patted his shoulder, and walked on, shaken. For once the neurotic little man might have got some straight facts. That was a very circumstantial touch about expediting the handling of prisoners by systematic lies—always the carrot and the stick.

Yes, everybody had been so god-damn agreeable since he climbed the Consulate steps! The friendly door guard, the Consul who nodded and remarked that his story was not an impossible one, the men he'd eaten with—all that quiet optimism. "Thanks. I'll remember you, Corporal Collins. You've been very helpful." He had felt positively benign toward the corporal, and now remembered that the corporal had turned around *very* quickly after he spoke. *To hide a grin?*

The guard was working his way down the aisle again and noticed that Royland was awake. "Changed your mind by now?" he asked kindly. "Got a good watch, maybe I'll find a piece of bread for you. You won't need a watch where you're going, fella."

"What do you mean?" Royland demanded.

The guard said soothingly: "Why, they got clocks all over them work camps, fella. Everybody knows what time it is in them work camps. You don't need no watches there. Watches just get in the way at them work camps." He went on down the aisle, quickly.

Royland reached across the aisle and, like Bloom, gripped the man who sat opposite him. He could not see much of him; the huge windowless plane was lit only by half a dozen stingy bulbs overhead. "What are you here for?" he asked.

The man said shakily: "I'm a Laborer Two, see? A Two. Well, my father he taught me to read, see, but he waited until I was ten and knew the score? See? So I figured it was a family tradition, so I taught my own kid to read because he was a pretty smart kid, ya know? I figured he'd have some fun reading like I did, no harm done, who's to know, ya know? But I should of waited a couple years, I guess, because the kid was too young and got to bragging he could read, ya know how kids do? I'm from St. Louis, by the way. I should of said first I'm from St. Louis a track maintenance man, see, so I hopped a string of returning empties for San Diego because I was scared like you get."

He took a deep sigh. "Thirsty," he said. "Got in with some Chinks, nobody to trouble ya, ya stay outta the way, but then one of them cops-like seen me and he took me to the Consul place like they do, ya know? Had me scared, they always tole me illegal reading they bump ya off, but they don't, ya know? Two years work camp, how about that?"

Yes, Royland wondered. How about it?

The plane decelerated sharply; he was thrown forward. Could they brake with those "jets" by reversing the stream or were the engines just throttling down? He heard gurgling and thudding; hydraulic fluid to the actuators letting down the landing gear. The wheels bumped a moment later and he braced himself; the plane was still and the motors cut off seconds later.

Their Luftwaffe sergeant unlocked the door and bawled through it: "Shove that goddam ramp, willya?" The sergeant's assurance had dropped from him; he looked like a very scared man. He must have been a very brave one, really, to have let himself be locked in with a hundred doomed men, protected only by an eight-shot pistol and a chain of systematic lies.

They were herded out of the plane onto a runway of what Royland immediately identified as the Chicago Municipal Airport. The same reek wafted from the stockyards; the row of airline buildings at the eastern edge of the field was ancient and patched but unchanged; the hangars, though, were now something that looked like inflated plastic bags. A good trick. Beyond the buildings surely lay the dreary red-brick and painted-siding wastes of Cicero, Illinois.

Luftwaffe men were yapping at them: "Form up, boys; make a line! Work means freedom! Look tall!" They shuffled and were shoved into columns of fours. A snappy majorette in shiny satin panties and white boots pranced out of an administration building twirling her baton; a noisy march blared from louvers in her tall fur hat. Another good trick.

"Forward march, boys," she shrilled at them. "Wouldn't y'all just like to follow me?" Seductive smile and a wiggle of the rump; a Judas ewe. She strutted off in time to the music; she must have been wearing earstopples. They shuffled after her. At the airport gate they dropped their blue-coated Luftwaffe boys and picked up a waiting escort of a dozen black-coats with skulls on their high-peaked caps.

They walked in time to the music, hypnotized by it, through Cicero. Cicero had been bombed to hell and not rebuilt. To his surprise Royland felt a pang for the vanished Poles and Slovaks of Al's old bailiwick. There were *German* Germans, French Germans, and even Italian Germans, but he knew in his bones that there were no Polish or Slovakian Germans . . . And Bloom had been right all along.

Deathly weary after two hours of marching (the majorette was indefatigable) Royland looked up from the broken pavement to see a cockeyed wonder before him. It was a Castle; it was a Nightmare; it was the Chicago Parteihof. The thing abutted Lake Michigan; it covered perhaps sixteen city blocks. It frowned down on the lake at the east and at the tumbled acres of bombed-out Chicago at the north, west, and south. It was made of steel-reinforced concrete grained and grooved to look like medieval masonry. It was walled, moated, portcullis-ed, towered, ramparted, crenellated. The death's-head guards looked at it reverently and the prisoners with fright. Royland wanted only to laugh wildly. It was a Disney production. It was as funny as Hermann Goering in full fig, and probably as deadly.

With a mumbo-jumbo of passwords, heils, and salutes they were admitted, and the majorette went away, no doubt to take off her boots and groan.

The most bedecked of the death's-head lined them up and said affably: "Hot dinner and your beds presently, my boys; first a selection. Some of you, I'm afraid, aren't well and should be in sick bay. Who's sick? Raise your hands, please."

A few hands crept up. Stooped old men.

"That's right. Step forward, please." Then he went down the line tapping a man here and there—one fellow with glaucoma, another with terrible varicose sores visible through the tattered pants he wore. Mutely they stepped forward. Royland he looked thoughtfully over. "You're thin, my boy," he observed. "Stomach pains? Vomit blood? Tarry stools in the morning?"

"Nossir!" Royland barked. The man laughed and continued down the line. The "sick bay" detail was marched off. Most of them were weeping silently; they knew. Everybody knew; everybody pretended that the terrible thing would not, might not, happen. It was much more complex than Royland had realized.

"Now," said the death's-head affably, "we require some competent cement workers—"

The line of remaining men went mad. They surged forward almost touching the officer but never stepping over an invisible line surrounding him. "Me!" some yelled. "Me! Me!" Another cried: "I'm good with my hands, I can learn, I'm a machinist too, I'm strong and young, I can learn!" A heavy middle-aged one waved his hands in the air and boomed: "Grouting and tile-setting! Grouting and tile-setting!" Royland stood alone, horrified. They knew. They knew this was an offer of real work that would keep them alive for a while.

He knew suddenly how to live in a world of lies.

The officer lost his patience in a moment or two, and whips came out. Men with their faces bleeding struggled back into line. "Raise your hands, you cement people, and no lying, please. But you wouldn't lie, would you?" He picked half a dozen volunteers after questioning them briefly, and one of his men marched them off.

Among them was the grouting-and-tile man, who looked pompously pleased with himself; such was the reward of diligence and virtue, he seemed to be proclaiming; pooh to those grasshoppers back there who neglected to learn A Trade.

"Now," said the officer casually, "we require some laboratory assistants." The chill of death stole down the line of prisoners. Each one seemed to shrivel into himself, become poker-faced, imply that he wasn't really involved in all this.

Royland raised his hand. The officer looked at him in stupefaction and then covered up quickly. "Splendid," he said. "Step forward, my boy. You," he pointed at another man. "You have an intelligent forehead; you look as if you'd make a fine laboratory assistant. Step forward."

"Please, no!" the man begged. He fell to his knees and clasped his hands in supplication. "Please no!" The officer took out his whip meditatively; the man groaned, scrambled to his feet, and quickly stood beside Royland.

When there were four more chosen, they were marched off across the concrete yard into one of the absurd towers, and up a spiral staircase and down a corridor, and through the promenade at the back of an auditorium where a woman screamed German from the stage at an audience of women. And through a tunnel and down the corridor of an elementary school with empty classrooms full of small desks on either side. And into a hospital area where the fake-masonry walls yielded to scrubbed white tile and the fake flagstones underfoot to composition flooring and the fake pinewood torches in bronze brackets that had lighted their way to fluorescent tubes.

At the door marked RASSENWISSENSCHAFT the guard rapped and a frosty-faced man in a laboratory coat opened up. "You requisitioned a demonstrator, Dr. Kalten," the guard said. "Pick any one of these."

Dr. Kalten looked them over. "Oh, this one, I suppose," he said. Royland. "Come in, fellow."

The Race Science Laboratory of Dr. Kalten proved to be a decent medical setup with an operating table, intricate charts of the races of men and their anatomical, mental, and moral makeups. There was also a phrenological head diagram and a horoscope on the wall, and an arrangement of glittering crystals on wire which Royland recognized. It was a model of one Hans Hoerbiger's crackpot theory of planetary formation, the *Welteislehre.*

"Sit there," the doctor said, pointing to a stool. "First I've got to take your pedigree. By the way, you might as well know that you're going to end up dissected for my demonstration in Race Science III for the Medical School, and your degree of cooperation will determine whether the dissection is performed under anaesthesia or not. Clear?"

"Clear, doctor."

"Curious—no panic. I'll wager we find you're a proto-Hamitoidal hemi-Nordic of at *least* degree five . . . but let's get on. Name?"

"Edward Royland."

"Birthdate?"

"July second, nineteen twenty-three."

The doctor threw down his pencil. "If my previous explanation was inadequate," he shouted, "let me add that if you continue to be difficult I may turn you over to my good friend Dr. Herzbrenner. Dr. Herzbrenner happens to teach interrogation technique at the Gestapo School. *Do—you—now—understand?*"

"Yes, doctor. I'm sorry I cannot withdraw my answer."

Dr. Kalten turned elaborately sarcastic. "How then do you account for your remarkable state of preservation at your age of approximately a hundred and eighty years?"

"Doctor, I am twenty-three years old. I have traveled through time."

"Indeed?" Kalten was amused. "And how was this accomplished?"

Royland said steadily: "A spell was put on me by a satanic Jewish magician. It involved the ritual murder and desanguination of seven beautiful Nordic virgins."

Dr. Kalten gaped for a moment. Then he picked up his pencil and said firmly: "You will understand that my doubts were logical under the circumstances. Why did you not give me the sound scientific basis for your surprising claim at once? Go ahead; tell me all about it."

He was Dr. Kalten's prize; he was Dr. Kalten's treasure. His peculiarities of speech, his otherwise-inexplicable absence of a birth number over his left nipple, when they got around to it the gold filling in one of his teeth, his uncanny knowledge of Old America, all now had a simple scientific explanation. He was from 1944. What was so hard to grasp about that? Any sound specialist knew about the lost Jewish Cabala magic, golems and such.

His story was that he had been a student Race Scientist under the pioneering master William D. Pully. (A noisy whack who used to barnstorm the chaw-and-gallus belt with the backing of Deutches Neues Buro; sure enough they found him in Volume VII of the standard *Introduction to a Historical Handbook of Race Science.*) The Jewish fiends had attempted to ambush his master on a lonely road; Royland persuaded him to switch hats and coats; in the darkness the substitution was not noticed. Later in their stronghold he was identified, but the Nordic virgins had already been ritually murdered and drained of their blood, and it wouldn't keep. The dire fate destined for the master had been visited upon the disciple.

Dr. Kalten loved that bit. It tickled him pink that the sub-men's "revenge" on their enemy had been to precipitate him into a world purged of the sub-men entirely, where a Nordic might breathe freely!

Kalten, except for discreet consultations with such people as Old America specialists, a dentist who was stupefied by the gold filling, and a dermatologist who established that there was not and never had been a *geburtsnummer* on the subject examined, was playing Royland close to his vest. After a week it became apparent that he was reserving Royland for a grand unveiling which would climax the reading of a paper. Royland did not want to be unveiled; there were too many holes in his story. He talked with animation about the beauties of Mexico in the spring, its fair mesas, cactus, and mushrooms. Could they make a short trip there? Dr. Kalten said they could not. Royland was becoming restless? Let him study, learn, profit by the matchless arsenal of the sciences available here in Chicago Parteihof. Dear old Chicago boasted distinguished exponents of the World Ice Theory, the Hollow World Theory, Dowsing, Homeopathic Medicine, Curative Folk Botany—

This last did sound interesting. Dr. Kalten was pleased to take his prize to the Medical School and introduce him as a protégé to Professor Albiani, of Folk Botany.

Albiani was a bearded gnome out of the Arthur Rackham illustrations for *Das Rheingold*. He loved his subject. "Mother Nature, the all-bounteous one! Wander the fields, young man, and with a seeing eye in an hour's stroll you will find the ergot that aborts, the dill that cools fever, the tansy that strengthens the old, the poppy that soothes the fretful teething babe!"

"Do you have any hallucinogenic Mexican mushrooms?" Royland demanded.

"We may," Albiani said, surprised. They browsed through the Folk Botany museum and pored over dried vegetation under glass. From Mexico there were peyote, the buttons and the root, and there was marihuana, root, stem, seed, and stalk. No mushrooms.

"They may be in the storeroom," Albiani muttered.

All the rest of the day Royland mucked through the storeroom where specimens were waiting for exhibit space on some rotation plan. He went to Albiani and said, a little wild-eyed: "They're not there."

Albiani had been interested enough to look up the mushrooms in question in the reference books. "See?" he said happily, pointing to a handsome color plate of the mushroom: growing, mature, sporing, and dried. He read: " '. . . superstitiously called *God Food,*' " and twinkled through his beard at the joke.

"They're not there," Royland said.

The professor, annoyed at last, said: "There might be some un-catalogued in the basement. Really, we don't have room for every-thing in our limited display space—just the *interesting* items."

Royland pulled himself together and charmed the location of the department's basement storage space out of him, together with per-mission to inspect it. And, left alone for a moment, ripped the color plate from the professor's book and stowed it away.

That night Royland and Dr. Kalten walked out on one of the innu-merable tower-tops for a final cigar. The moon was high and full; its light turned the cratered terrain that had been Chicago into another moon. The sage and his disciple from another day leaned their elbows on a crenellated rampart two hundred feet above Lake Michigan.

"Edward," said Dr. Kalten, "I shall read my paper tomorrow be-fore the Chicago Academy of Race Science." The words were a chal-lenge; something was wrong. He went on: "I shall expect you to be in the wings of the auditorium, and to appear at my command to an-swer a few questions from me and, if time permits, from our audi-ence."

"I wish it could be postponed," Royland said.

"No doubt."

"Would you explain your unfriendly tone of voice, doctor?" Royland demanded. "I think I've been completely cooperative and have opened the way for you to win undying fame in the annals of Race Science."

"Cooperative, yes. Candid—I wonder? You see, Edward, a dreadful thought struck me today. I have always thought it amusing that the Jewish attack on Reverend Pully should have been for the purpose of precipitating him into the future and that it should have misfired." He took something out of his pocket: a small pistol. He aimed it casually at Royland. "Today I began to wonder *why* they should have done so. Why did they not simply murder him, as they did thousands, and dispose of him in their secret crematoria, and permit no mention in their controlled newspapers and magazines of the disappearance?

"Now, the blood of seven Nordic virgins can have been no cheap commodity. One pictures with ease Nordic men patrolling their precious enclaves of humanity, eyes roving over every passing face, noting who bears the stigmata of the sub-men, and following those who do most carefully indeed lest race-defilement be committed with a look or an 'accidental' touch in a crowded street. Nevertheless the thing was done; your presence here is proof of it. It must have been done at enormous cost; hired Slavs and Negroes must have been employed to kidnap the virgins, and many of them must have fallen before Nordic rage.

"This merely to silence one small voice crying in the wilderness? *I* —*think*—*not*. I think, Edward Royland, or whatever your real name may be, that Jewish arrogance sent you, a Jew yourself, into the future as a greeting from the Jewry of that day to what it foolishly thought would be the triumphant Jewry of this. At any rate, the public questioning tomorrow will be conducted by my friend Dr. Herzbrenner, whom I have mentioned to you. If you have any little secrets, they will not remain secrets long. No, no! Do not move toward me. I shall shoot you disablingly in the knee if you do."

Royland moved toward him and the gun went off; there was an agonizing hammer blow high on his left shin. He picked up Kalten and hurled him, screaming, over the parapet two hundred feet into the water. And collapsed. The pain was horrible. His shinbone was badly cracked if not broken through. There was not much bleeding; maybe there would be later. He need not fear that the shot and scream would rouse the castle. Such sounds were not rare in the Medical Wing.

He dragged himself, injured leg trailing, to the doorway of Kalten's living quarters; he heaved himself into a chair by the signal bell and threw a rug over his legs. He rang for the diener and told him very quietly: "Go to the medical storeroom for a leg U-brace and whatever is necessary for a cast, please. Dr. Kalten has an interesting idea he wishes to work out."

He should have asked for a syringe of morphine—no he shouldn't. It might affect the time distortion.

When the man came back he thanked him and told him to turn in for the night.

He almost screamed getting his shoe off; his trouser leg he cut away. The gauze had arrived just in time; the wound was beginning to bleed more copiously. Pressure seemed to stop it. He constructed a sloppy walking cast on his leg. The directions on the several five-pound cans of plaster helped.

His leg was getting numb; good. His cast probably pinched some major nerve, and a week in it would cause permanent paralysis; who cared about *that?*

He tried it out and found he could get across the floor inefficiently. With a strong-enough bannister he could get downstairs but not, he thought, up them. That was all right. He was going to the basement.

God-damning the medieval Nazis and their cornball castle every inch of the way, he went to the basement; there he had a windfall. A dozen drunken SS men were living it up in a corner far from the censorious eyes of their company commander; they were playing a game which might have been called Spin the Corporal. They saw Royland limping and wept sentimental tears for poor ol' doc with a bum leg; they carried him two winding miles to the storeroom he wanted, and shot the lock off for him. They departed, begging him to call on ol' Company K any time, bes' fellas in Chicago, doc. Ol' Bruno here can tear the arm off a Latvik shirker with his bare hands, honest, doc! Jus' the way you twist a drumstick off a turkey. You wan' us to get a Latvik an' show you?

He got rid of them at last, clicked on the light, and began his search. His leg was now ice cold, painfully so. He rummaged through the uncatalogued botanicals and found after what seemed like hours a crate shipped from Jalasca. Royland opened it by beating its

corners against the concrete floor. It yielded and spilled plastic enve-
lopes; through the clear material of one he saw the wrinkled black
things. He did not even compare them with the color plate in his
pocket. He tore the envelope open and crammed them into his
mouth, and chewed and swallowed.

Maybe there had to be a Hopi dancing and chanting, maybe there
didn't have to be. Maybe one had to be calm, if bitter, and fresh from
a day of hard work at differential equations which approximated the
Hopi mode of thought. Maybe you only had to fix your mind savagely on what you desired, as his was fixed now. Last time he had
hated and shunned the Bomb; what he wanted was a world without
the Bomb. He had got it, all right!

. . . his tongue was thick and the fireballs were beginning to dance
around him, the circling circles . . .

Charles Miller Nahataspe whispered: "Close. Close. I was so
frightened."

Royland lay on the floor of the hut, his leg unsplinted, unfractured,
but aching horribly. Drowsily he felt his ribs; he was merely slender
now, no longer gaunt. He mumbled: "You were working to pull me
back from this side?"

"Yes. You, you were there?"

"I was there. God, let me sleep."

He rolled over heavily and collapsed into complete uncon-
sciousness.

When he awakened it was still dark and his pains were gone.
Nahataspe was crooning a healing song very softly. He stopped when
he saw Royland's eyes open. "Now you know about break-the-sky
medicine," he said.

"Better than anybody. What time is it?"

"Midnight."

"I'll be going then." They clasped hands and looked into each
other's eyes.

The jeep started easily. Four hours earlier, or possibly two months
earlier, he had been worried about the battery. He chugged down the
settlement road and knew what would happen next. He wouldn't wait
until morning; a meteorite might kill him, or a scorpion in his bed.
He would go directly to Rotschmidt in his apartment, defy Vrouw

Rotschmidt and wake her man up to tell him about 56c, tell him we have the Bomb.

We have a symbol to offer the Japanese now, something to which they can surrender, and will surrender.

Rotschmidt would be philosophical. He would probably sigh about the Bomb: "Ah, do we ever act responsibly? Do we ever know what the consequences of our decisions will be?"

And Royland would have to try to avoid answering him very sharply: "Yes. This once we damn well do."

About the Author

Once, when one of C. M. Kornbluth's short story collections was published, he was asked to write a short autobiographical sketch to include in it. This is it.

I was born in New York City in 1923, and was educated in the city schools as far as freshman year at C. C. N. Y., when I was dropped for the usual reasons. I had already begun to contribute to the science-fiction magazines and became a full-time writer after leaving college, though most people regarded me as an unemployed bum. I weakened once to the extent of getting a job as a hand-screw-machine operator, but quit after a few months to enlist in the army. In three years of service I acquired a wife, a combat infantry badge, two ETO campaign stars, a PFC stripe, and a constant ringing in the ears. After my discharge I settled in Chicago, where I combined writing blood-and-guts detective stories with acquiring an education according to the precepts of the University of Chicago. A friend managing the local bureau of a moribund news agency got me a job on its desk, and it was goodbye, Chancellor Hutchins. I rose to bureau chief eventually, paralleling the news job with contributions to the science-fiction magazines and such fantastic chores as writing a syndicated review of phonograph records for children. In 1951, at the urging of my wife, my agent, and my doctor, I resigned my job to come east as a full-time free-lance writer again. Since then I've sired two children and eleven books, including this one. I live now in a Tioga County, New York, farmhouse, and visit New York City infrequently. I drive a senile Ford timidly and not well; I like to cook, specializing in Italian and Chinese dishes. I have been accused of being a compulsive reader. My writing habits have changed over the years from white-hot all-night sessions to a-little-every-day and plenty of polishing. I have no formal hobbies, but am interested in practically every human activity except sports. I have no settled opinions about writing; currently I'm concerned most over the invasion of science fiction by exponents of the so-called "mandarin style."

The "constant ringing in the ears" turned out to be essential malignant hypertension, and a few years later it caused his death.